I have been thinking about your reason for coming here as you did," Hawk mumbled.

She swallowed against the tightness of her throat and waited.

"This matter of wanting to get to know me better—is that really why you did it?"

Krysta nodded. She took a breath, steadying herself. "It seemed a good idea at the time."

If he meant to mock her, he would do so now. She waited . . . hoping yet scarcely daring to hope. . . .

"The notion may have merit."

Krysta opened her eyes, belatedly aware that she had closed them as though in prayer, and stared at him. "Do you mean that?"

He frowned. "Do not read overmuch into my words. I merely meant it would not necessarily be a bad thing for us to know each other before we wed." Swiftly, he added, "That does not mean I approve of what you did. It was a harebrained scheme."

She was silent for a moment before she smiled. "We have hares in Vestfold. They are large animals with very powerful back legs, capable of leaping great distances. They survive the worst winters snug in burrows they dig deep beneath the ground and they seem able to thwart the wiliest predator." Her eyes met his. "Even the hawk."

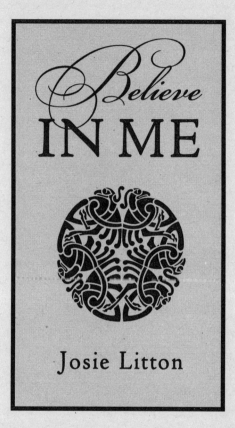

Believe
IN ME

Josie Litton

Bantam 🦚 *Books*

New York Toronto London Sydney Auckland

FOR

MM AND KT

FOR KEEPING ME HOPPING

Chapter

ONE

HOOVES POUND OVER THE HARD-PACKED road, dusty in the summer's heat, clods of dirt flung high as the horsemen ride for the proud fortress close by the sun-flecked sea. A day's hunting is well done. Thrown across the mounts' sweat-streaked hindquarters, the carcasses of boar and stag drip blood into the thirsting earth. Cheers resound through the bailey yard, welcoming the lord home, celebrating the kill.

Lord Hawk, master of Hawkforte, dismounts, handing the reins of his destrier to a stable boy. He is a big man, standing head and shoulders above other men, heavily mus-cled, hard faced, with watchful, sky-blue eyes and the lithe stride of a natural warrior. This day he is pleasantly tired, glad of the diversion offered by the hunt. Glad, too—though he would be loath to admit it—that another day has slipped by without the arrival of his bride.

His unknown, unwanted bride. He sighs and runs a hand through thick chestnut hair that curls at the nape of his corded neck. A man of his position should marry if only to sire sons. This he knows, even grudgingly accepts, but he would have preferred a woman of his own choosing, not this *faceless female sent as a pledge of peace in the effort to bind Norse and Saxon together that they might better stand against the rapacious Dane.*

For this reason his sister, the beautiful Lady Cymbra, had wed the powerful Norse jarl, Wolf Hakonson the previous year. Hawk can hardly do less himself for the promise of peace, yet he nurtures no hope that his union will be as successful as that of his sister and the man once known as the Scourge of the Saxons.

He will be glad enough if he can merely tolerate his bride, but he has no way of judging that until she deigns to arrive, something she appears in no hurry to do. However, on this day, there has been progress of a sort. . . .

M Y LORD . . ."
Hawk turned, seeing his steward approach across the yard. The man was hurrying but cautiously so, one shoulder turned just a little away as though with a view to quick retreat. Had it reached that point, Hawk wondered, when his own people had to go in fear of him because his temper had become so uncertain? He suppressed a sigh, hoping it was not true, for such weakness would afflict his pride as much as his stubborn sense of fairness.

"What is it, Edvard?" he asked, making an effort at cordiality. Already, the brief escape offered by the hunt was fading, returning him to the workaday world of decisions, judgments, compromises, and wise leadership he was expected to provide by the several thousand people who clustered in and around the fortress of Hawkforte and the thousands more spread out over his lands. He never questioned his duty, in fact he embraced it, but there were times when it weighed heavy all the same. Such a mellow day might have been spent in more amiable pursuits, perhaps dangling a line beside a brook in the hope that no fish would come along to require attention. He thought, too, that it would be pleasant to share such an interlude with someone who would ask nothing of him save his company. But that notion had scarcely stirred before the realities of his duty, which was to say his life, overrode it.

The steward, reassured that his lord was more approachable than of late, relaxed as much as his meticulous nature ever permitted. He was young for his position, which he had on merit rather than rank, and he meant to hold on to it. "Three servants of the Lady Krysta have arrived, my lord." He gestured toward a trio standing some little distance away near the smithy's shed, one of many such small buildings that framed the inner walls of the fortress. The slight motion of his hand, the faint pinching of his nostrils, and the shadowed look in his eyes expressed a range of emotion scarcely seen in the redoubtable Edvard. Surprise, concern, puzzlement, a veritable cacophony of feeling flowed from one who was normally the most imperturbable of men.

Hawk surveyed the little group for himself. There was a man—short and stocky, bent shouldered, with long black hair and beard, and coal-bright eyes. Beside him stood an aged woman dressed all in black, hair like a raven's wing, sharp nosed. Partly concealed by them both but still visible was a much younger woman, also blackhaired, delicately made with pixyish features and eyes . . .

Dancing, anticipation-filled eyes that even from a distance appeared to him to be the selfsame shade as a forest glen in high summer. He could almost feel the cool moss, hear the crystalline patter of water on stone, smell the fragrance of shy wood violets twined in the hair of a woman with skin like cream and . . .

Hawk returned to himself with a start. He was too far from the girl to see such detail yet had been so absorbed in his imaginings that he had forgotten all else.

That was absurd. She was only a servant, a rather small and disheveled one at that. There was no conceivable reason why she should be of any particular interest to him. Yet there he was again falling into those eyes and that sweetly entrancing smile that managed to remind him somehow of . . . of what, exactly? He'd seen it there in his mind for just an instant but it was gone too swiftly, leaving only a fleeting impression of sun-dappled water and the sleek, gleaming forms that leaped between air and sea in the wake of his fast-skimming boat.

Ridiculous. He looked away, looked back, caught himself doing so, and scowled. She saw his confusion and seemed to fold herself up, all but vanishing behind her two companions.

He was tired, that was it. He'd been at court until a fortnight ago and that was always wearying. Since returning home, the business of Hawkforte had occupied him without surcease. And then there was the matter of his damnable marriage hanging over him like the proverbial sword.

One no less sharp than the tongue of his half-sister who he saw too late was bearing down on him with all the grace and subtlety of an ill-tempered she goat. Hawk spared a thought for the rapacious Danes, whom he would have greatly preferred to face, and steeled himself for her usual tirade.

"This is beyond all bounds!" Daria proclaimed. "It is not enough that we are left to wonder when the Lady Krysta may find it convenient to appear, now we are expected to welcome her servants in her stead." She cast a dire look over her shoulder before returning her attention full force to her brother, who closed his eyes for a moment, summoning that most elusive of all virtues—patience.

Daria was his elder by a decade. By all rights, she should have been in her own manor and so she would have been had not her husband had the poor judgment to go against Alfred of Wessex just as the scholar-warrior was setting out to unite Britons against the Danes. Promptly widowed, Daria made no secret of her resentment against all those who had denied her what she thought of as her proper place, including the brother who had given her a home. Yet she managed Hawk's household well enough and generally had the sense to keep her endless complaints from his ears.

Not today though. Today, she so brimmed over with afflictions as to banish caution.

"What could she be thinking of to send these three with no warning?" she demanded, standing with her hands on her thin hips, glaring at him. "Did she consider the inconvenience to us? And why are they here? Does she think to find Hawkforte wanting? Does she imagine it poorer than what she has known in the barbaric northlands?"

With each question, Daria's shrill voice rose a notch until at the end she was fairly shouting. Hawk was a forbearing man but there were limits to what he would permit. His authority, and the simple prudence of any male, demanded he put a stop to such distemper.

"Curb your tongue, Daria, it pleases me not. See to quarters for them and be swift about it."

His sister sputtered in anger but the icy coldness of his gaze and the hard set of his features reminded her belatedly of the steely will he never hesitated to wield.

She was still glaring at Hawk when he gestured to the short, stocky man. As he approached, Hawk surveyed him more closely. The fellow was troll-like, thick through the shoulders, slightly stooped, with bandy legs as though he lurked under bridges waiting to surprise the unwary traveler. His bright stare beneath furry brows suggested he wasn't averse to such mischief.

"I be Thorgold, lord," he said. "Servant to the Lady Krysta."

"Do I take it your arrival means the lady will grace us soon with her presence?"

The biting edge to Hawk's words would have prompted most men to take a step back. Thorgold merely shrugged his broad shoulders and spread his gnarled hands.

"She comes when she comes, lord."

And that, it seemed, was that. Short of airing his irritation to the odd little man, Hawk had scant choice but to let it pass. He turned the trio over to Daria and returned his attention to Edvard, but not without a final glance at the girl. She was trailing after the other two as they proceeded across the bailey. Startled to be discovered watching him over her shoulder, she stumbled, caught herself, and flashed a look of pure chagrin that for some reason amused him mightily.

Several moments passed before he realized that Edvard's surprised expression came from the unaccustomed sound of his master chuckling.

T HAT SELFSAME SOUND WARMED KRYSTA ALL THE way through, sending little tingles down her back as she followed Thorgold and Raven, and the dour-faced woman, toward the servants' hall. She didn't dare another look over her shoulder but that was not for lack of temptation. Her common sense—in which she took great pride—managed to assert itself just barely enough to stop her.

He was so big. Easily the biggest man she had ever seen save for the brief glimpse she'd had a few months before of the mighty jarl of Sciringesheal, Wolf Hakonson, when he came to speak with her half-brother. Then was she summoned for a rare visit to her family's manor, never imagining why until she was told weeks later that she was to be given in marriage to the Wolf's own brother-in-law, the feared Saxon lord called Hawk.

He had the eyes of a bird of prey, she thought, yet when he laughed . . . A smile curved her full mouth set beneath a slightly upturned nose. When he laughed, Lord Hawk almost made her believe that her precautions were not even necessary. Being a woman of prudence, she set aside that notion, carefully to be sure, for it created a little bubble of happiness within her that she wished most fervently would grow.

If it were to do so, it would have to be protected from the sharp-eyed gaze and equally sharp-tongued speech of the Lady Daria, who, she gathered, had the running of the household. Indeed, everything about the lady appeared barbed, like an irksome nettle best avoided.

Daria led the way across the bailey toward a low, wooden building. Built of split logs notched and mortared together, and sheltered beneath a high-peaked thatch roof, the hall was plain in comparison to the vivid woodcarvings and paintings that ornamented Norse structures.

Entering, Krysta needed a moment or two for her eyes to adjust from the glare of day. Although ample in size, the building seemed eerily silent for all the servants were about their chores. She heard the faint buzz of a bee, smelled the aroma of dry rushes on the dirt floor, and slowly looked around.

At the center of the hall was a large hearth framed in stones and set beneath a smoke hole surrounded by soot-stained rafters. To either side of the hearth, running down both the long sides of the hall, were curtained alcoves for sleeping. It being day, the curtains hung open, revealing sparsely furnished sleeping quarters.

"You two may lay your pallets in here," Daria told the women, pointing to an empty alcove. "As for you—" She regarded Thorgold. "The men's hall is on the other side of the bailey. You may sleep there. I expect each of you to keep your quarters tidy at all times, appear for meals promptly, and do whatever tasks are assigned to you. Do you understand?"

Black-garbed Raven opened her mouth to reply but Thorgold forestalled her. "Perfectly, lady. We will give you no trouble."

"See to it that you don't. Your mistress has already created quite enough of a bad impression by not arriving here in a timely fashion. Frankly, if my brother were inclined to listen to my counsel, he would not embark on so ill-conceived a venture as this marriage is sure to be. He will rue the day."

Having rendered her judgment on the matter, Daria departed. Not a moment too soon. Thorgold had to put a restraining hand on Raven.

"Easy, she is of no account. Forget her."

"Fine for you to say," Raven muttered. Her thin neck arched, her head bobbing angrily. She took a breath, swelling her chest, then let it out and shook herself with a soft rustle. "I would suggest pecking out her liver but it is likely filled with bile and unappetizing."

Krysta laughed. She put an arm around each of her friends and gave them a reassuring squeeze. It had not been easy for them to come here. She knew their willingness to do so was testament to the love and devotion each had given her from the very moment of her birth. She returned it in full measure.

Much as she wanted to think only of her startling impressions of Lord Hawk, she knew duty came first. With a glance around the alcove, she wrinkled her nose. "I suggest we see what we can do to make ourselves comfortable."

Thorgold nodded, gave her a smile, and vanished out

the door. Shortly he returned with the first load of their belongings. As he shuttled back and forth, Krysta and Raven hastened to clean and straighten the humble chamber. Or at least Krysta tried. When it came to preparing a pleasant, safe place to nest, Raven had no equal. She bustled about, seemingly everywhere at once, and in no time the alcove was transformed.

Every trace of dust was swept away, simple wooden beds set up, and stools and a small table put in place. Bringing in the last load, Thorgold glanced about and nodded. "Best leave it at this. Much more and questions will be asked."

About to unpack a lush weaving of a forest glen in which small animals and various other creatures gamboled about, Krysta nodded regretfully. From what she had seen so far, Hawkforte's servants were housed snugly enough but allowed no luxuries.

"We'll leave the rest for later," she said, reluctantly setting the weaving aside.

With the chamber made suitable, she had her first chance to think about what she had so far accomplished. She was actually inside Hawkforte, had even seen its master, and no one seemed any the wiser. The little bubble inside her grew a notch. What had seemed a somewhat risky scheme requiring great caution was working out even better than she could have hoped.

Observing her smile, Raven and Thorgold exchanged looks. It fell to the old woman to speak. "It isn't too late."

"Whatever do you mean?"

"You could say you were too eager to wait for an escort but feared discovery on the roads if you traveled as yourself." Her thin shoulders rose and fell. "Who knows, he might even believe you."

"Only if you tell him now," Thorgold said. "Wait much longer and the man will know himself played for a fool. They don't like that." He smiled as though at amusing memories. "No, indeed, they don't."

Krysta jumped up from the bed where she had been sitting and stared at her friends in amazement. "I have absolutely no intention of telling him. That would put everything wrong. However will I learn what I must if I fail to persevere now?"

"What is there to learn?" Raven countered. "All men are alike . . . prideful, stubborn, ignorant . . ."

"Presumptuous, unseeing, clumsy . . ." Thorgold continued.

"They must have some redeeming qualities," Krysta protested. "When he looked at me, I felt—" She broke off, trying to recapture exactly what it was she had felt when those startlingly blue eyes met hers. She had sensed great strength, intelligence, and something more . . . something powerful and entrancing, drawing her into it. . . . Passion?

Was the master of Hawkforte a man of passion?

She shied away from the thought even as it tantalized her. As her husband, he would have the right to possess her as no one ever had. She knew the basics of what his ownership would mean but sensed there was a great deal more simmering just below the surface in the shadowed, roiling world of the unseen from which both terror and beauty could emerge so suddenly.

Passion aside, he'd had the wit to help forge an alliance that meant peace for his people and her own. That spoke of intelligence and self-discipline. She valued both, yet it was the lingering thought of a husband's rights and her own wifely duty that brought a flush to her delicate cheeks and caused her loyal servants to exchange knowing looks.

"Mortals," Thorgold murmured just before he ambled off to find his sleeping place. He would toss some belongings in the men's hall to make it look as though he were there, but the small bridge he'd noticed just before entering Hawkforte appealed to him far more.

"You should rest," Krysta suggested to her black-garbed friend when they were alone. The journey first by sea and then by horse had tired them all but Raven was the oldest of the trio by far, so old indeed that Krysta had no idea of her true age. Now that their destination was reached, it seemed only sensible that she take her ease.

But Raven would have none of it. "Perched on a horse is a poor way indeed to see a land. I would know more of this Lord Hawk's wealth and what sway he holds over this place."

With that, she was gone. Krysta had no chance to remind her to be cautious before there was a faint, fast-fading flutter of wings beyond the hall.

A short while later, having smoothed her gown and hair as best she could, Krysta also emerged, albeit in a somewhat more conventional manner. She stood for a few minutes, enjoying the touch of the sun on her skin, before surveying the busy scene.

The manor of Hawkforte was hard by the sea on the southeastern coast of Britain in the place she knew was called Essex. It dominated a point of land that controlled sheltered bays on either side. Watchtowers were set at intervals all along the high timber walls, giving a commanding view of movements by land or sea. Higher still was the central tower that rose above the bailey yard, standing fully four stories tall. Accustomed as she was to the strongholds of the Norse, Krysta still could not help but be impressed.

It being day, the wide wooden gates in the outer walls stood open. A steady stream of people, horses, and wagons moved through them. Krysta peered at the Saxons with unfettered interest, observing that contrary to the foolish rumors she had heard, they lacked both horns and cloven feet. A small smile tugged at her mouth as she saw her own good sense confirmed. They were people like anyone else. Soon they would be her people even as their master would be . . . well, no, not her master but her husband certainly, and she was determined that he would never have cause to rue that no matter what dour Daria had to say about it.

She would be the best possible wife the Lord Hawk could ever hope for, an ornament to his hall, a comfort to his days, a partner in his endeavors to bring peace between their peoples. What more could he possibly ask for? Truly nothing, and that being the case, he would love her as she must be loved were she not to suffer her own mother's fate.

A shadow moved behind her eyes. The dull echo of old pain rippled through her. Her mother . . . gone from her so long, who had risked her life for mortal love and lost. Her father had desired her mother, of that there was no question, but he had not loved her as she needed to be loved and so the tenuous connection between them stretched too thin to hold. With its snapping came the loss not only of the dream of love but also of a child, Krysta herself, left behind to the care of Thorgold and Raven. They had, as she grew, warned her that the same fate could befall herself. She had scarcely contemplated their warning, for that was when the thought of any man in her life seemed so remote as to be absurd, back before the summons to her family's manor, to stand beneath the hate-filled gaze of her half-brother and learn she was to be given in marriage to a stranger who, should he fail to love her, would all unknowingly destroy her life.

But that would not happen, she was quite resolved. Hawk *would* love her. Never mind that she had scant knowledge of men and even less of marriage. Aware that in her ignorance she might make some dreadful error that could ruin everything, she had hatched the admittedly unusual but, she thought, reasonable plan to come to Hawkforte as one of her own servants. Cleverly disguised, she would learn everything she could about the man whose wife she was to be. When she had done so, the servant girl would vanish—the black dye washed from hair that was naturally golden—and the Lady Krysta would appear, fully prepared to be the best—and best loved—wife the Lord Hawk could ever have.

It all made perfect sense to her; indeed, she was quite pleased to have thought up so resourceful a plan. True, Thorgold and Raven had tried to discourage her, until she reminded them, gently to be sure, that they were hardly experienced in such matters. The intricacies of marriage were at least as much a mystery to her beloved servants as they were to Krysta herself. But not for long. Oh, no, before very many days had passed, she was certain all her questions would be answered, her concerns resolved, and her course clear.

All perfectly sensible.

So where to begin? As she studied the activity in the bailey, she noted that the people looked healthy, well fed, and adequately if plainly dressed. Everybody seemed to have some task to do and was going about it diligently. There was even a little group of children sitting together as they carded wool.

Children fascinated her; she had been the only child in her own home. There she had lived from her birth until the day scant weeks before when she left for the journey to Essex. While her father lived, he had visited her frequently but he never even suggested that she leave her home and come to the family seat, where her half-brother and half-sisters, the children of his first marriage, resided. After his death, she had remained apart, content enough with her life. Yet she had always had the unsettling sense that she was merely biding time, waiting for something to happen.

Now it had and she could not repress her excitement, especially since she had actually seen the Lord Hawk. Eagerly, she scanned the bailey again but there was no sign of him. She was disappointed but not overly so, for there were still the children. Irresistibly drawn to them, she approached with caution, unsure of her reception, but when a hazel-eyed urchin looked up and smiled, her hesitation vanished.

"May I help with that?" she asked, indicating the wool they were carding. One of the little girls, apparently the leader of the small group, regarded her for a moment, nodded, and handed her a set of paddles set with wire teeth closely fixed together. Krysta settled down beside them on the dusty ground, studying how they went about their task and trying hard to do the same. Her first few efforts were clumsy. The paddles were more difficult to manage than she'd thought and she skinned her knuckles several times.

"Like this," the little girl said and placed her small hands over Krysta's, showing her the proper motion. With that help, she did better and soon felt she had the knack of it. When the children nodded approvingly, she couldn't help but be pleased.

They worked in silence for a short time before the little girl asked, "You're one of the foreign lady's servants, aren't you?"

Krysta nodded, disliking the lie but telling herself yet again that it was necessary. "My name is Ilka."

"People say Lord Hawk doesn't want to marry her. He's only doing it for the alliance."

Despite the tightening of her throat, Krysta managed to reply. "Perhaps he'll change his mind when he gets to know her."

"Perhaps." The little girl looked unconvinced.

"What's your name?" Krysta asked after a pause.

"Edythe." She introduced the others, who nodded shyly.

"What else do you do besides this?" Krysta asked.

Edythe shrugged. "All sorts of things. We help with the flocks, bring wood and water, cook, whatever needs to be done." She hesitated a moment before adding, "Lady Daria likes everyone to be busy."

"What about Lord Hawk? Does he think you should work all the time?"

Edythe cast her a glance from beneath sooty lashes. "Lord Hawk is a great and powerful noble. He has concerns far beyond here."

That told Krysta much. Understandably enough the Lord of Hawkforte left domestic matters to a woman. If he noticed at all that she was an extremely demanding person, he either did not care or saw no reason for change.

Or did he? He had, for whatever reason, agreed to take a wife who would be expected to manage his household. Perhaps he would appreciate someone whose view of such matters was very different from that of the Lady Daria. Or perhaps not. One more thing for Krysta to discover.

She would have sighed just then had not one of the children leaned over and whispered to Edythe, "She's going."

Following the direction of their collective gaze, Krysta observed Lady Daria departing Hawkforte in a lavishly appointed litter balanced between two pairs of horses. Several harried-looking servants followed on foot behind her. The lady was leaning out between the curtains, inciting the grooms to keep the horses under better control, complaining about the bumpiness of the road, and otherwise making her feelings known.

"Gone to market," Edythe explained. Quickly, she and the other children bundled up their carding. Before

Krysta's eyes, their demeanor changed from solemnity to exuberance.

"Now's our time to play," Edythe said and grasped Krysta's hand, drawing her with them.

They went, laughing and skipping, through the gates and down to the river that twined along the base of the hill. Krysta spared a quick glance at the moss-draped bridge that spanned the sparkling flow of water but chose not to inquire too deeply into what stirred beneath it.

The children were tumbling over one another like puppies. She was delighted to see it, having sensed that their earlier constraint was unnatural. Did everyone at Hawkforte, or at least all those not under the lord's direct command, have to pretend they were something other than they were to appease Demanding Daria?

At that irreverent thought, Krysta put a hand to her mouth to stifle a giggle but could not hold it back entirely. Sprawled on the riverbank, her small fingers teasing a stone she looked about to toss, Edythe glanced at her with wisdom that belied her years. "My ma says we have more fun sneaking off than we would if we could just play whenever we want."

"Do you think that's true?" Krysta asked, settling herself beside the little girl. Edythe was about eight, slender without being thin, with alert, intelligent eyes and a firm set to her small chin. She seemed to have a mature way of looking at the world that belied her tender years.

"I think my ma says it to make the best of things but that's all right, sometimes it's what you have to do."

Wisdom indeed, Krysta thought, yet did she dislike the idea that the good people of Hawkforte had to labor under such constraints. With all her heart, she hoped her husband would allow her to make such changes as would benefit them all.

But first there was the river to play in and a happy afternoon to while away twining garlands of daisies, chasing butterflies, and seeking out the tender raspberries the children knew well how to find. Krysta contented herself with listening as they talked among themselves, now at their ease.

She had no preconceived notions of children, but these children were very wise and aware. She wondered if the adults of Hawkforte realized how much these young ones saw.

"Fat Betty is with child again," Edythe remarked as she popped a raspberry into her mouth.

A little girl seated beside her made a small O with her mouth and opened her eyes very wide. "No! Is she really? My ma says she only has to look at a man to catch a baby."

"That's not how it's done," a lad named Howard informed them. "Besides, Fat Betty's husband's off in Brittany. He went months ago on Master Tyler's ship. So what's she doin' breedin'?"

Edythe sighed, rolled her eyes, and plucked another raspberry. "Goes to show, all those foreigners runnin' around town sure stir things up. Least that's what my da says."

"Good for business though," Howard remarked. "My da says we're plumper than he ever dreamed we would be this side of paradise. Lord Hawk knows a sharp sword, a strong arm, and a good mind are what it takes to get ahead in this world." He looked around proudly as he added, "That's why Da says I ought to be after learnin' to read. Says he gonna have a word with Lord Hawk 'bout that, see if the monks here can teach me."

The good sense of this was greeted with nods all around. A little girl, Aedwynna by name, blinked her big blue eyes, smiled sweetly and said, "My da says Lord Hawk's the toughest son of a bitch he's ever met but it's all right because he's our son of a bitch."

Edythe coughed delicately and cast an eye in Krysta's direction. She also said, "Aedwynna, don't say bitch, it isn't nice. Leastways not unless you're talking about your dog."

The little girl shrugged. "Oh, all right. Anyway, my sister gets so silly every time she sees Lord Hawk. Her and her friends go all giggly. They say that woman who's coming better be really, really nice."

Suddenly, she remembered who was listening. "She is, isn't she, Ilka?"

Caught off guard, "Ilka" did not answer at once, prompting Edythe to look at her with concern. "She's pretty and kind, and she'll be a good wife to Lord Hawk, won't she?"

"Oh, yes, of course. But you know . . . she might be an even better wife if she knew more about Lord Hawk, knew what he likes and doesn't like, for instance. That might help her to do a better job right from the start."

Edythe understood that immediately. "We could help. We could tell you things and you could tell her."

"I suppose you could. . . ."

"Well, then . . . Lord Hawk is very, very strong. He's had to be all his life because he spent most of it fighting up until a few years ago when King Alfred got the Danes to stop trying to take any more of England."

"I saw him once pick up a man the size of a horse," Howard declared, "and throw him all the way to the other side of the training field. The fellow wasn't hurt, fact they were both laughin', but it was really somethin' to see."

"I saw him lift up the whole back end of a cart loaded with rocks," another young boy chimed in, "and hold it while a man who was caught under it crawled out."

"That was Old Finney, he could've gotten killed right then. You know, he goes to mass every single day and lights a candle for Lord Hawk?"

"My ma always puts him in her prayers," Edythe said.

The other children nodded, one after another, as though this was common practice.

"My ma helps cook for the high table," Aedwynna said, "and she makes Lord Hawk's favorite rhubarb pie whenever she can."

"My ma weaves," said Howard. "She says he doesn't pay much mind to what he wears but she's still always trying to come up with colors and things she thinks he'll like."

"He definitely needs a wife," Edythe decided. "After all these years of Daria—" She shuddered.

"A good wife," little Aedwynna amended, and they all nodded firmly.

Edythe kept an eye on the passage of the sun and called a reminder to the rest when it was time to return. They were back within the walls of the fortress as Daria's litter bumped and swayed up the river road.

The berries were apportioned behind the wash house with Edythe handing out shares in what was apparently an established process. Krysta would have declined hers, not wanting to take from the children, but Edythe stood firm.

"You helped gather so you must have some, too."

Thus did she return to her quarters with an apron filled with summer's fruit and a bemused expression. Raven joined her a short time later.

"Wonderful berries," the black-garbed woman said as she settled on a stool beside Krysta. "I've been eating them all afternoon." Yet her appetite must not have been sated for she made quick work of a handful while she described what she had seen.

"Rich land, orderly farms, far more people living closer together than we're used to. I suppose that's because of the milder climate." She popped another berry into her mouth and continued. "There are watchtowers in both directions along the coast for miles. I saw several patrols, all wearing the colors of the Hawk. They looked as though they knew their business."

"Anything else?" Krysta asked.

Raven hesitated. She tilted her head to one side and peered at her mistress. "I saw him, too. He has a chamber at the top of the keep."

Krysta shifted on the stool, pretending great interest in whatever was going on outside the small window. "Was he alone?"

"No."

At her mistress's exasperated look, Raven laughed. "Oh, all right, he was with that fellow I think must be his steward. They were going over correspondence. He reads, by the by."

"Really?" That was surprising since few lords could claim such a skill. Her half-brother mocked the very idea of it, saying it was the province of eunuch priests. She smiled at the thought of him trying to fit Hawk into that category.

Her smile wobbled a little as she realized she would shortly see her intended husband. It was almost the supper hour. Tantalizing smells wafted from the kitchens and people were beginning to move into the great hall on the first floor of the tower.

"Come along," Raven said. Seeing her young mistress's hesitation, she added, "A few berries won't hold you. You need more than that."

Perhaps so, yet did she feel so swamped by sudden nervousness that she doubted she could eat a morsel. Had it not been for the reassurance of Raven on one side of her and Thorgold on the other, Krysta truly wondered if she would have managed to set foot in the hall of the Hawk.

Chapter

TWO

THERE WAS THE GIRL AGAIN, JUST NOW ENtering the hall with her two odd companions. She seemed unsettled, although Hawk couldn't imagine why. He surveyed her over the rim of his drinking cup while listening with one ear to the ever-diligent Edvard.

"Although the rains have not been as generous as we would wish, lord, yet the crops do well thanks to the channels you ordered dug three seasons ago. The harvest will be less than last year when rainfall was greater, but we should have ample grain for the stores."

"Ample . . ." Hawk murmured, still watching the girl. She held herself stiffly and darted an anxious look here and there, yet for all that she moved gracefully. Her body was slim, well-formed, with lithe strength that suggested an active life. But then he supposed it would be for she was a servant, undoubtedly accustomed to physical labors, although her skin was very smooth, giving no sign of excessive exposure to the sun. . . .

"Salt supplies are sufficient for our needs, yet we might be advised to lay in a larger quantity should there be an opportunity to do so at a reasonable price. As you know, due to the unsettled situation along the coasts, supply lines are subject to sudden interruption with the result that—"

Her hair was a deep black without shine. It was the only unattractive part of her.

Hawk's hand jerked, sloshing ale over the rim of the cup. What was he thinking? He had no business finding the servant of his intended wife attractive or unattractive, or for that matter noticing anything about her at all. Only a man born for folly would make so elemental a mistake, and Hawk was very far from that. As reluctant a bridegroom as he might be, he wanted the marriage for the peace it would bring, and he fully intended for that peace to extend into his own household. His wife's servant! God's breath, he must be in dire need of a woman if he was that susceptible to green eyes and a winsome glance. Yet it wasn't all that long since he had been at Alfred's court and eased himself with a pleasant widow who knew better than to expect more of him than a sweet tumble or two. . . . All right, more than two, but then he was a man in his prime who had deliberately turned away from the monkish life because he knew he would stumble over the obstacle of celibacy. Maybe when he was older . . . much, much older. Or better yet, dead.

His bride would arrive, the bride his brother-in-law swore—absolutely swore—was "not unappealing," whatever the hell that meant. Damn Wolf for refusing to say more. Hawk would do his duty by her, and if she proved cold, he would take a mistress. But *not* his wife's servant. The very thought appalled him.

". . . Charcoal could be a problem if you wish the smiths to increase production. While our sources for iron remain good, we might consider . . . Lord—?" Aware of his master's preoccupation, Edvard broke off.

Several moments passed before Hawk noticed the si-

lence. He waved a hand, trying to cover his lapse.
"Enough, Edvard, I am in awe of your diligence. But now
is the time to relax, enjoy your supper, perhaps even talk
of something other than production tallies." Around
them, the lieutenants who were privileged to share the
high table with their lord laughed. They had a sensible
appreciation of the steward, who was both a fair man and
one rising in power, but they didn't mind seeing him
mildly embarrassed.

Neither, it seemed, did Edvard, whose momentary
surprise gave way quickly to a grin. Tucking the slate
upon which he kept his numbers into his tunic, he took his
own seat. A pretty serving girl, the same one who of late
always seemed to be close by, seeing to his needs, gave
him a mug of ale and what even the preoccupied Edvard
knew to be an encouraging smile. That prompted a fresh
round of chuckles from the other men, including Hawk,
who was glad to shuck off gloomy thoughts of his impending marriage, if only briefly.

They were certainly in a good mood at the high table,
Krysta thought. As the deep, male laughter mounted, she
tried very hard not to stare but caught herself doing it
anyway. Laughter made her husband-to-be look younger
and more approachable. For just an instant, she considered doing as Thorgold and Raven had advised, going to
him and revealing her true identity. The idea was tempting, all the more so for the stirrings of desire awakening
within her. She had a brief, flashing glimpse of herself in
his arms but turned from it firmly. For all its enticement,
the idea was also fraught. Even if the Hawk forgave her
deception, perhaps even laughed over it as he was doing
now at some sally from one of his men, she would be no
closer to her goal of eluding the fate that had overtaken
her mother. She must—*must*—be loved by her proud
Saxon lord. Nothing, not even her own yearnings, could
be allowed to draw her from that course.

Seeking distraction, Krysta glanced around the hall. It was a large timber structure, similar to the hall where the women servants slept, but much more spacious and of an indisputably male nature. The walls were hung with banners, shields, and weapons, all glinting in the light of the center fire and the torches set on tall iron spikes. The lord's table was massive, made of polished oak and set with platters of beaten bronze. For Hawk, there was a high-backed chair of equally imposing design. His lieutenants, the steward, and the others privileged to be seated there were accommodated on stools of finely tanned leather. All in all, it was a display of wealth and power that left no doubt the master of Hawkforte was a man to be reckoned with.

Nor were the humbler folk forgotten. For them, there were large trestle tables and benches, platters of tin and pottery, and even cups of carved horn. For all, there was an array of foods carried out by servants under the watchful eye of the Lady Daria, who, from her own seat at the high table, glared over them. Alone among those closest to the Hawk, she and one other, a priest who sat next to her, did not share in the general merriment.

Raven's sharp elbow in her side drew Krysta from her thoughts. She jumped a little in surprise. "He's staring at you again," her servant informed her. Raven scowled down her long nose and sent a sidelong glance toward the high table. "Seems puzzled, he does, and who can blame him? What were you thinking of, gawking like that?"

Krysta darted a quick look at Hawk, saw that he was indeed staring at her, and ducked her head. Briefly, she wished a hole would open and consume her. A little sigh of relief escaped her as the man beside Hawk said something, diverting his attention.

Thorgold seized a platter of herring and began helping himself. He was as quick with a basket of bread, ignoring the chiding glances from those around them.

Raven took a few of the small fish, popped them into her mouth whole, and swallowed with a grimace. She looked with scorn at the partridges being carried to the high table. "Those would have tasted so much the better on the wing."

"Best hope the cook isn't too inventive," Thorgold chuckled, "elsewise, you could be seeing one of your cousins in the same condition."

Raven's small eyes flashed. "Not even these savage Saxons are that foolish."

"Hush," Krysta murmured. They spoke in Norse but there was no telling who might understand them. She had needed scarcely a glance around the great hall to tell her that much of Hawkforte's prosperity came from trade. Trade made possible by the might of its lord, who protected the fine harbor adjacent to the fortress and the ships coming and going from it. The Norse, too, were great traders and Thorgold had his own ways of acquiring little luxuries from far lands. If that involved lurking beneath bridges to exact a toll from unwary travelers, Krysta did not care to inquire too closely. She recognized fine velvets from Byzantium, the scent of spices from the legendary lands of the rising sun, jewels from beyond the great desert said to lie near the southern shore of the Mediterranean, and much more. Trade brought with it sophistication, which meant it would be a grave mistake to underestimate these Saxons, however jovial their manner.

Especially jovial when they were eating as they all were save herself. Realizing that would seem very odd, Krysta looked around hastily for something from which to make her supper. She smiled with relief to see the bowls piled with fresh summer greens and, nearby, rounds of cheese. With that, a bit of bread, and one of the tasty herring she was well content. At the high table, they were supping on roasted haunch of venison. A stew of the same meat was ladled out for all to share. Krysta made herself busy with the cheese, and after a moment the bowl of stock, herbs, and floating chunks of flesh passed by her.

She didn't eat much, Hawk noticed. Mayhap that accounted for her slenderness rather than did the usual hard work of a servant. Mayhap his wife-to-be was an indulgent mistress. Mayhap the unknown Krysta of Vestfold was a kind, gentle woman who would prove a balm to his life. Particularly if he stopped staring at her servant. God's blood, what was wrong with him?

The thud of his cup as he put it down hard on the table was lost in the general talk and laughter. For that, Hawk was glad. He wanted none of his people to notice his preoccupation—or his susceptibility. Both were weaknesses, therefore to be denied. He was relieved when the scop came forth, taking up his position near the central fire, and flung his arms wide, his deep voice calling out over the assembly, his words punctuated by the soft thrumming of the tabor held by the scop's young apprentice.

> "Hearken!
> I sing of great lords and noble deeds
> Deeds of valor and daring to smite our enemies
> Enemies who flee before us
> We who triumph by the mercy of God
> God-giving great leaders
> King-over-all, Alfred
> His strong right hand, the great Hawk
> Swift of wing, deadly of talon
> Holding us safe within his grasp
> Great lords and noble deeds
> Enemies fleeing
> Our lands our own
> Evermore!"

Cheers greeted this evocation but a quick hush followed as the tale resumed. Krysta settled in to listen, knowing how much there was to glean from the songs of the skalds and judging this teller-of-tales was of the same brotherhood.

He did not disappoint but went on to recite with eloquence and fervor the events of the age. He sang of Alfred's flight into the Athelney marshes to escape the invading Danes, his return to Somerset to rally his men and bring the armies of the fyrd to great victory over the Danes at Edington. Scarcely a soul in the hall breathed or moved. Though already well known, the story was told with such power as to seem to be unfolding at that very moment. When the scop sang of Alfred's skill as both maker and keeper of peace, the people smiled among themselves. And when his song turned to Hawkforte's master, they grinned and reached again for their drinking cups, casting amused looks at the lord, who appeared resigned to sitting through the recitation of his deeds yet again.

The scop intoned:

> "Then did the people weep,
> Weep for the loss of Lady Cymbra
> Taken by stealth in the night
> Night of the Wolf
> Come out of the north
> North did he take her to his great stronghold
> Sciringesheal by the sea
> There did the Hawk fly, straight and true
> True to honor and courage
> Bold to free fair Cymbra
> Returned to us safe.
> Yet safe through the ice lanes comes the Wolf
> Comes to reclaim his bride
> Wife and sister, healer of grace
> Grace to soothe the warriors' rage.
> Then did these two lords make peace
> Peace of Hawkforte, struck here in this place

Peace of families bound
Peace of children born and to-be-born
Peace of our peoples united
Evermore!"

Before the last word of the song began to fade, tumultuous cheers broke out. The people slammed their horn cups against the table, calling out their approval. Such exuberance made Raven skittish and Thorgold grumbly, but Krysta was enthralled. She had heard snatches of the tale that unfolded the year before in the rich port of Sciringesheal, lair of the mighty Norse Wolf, of a woman of great beauty taken by cunning, of a marriage forged from vengeance that became the seed of true love, of the Viking army that set sail to reclaim the stolen bride stolen in turn by her brother, the mighty Hawk, and of the war averted by wisdom and grace. Indeed, she had a particular interest in all that for it was the alliance forged by Wolf and Hawk that her own marriage was meant to strengthen yet further. With that, she had no quarrel. If her life could be an instrument of peace, she would not have it otherwise. But she would be loved, lest the cold, gray waters that had claimed her mother claim her in turn.

Such gloomy thoughts had no place amid revelry. She put it aside, and a short time later she slipped away with Raven and Thorgold to find what rest she could in this strange new place she must call her home . . . evermore.

BEFORE THE LAST STARS OF NIGHT HAD WINKED OUT, before the first cock of morn had crowed, the stirrings of sparrows in the eaves of the women's hall woke Krysta from uneasy slumber. For a moment, lying there in the gray shadows, she had no idea where she was. The air smelled of wood and smoke, the same as at home. The birds rustling in beds of ivy sounded no different. But the air was warmer, tangy with salt yet soft, and the murmur of waves in the distance was softer still for they made land on a gentler shore. Memory returned swiftly and with it the last wisps of sleep vanished as though they had never been. She rose and glanced at Raven, who still slept, head tucked against her chest. Softly, so as not to disturb her, Krysta dressed. She wore a simple wool gown dyed blue with a mix of dandelion root, woad, and juniper. Around her waist was a plain leather belt from which dangled the traditional tools of a trusted house servant—a knife, a thimble, a small felt case holding needles, precious scissors, and keys belonging to the chests that had come with her. Over her hair, she threw a finely woven white shawl, one end of which she tossed over her shoulder. Thus ready to face the day, she tiptoed past the other sleeping alcoves and stepped outside.

Her first surprise was the men on the walls. They were awake, alert, walking their posts. At such an hour? And not only a token watch but a large number, keeping guard through the night while she and everyone else in Hawkforte slumbered. More than anything else she had so far seen, that vigilance brought home to her the sheer power and determination of the keep's master. The keep's and her own . . .

Hastily, she looked away, noting the fires that were already lit here and there, including in the kitchens. A goodly number of servants were stirring despite the early hour. The gates remained closed save for a small door set to one side, through which other early risers were being admitted. Slipping through the shadows, Krysta made her way to that door. She waited until a gaggle of washer women were entering, then slipped out amidst the confusion of their greetings, their sallies, and their giggles. Making her way down the hillside, she felt a prickling at the back of her neck as though the fortress itself sternly observed her going.

Quickening her pace, she made for the woods near the bottom of the hill. Within the shelter of the first line of trees, she paused to catch her breath. Such a soft land, so gentle in comparison to her own, so enticing as to make her senses swim. A tiny brook gurgled softly nearby. Following it, Krysta found her way to a larger stream running over moss-draped rocks. Here and there, silver fish glinted and turtles dozed on fallen logs. The stream became a fall that spilled over boulders, flowing on into a tranquil pool that slipped almost unseen toward the sea. The ground turned from fecund soil to moist sand. Oaks gave way to pine. The sweetness of fragrant grass yielded to salt tang. She emerged from the coolness of the wood to stand suddenly on open beach. A bay stretched out before her, cradled within the curving arms of the land.

On impulse, she threw her own arms wide as though to embrace all that she saw. Her feet danced lightly over the sand. She whirled, laughing as she eluded the wash of foam advancing and retreating along the beach. Behind her, the sun rose in splendor, bathing the shore in golden light.

Bathing the woman, too, at her play. Her slender body moving this way and that, so lightly that she seemed not quite connected to the land, she appeared more sprite than human. From his stance on an outcropping of rock above the beach, Hawk watched, suddenly entranced even as he half expected her to vanish into the mist of sea spray. His keen eyes followed her progress along the beach. The breeze changed direction slightly and he caught a riff of her laughter, like crystalline droplets of sound. Abruptly, he realized he was smiling.

She amused him, that was all. There was something about her odd combination of shy awkwardness and innocent grace that pierced his reserve. It wasn't desire he felt, merely humor. Not that she wasn't lovely, she was that, but there were plenty of lovely women. He'd never had any trouble taking or leaving them as he was wont. After all, a man had to be ruled by higher considerations. Only a fool was led by his cock.

A shower of pebbles rolling from beneath his boots drew Hawk's attention to the fact that he was walking down the hilly slope to the beach. He hadn't meant to do that, but what of it? He'd come out for a bit of time to himself before the hurly-burly of the day. Who said he couldn't spend it strolling along his own shore. Indeed, she was the interloper, not he. She and those two other strange ones had come uninvited, unaccompanied by his tardy betrothed, and apparently now with nothing to occupy themselves save amusement. He was surprised Daria hadn't organized some work for them, but then he supposed she had no reason to allow them any usefulness that might reflect well on their mistress. Briefly, his mind drifted to Daria's likely reaction to being supplanted by the Lady Krysta. He'd have to deal with that, he supposed, and firmly, but he couldn't very well until the lady herself arrived and he had some sense of how assertive she was likely to be. From what he could see so far—or rather not see since she did not deign to present herself for his perusal—she was either extraordinarily bold in delaying her arrival or equally timid. Either way, he suspected he was going to be troubled.

And that being the case, there was all the more reason to take a pleasant stroll down the beach.

Krysta was bending to examine an opalescent stone gleaming in the little eddies of water near a rock pool when a shadow fell across her. She looked up, shading eyes that widened at the sight of the dark shape silhouetted against the rising sun. The Hawk. She knew him in an instant even though she could not make out his features. He was a very large man, easily standing head and shoulders above her, and she herself was tall compared to many of the Saxon women. Those shoulders were very broad indeed, so much so that they seemed to block out the sun. There was no softness about him, neither in his stance nor in the strength he radiated, save perhaps in the curls of his hair moving gently in the breeze. Krysta forced herself to focus on those curls where they clustered near the nape of his neck. Truly, they looked as fine and delicate as the silk on a baby's head. The thought made her smile.

"Good morrow, woman." His voice was deep, like water far in the earth. He held out a hand. She took it without thought and stood. His palm was large, hard, and callused. His skin was very warm. She snatched back her hand and squinted against the sun.

"Good morrow, my lord." She spoke clearly enough yet her voice sounded weak in her own ears, like the song of a reed cast upon urgent wind.

"Where is your mistress?"

The question was abrupt, the tone all the more so. Krysta stiffened. Without meaning to, she looked up, meeting his eyes. "My mistress . . . lord?"

"The Lady Krysta. Do you not remember whom you serve?"

Was he always so peremptory? So rude? This man whose love she must win? Her mouth thinned. "I remember well enough, lord. The Lady Krysta is coming here."

He ran a hand through those silken curls and frowned, his impatience manifest in the way he turned, half-away as though wishing to be done with her, yet turning back as though uncertain in his desires.

"I know that, woman. What I am wondering is why she is not yet here."

She had not anticipated that he would ask her. Indeed, she had not expected to have speech directly with him while she was no more than the servant of his absent betrothed. She had thought merely to observe from a safe distance.

There was very little distance between them now and she did not feel safe at all.

"I cannot speak for the Lady Krysta, lord."

A small jolt of fear went through her as he scowled. Was he a violent man, her betrothed? Yes, of a certainty he must be for he was a mighty warlord, but was he violent to those weaker than himself? Would he strike a servant unable to provide him with the information he sought?

Would he strike a wife who displeased him?

He sighed and shook his head. "No, I suppose you can't. Mayhap I should not have asked."

So easy was he then? So ready to forgive? A spurt of hope surged within her. Seeking she knew not what, perhaps to please him, she said, "But she does come, lord, most eagerly."

"Eagerly? Really?" He looked surprised, almost boyishly so, and what else was that there in his eyes blue as the sky? Hope?

Impulse took her. She wanted to confirm that hope and nourish it. "Of a certainty, the Lady Krysta is most eager for this marriage. She wishes for there to be peace between Norse and Saxon, and she believes this marriage is the best chance for that."

"You have her confidence then? She tells you what she thinks?"

Krysta hesitated. How much to say, to claim? How far dare she go? "I am but a servant, lord, yet do I believe I know my lady's mind at least in this matter, for she has made no secret of it."

He looked out to sea, looked at her again. "She has no concerns . . . no hesitations?"

"Ah, well, as to that, marriage brings great changes, does it not? Especially marriage in a far land and to an unknown lord. But my lady is resolved to do her utmost that all should be well between you."

"Arriving would be a good first step." He sounded disgruntled rather than angry. Even perhaps a little puzzled.

"Oh, but she will! And soon, I am sure. It is just that . . . she has always lived among the same people and leaving them is difficult. She needs must do all she can to see they will be well cared for."

"Surely her half-brother—what's his name, Sven?— can be expected to look after her people?"

Krysta hesitated. Frantically, she tried to think what a servant would be likely to say about Sven. She had met her half-brother only thrice in her life, once after their father's death, the second time when she was summoned to be presented to the jarl Wolf Hakonson, the third to be told she was being given in marriage to the Lord of Hawkforte. Despite such brief acquaintance, she had an unpleasant feeling about Sven. He struck her as a man of empty smiles and even emptier promises.

"Even so, lord, I believe the Lady Krysta feels a personal responsibility for her people." All perfectly true, for she had racked her brains and worn herself down with worry until the few dozen families clustered at her cliff-side manor were safely snug, with relatives in distant villages.

"That is . . . good."

Krysta began to smile.

"Unless, of course, it is vanity."

The smile turned to open-mouth amazement. She gaped at him. "V-vanity . . . ? It is vanity to care for her people?"

He shrugged. "Sometimes, people have difficulty telling the difference between caring about something and just trying to control it."

"I assure you, the Lady Krysta knows the difference."

He nodded as though to note her assertion but not necessarily believe it. "You are loyal to her, as would be expected."

"I am not merely loyal, lord. I *know* the Lady Krysta and I can assure you, she is not interested in controlling anything."

He speared her with a sudden look that sent a shiver to her toes. "She's not a lackwit, is she?"

At this rate, she'd be swallowing flies before long. Krysta shut her mouth hard. She took a breath and another before she tried to speak. "Might I ask, lord, why you should wonder such a thing?"

"Most people want some control over their lives. Only the most inept seek to be told everything to do, when to do it, and so on. She's not like that, is she?"

Patience, her mind counseled. *Hope,* her heart pleaded.

"No, lord, she is not like that."

He bent down, picked up the opalescent rock she had been admiring a few minutes before, and sent it spinning out over the water where it splashed, once, twice . . . five times before settling out of sight.

"What is she like?"

A boy's gesture, a man's question. *What is anyone like?*

"She . . . cares about her people, as I have said. She wants peace between Norse and Saxon. She will miss her home but she is determined to find a new one here."

She spoke wistfully, Hawk thought, another who would miss her home. He stared at the girl whose company he had not meant to seek, whose name he deliberately had not asked, the girl with green eyes and freckles across the bridge of her nose. She was a pretty thing, not with the stunning beauty of his sister Cymbra, whose presence was enough to make men walk into walls, but pretty all the same. More even than pretty when she smiled . . . or looked thoughtful . . . or merely stared back at him as she was doing now.

He looked at his hand reaching out as though to touch her cheek and had no idea how that had come to be.

She swallowed hard and stepped back. "Lord . . ."

"*Caauuuaaawwww* . . ." Black wings flashed overhead. Hawk looked up as the raven swept past, little higher than his head, circling. He heard fluttering, turned, saw other ravens perched in the trees just beyond the beach, black shadows amid the branches.

"*Caauuuaaawww.*" Had there always been so many at Hawkforte? He didn't remember that but thought little of it. Birds came and went.

The green-eyed girl's reaction was different. She looked surprised, then annoyed. Mayhap she did not like birds.

"I must go, lord." This was said on the wing, as it were, for she was already halfway up the beach. He almost moved to stop her but caught himself. His betrothed wife's servant. Folly unimaginable.

He lingered awhile yet on the beach before impatient duty sent him back whence he had come. The gates of Hawkforte stood open, carts and wagons streaming through. Beyond those gates lay the town and beyond it more walls and more gates, all well guarded by the Hawk's own men, trained to his exacting standard of vigilance and deadly skill. It was a fat, prosperous town, straining at the walls that contained it. Soon, mayhap as soon as the coming year, he must needs begin to build a new ring of wall to let the town expand. There were so many merchants coming in search of his protection, growing wealthy beneath the shelter of his sword, and drawing many more to do the same. So, too, were there scholars, for Alfred had begun that fashion and Hawk had followed it gladly. Men came who were at home in books, marvels that they were, who could speak of events long distant as though they had happened but yesterday. Others came with talents of their own. Hawkforte boasted some of the finest smiths in all of Essex, if not beyond. The same for tanners, carpenters, and the like. There were monks to illuminate the manuscripts that poured from the abbey Hawk had founded, apothecaries to tend to his people's ills, men who built marvels never seen before in these lands, who had conceived the idea for the channels that kept the crops green in a year of scant rain.

It all made for a loud, messy concoction, this burgh of his, but he was proud of it in a way he had never expected to be in a life that seemed destined for little more than blood and sweat. Thanks to Alfred's vision, something better had proved possible and Hawk was determined to protect it at all costs. Yet, too, did he wish to enjoy it. He went among his people now without display or hindrance, on foot and dressed simply in a well-worn tunic of unornamented brown wool. Only the sword belted to his side gave hint of his rank, that and the deference of his people. Hats were doffed in his direction, he received shy smiles, and an old woman pressed a warm raisin bun into his hand. Hawk was glad of it, having come out without first breaking his night's fast. He bit into it as he walked.

He moved slowly along the rows of shops and stalls, pausing to speak to a merchant here, a peasant there. There was a time when he had known virtually everyone at Hawkforte by name. The place had grown too much for that still to be the case, yet he tried. A man, Toby as he was known, put an arm around the shoulders of his sturdy young son and announced that the lad was beginning his apprenticeship as a wheelwright that very day. Hawk riffled the boy's hair and offered his congratulations as family and onlookers alike beamed their pleasure.

He moved on past a tavern popular with ship captains and their crews. Trestle tables were just being set up outside, yet a few stalwarts were already enjoying a morning tongue-tickler. Hawk received invitations to join them but declined cordially. He was climbing the mount toward the fortress itself when a flicker of movement at the corner of his eye stopped him. Instinctively, his hand went to the hilt of his sword.

Thorgold snorted. He unfolded himself from his perch beneath a stone arch that held up part of the road and grinned at Hawk. "Easy there, lord, 'tis only old Thorgold. Good morrow to ye."

"And to you," Hawk responded automatically. He felt foolish reaching for his sword, although not as foolish as he had felt reaching for the green-eyed girl. That sensation prompted him to speak more sternly than he would have otherwise. "What do you here?"

"Restin' my bones, lord. 'Tis a long journey we've had."

Still irked, Hawk said, "It must be as it is taking your mistress so long to make it."

The strange fellow—bearded and stooped, barrel-chested above bandy legs—chuckled. "Impatient are ye? Well an' ye' should be. She's a fine lass, she is."

"Lass? Are you that familiar with her then?"

"Ye could say so. Known her since the day she was born."

Foolishness was dogging him this day. He might as well add to it. "Tell me of her."

Thorgold grinned. "Are ye that eager to know her?"

"Eager? No, merely curious."

The old man pursed his lips, nodding sagely. "Ah, curiosity, now there's the thing. Men have wandered the earth because of it." He cast a sideways grin. "Or mayhap they only wanted to get away from the womenfolk. Trouble they can be, sad to say. Harpin' on this and that, never done. Voices like . . . well, I won't say ravens 'cause I want no trouble myself. But raucous they can be when they've a mind. Know what I mean?"

Hawk thought of Daria and sighed. "I suppose I do."

"Ah, but then there's the other kind. Soft as a spring rain, strong as water running over rock. Wears down the rock, it does, but gently like. Rock hardly knows what's happening to it. Doesn't seem to mind neither."

"I am not a rock," Hawk said. He looked up at the sky so blue as to sting the eyes, down and around at the trees cut back from the fortress walls. Ravens were sitting in them. So many ravens. "I am a man."

Thorgold chuckled again. He seemed pleased with the response. It made him generous. "She likes hair ribbons."

"What . . . ?"

"Ribbons, for her hair. She likes 'em. All different colors, doesn't seem to matter. Ever since she was a little thing, she's liked hair ribbons." He stared back at Hawk staring at him. "Keeps 'em in a little chest, she does. All curled up like flowers."

"Are you suggesting I acquire some hair ribbons?"

Thorgold shrugged. "Couldn't hurt."

"What about jewels, furs, silks?"

"Hair ribbons."

"A fine mount, luxurious hangings for her chamber, rare perfumes?"

"Hair ribbons."

"A mirror from the farthest reaches of Araby, cedar chests filled with spices, a harp strung from the tail of a unicorn?"

"Hair ribbons. And I'd forget that about the unicorn, if I were ye. They can't be caught."

Hawk fought a smile, didn't win. "Are you telling me I'll be an old, old man and still buying her hair ribbons?"

"Ye will if ye be lucky, lord. Are ye? Is the fey gift of fortune sittin' on those broad shoulders?"

"Damned if I know." Was it? He'd had good fortune in his life and bad. The Essex of his childhood had been a more dangerous and uncertain place than it was now. Yet no man of sense drew more than two easy breaths in a row. His mother had died too soon, yet gentle memory remained, elusive, sometimes filling him with yearning at unexpected moments. Odd things would set it off—a snatch of song, a whiff of scent, the murmur of a voice that was almost but not quite familiar. He was accustomed to it. By contrast, he scarcely remembered the selfish, unthinking girl who had perished in a foolish accident of her own making shortly after their marriage, taking their unborn child with her. He had done well in the terms of the world and was glad of that, yet were there times when he found himself wondering if there was anything more to be hoped for, something as yet undiscovered and unexperienced.

A signal horn rang out, the warning of riders approaching Hawkforte. Its master took a quick step, levering himself up onto the arch, and looked out beyond the town. He spied the banner of the royal equerry fluttering above a party of a dozen horsemen.

Chapter

THREE

THEY WERE LIKE MEWLING BABES, BRAYING their laughter, posturing, expecting their every whim to be obeyed. Watching the men newly arrived from the court at Winchester, prattling on with her *dear* brother, Daria sneered. They were such dung-for-brains, all of them, imagining themselves to be of worth and consequence when they could not even recognize the person of true consequence among them. And Hawk was the worst of them. Malicious fate had made them siblings of a sort. He suffered her presence under his roof because it was his duty to do so. She knew it and hated him for it. But he went his own way, brushing her off as lightly as he would a fly, scarcely noticing that she existed. She would change that. Oh, yes, make no mistake, she would change it once and for all.

Daria looked away from the men at the high table, trying to block out their deep laughter, but the very smell of them overtook her. She was engulfed in the scents of leather, wool, sweat, and something intrinsically male she did not care to know. Her senses whirled and for a moment she thought she would be ill, vomiting it all up right there for everyone to see.

Father Elbert's pale hand on her arm steadied her. "Be at ease, lady." His voice was low, sibilant, oddly soothing. She stared into his narrow face lit by coal-black eyes and felt the tumult of the hall fading. Slowly, she exhaled, willing her weakness away.

"How I despise them," she murmured, conscious of the need not to be overheard. Anyone observing them would see only a holy man in consultation with a righteous woman, her gaze suitably downcast, her manner humble. Appearance was all.

"As you should, lady, but the time of repentance is coming. They shall pay for all their crimes."

"They cannot pay enough, it isn't possible." She glanced again at Hawk—big, hard muscled, blatantly masculine in a way that made her strangely unsettled. Her late, unlamented husband had been a weakling, too stupid to do as she directed, too inept to seize the power that had gone to Alfred instead, an utter failure who, instead of making her the queen she was born to be, had dared to die and leave her to live on charity and dreams of revenge. Dreams that could not come true soon enough.

She had failed once, when that cow Cymbra everyone thought was so beautiful managed to survive being taken captive by the Norse Wolf and thwart the plot to provoke him into killing her, becoming instead his cherished bride. Merely thinking of that was enough to make Daria's gorge rise again. She would not fail this time—she couldn't. Hawk's unwanted Viking wife was due to arrive any day. Turning him completely against her *and* the peace she represented would give Daria more pleasure than anything else in her bitter, resentment-filled life. She glanced down the high table where Hawk sat in conversation with the lords from Winchester. A fierce, dark sense of anticipation rose within her. How eagerly she awaited his destruction, how fiercely she would relish it.

The prickling at the back of his neck distracted Hawk. He turned slightly, not taking his attention entirely from the man with whom he was speaking but seeking the source of his sudden unease. Such was his life that he had learned long ago the folly of ignoring his instinct for danger. But danger in his own hall, among his own people? Not impossible, to be sure, yet it was unlikely. He knew all the men lately come from the royal court, had fought beside them, shared hardships and hopes, and he trusted them. They were the pick of Alfred's most loyal nobles, the men who were rebuilding England, and he was proud to be counted among them. As for the rest . . .

His glance drifted past Daria, swiftly as always for he disliked being reminded of her. So, too, did he spare scarcely a moment's thought for his house priest, the dour Father Elbert. Hawk was of a mind to replace the fellow, he just hadn't gotten around to it yet. That left visitors to his hall, merchants passing through, some he recognized, others he did not. And, of course, the servants of his absent bride, the trio seated together at the farthest table. He had made a point of not looking at the girl but now he did so, finding the sight of her oddly refreshing, as though he had wandered into a cool, sylvan glen. He could almost hear the droplets of water falling through moss-laden rocks. So clear was the sensation that Hawk had to shake himself out of it.

He frowned, struck yet again by his unwonted susceptibility to the girl, and turned his attention to her companions. The black-garbed woman was busy cleaning the meat from a small pile of bones on her trencher. Pigeons had been served and he supposed that was one of them. Beside her, Thorgold was quaffing ale. He saw Hawk looking at him and raised his cup in salute. The girl noticed and looked in the same direction. Her gaze met Hawk's and he saw, actually saw across the length of the hall, her cheeks redden. She looked away hastily but not before he was struck by a bolt of lust so intense as to rob him of breath. The sensation stunned him. He was no randy youth to be overtaken by winsome eyes and a fair form. Far from it, he was a man of power and discipline. Yet just then he felt as though the years had fallen away and he was no more than a callow boy confronted by the first mysterious stirrings of his body.

Absurd. Absolutely, utterly absurd. Also mad, for she was, he reminded himself for perhaps the hundredth time, his betrothed's *servant*. Even if his soon-to-be wife was the finest woman to walk the Earth, such lunatic behavior could turn her into another Daria. The thought of being shackled to a shrill, harping woman who would actually have some claim on his time and attention filled him with sensible dread. Something would have to be done. Perhaps he could persuade the Lady Krysta to send her servants home. He could provide her with all the servants she could possibly need but she might resist all the same, preferring the company of those familiar to her. So he would begin his marriage by making his wife sad and lonely, all in order to avoid making her jealous and enraged. He sighed, wondering how large a supply of hair ribbons he should set about acquiring.

He seemed vexed, Krysta thought, and wondered at the cause. Wondered, too, about the odd look he had given her just before ignoring her completely. That look had made her feel warmed clear through and oddly tremulous. How extraordinary that someone could make her feel that way merely by looking at her. How exhilarating that the person doing it was to be her husband. She felt buoyed, as though she floated on a cushion of water, elated yet calm all at the same time. That made no sense, she was contradicting herself. *He* was contradicting herself, making her feel all sorts of at-odds emotions that jumbled together inside her. He kept looking at her, on the beach, in the hall, in her dreams. She had thought to stay beyond his sight so that later he would not recognize the girl who came to him as his wife. Now she had to wonder if there was still a chance that would work, and if it did not, how would she explain? Laugh it all off as a joke? Admit her fears, cajole him to excuse them? Neither appealed to her but she might have no other choices. Not that it mattered in the end, not so long as he loved her.

He desired her, she knew that in some essential way of knowing she had never known before. But desire was not love. So, too, did she know that. How to bridge the gulf? Krysta toyed with the food before her, finding she had no appetite. Raven was too busy with another pigeon to notice, but Thorgold did. He shot her a sympathetic look before returning to his ale.

For all that, Krysta slept surprisingly well and longer than she was accustomed to. She woke to squeals of delight coming from just beyond the women's hall. Finding it empty save for herself, she dressed hurriedly and went out into a warm, bright day. Almost at once she spied the girl child Edythe, leader of the motley crew that tumbled at her heels. So, too, did Edythe see her and grin broadly. "Daria has gone to market again. One of the kitchen boys heard her say she wouldn't be back until supper."

Before Krysta could think, she returned Edythe's grin and asked eagerly, "What shall we do first?"

The flicker of surprise in Edythe's gray eyes alerted Krysta to her misstep. How foolish of her; adults would not normally join in the antics of children. But her own childhood had been barren of such companionship and she had missed it truly. Not that she wasn't grateful for all she had known, only that she wished to know just a little of what it meant to be an ordinary child in an ordinary world.

"I meant what will you do first?"

Edythe continued looking at her. "I don't know." She hesitated a moment, weighing the novel situation. Kindness, or perhaps curiosity, won out. "But you can come with us if you want."

"I would be in the way," Krysta said softly.

Edythe shrugged. "You weren't yesterday." She turned to go, looked back over her shoulder. "C'mon then."

Krysta went, trailing after the little girl until they linked up with her friends, who, after their initial surprise, accepted her reappearance among them with the ease of open-hearted children. They went first to the river for an extended bout of frog hunting, which gave way to a frog-jumping competition won by a shy little sprite of a boy who glowed with pleasure when Edythe declared his frog the victor. From there, they gathered berries and wild greens, lolling in the grass to eat them. The day warmed and they paddled in the river, venturing along it all the way to the beach, where they rooted about for clams and mussels, finding a bounty of both. Thus laden, they returned home to deliver their treasures to their mothers, who received them gladly. The women spared a few curious glances for Krysta but did not question her. Indeed, no one had questioned her since her arrival at Hawkforte save for its master. She wondered if being a servant, and a foreign one at that, rendered her in some way invisible or if this was only an expression of courtesy on the part of people naturally inclined to respect the privacy of others. Whatever the answer, she observed that the parents were indulgent, kind to their children and glad to see them have a day of leisure. Nor did it end then, for Edythe led them back out to a circle beyond the fortress walls where, so she informed Krysta, the older boys bound for knighthood trained. They were done for the day, gone off to polish their weapons and talk of manly things, thus leaving the circle available for gentler pursuits.

The children danced. They whirled around in circles, sometimes alone, sometimes holding hands. They sang, nonsense songs mostly that they made up as they went along. They whistled, clapped, stamped their feet, flung their arms to the sky, and laughed. Krysta watched, entranced. She had never seen so much lovely, glowing energy blossoming in one spot. Instinctively, she was drawn into it. Edythe took her hand, grinning up at her, and suddenly Kysta, too, was dancing, around and around, the steps becoming more intricate, the tune playing in her mind, the song forming on her lips. The children became a line behind and around her, following where she led, their darting bodies creating ancient patterns that coiled back upon themselves before bursting out again in new shapes, new forms, new energy. It was a dance for starlight and hidden places, for strands washed by moonbright foam, for children of another ken. Yet here it was in the bright sun of a Hawkforte afternoon, among children who held within them, all unsuspected, marvels beyond reckoning. Those might be hidden but their exuberance was plain for all to see. Certainly it did not escape the Hawk, who, coming off the training field thinking of nothing more than a good steam and a mug of cold cider, stopped suddenly at the sight of them.

Children dancing? Had he ever seen that before? Of course, he must have for children were ever-energetic, yet did memory elude him and without it came the stirring unease that perhaps such merriment should be more in evidence in his domain. Since it was not, he sought some explanation for its sudden appearance and found it quickly enough. The green-eyed girl was right there in among them, noticeable only because she was taller but otherwise gamboling along with the rest. The air seemed to shimmer around her. The glow must be dust raised by their feet, glimmering in the sun. Yet it had rained in the night, softly like a benediction, and there was no dust. Only that glimmering, shimmering ripple of the air right to the edge of the circle.

He blinked, looked again, saw the children and the green-eyed girl bathed in radiance. He was no dancer but he knew the morris dances and the other revels, still indulged in on the holy days or, more often, the night before them. This dance he did not recognize. The steps were more complex. Yet did it seem he had seen it somewhere . . . sometime . . . as though in a dream. A tune rippled on the air, very faint, taking him by surprise for he saw no players to make such music. He heard a reed, high and fluting, and beneath it the throb of a drum beaten lightly. Then it was gone and the children had stopped, suddenly, as though frozen in place. They were staring at him.

Only then did he realize he had come almost into the circle, so absorbed was he in watching the dance that he might have joined it.

"My lord . . ." the green-eyed girl began. He sensed an explanation forming, perhaps a request for pardon. He felt the tension of the children, looked around at their faces set in expectation of reprimand or worse. Thought of the child he had lost unborn when his feckless wife went to her death, felt the old pain of that for the first time in more years than he could count.

"You should dance more often," he said, and smiled.

They stared at him as though he had grown a second head. All but the green-eyed girl, who, after a moment, cast him a smile of gratitude and . . . vanished. No, she didn't really, but they all moved off suddenly before he might have a chance to reconsider the good humor they apparently did not trust. In an instant, it seemed, she was gone, yet did she linger in his thoughts after his steam and

the mug of cider, after the evening's meal was eaten, the
stories sung, the fires banked. Later, even as he slept, she
danced through his dreams, laughing.

God's blood, he was a fool after all.

THE AIR WAS TOO STILL; IT CLUNG TO HER LIKE A
shroud. Krysta turned over restlessly, the ropes of
her bed creaking beneath her. Raven fluttered nearby,
grumbling. Loath to disturb her, longing to escape the
burr of sleeplessness, Krysta rose. She slept nude—who
did not?—but donned a shift for modesty's sake before
stealing forth from the hall. The night air was warm with
an exotic scent of far-off lands carried on the sea breeze.
She looked up and saw the sea above, the ribbon of stars
stretching from horizon to horizon, not a wisp of cloud to
mar them. The moon had long since set, the stars the only
light save for the flare of watch fires at intervals along the
walls. Coils of dark smoke rose from them, drifting
around the silhouettes of men who paused in their patrol
to speak a few words and survey the night together.

Hugging the shadows, she drifted toward the inner
edge of the walls. There was no clear thought in her mind
of where to go or what to do until she saw the embers
glowing red in the smithy's forge. All day the ring of hammer on metal sang out from there yet now was it stilled,
the only sounds the faint call of an owl and, closer by, a
rustling in the straw. That and a soft mewing. She crept
closer, scarcely breathing. The tabby raised her head, eyeing Krysta with frank appraisal. After a moment, she
blinked and returned her attention to the tiny kittens clustered at her belly. There were six in all, most still suckling
but a few, milk-full, asleep. Balanced on her knees, Krysta
observed them from a courteous distance. She had seen
kittens many times before but never quite this young,
pink and blind from the womb. Likely they had been born

this very night. Their mother had picked a goodly spot, warmed by the forge but tucked back in a corner well padded by straw. She appeared to know her business. As Krysta watched, the tabby laved her kits with a rough tongue, making their skin flush red. She broke off once, distracted by the scurry of a bold mouse who, under other circumstances, would have made a fine late-night snack. It escaped unscratched, thanks to her preoccupation.

"I'll bring you herring tomorrow," Krysta murmured. "You shouldn't have to hunt while your babes are so young."

The tabby blinked again as if in acknowledgment and returned to her task. Krysta continued to watch her, finding the sight of maternal care oddly soothing. So much so that she woke with a start as her head hit her chest. She had no idea how much time had passed but her legs were cramped. She moved them stiffly, bending to rub the calves as she hobbled from the forge.

He saw her first bent over, indiscernible in the predawn light. To the east, the horizon was rimmed with gray. To the west, stars still shone brilliantly. A freshening breeze blew off the sea, ruffling the tunic Hawk had cast on hurriedly when he woke from the sort of dream he had not had since tender manhood. Either his betrothed arrived promptly—and proved herself a warm and willing woman—or he must needs acquire a mistress. A man of his responsibility and supposed dignity could not afford such preoccupation with the gentler sex as he had known in his youth. For whatever reason, his juices were stirring. Best he heed them.

He was set on that, having decided in his mind, when he spied the girl coming from the forge. What did she want there in that place of fire and steel? What possible purpose could she have? And why, if she was wont to wander about at night, had she not clothed herself more properly? So far as he could see, she wore only a shift that the night wind shaped to her body. A very nice body, so he thought, slender and lithe. Never mind that, why was she creeping about? Or was she? She seemed in some distress.

For so large a man, he moved with stealthy grace. Between one breath and the next, he seemed to materialize directly in front of Krysta. She gasped, fear washing out the pain in her limbs. For an instant she didn't recognize him, and her fear mounted. What folly to be caught alone, scantily dressed, in the dark by an unknown man who might intend . . . what? A moment later, he moved and she knew him, not by his features, which she still could scarcely see, but by the essence of him, somehow already familiar to her.

"My lord . . ."

"What do you here?" He did not wait for her reply. "Have you no better sense, woman, than to wander about in the night wearing no more than . . ." He flicked a finger at the thin fabric of her shift where it billowed along her arm. She stepped back so suddenly that she would have lost her balance had not he caught her. They stood, scarcely a hand's breadth apart, his arm a band around her waist. So many impressions, flooding her so suddenly. The heat of him and the strength, the puzzlement in his eyes, the need to smooth his troubled brow, to offer comfort and far more.

Over his right shoulder, a star fell. The streak of silver distracted Krysta just long enough for reason to return. "Look," she said, and when he turned to do so, she slipped from his hold like water through the crevices of a stone.

He caught at air, scowled. She thought to flee, thought better of it. He was a hunter, it was wiser not to give him anything to pursue.

"What was your mistress thinking to send you here? She found two servants of rare ugliness, couldn't she have found a third?"

"They are not ugly," Krysta protested, instantly affronted. Thorgold and Raven were beautiful in her eyes.

The Hawk closed his for a moment, summoning patience. "It matters not. Why did she send you?"

Ah, why indeed? To spy on him, to ferret out the essence of his nature, to conspire that he might come to love . . . herself. Oh, yes, that would explain itself easily enough.

"To see to her comfort, lord."

His laugh was mocking. "Then she sorely misjudged the situation, didn't she? Is she truly that innocent?"

Was she? Just then it was not innocence Krysta felt. Knowledge was stirring in her, ancient, feminine, irresistible. But he was waiting, his silence demanding an answer. "She is . . . as she is, lord."

What more could she say? She was as she was. He would love her for it or destroy her. It was in God's hands.

A moment more he stared at her. His broad chest rose and fell as a sigh escaped him. Into that silence, he spoke a single syllable. "Go."

She went, swiftly and without looking back, knowing there truly was no escape.

T HE AIR, HEAVY AT THE START OF DAY, GREW HEAVIER as the hours passed. By afternoon, the sky was a lowering gray tinged with yellow. Dogs went about with their backs arched or slunk low to the ground. Horses whinnied anxiously. People hurried about their tasks, women doing their wash early and taking it in before it was fully dry. The sea grew unnaturally calm without a breath of wind to stir it. Inhaling deeply, Krysta felt her chest ache or perhaps it was her heart. Pierced by longing for the crisp, pine-scented breezes of home, she ventured down to the beach. The tide was out but the birds who should have been taking the opportunity to feed were nowhere to be seen. Even the gulls were absent. She stayed only a short while, driven off by the mournfulness that hung over the place.

Back within the burgh, merchants were taking in their stalls and lowering their shutters. The lanes were being stripped bare. Even the wooden troughs from which horses drank were being moved inside. The sky hung ever lower, seeming to brush the tops of the distant hills. Apprehension prickled down Krysta's back. She had seen wild storms at home when cyclones raged off the North Atlantic but this was different. The strange color of the sky and the leaden air set her nerves on edge. She looked for Raven and Thorgold but found no sign of them. Gone to ground somewhere, no doubt.

Even the smith was finishing his work early. He grinned when he saw the basket of herring she carried and waved her on to where the tabby lay enthroned. The gift was accepted with blinking courtesy and promptly devoured. Krysta lingered a few minutes, watching the kittens sleep, then took her leave. Just outside the forge, she was buffeted by a sudden swirl of wind. She tucked her head down and made for the women's hall at the other side of the compound. But before she could get very far, the sky opened and a sheet of rain soaked her to the skin. Staggering at the sudden onslaught, she looked around for closer shelter, saw the stables, and ran for them. Inside, the door closed firmly behind her, Krysta sighed with relief. The tumult of the storm was growing ever stronger. A sudden clatter of wind smashing against the wood-plank walls drove her deeper within. Water dripped from her gown. She bent over to wring out the hem just as a bolt of lightning rent the sky, bringing with it a crack so loud as to deafen her momentarily. A mere glimpse of the finger of fire caught through a shutter torn from its hinge was so bright as to be almost blinding. Dazed, uncertain what to do, she looked around in all directions. The whinnying of a horse and the deep-voiced response of a man drew her toward the far end of the stables. She thought to remain out of sight, comforted merely by the presence of another, but such was not to be. Just as she neared, the man turned. She saw his features in the glow of yet another bolt of lightning, like harshly beautiful stone.

"God's blood." It sounded like a plea for deliverance.

"I'm sorry, I was caught in the storm. The women's hall was too far."

The words tumbled over each other. The air seemed to crackle with a strange smell that made the fine hairs at the back of Krysta's neck rise. Hawk stepped away from the stallion he had been steadying. What was the point of trying to calm the horse when he couldn't calm himself? All day, he had stayed away from this woman, driving himself and his men on the training field and at the hunt. When despite all that she remained steadfast in his mind, he had made the decision to send her to his dear brother-in-law with proper escort and a message inquiring as to the whereabouts of his absent bride. The whole sorry business was the result of Wolf's conniving, let him sort it out. Now here she was, right in front of him, tempting as a draft of cool water to a parched man, dangerous as the storm that had thrown them together . . . again.

Wolf would say it was Loki's doing. The god of mischief delighted in tormenting hapless humans. Hawk supposed it was as good an explanation as any.

"Come here."

"No." She spoke without hesitation, clearly and unmistakably. Something stirred within him, the suspicion that it was an odd sort of servant who would reject an order so readily. A moment more and the thought was gone, burned out by the driving need to compel her obedience.

"No?" He smiled. "You are a woman, are you not? And a servant? And on my lands? How then do you tell me no?"

Her chin lifted. "You are not my lord." It was a weak excuse and they both knew it.

His smile deepened. "You have nothing to fear. I merely wish to confirm what I already know."

She had been afraid the moment he spoke but now a bolt of true dread shot through her. What he already knew? Did that mean he had seen through her masquerade? Yet he had called her servant as though she were a thrall unable to gainsay her master.

"I am a freewoman, lord, and unwed. I can say no to any man. Unless . . ." Her eyes narrowed, surveying him. "Unless you care not what a woman says." The curl of her lip made it clear what she thought of that.

"I care," he said and she relaxed just a little. "And I have told you, you have nothing to fear. Now come here."

"I would rather not."

It was the work of an instant to reach out and take her. He knew she could not possibly resist him. He was a warrior, honed to battle, and a natural hunter. Beside him, she was helpless. Or was she? Somehow, he could not imagine hurting her.

"You know what is between us. I have seen that in your eyes."

His bluntness took her unprepared. Was he truly saying that he desired her . . . her, the servant of his betrothed? Did he have no care for what that would mean to her . . . his betrothed? Were the feelings of his wife-to-be of no concern to him?

"I will not lie with you." The wind chose that moment to die away. Her voice sounded unnaturally loud in the sudden stillness.

"I did not ask you to."

Her cheeks flamed. She assumed she had mistaken the situation and was humiliated. "I thought . . . Never mind." She turned to go, thinking to escape while the storm was at an ebb. Hawk thought otherwise. His hand lashed out, grasping her arm. Before she could react, he drew her to him.

"You are a woman, like any other. I have only to convince myself of that and this foolishness will end."

She had time to draw a breath, just one, before his mouth was on hers. Her first, instantaneous response was shock. She had never been kissed, although truth be told she had imagined it from time to time, especially of late. But no imagining had prepared her for the reality of his touch, not harsh or cruel but enticing, tempting . . . drawing her out of solitude, presenting her with intimacy. His lips were firm, parting hers, the heat and taste of him suddenly in her mouth. She gasped and dug her hands into his broad shoulders, buffeted by a force she had not known existed. He made a rough sound deep in his throat and gathered her closer.

Her spirit leaped in instant recognition. The wildness within her answered his own. She savored the thrust of his tongue, teasing with hers, suddenly bold where she had mere moments before been utterly unaware. Oh, yes, this was what she wanted, had always wanted in the blood and the bone. This was a man to make her own, to enlarge her soul, father her children, travel with her through life's journey. She knew all that in a heartbeat and she rejoiced in it. Without thought, she tangled her fingers in the thick silk of his hair and drew him closer, claiming him. The kiss became hers, kissing him, prelude to drawing from him the essence of life itself.

He broke away, gasping, his cheeks stained dark, and stared at her in disbelief. "What are you doing? I thought you loyal to your mistress. Is this some game you play?"

A game? She reeled back, stunned by his reaction. It was a game only if life itself could be called such. But she had done something wrong, out of step, far worse than when she presumed to play with the children. It was her lack of experience, her ignorance about the ways of people, that was to blame. No, it was herself and the fierce, unbridled urgings he unleashed within her.

"I did not mean—" she began, but he stopped her with a quick slice of his hand through the storm-heavy air.

His breath came harshly. "Were you another, this would not end here, but it needs must if there is to be peace. I am sending you back to Vestfold, let your mistress make of that what she will."

"Sending me back? No!" How could she possibly arrive if he was sending her away? She had thought to slip off and return appropriately transformed. If she was dispatched, no doubt with escort, there would be no chance for that. He would be left to curse his ever more tardy bride while the peace they both wanted became ever more elusive.

"I am not yours to send away," she tried.

His gaze scorched. "You will be mine if you remain and that I cannot allow. Now get you from here lest we both forget the duty owed your mistress."

It was on the tip of her tongue to suggest that her mistress was a kind and forgiving woman, ever understanding, ever tolerant. She sought to betray herself with . . . herself. What a travesty.

She went, welcoming the shock of the cold, wet air even though it did nothing to dampen the heat within her.

Alone, Hawk slumped against the side of the stall and took a deep, shuddering breath. He had been wrong to think this foolishness. It was far worse, a sweet madness making him forget all else—duty, honor, even simple sense. She would leave in the morn, he would make damn certain of that. And he would bring all his formidable will to bear on the task of forgetting she had ever existed. He might even have some scant hope of succeeding.

With a heavy sigh, he turned to go. Light from the oil lamp he carried fell across his hand and arm. Halfway out of the stable, he stopped suddenly and stared at the dark stain that lay across his palm and up beyond his wrist. That was odd; he couldn't remember touching anything that would have left such a stain. Not that he would remember necessarily or that there was anything unusual about a bit of dirt. But he had washed his hands shortly before the storm began, prior to sitting down for a few minutes with one of his precious books. The stain had not been there then.

A black stain, still wet as he discovered when he dabbed a finger to it. A heavy, dull black . . . like the green-eyed girl's storm-wet hair he had touched in drawing her to him. The same girl who so readily disobeyed a direct order from a man hardened warriors would not cross. The servant with no duties whose hands were soft as down. A suspicion formed in his mind. He all but dismissed it in an instant, thinking it beyond all bounds of foolishness. Yet did it linger. . . .

KRYSTA DID NOT APPEAR IN THE HALL THAT EVENING. She stayed out of sight, wrestling with what to do. All night she tossed and turned, trying to decide on some course that might yet bring a fair wind. She could confess all and throw herself on his mercy, but the mere thought filled her with dread. She could sneak off on her own before he sent her away, then return somehow as though just newly arrived. If Thorgold and Raven went with her, perhaps they could claim to have encountered their mistress on the way. But what chance was there that would work? Hawk had seen her too often and too clearly. She should have thought of that before embarking on what had seemed so sensible a plan, the selfsame plan now lying in tatters about her.

She rose at first light, dazed by sleeplessness, still trying to decide what to do. To her relief, she saw no sign of preparations for her departure. But that meant nothing.

No doubt the Hawk's men were ready to ride in an instant. Her stomach churned with hunger but she could not bear the thought of eating. She heard Daria's shrill voice coming from the kitchens and turned instinctively in the opposite direction. Scarcely had she done so, and before she could take more than a step, she ran right into the steward, who must have come up directly behind her.

"Your pardon," Krysta said quickly and tried to move away, but the young man moved as well, blocking her.

"His lordship wants you."

"W-what do you . . . ?" she stammered.

"He wants you," Edvard repeated with a hint of impatience. "Upstairs in the tower room." When still she hesitated, he gave her a little push in the right direction. Worse yet, he stood right there, watching to make sure she went.

Krysta climbed the tower steps slowly. She was thinking desperately of what to say. If only she had a little more time, she might be able to come up with a plan of some sort or another. But time had run out and now there was nothing left to do save hope for the best. And pray, that might also help.

The door to the tower room was partly open. She took a deep breath, gathered her courage, and pushed through it.

The chamber took up the entire uppermost floor of the tower. It was dominated by the largest bed Krysta had ever seen, hung with richly embroidered curtains and covered with luxurious furs. She might have noticed nothing but that bed had it not been for a sight more arresting to the eyes. In a corner of the room, Hawk stepped into a tub of steaming water. She caught just a glimpse of his bare flanks before he lowered himself, preserving modesty but leaving plain for her befuddled sight the vast expanse of his heavily muscled chest and arms. That and his predator's smile.

"Don't just stand there," Hawk said. "Make yourself useful. I need my back scrubbed." Before she could get her mouth around a response, he ducked under the water, came up flinging drops in all directions, and began lathering his hair. She watched with unwilling fascination. His skin was bronzed and beneath it muscle and tendon moved with easy grace. His nipples were small and flat. Under his arms were tufts of hair that looked even silkier than that on his head. He ducked again to rinse and came up with water streaming down his face. Opening one eye, he glanced at her. "Mayhap you did not hear me."

She had heard him all right, well enough to know what the edge in his voice meant. He was bound and determined on this, for some reason. Mayhap he regretted letting her go the previous day and meant to remedy that, a thought which set her heart to racing. Or mayhap he merely wanted to humiliate her before sending her on her way. Whatever his intent, angering him seemed a poor choice.

Not that there were any good ones to be seen. With utmost reluctance, palpable in every step she took, Krysta approached the tub. She did not take her eyes from him but, once convinced she meant to obey, he ignored her completely. She blushed red and looked away quickly as he matter-of-factly went about his ablutions, grateful though she was that the water afforded some protection to her innocence. Or what remained of it after the awakening of desires she had not known she possessed.

Just then she was discovering yet another of them, the desire not to let him have his way completely. He wanted his back scrubbed, did he? With docility that should have alerted him, she knelt beside the tub, picked up a cloth, and dunked it into the water. Applying it and all her strength, she set about to scrub the skin right off his back.

Hawk laughed. Damn him, he thought her amusing. She redoubled her efforts. "Sheathe your claws," he said, still chuckling. "I've slept on rock and never noticed. I doubt you can have any ill effect."

"It won't be for want of trying," she muttered. There was no give in him at all. She might as well have been scrubbing stone. Warm, smooth stone so firm beneath her touch . . . She jerked back as though burned and tried to rise, only to be stopped by his hand clamped on her wrist. "You haven't finished," he said. His brows rose mockingly. "I thought the Norse prized cleanliness. Can't you even manage a simple bath?"

"If you took it properly, in a sauna like a person should rather than soak yourself like salted beef in a pail of water . . ."

"There is a sauna here and I enjoy it. But a man still wants a real bath from time to time."

His fingers were rubbing soothingly where he held her, as though to ease away any small hurt he might have inflicted. Had there been any? She couldn't remember. A shiver of pleasure danced beneath his touch. His eyes were as blue as the sky at high summer, thickly fringed by sun-kissed lashes. A night's growth of beard softened the harshly beautiful lines of his face. She had a sudden, almost irresistible urge to touch him slowly and lingeringly, so that she might learn every inch of him.

"You have a sauna?" Anything to distract herself from thoughts becoming more wayward by the moment.

He nodded without taking his gaze from her. "The only good idea the Danes ever had."

"Better than invading England?" The question was out before she could stop it. Foolish, foolish! She should have kept silent, concentrated only on getting away. What was she thinking to converse with a naked man holding her captive?

His gaze drifted to her mouth, watching her lips move as she formed the words. "I suppose it depends on your perspective," Hawk said absently. "To the Danes,

that's an excellent idea. To us . . ." He shrugged, in that
gesture accepting the great struggle that had dominated
his life. The struggle he was bound and determined to win
even to the extent of forging an alliance between English
and Norse against their common enemy, and taking a
Norse wife to cement that alliance.

A Norse wife . . .

"Enough talk of war," he said. "I have other matters
on my mind." All night he had chewed over his suspicions, now convinced he had to be completely wrong, now
not certain of anything at all. In the end, impulse had won
out, which was unusual, for he always thought before he
acted even in the heat of battle when the razor-sharp
quickness of his mind had saved his life more times than
he could recall. But such thought was lacking where she
was concerned. She fogged his mind, sowing confusion
with every smile. How fortunate she was not smiling at
the moment. Indeed, she looked as though she might
never do so again.

"You said you would not lie with me."

Her eyes widened. He watched, fascinated, as color
crept over her cheeks. "I spoke in haste. . . . I meant—"

"Oh, then you will lie with me?"

"No! I mean, we should not speak of such things. My
mistress . . ."

"Your absent, tardy mistress." His eyes narrowed. To
be safe, he tightened his hold on her wrist but carefully,
for he truly could not imagine hurting her. Provoking her
was another matter altogether. "Forget her, she is of no
account."

"*What?* She most certainly is of account! Did you
yourself not say we both owed her a duty?" His precautions were well taken. She tugged hard, trying to free herself. He continued to hold her easily.

"Duty is a cold bedmate. I prefer mine warm and
willing. Better yet, as hot and yielding as you were yester-

day. Come here." He did not wait for her response but began drawing her closer until she was half bent over the tub, her eyes so wide with shock he thought he might fall into them.

"I will not! How can you even think such a thing? Let me go! Stop it."

He tugged a little harder. Just enough. She lost her balance and toppled over into the water. Indeed, she would have landed right on Hawk had he not removed himself agilely from the tub just as she entered it. There was only so much temptation a man could take and he thought it prudent to limit his. He stood, heedless of his nudity, watching her thrash about. Watching, too, what happened to the water. When the first traces of black color began running off into it, his expression changed. Uncertainty had held his anger at bay. Certainty unleashed it.

He yanked a towel from the nearby stool and wound it around his loins as he awaited the emergence of the soaking, sputtering, dye-stained Lady Krysta. His bride.

Chapter

FOUR

ER EYES STUNG. KRYSTA RUBBED AT THEM as she struggled to her knees in the tub. She couldn't believe he had pulled her in. What was he thinking? What did he intend? What should she . . . ? Her thoughts skittered to a sudden halt as she stared down at herself. Black dye ran over her gown, flowing into the water and, she realized belatedly, stinging her eyes.

A cloth landed in her face, tossed by a heavy hand. She grabbed for it as a harsh voice said, "Clean yourself and get out of there. Try not to make a mess while you're doing it."

The realization that she was undone roared through her. *He knew.* And he was clearly furious. One quick peek over the top of the towel was enough to confirm that. Confirm, also, that he was scarcely clad, barely enough for modesty's sake. He stood with his legs braced apart, his powerful arms crossed over his chest, looking at her as though she were a bit of unpleasant something washed up at his feet.

Not a good beginning.

Her sodden gown and hair weighed her down but Krysta managed to drag herself out of the tub. She was trying to wipe the rivulets of dye from her face when she froze suddenly. Hawk had closed the distance between them so swiftly she had no warning. He stood directly in front of her, affording her an impressive view of his bare chest, and took hold of a strand of her hair. Examining it with the enthusiasm he might have given to a lump of seaweed, he asked, "What color is it really?"

Krysta coughed. Some of the water had gotten down her throat but she scarcely noticed that added discomfort, so small was it in relation to all else. "B-blond . . ." He obviously didn't like that color, for his derision increased.

"You expected . . . what? That I would not recognize you when you finally did appear simply because your hair had been darker?"

The knowledge of her own foolishness struck her so forcibly as to render her unable to answer. He let her hair drop and turned away, as though the continued sight of her was more than he could tolerate. "Get out of those clothes."

"W-what?" Her voice returned but weakly, thinned by shock.

He glanced at her over his shoulder. "Get. Out. Of. Those. Clothes. Is that clear enough?"

His back to her, he plucked a tunic off the stool and dropped the towel from around his loins. As he shrugged into the garment, Krysta's eyes widened. His back was broad, sculpted by bands of muscle, his waist and hips narrow, and his buttocks . . . Krysta had never before given a moment's thought to any man's buttocks. Now she found herself riveted by what had to be the most perfectly shaped pair in creation. He turned to catch her staring at him. For a moment, he looked surprised but suppressed that and eyed her narrowly.

"Not long ago, I asked you, not knowing you were

you, if you were a lackwit. You assured me you were not. Were you lying about that, too?"

That stung enough to rouse Krysta from her daze. "There is *nothing* wrong with my wits, and if you would but let me explain you would see that."

"Oh, you will explain, *my* lady." He laughed harshly. "Be assured, you will explain most thoroughly. But first, get out of those clothes. If I have to tell you yet again, I will strip them off you myself."

Before she could offer her opinion of that, he strode to the door, flung it open, and bellowed for the servants. They stumbled in, tripping in their haste, only to freeze at the sight of Krysta standing there, dripping and dye-stained.

"Empty the tub," Hawk directed, "and bring water to refill it. A great deal of water." For good measure, he added, "Don't bother heating it, just get it up here."

They rushed to obey, no doubt in haste to be away from their infuriated lord but also unable to keep so juicy a bit of gossip to themselves for very long. Krysta longed for them to linger, or for more to come, or for herself to fly out the window, anything just so she was not left alone with the Hawk bent on vengeance.

"My clothes will dry better on me," she ventured. "The servants needn't be bothered with water. I'll fetch a few bucketfuls for myself or just go down to the river." As she spoke, she tried sidling past him only to stop when he laughed.

She was grappling with the notion that he found all this amusing when he said, "You flatter yourself."

"I what?"

"Flatter yourself if you imagine I want you out of those clothes because I desire you. You're filthy. You look like something a self-respecting cat wouldn't drag in. It is to your advantage—*yours*—to at least look human before we discuss the reasons for your outrageous behavior. Now get out of those clothes!"

He clamped down hard on his temper but not before Krysta realized that she stood on the edge of a precipice. She should have stepped back. Any sensible person would have. But she was beginning to suspect that despite what she'd always thought about herself, good sense might not be her strong point.

"I will if you leave."

Under other circumstances, his expression would have been comical. Now it was chilling. "Leave? You are telling me to leave . . . my quarters . . . in my stronghold? Leave?"

"Not telling, asking. If you want me to undress and bathe, please leave. And I'll need fresh clothes. Obviously, I can't put these back on. If you would be so kind as to send someone to the women's quarters, my chests are there."

"You have no instinct for survival at all, do you?" He said it almost pleasantly, as though that was an interesting discovery.

It was that pleasantness, the suggestion that her plight was entertaining to him, that pushed Krysta over the edge. Beneath the trails of black dye, her cheeks flamed. She gripped her ruined gown between her hands and began twisting it as though it were her intended lord and master's neck. He observed that, too, with some interest and just a hint of trepidation. It stirred his own instinct for survival, however belatedly.

"Survival?" She spoke the word with scorn. "As though I would be satisfied with so little. It's possible to survive in a hole in the ground but it's no way to live. I want peace for my people and yours. Peace! A chance to live with safety and hope instead of always wondering when the next attack will come, the next men carried home dead, the next farmsteads burned. I thought you wanted peace, too, but now I think I must have been wrong. Allow me to inform you, *my* lord Hawk, the path to peace does not lie through the beds of other women!"

He stared at her dumbfounded. She put her hands on her hips and glared at him. "You heard me and don't try to deny it! You wanted to lie with me when you thought I was a servant. That's what you would have done if all this"—she gestured at her hair—"hadn't happened."

"I was sending you back to Vestfold so that it wouldn't happen!"

"Then you admit it, you wanted to lie with me when you had every reason to think I was another woman. You would have betrayed me with . . . myself." That didn't sound quite bad enough so she hurried on. "And with who knows how many other women. Oh, I know it's common practice. But to not even be able to wait until we were decently married before violating your vows—"

His head was spinning. He, who had faced hordes of screaming Danes with perfect equanimity, slashing and hacking his way through them as though partaking of healthful exercise, couldn't seem to find his balance. His sputtering spitfire of an intended bride spoke to him as no one had ever dared. She challenged him at every turn and apparently expected him to accept such behavior as her right. Belatedly, he remembered what he'd heard about Norse women. They were headstrong and independent, as liable to cuff a man as to kiss him, and fiercely possessive of what they regarded as their own. Dragon had warned him but Hawk had thought he was exaggerating.

He had himself a termagant by the tail and unless he was very careful, she was going to upset his entire, carefully ordered existence. "Enough!" His roar shook the rafters and so affrighted the returning servants that they splashed water all over the floor. That made them even more nervous, so that in scrambling to empty the tub they spilled yet more water. Hawk watched them in disbelief, sure he was seeing a warning of things to come.

Servants were on their hands and knees trying to mop up the mess. Others were frantically running about bringing in yet more water. People with no business in his tower were finding a reason to appear, staring into the room in horrified astonishment. The spectacle was even attracting birds, for just then a raven landed on the windowsill and cawed raucously.

"Be quiet," Krysta said.

Hawk had no idea whom she meant and didn't care. Throwing his hands into the air, he stormed out. He was halfway down the tower stairs before he realized that he had done exactly what she wanted.

HER FIRST TASK, KRYSTA DECIDED, WAS TO SOOTHE the servants. After all, they were to be her servants and they were obviously very upset, understandably so given their master's display of temper. Not that she could really blame him for being angry. Thorgold had warned her that men did not like to be tricked.

"Thank you for bringing the water," she said, smiling kindly.

The servants darted startled glances at her and one another but not one said a word. They hastened about their tasks, making short work of them now that Hawk was gone, and departed swiftly. No trace of their presence remained save a few scattered drops of water around the refilled tub.

Alone, Krysta stood in the center of the room and wrapped her arms around herself, trying to still the trembling that rose from deep inside. Had she truly told her soon-to-be husband that the path to peace did not lie through the beds of other women? Had she truly scorned the very notion of survival and virtually dared him to fulfill his pledge of peace? Had she taken leave of her senses . . . or what passed for them?

With a quick glance at the door the servants had closed behind them and an equally quick prayer that Hawkforte's master would not suddenly decide to return, Krysta stripped off her sodden, dye-stained gown. The water in the tub was freshly cold from the kitchen well, as Hawk had instructed, but it came as no surprise to one who was used to bathing in rivers and the pools formed by runoff from melting glaciers. Krysta settled into it with a sigh of contentment. She plucked the cake of soap from the nearby stool and began washing her hair. Within minutes, the water in the tub was black. She climbed out, emptied it through the cleverly designed drain that ran down the outside of the tower, and filled it again from the extra buckets left by the servants. This time, the water stayed clean. Having lingered as long as she dared, Krysta got out and wrapped a length of sheeting around herself just as a knock sounded at the door. She called out permission to enter, and Thorgold pushed the door open and lumbered in, dragging one of her trunks behind him.

"Raven said you'd be wanting this."

"Thank you! I was just wondering how I would manage with no clean clothing."

"I'd say you're managing well enough." Thorgold grinned. "His Mightiness came down out of his tower looking like the Furies themselves were after him. You should have seen folk scatter."

"Oh, no," Krysta moaned. "I thought he must be angry but I hoped it wouldn't be quite that bad—"

"I wouldn't say he was angry." Before she could make anything good of that, Thorgold added, "Enraged would be more like it, not to mention befuddled." His laughter was a deep rumble starting somewhere around his hairy toes. When he saw Krysta's downcast eyes, he sobered.

"There now, girl, don't fuss yourself. Done's done, I always say. It's what you do now that matters."

"I don't know what to do now," Krysta said miserably. She sat down on the stool, wishing she could just disappear. Too well, she remembered the look on Hawk's face when he called her something a self-respecting cat wouldn't drag in. How could she hope to win the love of a man who held her in such contempt?

Yet he had desired her . . . before he had discovered the truth of who she was and what she had done. Innocent she might be, but she was not so ignorant as to mistake what had been between them from the beginning.

Thorgold sighed, uneasy with such female doings yet still wanting to help. He pointed to the chest. "Raven said to wear the gown that's on top."

When he was gone, Krysta knelt beside the chest and opened it. Before her lay a gown she had never seen before. It looked like a froth of sea foam so insubstantial that a whisper of breeze would blow it away. Yet when she lifted it, it felt solid and even heavy in her hands, strangely so until she realized that the color came from uncounted crystals no larger than grains of sand stitched one by one into the fabric. At once fragile yet strong, the gown seemed to embolden her. She rose hurriedly and slipped it over her head. It molded to her form as though made for her yet she knew it must have been created for another woman, the mother Krysta had never known.

There was only one mirror in the room, set beside a basin and a rather lethal-looking razor she supposed Hawk used for shaving. Her reflection in the polished bronze showed tear-bright eyes and a mop of tangled hair. Freed from the dye, her hair had reverted to a curling, waving froth that defied all attempts at control. She could do nothing but catch up part of it with a matching ribbon and leave the rest tumbling over her shoulders.

Having bathed and dressed, she tidied up after her-self, delaying the moment when she would have nothing left to do but leave the relative safety of the chamber. Rather than hasten that moment, she looked around for some—indeed, for any—way to occupy herself. Her gaze fell on the table beside the window and most especially on the object lying on that table.

A book.

Krysta had seen perhaps a half-dozen books in her life and actually owned three, thanks to the generosity of her late father. She remembered Raven telling her that Hawk could read, yet the sight of so rare and precious an object still surprised her. She approached it tentatively and for some little time was content merely to study the ornate leather cover. But inevitably, the moment came when she found herself reaching out and very gently, with the greatest care, opening the book. At some point, she sat down in the chair beside the table but she had no aware-ness of doing so. The book held her heedless of all else.

HIS ANGER WAS UNRELIABLE, HAWK NOTED. Scarcely an hour since he'd stormed out of the tower room and already the rage that had propelled him was be-coming a memory. The wind blew his foul mood away as surely as it filled the sail of his skiff dancing over the waves beyond the harbor. He looked back toward Hawkforte where it lay nestled in the curve of golden beach and white cliff. The sight of the burgh never failed to make his spirits lighten whether he was returning from a short sail or a journey of many months. It was his home and his sanctuary, but more than that it was his triumph against a violent and uncaring world. He cherished Hawkforte in the private places of his heart, but now the town that lay so serenely in the embrace of land and sea had an added meaning. Within its walls was the woman

who was to be his wife, she who represented the hope of
peace between both their peoples. She who he had just begun to wish might bring him a measure of the happiness
he had seen was possible with his sister and her husband.
She who had tricked him . . .

But not for long. That was balm to his pride yet he
wondered how long she had thought to continue her masquerade and to what end. Why risk his anger if she was
found out?

He supposed she had some reason, and perhaps he
would learn of it eventually. Of rather more significance,
he had met his bride at last, much good it did him. The
mystery of her should by all rights be solved, but instead
had only deepened.

He had lied when he claimed not to desire her but a
man would be a fool not to keep some things to himself. A
fool ten times over to let a woman know the power she
wielded over him. He lusted after his fey Norse bride as
he could not remember ever lusting after another woman,
which struck him as ironic given that she had accused him
of meaning to betray her with herself. The memory of
how she looked as she dragged herself from the tub, wet
and bedraggled yet with fire flashing in her eyes, made
him chuckle. But amusement fled, giving way to something deeper and hotter, as he recalled how she looked at
him when he dressed. Lust, it seemed, was not his alone.

A smile tugged at the corners of his mouth. His eyes
narrowed against the glare of sun bouncing off water. He
turned the skiff into the wind and raced along the shore-
line. From tenderest boyhood, he had loved the sea. There
was no greater freedom than those moments when he
could leave the land behind and become one with the
mighty currents of air and water. That such surcease from
daily care could never be more than temporary made it all
the more precious.

He sailed the rest of that morning and into the

afternoon. Fishermen in their small, swift hide boats waved to him. So did the captain of an incoming merchant vessel, who lowered his banner in salute when he spied the skiff's hawk-emblazoned sail. A herd of fat seals frolicked past. They had just vanished from sight when Hawk was startled by something else in the water, dark and sleek, that seemed to lift its head to look at him. For a moment, there appeared to be several of them, but mayhap they were no more than shadows for they were as swiftly gone.

Gulls circled overhead, tracking the schools of gleaming herring that looked like darting streaks of silver beneath the water. The seals chased them, too, as did the men standing in their tiny vessels to fling their seining nets far out over the swell, then pulling them back into shore fat with their catch.

The sun was slanting to the west, bathing the sea in gold, before Hawk finally turned his skiff landward. He had stolen a day and felt no remorse for it, especially not when he considered the change the hours of freedom had wrought in him. He felt far better able to deal with his trickster bride than he had that morning. Indeed, he found himself looking forward to it. The cheerfulness of his mood lasted right up to the moment he came within sight of the harbor.

Daria was waiting for him on the quay. Seeing her there, a dry specter ever ready to cry doom, Hawk almost headed back out to sea. Only stern discipline enabled him to secure the boat and climb the stone steps. Scarcely had he come into sight than Daria drew breath and let it fly like barbed arrows.

"Do you know? Of course, you must. How dare she! What game is that stupid girl playing? And the insult to you—" She moaned and clutched her breast like a mummer in a bad paschal play. "I can't imagine why you haven't had her lashed already, her and those dreadful servants. How is she ever to learn her place if you tolerate such disrespect?"

Hawk had learned long ago that his half-sister thrived on irritation and anger, all the negative emotions. He refused to let her feed off her own fury. "Calm yourself, Daria. In your haste, you misspeak. It is for me to decide what to do and only for me."

She ducked her head and looked up at him sideways with false humility. "Yes, of course, how foolish of me. But whatever could she have been thinking? Perhaps her mind is not as it should be. Surely, her reason must be questioned."

He began walking down the quay briskly, forcing Daria to run to keep up with his long stride. "Her reason is for me to know and judge. For you and everyone else, it is enough that she is who she is. Make no mistake, I agreed to take the Lady Krysta as my wife sight unseen because she brings the promise of peace *and* a dowry large enough to choke a horse. A dowry to be put to swift work making the defenses of Hawkforte yet stronger against the Danes. Nothing—absolutely nothing—matters more than that. Do you understand me?"

For a moment, something deep and dark flared behind her eyes but it was gone so swiftly Hawk could not be sure he had seen it. "Surely I understand," Daria said. "You have always been very clear as to what is important and what is not. Only my care for you compels me to say that there will be difficulties because of her. The people will not accept her readily, not after this display of foolishness. Best you be prepared for that."

Tempted though he was to dismiss her warning, Hawk could not. At the very least, his people would be surprised and puzzled. As loyal to him as they were, it was likely they would condemn Krysta for her deceit. He frowned at the thought. Much as she deserved punishment, she was his wife-to-be and she needs must have the respect of his people. They would take their lead from him, which left him with few options for dealing with her. Yet another problem she presented, and they not even wed yet. It did not bode well for their future.

Leaving Daria behind, he strode on to the fortress. The bailey yard was busy as usual and all looked as it should but Hawk wasn't fooled. He caught the quick, apprehensive glances from all directions and knew that word had spread. No doubt his people were brimming over with curiosity but they had the sense to hold their tongues in his presence.

Briefly, he considered seeking out his errant betrothed but decided to postpone so dubious a pleasure at least a short time. He never had finished his bath that morning and since then he'd been sprayed with enough salt water to leave his tunic stiff and scratchy. Glad of the refuge, he withdrew to the sauna after sending a servant for fresh clothes.

The chamber half-submerged in the earth and roofed with stone would have been cool were it not for the fire kept burning in a metal box topped by heaps of polished rocks. Hawk added fresh wood and poured a ladle of water over the rocks before stripping off his garments. He washed himself down, then stretched out on a bench and let the heat take him. With it came memories. It was in this very sauna that his brother-in-law, the aptly named Wolf, had put forward the idea that Hawk should also make a marriage to strengthen the alliance between Norse and Saxon. Wolf had come to Hawkforte as an invader backed by a mighty Viking army to reclaim his bride, Hawk's own sister, the Lady Cymbra. Hawk still felt a twinge of guilt for having taken her from Wolf's stronghold at Sciringesheal, to which she had been brought a captive but where she had become a beloved wife. Not understanding that, Hawk had taken her by stealth . . .

some might even say by trickery. That thought made his brow crease. His situation wasn't the same at all. He'd had every good reason to believe he should bring his sister home. What possible reason could Krysta have for what she had done?

No doubt she had some excuse prepared by now, perhaps a whole host of excuses, but he wanted her actual reason even though he suspected he had little hope of getting it. He was still mulling that over when his stomach growled, reminding him that he had eaten nothing since morning. Reminding him, too, that the day was aging and he could not remain in the sauna forever. Steeling himself, he plucked up the fresh clothes left for him, walked down the short track to a deep pond, and plunged into its refreshing waters. When he emerged, he felt invigorated and ready to face whatever might come . . . or so he hoped.

Entering his hall, Hawk took a cautious look around. The servants were at work preparing for the evening meal. They glanced his way before returning to their duties with great diligence. Daria was making herself scarce, for which he was grateful. He hesitated, half hoping Edvard would appear with some matter that required Hawk's immediate attention. When there was no sign of the steward, Hawk mounted the stairs to his tower. He went rather more slowly than usual, mindful of the servants' eyes on him and not as eager as he might have been to discover what awaited him above.

He found his door ajar and eased it open with the same care he might have used to gain entry to a Danish stronghold. It swung soundlessly on well-oiled hinges. The room was as he had left it but tidier, the tub and all traces of it gone. The bare wooden table, the one where he sat going over the endless tallies of his estates, the correspondence from Winchester, and the tide of petitions that came to him from all directions, the table where he occasionally snatched a few precious hours to read his beloved books . . . There was a book open on that table now and it was being read but not by himself. His bedraggled, dye-stained betrothed had been snatched away and in her place sat a creature spun of sunlight and sea foam, surely not human and yet seemingly so, if the blush that overcame her when she glimpsed him was any indication.

Slowly, she set aside the book—with care, he noted. She rose as though preferring to face him on her feet. She tried to smile, but the effort wobbled. "My lord . . ."

She sounded the same, her voice soft and faintly husky. Looking more closely, he saw that she appeared much the same. Her eyes were still a hue of green he had never seen before. And her nose was still splattered with freckles. For all that, he was most grateful, elsewise he truly doubted he would have recognized her.

She was not, even now, precisely beautiful if judged by the standard of his sister, who was said to be the most beautiful woman in all Christendom. But what she lacked in classical perfection, she made up for in her uniqueness. He caught himself staring at her and tried to look away but had no success. She was, after all, his almost-wife and he supposed he could be pardoned for being curious about her.

"What are you doing?"

His voice sounded gruff to Krysta and he looked gruffer yet, frowning down at her from his considerable height. He seemed to have brought the outside in with him, filling the chamber with the power of wind, sea, and earth. She wasn't afraid . . . precisely . . . but she did take a step back before catching herself. It was absurd to retreat when there was nowhere to go. She gestured to the book now lying closed on the table. "I was very careful."

He followed the direction of her gaze, his frown deepening. "You read?"

It was not a foolish question for there were many who

were pleased enough merely to gaze upon the intricate designs that decorated the vellum pages without any understanding of the words written upon them.

She nodded and searched his gaze anxiously for censure but to her great relief there was none. He merely looked surprised. "A rare accomplishment," Hawk said. Later, he would deal with the notion of having a wife who read and who might therefore share his love of books. Just then it was enough to wonder what other skills she might conceal.

"What do you think of it?" he asked, indicating the book.

"It is beautiful but disturbing. Who is this man . . . Boethius?"

"A Roman who lived several centuries ago. He loved music and mathematics but, as the book says, he found his greatest consolation in philosophy." Hawk stared at the book a moment longer. "He wrote it in prison shortly before he was executed for something he had not done. If the doing of this truly consoled him, all to the good."

It was Krysta's turn to frown. "This book is not so old. The vellum is still fresh. Moreover, there is commentary within it from the present day. How comes all that to be?"

"The commentary is Alfred's, as is the translation. The king is a great admirer of Boethius even if he does not agree with him completely. It is thanks to Alfred that copies of this and other books are made so that they may become known to those with skill to read or wit at least to listen."

"Then your king is a scholar as well as a warrior." Krysta nodded thoughtfully. "I understand better now why you serve him."

"It is my duty to serve him."

"Only duty makes you loyal?" She spoke softly, knowing she might be trespassing upon his private thoughts yet driven all the same to take the measure of this man who would determine her fate, did he but know it or not. "Does nothing else inspire it?"

He did not answer her at once but considered his reply before he spoke. "Trust comes before loyalty and is necessary to it."

She paled, understanding too well how low she stood in such regard. "I can explain—"

"Can you?" He leaned against the wall beside the window, his arms crossed over his broad chest, looking as though he was no more than mildly curious. She was not fooled. Already she knew him to be a man of deep currents. The surface of him could look unrippled, but below anything might be happening, anything at all.

"Let me guess," he said. "You disguised yourself because you feared capture by the Danes. Once you arrived, the natural shyness and modesty of a maid hindered you from announcing yourself."

It was perfect, an excuse with which no one could argue and which reflected well on her. Even as she wondered why he was offering her so easy an escape, Krysta almost succumbed to the temptation to take it. All that prevented her was the barrier of truth.

"An interesting idea," she said wistfully, "but not one that had occurred to me. I came as I did because I thought if I could learn to know you a little from those in your household before we wed, I would be a better wife."

She had a glimpse of his surprise before it was hidden behind the mask his eyes so easily became. Sardonically, he said, "I suppose I cannot dispute such selfless intent. You did it for my own good, is that it?"

Short of revealing to him the entire truth, including her desperate need to be loved by him, Krysta could say little more. Still, she tried. "No, not entirely. We will both benefit if this marriage is a success, as will both our peoples."

They had come full circle to the subject of duty, Hawk noted. He stepped closer to her, pleased that she did not try again to withdraw from him. Slowly, he raised a hand and touched the glittering disarray of her hair. He had never seen hair quite like this before. It was thick and riotously curled as though a dancing wind had swept over it. Yet when he touched it, it felt like silk clinging to his fingers. An unwilling smile tugged at his mouth as he saw she had tried to take the wildness from it with a hair ribbon, which had itself become entangled. She was so close that he could smell the perfume of her skin like the roses that bloomed only by the sea and lent their fragrance to the freshening air. A pulse beat in the golden column of her throat. He stared at it for a long moment before a sigh escaped him. He plucked the ribbon free and set it to order with a gentle touch. She turned her head toward him in surprise.

"Where has your anger gone?"

He wondered the same but wasn't about to admit that. "To wait until I decide whether I have need of it."

Deep currents, she thought again, and nodded. The little bubble of hope that earlier that day had seemed pierced and gone suddenly reappeared. It seemed a tiny, opalescent pearl glowing within her, filled with rare and beautiful light.

"Come," Hawk said and held out his hand.

On the beach, she had drawn back from his touch as though scorched. Now, she laid her hand in his and left it there.

Chapter

FIVE

WITH A CRY OF ALARM, KRYSTA ROSE out of the depths of sleep struggling against the thick weight pressing in all around her. Desperately she fought to free herself, flailing her arms and legs against the hideous villain bent on smothering her.

"Aichoo!"

Feathers knocked loose from the mattress she was pummeling tickled her nose, the sneezing they provoked clearing her head sufficiently for her to remember where she was. She threw off the lush fur cover and sat up, feeling the perfect fool and glad there was no one to observe her silliness.

She was lying in an immense bed the same size as the one in Hawk's tower. It was, so she had been told, the bed King Alfred himself used when he came to Hawkforte. The chamber kept prepared for royalty was hers . . . for the moment. Still sleep dazed and bemused, she glanced around. Last night, the room had been visible only by firelight, lit by the torches the servants carried to escort

her to her rest and by the copper braziers filled with glowing coals that made corners of the room gleam like living
fire while filling the rest of it with dancing shadows.

Today, by the sunlight streaming through the windows, she saw the luxurious appointments, the carved
wooden furnishings, tapestries, and mats of woven rushes
to cushion the floor. The bed itself was draped with embroidered hangings and piled with the furs she had
thought crushing her.

Never in her life had Krysta occupied such lavish
quarters nor had she ever been so entirely alone. Always
before, she knew either Raven or Thorgold was nearby,
but now she had no idea of their whereabouts. She had not
seen them since the preceding evening in the hall, and then
they had not been able to exchange even a word. Tugging
up the bed gown that had slipped over her shoulder, she
recalled the moment when she entered Hawkforte's hall
on the arm of its master. So thick was the curiosity that
greeted them she thought Hawk would need his sword to
slash their way through it. But he had merely continued
on as though his people were not staring at them in
stunned amazement, their gazes guarded, their manner
poised to condemn her did he give the merest sign. At the
high table, he paused for a moment, looked about him,
and then, as though it were the most ordinary of matters,
raised her hand in his and announced to all and sundry:

"The Lady Krysta of Vestfold."

And that, it seemed, was that. He said not another
word about her transformation and offered no explanation for her masquerade. But he did summon a second
chair almost the size of his own for her to sit beside him.
Seeing their lord's honored welcome of his bride-to-be,
his lieutenants inclined their heads to her but not a one
spoke to Krysta directly. They did, however, glance at her
from time to time cautiously as though taking the measure

of a creature previously unknown. Someone who had challenged the Lord of Hawkforte and emerged unscathed . . . apparently.

So did the meal progress though Krysta managed to eat very little of it. She was too vividly aware that Hawk's people were weighing her in the balance and prayed they would not find her too wanting. Only Daria dared to make her opinion known and then only because the bitter woman seemed unable to contain the waves of anger rising off her. Father Elbert tried to whisper to her but she waved even him off and continued glowering her way through supper.

It was over finally, leaving Krysta all but limp with relief. Hawk remained at table with his men but signaled the servants to accompany her to her quarters. He rose as she did, bowed over her hand, and wished her a cordial good night, all in the full view of their fascinated audience, who could not resist putting their heads together over that. Sleep seemed an impossibility yet it had come so suddenly as to take her unaware. Scarcely had she laid her head upon the pillows than she woke to the glare of morning.

Late morning, it seemed, when she peered more closely at the light. Shocked to discover that she had slept much longer than she had ever done before, Krysta jumped from the bed and began looking for her garments. She found her mother's dress at last, folded carefully away in a large wooden chest at the foot of the bed. In the same chest were all of Krysta's garments. With a start, she realized that other of her belongings—her precious books, the water-polished stones brought from the bay in front of her cliffside home, even a small box holding pressed flowers from that same cliff—were set out about the chamber.

Wondering at the thoughtful hand that had made her feel just a little at home, Krysta drew a chemise, stockings, and a simple day gown from the chest. She found water in an ewer on a table beside the windows. Halfway through scrubbing her face, she realized that the water was warm. A servant must have come in while she slept. Worried that she be thought a layabout, she hurried her ablutions and was quickly dressed. But before she could summon the courage to open her door, there was a soft knock. At her invitation, a young woman bearing a tray entered and gave Krysta a cautious smile.

"Good day, my lady. I hope you slept well. My name is Aelfgyth. So it please you, I am to be your maid."

"My maid?" So surprised was she that Krysta almost blurted out that she had never had a maid. Servants, to be sure, but Raven and Thorgold both were independent souls who still tended to see her as the child they had nurtured. They were as likely to do as she said simply because she said it as they were to fly to the moon. In truth and all things considered, less likely. Still, she did not think it wise to parade her lack of experience in such matters.

"I am sure we will get on well together, Aelfgyth." With a glance at the tray the young woman had set on the table, Krysta saw with pleasure that it held fresh baked bread, berries, and a round of cheese—food she would have selected for herself.

"Your serving woman says you do not eat meat," the young woman said, a little anxiously as though conversing with Raven had been no easy matter. "Else I would have brought some of the sausage Cook made this week. It is very good."

"I am sure it is." Krysta smiled and gestured at the tray. "This suits me very well. Be assured though that I do not expect my meals brought, nor do I usually sleep so late. Indeed, I don't believe I have ever done so in my life."

"No doubt yesterday was eventful," Aelfgyth murmured diplomatically. She hesitated a moment before adding, "When it pleases you, my lady, the steward Edvard is waiting to attend you."

The redoubtable Edvard was waiting on her? Krysta's surprise must have shown, for Aelfgyth said, "His lordship is on the training field with his men but he left instructions for Edvard to show you about the manor and answer whatever questions you might have as to the running of it."

Edvard was to show her the domestic side of Hawkforte, not Daria. Doubting though she did that the steward was pleased with such an assignment, she was grateful to be spared the company of her future sister-in-law if only temporarily.

Reluctant to keep the steward waiting any longer than he already had been, Krysta made short work of her meal and hastened from the royal chamber. She found Edvard on the steps to the main hall, where he was going over his accounts. At her arrival, he rose quickly, stuffed the roll of parchment into his tunic, and bowed. As he straightened, he and Aelfgyth shared a look so swift it might have eluded Krysta had anxiousness not made her unusually alert. At sight of Aelfgyth's smile, his brows rose but he lowered them swiftly and gave prudent attention to his master's soon-to-be bride.

"Good morrow, my lady. I trust you slept well?"

"Well and too long. Aelfgyth tells me you are to show me the manor."

"As my lord has directed." Edvard paused, frowning. Confronting the remarkable creature who had appeared suddenly last eve bearing no apparent ill effects from having deceived a man known the length and breadth of England for acting with ruthless speed against any who displeased him, the steward thought some further explanation might be in order. "For certain, the Lord Hawk would see to the matter himself were he not engaged in training his men. That task must take precedence over all others in our unsettled times. Hawkforte may appear a peaceful burgh, but the appearance and the reality both are earned only through constant and devoted diligence to duty, which we are most fortunate to receive in the person of the Lord Hawk himself."

Having worked her way through this thicket of words and concluded that the steward was trying to assure that she should feel no slight at being escorted by him rather than by Hawk, Krysta made swift to reassure him that she had no objection to his company. Inwardly, she admitted that she was just a little relieved not to have to face her formidable betrothed right then.

Edward said not a word of Daria, nor was that specter in evidence anywhere they went at Hawkforte. From the cool stone interior of the dairy half-buried in the ground through the dozens of dependencies—where wool was spun, woven, and dyed; food smoked, pickled, or stored; iron heated and bent; wood sawed, soaked, and shaped; grain ground; leather tanned, and on and on ending finally with the pigeon coops perched high above on the towers—Hawkforte's residents greeted her with cautious curiosity. Edvard maintained a stern demeanor that served to remind people of who and what she was, as though any needed reminding considering the banquet of gossip with which she had provided them. Yet did she find herself looking over her shoulder from time to time, just in case the Hawk should appear. No sign of him was to be had, and as the hours passed in diligent perusal of her new home she found herself impatient for some sight of him. Surely he was not . . . avoiding her?

"Is the Lord Hawk often so long occupied on the training field?" she asked as pigeons fluttered in their coops and the small boy who tended them peered at her through the tangle of his bangs.

The question startled Edvard. He gave off elaborating on the merits of the locally grown grapes still cultivated in the ancient Roman vineyards versus those native to the sunnier climes of the Mediterranean and looked at her cautiously.

"Training is very important. Lord Hawk maintains a sizable garrison and it would not do for the men to have too much idle time."

"I suppose not. . . ."

She turned away, looking out over the walls. Between her high perch and the sea whence she had come lay golden fields, plump orchards, orderly vineyards, and timber-rich forests. To eyes bred for harsher climes, such blatant plenty seemed a skald-spun dream.

Edvard spoke at her shoulder. "It was not always as you see it now. There was a time when those fields were trampled and lifeless, the town a tiny burnt shell, and those huddled within this fortress clinging to only the faintest hope that the Danes could be driven from the land."

"All this before King Alfred rallied the fyrd and gave battle to the Danes?"

"Yes, before men such as the Hawk rode with him, fighting at his side through more battles than anyone could count, living days in the saddle with scarcely any food or rest until it must have seemed to them that there was nothing left in the world save blood and death." The wind whispered in a moment's silence. It died away as Edvard went on. "He never speaks of it, not a word. Others will brag of their exploits in battle, but the Hawk says nothing. He was only a boy yet he fought with the strength of a grown man and he saw things no boy should ever see. Alfred himself hailed him as the greatest warrior of our age. He offered him any prize short of the throne itself. Do you know what Lord Hawk said he wanted?"

Krysta shook her head.

"To go home, to heal the land, and hopefully to have the land heal him."

"You were with him?" Her voice was tight with emotion.

"No, I was little more than a mewling babe hidden with my parents in the forest, my mother boiling bark and roots to try to keep her milk coming so that I might live. The Lord Hawk brought peace to this land and its people but that same peace eludes him. He knows full well it is the fierceness of his reputation that keeps the Danes at bay. So does he drive himself on the training field, at the hunt, in all ways that the spies of the Danes can see and report."

"Spies?"

"Of course there are spies here, did you think not? The Danes are not reconciled to their loss of these lands. They paw the ground like tethered bulls, awaiting the first sign of weakness to gore us yet again."

"I had not thought of that," Krysta admitted and felt foolish for so obvious a lapse. The land might look prosperous and at peace to her, but to other eyes it would appear all that *and* a prize to be coveted.

"Then think on it now, my lady," Edvard said. "It is the dread repute of the Hawk that protects us. Any hint of weakness is the door through which catastrophe will enter."

Her shoulders stiffened. She faced the steward proudly. "I see no weakness in Lord Hawk."

Edvard did not relent. "And surely you would never seek to prompt any."

"I seek only to be a good and loyal wife." She spoke gently in deference to what she recognized as his true loyalty to his lord.

The young man's expression softened slightly. "Then we will all hope you succeed, my lady, for there is not a man or woman or child here who does not wish the best for Lord Hawk."

Thus on notice that the people of Hawkforte expected

her to prove herself, Krysta was relieved when the tour of the manor concluded a short time later. She thought to seek the relief of solitude in her quarters until the supper hour so that she might reflect on all she had seen and learned. But when she passed through the great hall on her way to her chamber, she found Daria lying in wait for her.

So suddenly did she emerge from the shadows that she took Krysta by surprise, prompting a small, startled cry.

"Oh . . . Daria. I didn't see you."

The older woman's thin face bore two stark patches of color high on her cheeks, emphasizing the flat glitter of her gaze. "No doubt your mind is too full of frivolous thoughts to take note of your circumstances." She sneered, her mouth twisting in derision. "You are a fool. The only sensible thing you can possibly do now is leave."

Coming from another, such rudeness would have surprised Krysta. But from Daria it seemed as natural as the curl of smoke from a wood fire, a reminder of embers lurking just below.

"I don't think that would be sensible at all," Krysta said.

"Don't you? Then you don't understand the situation. You have *enraged* Hawk. Do you understand? He is so consumed with fury that he cannot trust himself to be anywhere near you. He's already had one stupid, selfish little wife and she did not live long. He is not a man who suffers fools gladly. He is in love with another woman, a lady of true nobility and worth whom he wishes to make his wife. Indeed, he would already have done so were it not for this idiotic alliance."

Before the barrage of so much that was new and shocking—a previous wife, dead . . . another woman he loved?—Krysta felt as though she had been plunged into a turbulent sea, both cold and smothering. Yet did a lifeline seem to beckon, disputing Daria's claims at least in part.

"Hawk is not angry. Certainly he gave no indication of that yesterday eve."

Daria dismissed that with a snort. "Of course he did not. He never shows his emotions before his people. But he's been out on the training field all day barely restraining himself from hacking his own men to pieces. You truly have no idea of the havoc you've wreaked, do you?"

"I have done nothing so severe as to merit this. You are exaggerating—"

"Nothing? God's breath, you are even stupider than Adda!"

Daria's poison tainted the very air around her, yet even recognizing that, Krysta could not stop herself from asking, "Who is Adda?"

"Who *was*," Daria corrected triumphantly. "She was Hawk's first wife, that sniveling child. Her death was a relief to us all."

"How did she die?"

"She fell from a cliff, that same one right out there." Daria pointed toward the sea. "And good riddance to her, she deserved no better. We weren't even able to recover her body. Denied proper burial, her soul is condemned to wander forever. But of course that wouldn't worry you as you are not a Christian."

"I *am* a Christian. My father saw to it that I was reared as such." She did not add that she suspected him of doing so as an antidote to what he perceived as the dangerous influence of her vanished mother.

Daria looked taken aback but she recovered quickly. "No matter. You may call yourself what you will but your heart is pagan. The Norse can never be anything else. That is why you dwell in the frozen wastelands beyond the grace of Our Lord."

"Our land is as God willed it to be. However, I doubt

He willed you to be so ignorant and prejudiced. If that had been His wish for anyone, He would not have sent His Son with tidings of love and redemption for all."

For a moment, mounting fury held Daria in thrall. She did not move or speak but stared at Krysta with unconcealed malice. The silence drew out between them like a rank fog. Daria's mouth worked for some moments before she could manage sound from it.

"Beware how you speak of the Lord lest the words leap from your tongue as poisonous frogs, revealing to all the cursed witch you are."

This was more even than Krysta could have expected and far more than she could bear. All her life she had lived among people who loved her, yet so sheltered an upbringing had not weakened her. To the contrary, it lay at the core of her strength.

With quiet dignity, she said, "Enough, Daria. I sorrow for the demons that ride you but I will not allow you to speak to me in this way. If nothing else, it is disrespectful to the Lord Hawk, whose bride I will be. Accept that and mayhap there can yet be accord between us."

"*Never*," Daria spat. She glared at Krysta, then turned and stomped off, leaving the air to vibrate with her anger.

When she was gone, Krysta moved over to the window and took a cleansing breath of fresh salt air. Steadier, she sat down on the bench overlooking the sea. It was a hopeless fancy, yet she wished that she could see over the vast miles to her beloved home. And if she could, what would the sight of home bring except a deep longing in her heart?

"What ails you?" Raven asked. She settled on the bench beside Krysta and peered at her with keen black eyes that missed nothing. "If your face was any longer, it would be hanging down to your knees. Did I not see you in all your glory just yestereve, sitting right beside your proud lord and him not giving off a flicker of displeasure?"

Krysta shrugged a shoulder but could not quite cast off self-pity. It had a tendency to cling. "Did you think that meant all was well?"

Raven made a small clicking sound, evidence of her impatience. "I thought it meant you'd done a damn sight better than I thought you would, but then I've never understood the ways of men. So what troubles you? No, wait, I'll guess. Dreadful Daria has been hereabout, spreading her own special brand of venom."

"Is it so obvious?"

"It is, to me and everyone else. They're all whispering about how you looked last night, how Lord Hawk looked, how he looked at you when you weren't looking at him, and so on and so forth." Raven shook herself at such foolishness. She tilted her head to one side and gazed at Krysta solemnly. "Of course, all they dare to do is whisper. That one still has power, she does, and she means to hold on to it."

"I have no wish to bring strife into my husband's home."

Raven snorted. "Strife is already here, girl. Strife is all that bag of bones knows. Not a hint of meat on her and not a bit of use to her save for making folks miserable. Besides, it's up to his lordship to decide what he wants or doesn't want in his home. From what I saw last night, what he wants is you."

"Wanting isn't loving."

"It's where most men start, so I hear." Perceiving that little had changed in Krysta's mood, Raven sighed. "There now, you're made of sterner stuff than this. I can't believe she has brought you so low."

"It isn't really her, it's what she told me. Did you know that Lord Hawk was married before?"

Raven glanced away. "I might have heard mention of

it. She died a long time ago. They say he never speaks of her."

"He never speaks of the battles he fought against the Danes when he was no more than a boy, either, but that doesn't mean they weren't important to him."

"He thought poorly of her, so folks say. They're hoping you'll do better."

"Mayhap I would if he weren't already in love with another woman."

Raven's head snapped up. "What's that you say? What woman?"

"Daria didn't tell me her name, she only said there was another woman he wanted to marry. She called her a lady of true nobility."

"And you believed her? What's addled your brains, girl? If he had a notion to marry someone else, what of it? Doesn't mean he loved her. Love and marriage have nothing to do with each other." She caught herself. "Leastways, not usually. Besides, if Dreadful Daria said she was *a lady of true nobility,* that likely means she's as stiff a stick as Daria herself. No wonder Lord Hawk hasn't been brought to the altar yet. He ought to be down on his knees thanking the Danes for making so much trouble as to bring about this alliance against them."

"Somehow, I don't see Hawk giving thanks to the Danes," Krysta said with a reluctant smile.

But the idea had a certain appeal, so much so that she was still amused by it after Raven departed. The hall was quiet, preparations for supper not having yet begun. Dust motes danced in rays of sunlight filtering through the windows. She drew her knees up, leaned her head against them, and looked out over Hawkforte. She knew the manor far better now thanks to Edvard's tour but so much more remained to be discovered. Of the town beyond the fortress, she knew almost nothing. She could see it was prosperous, and if the new wood of many of the buildings was any indication, it was also growing rapidly. But the people remained a mystery to her. She had never lived in so large and crowded a place, had never even imagined doing so. One more thing to which she would have to adjust. She was mulling that over, wondering how she might make a place for herself amid strangers, when Hawk entered the hall.

Adrift in her thoughts, Krysta did not see him. He stopped at first sight of her and stared. The dull-haired serving girl of the last few days was gone but so was the ethereal goddess of the preceding eve, seemingly crafted from sea foam and sunlight. In both their places was a young woman—a very *serious*-looking young woman— simply dressed, her cheeks and brow slightly sunburned and her eyes pensive. She looked sad to him and he felt a sudden need to change that. Without questioning the impulse, he crossed the room and knelt beside her.

"Did Edvard tire you overmuch?"

She started, so surprised was she by his sudden appearance. He loomed beside her, so big and so very near. His hair was matted to his head, his cheeks darkened by a day's growth of beard. He looked sweaty and grubby, and absolutely wonderful.

"No, not so much. Have you been training all this time?"

He nodded though he scarcely knew what she had asked. Her voice flowed through him, soft and faintly husky, gentle as a caress. "Did you see all you should?"

"I think so." She smiled faintly. "Edvard was very thorough."

Hawk smiled in turn. "He is ever that." He rose and took a seat beside her. She moved over to make room for him. They shared the bench companionably. "What do you think of Hawkforte?"

She said what had been in her mind before he came to eclipse all other thought. "It is very big."

He looked surprised. "Do you think so? Winchester is far larger."

"I can scarcely imagine that. My home—my old home—would fit in a corner of the burgh. My brother's holding is far larger than that, nearer to Hawkforte's size, but in land rather than in people."

Hawk nodded, thinking of how the Norse lived. "I have been to Sciringesheal. That is a good-sized town and a busy port."

Krysta hesitated but curiosity overcame her. Best she should learn the measure of this man now. "Is it true you went there to take back your sister from the Wolf?"

He cast her a swift look but did not appear offended. "Is that what people say?"

"They do, and the skald sang of it the first night I was here."

"The truth is I went to Sciringesheal to kill the Wolf. I believed he had kidnapped my sister and I feared her dead, or worse yet suffering terribly. I wanted nothing so much as his blood on my sword."

"Why then does he live?" Krysta asked softly.

"Aside from the fact that in any duel between us, victory might favor either one or perhaps neither? We could have ended by killing each other, but Cymbra insisted she was happily wed and begged me to believe her. Instead, I thought she was lying to protect me and took her away by stealth." He sighed. "To her credit, she forgave me, as did Wolf after he arrived here to reclaim her. The idea for the alliance between Norse and Saxon was Wolf's to begin with but he quickly enlisted Alfred's support. You know the rest."

She did, or at least she could easily surmise it. The king had thrown his wholehearted support behind an alliance and the marriages meant to support it. Whatever Hawk's feelings for that *lady of true nobility*, he would never gainsay his king.

"I am glad it worked out well for your sister and Lord Wolf," she said and meant it truly, even as unspoken in her heart was the hope they might somehow prove to be as fortunate.

"They are in love." He spoke the last word as though it was a strange, odd thing come clumsily to his tongue. A word from an unknown language that had been explained to him yet remained mysterious.

Sadness weighed heavily on Krysta's shoulders. She kept them straight but with an effort. Were she braver, she might have asked him if he believed in love. But the thought of his likely answer terrified her. Best to remain in blissful ignorance where hope at least had a chance to grow.

"I have been thinking about your reason for coming here as you did."

She swallowed against the tightness of her throat and waited.

"This matter of wanting to get to know me better—is that really why you did it?"

Krysta nodded. She took a breath, steadying herself. "It seemed a good idea at the time."

If he meant to mock her, he would do so now. She waited . . . hoping yet scarcely daring to hope. . . .

"The notion may have merit."

Krysta opened her eyes, belatedly aware that she had closed them as though in prayer, and stared at him. "Do you mean that?"

He frowned. "Do not read overmuch into my words. I merely meant it would not necessarily be a bad thing for us to know each other before we wed." Swiftly, he added, "That does not mean I approve of what you did. It was a harebrained scheme."

She was silent for a moment before she smiled. "We have hares in Vestfold. They are large animals with very powerful back legs, capable of leaping great distances.

They survive the worst winters snug in burrows they dig deep beneath the ground and they seem able to thwart the wiliest predator." Her eyes met his. "Even the hawk."

The sound of his laughter surprised them both and so startled a serving lad carrying bowls into the hall that he backed out hastily, juggling his burden in an effort not to drop it.

"You don't look anything at all like a rabbit," Hawk observed. As compliments went he supposed it wasn't much, but he had little experience in such matters. Moreover, he was suddenly preoccupied with the thought of *legs*, long, smooth, silken legs wrapped around him.

"I need a bath," he said and stood up. He wasn't retreating, precisely. He just needed a little time to himself to adjust to the discovery that his intended bride had a sense of humor. He valued honor above all else, and he prized intelligence. He was no more immune to beauty in a woman than was any other man. But secretly he thought a sense of humor among God's greatest gifts.

Krysta resisted the impulse to ask if he wanted his back scrubbed again, but only just. At the mere thought of saying such a thing, much less the real difficulty she had not saying it, she pressed her lips firmly together, but she couldn't keep them there, so strong was the smile that demanded to be let loose.

"Edvard didn't show me the sauna."

"I'll have to do that . . . sometime. I'll see you at supper." He waited, needing to see the little nod she gave.

Later, lying in the tub in his own quarters, he leaned his head back against the rim and searched the ceiling for answers. How did one get to know a woman? And what did such knowing mean? Men said they knew a woman when they had possessed her but Hawk dismissed that as an empty claim. He had risen from enough beds more aware than ever of the essential mystery of women to believe that fucking was the route to knowing any of them.

Not that it didn't have its uses, it surely did. But this notion Krysta had that they should know each other before they wed—how could that be done?

He had never spent any time with women, not really. The only woman he cared for was Cymbra, and he had deliberately sent her away to her own residence to keep her safe from the strange gift that made her both a great healer and vulnerable to the pain of anyone near her. Even after she'd learned to control that gift, he had still kept her secluded, realizing full well how men would fight for her once they glimpsed her beauty. Wolf had settled that problem, for which Hawk was duly grateful, but now he was with the problem of how to get to know Krysta.

Men learned to know each other on the training field and in battle. Bonds forged in armed camps lasted a lifetime, whether that be measured in hours or decades. Yet he could hardly invite Krysta to join him in swordplay, at least not the sort that involved a blade. His contrary mind, ever irksome, suggested another sort of play in which they might indulge but he repressed that firmly. Taking her to his bed would make her his wife in his own eyes and those of his people. The blessing of the Church would be mere formality.

Not that he wasn't tempted. The cooling water did nothing to discourage his desire for her and, indeed, nothing concealed it. The mere thought of her was enough to arouse him, a fact he observed ruefully. But this business of a *wife*, that was altogether different from a temporary mistress or chance encounter. It was for the long term, therefore patience was counseled.

She could read. That might be a starting place. They could talk of books. He had read more than fifty books in his life. He would regale her with them, she would be suitably impressed, and they would . . .

He sighed, trying to imagine such an unlikely course. Mayhap there were better ways. His mind chewed on it until the sun slanting through the windows alerted him to the passing hour. He rose and dried himself quickly before dressing for the evening meal. When he caught himself pulling out a tunic the color of which he thought might appeal to Krysta, he groaned in disgust and threw it back into the chest. But a moment later he took it up again and donned it, telling himself it was merely the easiest to hand.

So did the master of Hawkforte descend to his hall, and to the woman who awaited him there.

Chapter

SIX

KRYSTA TOO WAS FRESH FROM A BATH. SHE had dressed with care, choosing a gown the same shade of teal blue as sometimes lingered in the sky at the turning of the sun. She had never seen the gown before and only now realized that her chests must contain quite a few items that were entirely new to her. Either they had belonged to her mother and been held in waiting for her, or Raven had been procuring them all this time, no doubt with Thorgold's able assistance. Glad though she was for their foresight, she had to wonder what had made them believe she would need such garments. Certainly the thought had never occurred to her.

Her half-brother Sven had called the Saxons dirty and said they lived in their own filth, but she had seen no evidence of that. In the warmth of summer, people seemed to bathe regularly and the women were forever sweeping out their cottages, airing their bedding and the like. Nor had it escaped her notice that after Daria retired for the night, the servants were inclined to pair off and drift down to the river. Their laughter floated on soft evening breezes, along with what sounded like energetic splashing.

She was glad, then, to be able to appear before them suitably groomed and garbed. Glad, too, of Aelfgyth's kind help. The young woman insisted on brushing Krysta's hair for her, murmuring compliments on the color even as she struggled with the riotous curls.

"Did your mother have hair like this, my lady?"

Krysta glanced away from the small bronze mirror that revealed a reflection she had scarcely ever seen. "I don't know. My mother went away when I was very young."

Aelfgyth's hands stilled for a moment before resuming their soothing rhythm. "She died?"

"No, she just went away. Raven and Thorgold have told me only that she was very beautiful, nothing else."

"Forgive me if I ask too much, my lady, but is that customary among the Norse? I mean for a wife to leave her husband like that? It happens here sometimes when folk follow the old ways and handfast before seeking the blessing of the Church. They are only sworn to stay with each other for a year or unless a child is conceived, so sometimes such couples part."

"The Norse do that as well but I don't think many wives leave their husbands after a child is born. Still, I suppose it happens."

Aelfgyth was silent again for so long as she could contain her curiosity. Swiftly enough, she said, "Could you not visit your mother?"

Krysta hesitated. She had surprised herself by mentioning anything about her upbringing and knew not how to put the question aside with due delicacy. Finally, she said, "She went very far away. I could not follow. At any rate, my father was a good man and I would have missed him sorely as I did when he died a year ago."

The maid nodded sympathetically. She finished

smoothing Krysta's hair as best she could and secured it with a ribbon the same shade as her gown. "You look lovely, my lady."

Krysta mustered a smile but it wobbled away before she stepped from the room. Last night, she had thought only of how the Hawk's people would react to her sudden transformation. This night, her thoughts were solely of him. He was already in the hall when she arrived, talking with several of his lieutenants and the redoubtable Edvard. The conversation broke off as she entered. Hard-faced men shot her quick, sharp looks. A few nodded in her direction but none spoke to her directly, yet was she suddenly, acutely aware of being the focus of all eyes. Her throat tightened and for just a moment she had to fight the impulse to run back up to her tower room. But Raven was right, she was made of sterner stuff. She held her place, back straight and chin tilted proudly, through the seemingly endless moments until Hawk stepped forward. It truly was only moments, for which she was grateful. Grateful, too, for the swift glance of approval he gave her.

The chair he had called for last evening remained in place beside his own. He handed her into it and sat down, his lieutenants quickly following suit. There was a general rustle throughout the hall as everyone did the same. Only the servants who worked at meals were left bustling about with heavy platters and skins of wine. She caught a quick glimpse of Raven and Thorgold in their accustomed places. They both looked cheery, Thorgold going so far as to grin.

His good humor might have had something to do with the feast being laid before them. With a day's warning that the Hawk's bride had arrived, the cook and his army of assistants had outdone themselves. An entire roasted pig was paraded in on a litter carried by four serving boys. The cheers greeting this sight had barely died away before haunches of venison and lamb followed, along with platters of succulent crabs, eels, and oysters. Heaps of round loaves of bread were distributed and bowls of fresh greens offered.

As was fitting, Hawk was served first, but he in turn served Krysta, offering her only the choicest morsels. Such courtesy was duly noted by his people, who smiled and nodded among themselves. Surprised by the outpouring of such delicacies, Krysta was momentarily distracted. She returned to herself just as Hawk was about to place a slice of pork on her side of the silver platter they were sharing.

"Oh, no, thank you," she said hastily.

"You do not care for pork?"

"I'm sure it's excellent but I don't eat meat." She smiled apologetically. "However, everything else looks wonderful."

Hawk frowned. "You must eat meat elsewise you cannot be healthy."

Krysta hesitated, seeking some way to respond without appearing to disagree with him. She shrugged lightly. "No doubt what you say is true for some but I have never eaten meat and I assure you, I am perfectly healthy."

"Never?" He was genuinely shocked. The only people he knew who eschewed meat were a few monks and none of them struck him as particularly vigorous. For everyone else, meat was much sought after and always appreciated. "Surely your parents had better care of you than that."

"My father provided for me very well. I wanted for nothing."

He was about to dispute that when her omission distracted him. "Your father? What about your mother?"

Krysta suppressed a sigh. To be called upon for the second time in less than an hour's span to explain something she had never spoken of with anyone save Thorgold and Raven was unsettling, yet did she gird herself to reply honestly. "My mother left a short time after I was born. During their time together, my father had given her a manor of her own a day's ride from his main holding. It became mine and there I remained until I left to come here."

Hawk set down the pork she did not want, placing it on his own side of the platter. Her brief explanation raised far more questions than it answered. Yet was he reluctant to probe too sharply where hurt might well linger. "Where did your mother go?"

"Away." Hastily, she added, "But my father was a good man and, as I have said, I was well provided for."

"No doubt . . . But why did your mother have her own residence instead of sharing your father's?" He paused, not wishing to force an answer but driven to know all the same. "I understand that among the Norse the custom of a powerful man having more than one wife has not entirely died out." He was imagining a senior wife who would not have welcomed into her own home the winsome beauty Krysta's mother undoubtedly had been, but that notion was quickly set aside.

"It most certainly has died out in my family," she informed him tartly. "My mother was my father's second wife only because the first had died. He had children by that first union, my half-brother Sven among others, and I gather he thought it best to keep his lines apart."

It still seemed an odd arrangement to Hawk but he said nothing more of it. He knew something more of her than he had a few moments before, and that pleased him. Moreover, he thought he had a glimpse into why she was so concerned that their marriage be a success. Her own parents' union had not been, elsewise her mother would not have left or, he thought more likely, been sent away. Understandably enough, she wished to avoid the same fate. That conclusion left him well satisfied. The business of getting to know a woman was not so hard after all.

In good humor, Hawk decided to overlook her curious notions about food until a later time. In the meanwhile, he made sure she had a decent meal of crab and oysters, which, truth be told, he also enjoyed. It also pleased him to hear her impressions of Hawkforte, which he drew from her steadily in between succulent bites and the sips of wine he urged on her. Edvard seemed to have done his usual thorough job, for Krysta had seen aspects of the domestic side of Hawkforte unknown even to its master. He knew cloth was woven . . . somehow . . . just as he knew food was preserved, clothes made and washed, children and animals tended, and a hundred sundry other tasks done that were so much a part of ordinary life as to be noticed only in their absence. But he had never inquired into the actual doing of them until now. Not that he had suddenly become interested in such matters. Rather, he was too absorbed in the delectable soft tones of Krysta's voice and the pleasure of watching her full, rose-hued lips move for it to matter much what she was saying.

Indeed, so enjoyable did he find the experience that when she fell silent, the master of Hawkforte, the stern taskmaster of several thousand fighting men, the war leader who scarcely ever let a day pass without rigorous training, tossed down the remainder of his wine and said, "Come riding with me tomorrow."

IT WAS IN HIS MIND TO SHOW HER HAWKFORTE HIS OWN way. He hoped that under his guidance she would feel some small measure of the tug he experienced whenever he returned from a journey and caught the first sight of smoke rising from his fires. At any rate, it seemed the thing to do. The stable boys had received his instructions and carried them out to the letter. The pretty little mare they led out for his inspection was agile and obedient. She was pure ebony from end to end, the color so rich as to glow with a silver sheen. When he rubbed her nose, she blew softly and tried to nuzzle into his pockets for the apple he ended up giving her sooner than he had intended. With a laugh, Hawk reflected that such behavior was useful in both a horse and a woman. He was indulging that notion when Krysta arrived. She had almost, but not quite, managed to tame the mass of her curls beneath a veil that matched her dun-hued gown, chosen, he suspected, because it would continue to look well when splattered with mud. He smiled approvingly at her foresight but sobered when he saw the expression in her eyes. She was unmistakably wary if not outright afraid. When the mare pranced gracefully, no more than showing off, Krysta backed up hastily.

"I think perhaps you should know that I haven't ridden all that much."

Hawk was surprised. Everyone rode; even a peasant could sling his leg over a donkey and get where he was going. Ladies no less than lords took great pride in their ability to sail over any obstacle and ride for miles without tiring.

"How much is 'all that much'?" he asked.

She looked away, her cheeks coloring. "Almost not at all." Hastily she added, "In Vestfold there really isn't all that much reason to ride. We use boats to get everywhere."

He supposed that made sense, although every Viking he had encountered rode extremely well. Still, he had to take into account her unusual upbringing.

"Here we ride," he said gently, "and so will you. It really isn't difficult."

As she continued to look doubtful, he drew the mare forward and gently placed Krysta's hand on her nose, then laughed at his betrothed's reaction.

"She's so soft!"

"She is that and she's very well behaved." He gestured

to a stable boy to hold the mare's reins. Krysta's eyes widened when Hawk placed his hands on her waist and lifted her easily into the saddle. For the first time, Krysta found herself looking down into the face of her husband-to-be. The strangeness of that heightened her unease.

"Oh, I don't think . . . I'm not really ready to . . ."

"Of course you are. Now hold the reins like this." She fumbled with them for a moment but caught on quickly. When he was sure she was seated securely, Hawk called for his own mount. The gray stallion was led out prancing and snorting, causing the mare to shy. Instinctively, Krysta reached down and patted her side, murmuring to her reassuringly. Beneath her touch, the mare quieted. Pleased, not to say surprised, Krysta laughed. All night she had tossed and turned, worrying about how she would manage to ride with Hawk. Not for the world would she have attempted to refuse but she had dreaded making a fool of herself. Now, it seemed, she would not.

Near giddy with relief, she beamed him a smile so beguiling as to rob him of breath. They rode out past the high walls of the fortress, down the path that led behind the hill and away from the town. He kept the pace slow at first but picked it up as she gained confidence. They were trotting when they came up out of the wood onto the broad cliff above the sea. Gulls whirled overhead and sunlight sparkled off the water. The tang of salt mingled with the perfumes of wild grasses and flowers. Although the day was still young, the air was already warm.

Hawk turned his horse in a half-circle and looked back toward the town. When Krysta did the same, she gasped. They were on the other side of the bay with all of Hawkforte spread out before them, from the busy town clustered at the water's edge to the proud fortress on the hill above. She could see boats moving in and out of the harbor, and could even make out carts moving along the docks. When she squinted, she thought she glimpsed the guards on patrol along the walls.

"It's beautiful," she said softly, seeing the town for what it truly was, a place of hard-won peace and prosperity.

Hawk nodded. "It is that."

She looked into his rugged features, the skin drawn tautly over bone and sinew, and had to fight the urge to reach out to him. "Edvard told me it used to be very different."

"It was a charnel house," Hawk said bluntly. "Burned fields, burned homes, and burned hopes." He gestured toward the line of trees closest to the town. "Do you see there, how those trees are younger than the ones farther out? The Danes even burned the forest, at least that part of it they didn't cut down and haul away to their shipyards. When they realized they weren't going to be able to hold this place, they tried to lay waste to it. Even the wells were poisoned."

"It must have taken great courage and determination to remain here and rebuild," Krysta said softly.

"It took desperation. There was nowhere else for those left alive to go. So many people had fled farther west that the land there couldn't support them and they faced starvation." He leaned forward in the saddle, his arms folded over the pommel, and looked out toward the town. "I vowed there would be peace here. At the time, I had no idea how I would fulfill that vow but I knew I would give my life to it."

Krysta said what was in her heart. "Your people are fortunate to have you as their leader."

He shook his head. "We are all fortunate to have Alfred of Wessex. Without him, we would have been a few lone men trying to hold off the Danes." He raised his hand, the sun-burnished fingers splayed wide.

"Separately we could not have accomplished anything except more death." He folded his hand into a mighty fist. "Together we were able to change everything."

Hawk shook himself abruptly. "I did not mean to speak of such things. This is supposed to be a day for relaxation."

"I would rather it be a day for getting to know each other," Krysta said.

He laughed a little, as though that thought still made him uncomfortable. "It should also be a day for you to learn to ride. Come."

She followed him down a path that led from the cliffside by easy stages to the beach below. Even so, Krysta held her breath a time or two as the mare picked her way daintily in the stallion's wake. When they reached the sand, she let out a sigh of relief so heartfelt that it prompted a grin from Hawk.

"There, that wasn't so bad, was it?" he asked as he helped her from the saddle.

More aware of his strength and nearness than of her fast-fading fear, Krysta shook her head. "It was fine."

She was lying and he knew it but her spirit pleased him so he let the small untruth go by. Besides, he was preoccupied with the way her slim waist fitted between his hands, hands he had only to raise slightly to caress the swell of her breasts. The temptation to do so was strong within him, as was the even greater temptation to lay her down on the sand and satisfy the passion that had been between them from the beginning.

But the business of *knowing* lingered, that and the stray thought that just perhaps what Cymbra and Wolf shared might not be unique to them. He had never considered love except to dismiss it as fantasy, but now he found himself wondering. . . . That he should wish for anything so foolish was impossible. He was merely surprised and a little puzzled, that was all.

Thinking she needed a rest from the saddle and remembering her pleasure on the beach below Hawkforte, he left the horses tethered to a bush and took her hand in his. Together, they strolled along the shore. Hawk could not remember ever walking along a beach with a woman. Indeed, he could not recall walking with one anywhere save into supper at Alfred's Winchester palace. He felt at a sudden loss as to what to say to her. It seemed doubtful she would want to hear about the new spear he had designed and which his men were learning to use. Nor did he think she would enjoy discussing the battles he sometimes worked out in his mind, designing strategies to repel their enemies. The women he knew at court excelled at intrigue and loved politics; never would he make the mistake of underestimating any of them. But Krysta seemed different. There was a softness to her, a quiet gentleness that roused memories of his mother. Yet, he reminded himself, she was no milksop; she had flown at him like a Fury. He smiled a little, remembering how she had looked dripping wet and dye-stained. The sons he got of her would not lack for spirit, nor, he suspected, would the daughters.

It was a mistake to think of that for immediately he felt himself growing hard. Surprised and a little ruefully pleased, he let go of her hand and reached down to pluck a pink-gray shell from the damp sand. The shell was intact and polished to an opalescent hue. He turned it over between his fingers, struck by the simple perfection of the shell and its ability to survive the tumult of the seas. He was about to toss the shell back into the waves when he reconsidered and handed it to Krysta instead. She took it with a shy smile. He stood for a moment, absorbed in that smile, before abruptly returning to himself.

"Sometimes there are dolphins by those rocks over there."

She followed his gaze toward the blue-green water

lapping at boulders that looked as though they had been scattered along the beach by a playful giant. "I have never seen dolphins. They do not come so far north as Vestfold."

"Let's see if they're about."

They continued on to the rocks but as they approached, Hawk cautioned, "Be careful. They're wet and slick."

Krysta nodded but she was preoccupied by the sea. As always, the sight and scent of it filled her with longing. The wind stung her eyes, and brought tears to her cheeks. She brushed them aside impatiently. A shape moved far out in the water, coming swiftly nearer. She peered more closely, wondering what she might see. The head rose suddenly and she laughed with sheer delight as she saw the wide smile of the dolphin.

"Oh, how wonderful!" she exclaimed and moved forward, unthinking, wanting only to see more. She was very near the edge, and Hawk was just reaching out his hand, when she stepped on a patch of seaweed clinging to the rock. Her balance faltered. She stretched out both arms, trying to steady herself, but the effort was futile. With a gasp, she fell into the frothing water.

Hawk froze. The man who had never hesitated in a hundred battles, whose reactions were lightning quick, stood for an instant staring down into the sea and felt only disbelief. His intended bride could not possibly have just disappeared beneath the waves. The day begun with such promise could not possibly have turned so suddenly, savagely dark.

Could and had. With a roar of rage at capricious fate, Hawk threw off his cloak and dived into the water. He surfaced moments later and looked around frantically. When still he did not see Krysta, he inhaled deeply and dived again. For long, agonizing moments, he searched for her but without success. Burning lungs forced him to rise again. He gasped in air and was about to dive once more when a swift shape moving nearby caught his attention.

Krysta surfaced, laughing. Her hair dark and sleek around her head, her body moving with lithe ease despite the weight of her gown, she looked utterly delighted. "This is wonderful! Why did no one tell me the water is so warm?"

Before he could do more than gape, she dived from sight. He treaded water, looking around in all directions. Moments later, she surfaced again but easily fifty feet from where she had gone under.

"You can swim," Hawk said, rather stupidly he thought for it was hardly necessary to comment on something so supremely evident.

Krysta grinned. "Raven and Thorgold claim I was born swimming. I suppose they're exaggerating but I've always loved the water." She disappeared again and this time surfaced near him. Her face alight with happiness, she said, "I've swum in a few rock pools that were this warm but the sea near Vestfold is always colder even in high summer. This is incredible."

Hawk, who was finding the water pleasant but cool, could only sigh. He was, of course, infinitely relieved that she had come to no harm. But the sheer terror he had felt when she vanished beneath the waves lingered within him. He could not remember ever feeling such fear, even on the battlefield where fright was the boon companion of the sensible man.

Fear made him sterner than he would elsewise have been. "The water is not so warm that you cannot take ill from it. Enough of this."

She looked surprised and disappointed, but she did not argue. At least she was obedient, he told himself as they regained the beach. But as she bent over, wringing out her sodden gown, Krysta said, "I suppose it doesn't make much sense to swim in all these clothes." She glanced up at him hopefully. "At home, I swam in a shift." She did not add, although some imp of mischief tempted her to, that there were times when she swam in nothing at all save the silken sheath of her hair.

He looked at her disbelievingly until he realized she was serious. With a scant ounce of encouragement, the Lady Krysta would be happy to return to the water . . . in her shift. And just what was he supposed to do? Sit on the beach and enjoy the spectacle? Or perhaps join her? Oh, yes, that would be an excellent idea. The lust he had battled all morning surged abruptly. He cursed under his breath and tossed her the cloak he had abandoned before leaping in to what he supposed was her rescue.

"Here, put this on."

She caught the cloak but said, "Thank you but I'm not cold."

She was also apparently oblivious to the way her wet gown clung to her, outlining the high curve of her breasts, etching even the shape of erect nipples, down along her willow-slim waist to the chalice of her hips and the long, slim legs beneath. Hawk had never considered himself a man of great imagination but he needed none at all to envision what she would look like bare to his gaze. She was his promised wife. Many couples lay together before marriage and many brides received the blessing of the Church after their first babe was planted in their womb. No one would gainsay him. *No one* . . . save just possibly the Lady Krysta herself, and judging by the kiss they had shared in the stable, overcoming her reluctance would be both easy and pleasurable.

But he was a man of discipline—*dammit*—and no woman, however tempting, was going to make him forget that. He would make her his wife in his own time and on his own terms.

"Put the cloak on," he said again, and this time his tone alerted her to danger. Her head snapped up and she looked straight at him. A flame of color blossomed over her cheeks. She glanced away hurriedly. When she mounted the mare, the cloak was wrapped snugly around her.

They returned as they had come but in silence. Despite the tumult of his thoughts, Hawk kept a close eye on her. She rode far better than she had scant hours before. She learned quickly and had a natural agility that served her well. He caught himself remembering how she danced and quickly steered his thoughts in other directions, only to encounter the image of her sleek and unfettered, moving through the water with what seemed like more than human grace. Such distraction as she was prone to be would be eased on the training field. He'd pluck half-a-dozen of his men who had imagined they were in for a soft day and work himself until fatigue blocked out all else.

But his plan was for naught. Three longships, their ominous dragon prows rising high above the water, had appeared suddenly around the point and were heading straight toward the docks. Hawk rose in the saddle, gazing out at their wind-filled sails and the proud emblem emblazoned on them. He cursed again and dug his heels into the stallion's side, urging his mount to a gallop.

SEVEN

L ET ME GUESS," HAWK SAID. "YOU HAPPENED
to be passing by and thought you'd drop in for a
visit."

The man across from him grinned. He was
as large and heavily muscled as Hawk himself, with brown
hair shot through with gold brushing his massive shoulders and eyes like flame-lit topaz. He wore a plain tunic of
finely spun black wool and polished leather boots, but no
adornment to hint at his true rank and power save for a
sword of finely crafted steel. Yet was there no mistaking
the aura of nobility that clung to him, an aura in no way
diminished by the trick of nature that had made him an
unusually handsome man.

So far, no fewer than six serving girls had tripped past
on one pretext or another. Hawk found himself wondering if more lustful looks had ever been directed toward
any one man in less time but his guest seemed to think
nothing of it. He didn't ignore the girls, on the contrary,
he bestowed upon each a smile of true friendliness and regard. Hawk sighed, remembering that the Viking genuinely adored women, believing them the best gift the

gods could bestow upon mankind. They, in turn, seemed to sense that and returned his affection with what could only be described as unbridled enthusiasm.

"What sort of a friend would I be if I went by without a word?" his guest asked after a pretty redhead swept past, wiggling her hips fast enough to cause a draft. "Besides, I thought you might want news of your nephew."

Hawk looked at the man known from the ice fields of the north to the souks of Byzantium as Dragon and grinned. "And how is the little lion?"

That his sister had married into a family with the same penchant for bestowing evocative names on their males no longer surprised him. He had come to accept that in the feared Norse Wolf, Cymbra had found her true mate. The birth of their son at Hawkforte just a few months before had brought great joy to all, not least because it dissuaded Wolf from dismantling the stronghold plank by plank and stone by stone, as he had threatened to do in revenge for Hawk's misguided rescue of his sister.

Amazingly, they had put all that behind them as they forged the alliance of Saxon and Norse to stand against the Dane. Hawk's marriage to Krysta would doubly bind the alliance, which meant that only the man seated across from him would be left unwed, but not for long.

"The little lion continues to shake the walls of Sciringesheal whenever he bellows. Fortunately, he's a happy sort and doesn't do it too often. Cymbra's a wonderful mother, of course, and an equally wonderful wife. Wolf is disgustingly content. It's hard to believe he used to be known as the Scourge of the Saxons."

Hawk shrugged. "You know what they say, reformed scourges make the best husbands. And speaking of which, has your brother found a bride for you yet?"

Dragon flinched and took a long quaff of his ale. "I told him I wanted a meek little woman who would rub my feet and bear me sons. He said any such would bore me so much I'd be dead before the bridal flowers wilted. With that much difference between us, I'm counting on a long delay." He nodded at Hawk. "Besides, he's got you to preoccupy him." Dragon paused, took another swallow, and eyed his host. "What do you hear from Vestfold?"

Innocently, Hawk replied, "I had a letter from Cymbra last month. She's hoping to persuade Wolf to pay Hawkforte another visit before too long, just not bring an invading army with him this time."

"That's nice but I was referring to your impending marriage."

"Oh, that. Your brother kindly rammed through— that is, negotiated—the bridal terms so I really haven't had much to do with it. I gather all is in order regarding . . . what's her name . . . Kwirka? Klonka?"

"Krysta," Dragon corrected. "Lady Krysta of Vestfold. It might help if you could remember your betrothed's name."

Hawk nodded solemnly. "I bow to your expertise in such matters. How long do you think you'll be staying? We can get in some hunting."

"Wonderful, but about the Lady Krysta . . ." Dragon's brow furrowed. He put his goblet down and sighed deeply. "There may be a slight problem."

"Problem? What sort of problem could there possibly be? I assume the dear girl is eminently acceptable and all will proceed on course." He looked at Dragon. "That is true, isn't it? You're not suggesting otherwise?"

"Oh, no, certainly not. Eminently acceptable . . . of course . . . absolutely. The only *small* complication might be that at the moment her half-brother Sven, who appears to be closely related to a slug, doesn't seem entirely certain of the dear girl's whereabouts."

Hawk gave himself a moment apparently to absorb this. He was enjoying himself hugely. Since his first encounter with the Hakonson brothers—Wolf and

Dragon—he had felt caught in a maelstrom not of his making. While he agreed wholeheartedly with the objective of the alliance, he didn't mind getting a little of his own back, however briefly. Watching Dragon twist on the hook of diplomatic catastrophe was proving to be unexpectedly pleasant.

"You aren't suggesting he's lost her?" Hawk asked with feigned alarm.

"Of course not! The fellow's a dullard. Undoubtedly it's all a misunderstanding. I did have the idea that perhaps, just perhaps, she might have come this way but apparently not. . . ." He trailed off as the look in Hawk's eyes struck him as suspicious. "You haven't seen her, have you?"

"Well, now it's odd you should mention that. The strangest thing happened. Three of the Lady Klonka's servants . . ."

Dragon closed his eyes, searching for patience, and therefore missed Hawk's grin. "The Lady Krysta."

"Whatever, three of her servants showed up here. There's a strange, grubby fellow who looks like a troll, a woman named Raven, and one other . . . odd girl, very black hair that has a tendency to run when it gets wet."

Dragon shook his head in puzzlement. "Her hair runs?"

"More specifically, the dye in it runs. Turns out it's actually blond. Turns out she isn't actually a servant. *Turns out* Klonka—"

"Krysta!"

"—had some outlandish notion of coming here in disguise in order to get to know me before we were wed."

Dragon, sensible man that he was, looked suitably appalled. "Tell me you're making this up."

"Couldn't possibly. Besides, you're supposed to be the one with imagination."

"She's here?"

"Oh, yes, most definitely here."

"Praise whatever gods want to take credit for it," Dragon said fervently. "I thought Wolf was going to dismember her half-brother limb by limb when the fool turned up at Sciringesheal and announced she was missing."

"Seems a reasonable thing to do but you might have some sympathy for the poor fellow. She's . . . unusual."

"Wolf said she was beautiful, soft-spoken, and had lovely eyes. He went so far as to claim that if she were Saxon instead of Norse, he'd be after me to wed her."

"Forget that," Hawk snapped. He caught himself half-rising out of his seat and sat down again abruptly but not before Dragon noticed.

The Viking grinned broadly. "Like that, is it? I'm glad to know the two of you are getting along."

"I didn't say we were getting along. She's just a woman and an unruly one at that."

Dragon was close to outright laughter but managed to contain it, if only barely. "Those are the best kind."

"It may be a joke to you but it isn't to me. I've already had one wife who couldn't be trusted and I don't want another. Not that I think she's dishonorable in any way, just that she may not have the best judgment in the world. Coming here as she did was a hell of a risk."

"So she has courage. That's bad?"

"I'd prefer for her to have sense. She's . . . unpredictable."

The man who adored women nodded in understanding. "Ah, I see. You want order, no surprises, calm, boring—"

"When you've lived with as much disorder as I have, boredom has a real attraction." Hawk sighed and ran a hand through his hair, unaware that he'd already raked it into a hopelessly tangled mess. "She fell in the water today. I thought she was going to drown. I felt . . . I don't even know what I felt but it was awful."

"She's all right?" Dragon asked, concerned.

"Of course she is. Turns out she swims like a fish . . . or something. She thought it was wonderful, came up laughing and wanted to stay in. Hinted she ought to be allowed to strip down to her shift. Now there was a good idea!"

"She's *that* innocent?"

"Apparently. She's had a rather odd upbringing."

Dragon gave up restraining himself and yielded to deep-throated laughter. When he caught his breath, he said, "Beautiful, soft-spoken, lovely eyes, unpredictable, *and* utterly innocent. I can see your problem, friend. I think I will stay awhile. This is too good to miss."

"Your sympathy overwhelms me," Hawk muttered. "Just remember, your turn will come."

That sobered Dragon but he cheered a moment later when the redhead wiggled by again. Following her with appreciative eyes, he murmured, "The fates are female. They may spare me yet."

They just might do that, Hawk reflected, but he had no illusions that they would show him any mercy, not when they already had his insides knotted up over a fey girl who had damn well better never scare him like that again. He glanced idly at the redhead and signaled for more ale, even as he wondered how much longer it would be before the storm he felt gathering finally broke.

One more heartbeat . . . one more breath . . . if that creature with a head like a scarlet woodpecker's didn't move on by then, Krysta wasn't sure exactly what she'd do but it wouldn't be pretty. The woman was strolling up and down in front of Hawk, who looked to be in real danger of getting walloped by her revolving hips, if she didn't poke him in the eye first with what she had just barely tucked into her low-cut chemise. Krysta's gaze narrowed. Was that a *nipple* she saw?

Outrage won over discretion. Having meant only to creep down and get a look at the visitor, she found herself forgetting all her good intentions about staying out of sight. The relief she felt when Raven brought word that the longships belonged to neither attacking Danes nor her own half-brother had faded quickly when she learned it was the Wolf's own brother, the feared Lord Dragon of Landsende, who had come. No doubt her departure had been discovered and she was in deep trouble, but she could not think of that just now. Indeed, she could think of nothing save the anger boiling up inside her.

It *was* a nipple. The unspeakable nerve!

"My lord," Krysta said loudly enough that both men swiveled around in their chairs to look at her. Clutching her courage, she emerged from the stairwell and threw the red-haired strumpet a look that should have turned her to dust on the spot. Incredibly, the girl merely grinned and shrugged her smooth shoulders so that her chemise dropped a notch lower.

Hawk saw that she was angry—a blind man could have seen it—but had no idea why. He stood up quickly and offered her his hand.

"Krysta, do you know Lord Dragon, jarl of Landsende?"

Krysta spared that worthy no more than the barest glance. "I know of him. My lord, I . . . wished to thank you for the wonderful ride. I was wondering if we might do it again soon . . . very soon—" The redhead was lounging against the table, hiking up her skirt to display a well-turned ankle and smooth calf. "Now, perhaps." In a belated attempt at courtesy to the man she had scarcely bothered to glance at, she added, "If Lord Dragon wouldn't mind."

"Not at all." Dragon jumped to his feet, grinned at

Hawk, put his arm around the redhead, and said, "No doubt I can find something to occupy me." He smiled down at the woman snuggled against him. "I can, can't I, sweetheart?"

"Oh, most definitely, my lord," the delighted woman purred.

"There you are, then," Dragon said. "You two do whatever strikes your fancy. I'll be occupied for hours." He looked at his companion again. "Or days, who knows? Don't give me a thought."

Belatedly and excruciatingly aware that she had mis-interpreted the situation completely, Krysta said, "You are very gracious, my lord."

"Not at all, dear girl," Dragon said. "Merely practi-cal. You're here, Hawk is managing well enough, high summer comes, and I know not a single reason not to en-joy it."

She looked at him then, finally looked at the man most women could not help but stare at. He was pleasant enough, she thought, but no match for her Hawk. He seemed kind, which surprised her, given his fearsome rep-utation. And he was right about the season. It was that precious time for long hours of warmth, delights explod-ing on the tongue and languorous sighs beneath star-lit skies.

She turned to the golden-haired man at her side and smiled into his perplexed eyes. "I know a place where the wild strawberries are ripe."

He went with her, how could any man not? Behind them, Dragon laughed, relieved and glad. A little envious, too, perhaps, but he would not think of that. Besides, he had the redhead to amply occupy him.

D RAGON STAYED FOR A WEEK. BY DAY, HE HUNTED and sailed with Hawk or joined him with his men on the training field. The harvest began and almost all the residents of Hawkforte, even those who had other occupations, were busy in the fields. Their lord gave it to be understood that the celebration of his and the Lady Krysta's nuptials would await the completion of the harvest. As this was the custom, his people accepted it readily enough.

Only the warriors continued their usual routine. By night, everyone who could gathered to hear the stories Dragon spun. Wonderful, incredible, exhilarating stories that held his listeners spellbound. Even the tellers of tales among the Saxons themselves were content to sit back and listen to the man they recognized as a master. Fate had called him to be a warrior but he was a skald to the bone.

He told of the creation of Asgard, the abode of the gods, linked with earth by the bridge Bifröst, which appeared to men as a rainbow. "After the gods defeated their enemy, the giants," Dragon explained, "the great god Odin and his companions, Hoenir and Lodur, decided to make mortals from the trunks of trees. They called the first man Ash that he would be strong and mighty, and named his wife Vine, that she should cling to him, being loyal and faithful. It was fitting that they named the man Ash for the great ash tree Yggdrasil stands at the center of the earth. Its roots reach down into the netherworld and its branches ascend to the heavens. Odin's favorite steed, Sleipnir, browses in its leaves. Beneath Yggdrasil there is a holy place where the gods meet each day to mete out justice. You may hear their mediations in the rumble of distant thunder that sometimes disturbs the sky."

All this was known to Krysta for she had been reared on such tales despite her otherwise Christian upbringing. Yet she enjoyed hearing Dragon tell the familiar legends, for his accountings were clearer and more vivid than any she had heard before. Too vivid for Father Elbert and Daria, who spent the evenings scowling and putting their

heads together to mutter of "heathen doings." They were
ignored by all, the Norse giving them no heed and
the Saxons so inured to their sourness as to pay them no
mind.

The weather being warm, they dined outside, the
long tables and benches surrounded by high torches that
gave light and kept the insects away from the revelers. The
nights were clear and star-filled. On the last night of
Dragon's visit, the moon was full, prompting him to tell
this story:

> *After the gods had dwelt in Asgard for a time, it*
> *came to them that there was no wall around their*
> *home to protect them. Despite their might, the*
> *gods remembered the fierceness of their enemies,*
> *the giants, and they wondered if they could truly*
> *be safe from them without a wall. As they were*
> *debating this, a stranger appeared in Asgard. He*
> *offered to build a mighty wall around the entire*
> *realm and promised he would have it done to their*
> *satisfaction within a single year. The gods were*
> *tempted to agree but first Odin, wisest among*
> *them, asked his price. The stranger faced great*
> *Odin boldly and said, "When I have built your*
> *wall, give me Frigg, fairest of all the goddesses.*
> *Oh, and I also want the sun and the moon." Odin*
> *was outraged for not only would he never consider*
> *giving any goddess to a stranger but most*
> *especially he would not give his own wife. Truth be*
> *told, there were many times when Odin and Frigg*
> *argued, yet was she his and did he mean to keep*
> *her. Great Odin was about to dismiss the stranger*
> *from Asgard, when Loki, the trickster god, spoke*
> *up. He said they should agree to the stranger's*
> *terms but on condition that he build the wall in*
> *only half a year. Surely he would not be able to do*

*this, so he would be paid nothing and at the least,
the gods would have half a wall for free.
Reluctantly, Odin and the others agreed, although
Frigg still was not happy and wept tears of gold.
Almost half a year passed and to the shock of the
gods, the wall was almost complete. The stranger
was about to win his bet and take fair Frigg from
them, not to mention the sun and the moon.
Fortunately, Loki had an idea. "The stranger
needs his powerful black horse to haul the stone to
the wall," Loki said. "I will lure the horse away
and the wall will not be completed." Loki changed
his shape into that of a lovely white mare and as
expected, the stranger's black stallion followed her
into the woods. Realizing his horse was gone and
he could not complete the job, the stranger was
enraged. So angry did he become that he dropped
his disguise, revealing himself to be a giant, enemy
of the gods. At this, Odin summoned the strongest
of the gods, mighty Thor, who struck the giant on
the head with his immense hammer, making
thunder ring throughout the heavens. Thus did the
giant depart Asgard, the gods finished the wall for
themselves, and eventually Frigg forgave Odin for
almost losing her. Even Loki was welcomed back.
When he returned, he brought with him a
wondrous black horse with eight legs, named
Sleipnir, which he gave to Odin. And that is how
the gods of Asgard acquired their wall and how
Odin acquired Sleipnir.*

"Let's see now," Hawk said when the applause had died
away. "Loki went into the woods disguised as a white
mare intent on luring away a black stallion, and returned
sometime later with an eight-legged black stallion. Did
anyone ever ask Loki just how Sleipnir came to be?"

Dragon grinned. "I don't believe anyone ever did, or leastways Loki never said. But we all know a trick may turn around and trick the trickster." He gazed pointedly at Krysta. "Although sometimes a lucky trickster will escape unharmed."

Although he looked at her in a friendly fashion, Krysta understood full well what he was saying. She was most fortunate to have escaped unharmed from the trick she had played on Hawk. Only the most foolish of women would tempt fate—and the patience of her lord—again.

"Loki never seems to learn his lesson," Krysta said softly. She turned her eyes to Hawk. "Humans are wiser in that regard."

Her response pleased him but before he could reply, Edvard broke in. The young steward had imbibed a little more than usual, perhaps encouraged by pretty Aelfgyth's frequent smiles, and his usual reserve had fallen away. "What about what Odin did?" he challenged. "Agreeing to barter his wife for a wall, even if he didn't believe he'd end up having to pay, was very foolish."

"That's true," Dragon agreed. "But Odin never seems to know how to handle Frigg. He's always doing things that anger her and embolden her to defy him."

"If Odin stayed at his own hearth more," Krysta said, "not to mention in his own bed, he wouldn't need to worry about *handling* Frigg and she wouldn't be so inclined to oppose him."

Barely had she spoken than Krysta blushed. She realized in an instant how everyone would construe her words and wished desperately that she could snatch them back. It was one thing to tell Hawk when they were alone that the path to peace did not lie through other women's beds. To announce the same to all and sundry was more than a man was likely to tolerate.

"What I meant—" she began.

"I think we all know what you meant," Hawk said. To

her amazement, he smiled. Leaning closer, he said for her
ears alone, "It takes a very confident woman to stake such
a claim. Are you sure you're equal to it?"

Krysta's flush deepened. He knew perfectly well she
couldn't be sure, just as he knew she had never been with
a man and thus had no way of knowing how adept she
would prove. But not for the world would she admit any
of that to him. With a light shrug of her shoulders, she
said, "I rather think that depends on you, my lord.
Wouldn't you agree?"

She watched, fascinated, as passion flared in his eyes.
He was half out of his chair, looking for all the world as
though he intended to take her away right then and there,
when Dragon said, "All this talk of marriage brings to
mind another story. I had this from an Irishman I met in
Byzantium. He swore it was true and claimed even to
know the poor fellow involved:"

*The mighty lord of an Irish clan was out one day
in his curragh. He had gone out alone, away from
the bustle of his court, because he needed to think
over a problem he faced. You see, this lord knew
that he should marry but he could not decide
which young woman he wanted to take to wife.
There were so many to choose among that he found
himself drawn first to one, then to another. Yet he
knew his duty, and as he rowed across the bay
near his holding, he was resolving how he might
do what was right. Just as he was thinking about
the daughters of the neighboring clan chieftains,
he saw a strange shape moving through the water
near him. So startled was he that he rose up in the
curragh, seized the net he was carrying, and threw
it out into the water. His aim was sure and the net
engulfed the creature even as it tried to flee. The
lord pulled in the net and to his utter amazement*

*found himself gazing upon a young woman of
extraordinary beauty. With no adornment save her
own milky white skin and ebony hair, she was by
far the most desirable woman he had ever seen.
Straightaway, he made up his mind to marry her.
The lord took his bride home and presented her to
his people. Although they were surprised, to be
sure, none would gainsay him. The lord and his
lady from the sea were wed, and in due time they
had strong sons and daughters. All seemed as it
should be save for one strange habit of the lord's.
Regularly, every few days or so, he would go off
by himself to a place only he knew. He only stayed
a short time but he never failed to go, and
whenever he went, he ordered his wife locked in
her chamber so that she could not follow him. This
went on for years until finally one day the lady
asked her eldest daughter to follow her father. The
girl did as she was bid and reported back to her
mother that the lord's destination was a small cave
not far from their holding. The girl had not dared
to follow him inside, but this did not seem to
trouble her mother. She thanked the girl, then
kissed her gently and told her how very much she
loved her and all her other children. The next day,
the lady vanished. She was never seen again,
although the gown she had been wearing was
found in front of the cave to which the father had
gone these many years. As her children wept for
her, their father confessed the truth. When he
drew their mother from the sea, he found
something else in the same net that held her, the
skin of a skelkie. Right away, he knew it for what
it was and recognized that the beautiful maiden he
had captured was an enchanted creature who
could only stay with him so long as she could not*

*repossess her skelkie skin. Faithfully, he cared for
it, going to the cave every few days to make sure it
remained wet as it must and in good condition, for
if it did not, he knew she would die. But never did
he want her to leave him, so he kept the
whereabouts of the skin a secret. Once a skelkie
rediscovers her skin, she can do naught but return
to it and to the sea, as his wife had finally done.
As long as he lived after that, the lord went to the
sea every day and looked out over it, as though
searching for his lost wife and beseeching her to
return to him. From time to time, a shape could be
seen far out in the water looking back at him, but
she never came near again.*

"A strange story," Hawk said thoughtfully. He had heard
more than a few odd tales but never one odder than that.
Offhand, he wasn't inclined to believe it, yet he had to admit that some of the strangest tales turned out to be the
truest. For instance, there was the one about an island to
the west with mountains that spewed rivers of fiery mud.
What sane man would believe that? Yet he knew men of
impeccable sense who swore to have seen it with their own
eyes.

Dragon seemed to feel the same way. "I admit it
sounds unlikely but who knows? Besides, if any place har-
bors such creatures, it would be Eire. Have you ever been
there?"

Hawk had not and didn't expect he would ever make
the journey. He had his hands full trying to help Alfred
put England to rights.

"The Norse have established a holding at a place
called Dubh Linn," Dragon went on. "Unless the Irish
manage to unite their many clans, it is likely that far more
of their fair isle will be lost before long."

"What is it that compels you Norse to prefer the

lands of others to your own?" Hawk meant no offense by
the question, he was genuinely curious. The Danes he
thought he understood well enough for they were driven
by the same lust for wealth and power as seemed to strike
many Saxon men. But the Norse, who were cousins to
those very same people, seemed to seek both less and
more, preferring land above all else.

"Mayhap there is not enough of our own," Dragon
said good-naturedly. "Our lands are beautiful but harsh.
Little can be grown save in the scant months of summer.
In deepest winter, not even the sea can be harvested. We
tend toward large families, so some of us must seek our
livelihoods elsewhere."

This seemed a reasonable enough answer and Hawk
was mulling it over when he noticed that Krysta suddenly
appeared paler. So bright was the moon as to make the
torches all but unnecessary. In the glow of silvery light,
the flush that had stained her cheeks scant minutes before
seemed to have disappeared. Even as he watched, she
pressed her lips tightly together and stared down at her
hands twisting in her lap.

"Is something wrong?" he asked quickly, wondering
what could have upset her so.

She stared at him with wide, dilated eyes. He was
shocked to realize that she seemed genuinely afraid.

"Nothing is wrong," she said, and managed a wan
smile. "I'm merely tired."

Not for a moment did he believe her. Something had
distressed her deeply but he had no idea what it could
possibly be. Swiftly, he glanced around the table. Daria
and the priest had their heads together and were scowling;
he saw nothing unusual in their behavior. Edvard had settled a pretty maid on his lap and was chatting with her
happily. Hawk's lieutenants were drinking and laughing
with their Norse guests—nothing out of place there. He
glanced further down along the tables and saw Krysta's

odd servants, Thorgold and the Raven woman, both apparently content. What, then . . . ? He ran over in his mind what had happened in the past few minutes but could find nothing to account for Krysta's strange behavior. Granted, Dragon had teased her about her trick in coming to Hawkforte disguised, but she'd taken that perfectly well and had seemed to recover from her own boldness in declaring her sympathy for Frigg. But was that it? Had his so-obvious desire for her caused this distress? Yet had she seemed unafraid of passion when they kissed in the stable.

He told himself that he had to remember she was but a young and untried girl, newly arrived in a far land and confronted by a stranger to whom she had been given with no thought to her own feelings, a stranger who would henceforth have complete control over her life. Granted, the same fate befell most women, but he supposed that did not make it any easier or pleasant.

Reluctantly, he thought of his first wife. They had been wed so short a time and so many years had passed since then that he could not recall her features with any clarity. Yet could he remember her reluctance in the marriage bed and the habit she had of shirking from him whenever he came near. In all modesty, he knew he had not lacked for gentleness or skill, but that had not mattered. The thought of enduring such a marriage again filled him with dread. He was willing to do virtually anything to avoid it.

Even to restrain the desire he had felt since the first moment he saw his Norse bride-to-be until he could be certain that she shared his passion.

He sighed inwardly, knowing he set himself a task from which most men would shirk. But he was a warrior and a leader. He would damn well find as much patience as was needed. On such grim thought, he drained his ale and did not object when the servant filled his goblet again.

Chapter

EIGHT

"YOU'RE MAKING TOO MUCH OF IT," RAVEN
scolded. "It was only a story, nothing more.
Why take it so to heart?"

Krysta looked away from her grim study
of the sea. Dragon was gone on the morning tide but his
words still echoed in her mind. She had slept poorly, if at
all, and now her head throbbed so much that even the
sound of her voice was painful. "You heard the tale. Do
you honestly believe he told it just by chance?"

"Why, yes, that's just what I think. It was a story,
nothing more."

"Before he told it, he spoke of tricksters and looked
right at me."

Raven sighed and fluttered her thin arms. She settled
on the window seat beside Krysta. "One has naught to do
with the other. He has no idea—"

"He could have heard something. Indeed, how could
he not? Once Father died, Sven was eager enough to tell
all and sundry before he discovered I had value to the jarl
of Sciringesheal. Only then did he still his tongue, but
how am I to know the damage was not done?"

Raven reached out a thin hand and laid it over Krysta's. Gently, she said, "You are here, are you not? Think you the jarl of Sciringesheal would send a tainted woman to bind up peace?"

"I think he would send the Norns themselves, if he thought it would suit his purpose."

Raven cackled. "Fierce Harpies of the battlefield who decide who lives or dies probably would not serve well in this case." She looked at Krysta fondly. "Better to send a lovely young maiden to gentle a warrior's heart."

"Well and good, but I tell you, Lord Dragon knows. Or at least he suspects. Why then would he not tell the Hawk?"

"Tell him what? A tale whispered by your dullard of a half-brother? If Lord Sven declares the sky to be blue, a wise man sticks his head out of his lodge to check. Everyone knows this. The Dragon is no fool, far from it."

"He would not have to know Sven said it, only that it *was* said. You know how tales spread."

"I know you have become a worrier where you were never one before." Raven peered at her closely. "What accounts for that?"

"I know not what I have become or why," Krysta murmured. "I only know I am not myself any longer. Something is happening to me. I would stop it if I could but I seem to have no power over it."

Raven clucked in distress but sought to reassure. "How not yourself? You are the same person you were when you left Vestfold, the same you have always been."

"No, I am not. I feel a stranger in my own skin. I scarcely recognize myself." Outside, beyond the window, tiny wavelets lapped against the beach. The air was still and heavy with hardly a breath of wind. Like the stillness within her . . . the waiting.

"You are in a strange place," Raven said. "Of course you feel different."

Krysta hesitated. "It's not the place. Whatever I'm doing, waking up, eating, listening to Edvard, whatever, Hawk is always in my mind."

"He is?" Raven looked surprised. "Why?"

"He is to be my husband, surely that is reason enough to think of him?"

"I suppose so, but how much is there to think about? After all, he is only a man."

"Only?" Krysta laughed faintly. "I wish I could see him that way."

Raven clucked and busied herself smoothing her gown. Finally, she said, "I should have been prepared for this. It was so with your mother."

"It was?" Krysta was surprised. Her mother was spoken of so rarely that she had little sense of her. "I know she wanted Father to love her and he could not. . . ."

"He was a good man but his heart was given to duty. There was no room left for love."

"Yet she loved him."

"She could not help herself. I don't pretend to understand it. Some say love is a weakness, some call it a fever in the blood. Don't ask me, I have no experience with it. But I do know your mother had great strength, as do you, yet she could not resist love when it came to her."

"But I am not in love," Krysta protested. "I scarcely know the man."

Yet even as she spoke she remembered the kiss they had shared in the stable and her instant, irresistible sense that she recognized him in some way she could not understand. Perhaps knowing did not take so very long, not really. Perhaps it happened in the spirit and the heart while the mind remained all unawares.

"I am not in love." It was a wishful claim, nothing more.

"Did you not expect this?" Raven countered. "Did you think to make him love you without loving him in turn?"

"I thought he would love me *first*, then would I be safe to love him."

"There is no safety in love. You want to be safe? Go find a cave and hide in it. But to live, truly live, you must not conceal yourself. Every flight—whether of wing or of heart—is risk."

"Risk that killed my mother."

Raven stiffened. "Never say that! Never have I said she died."

"She walked into the sea." The words nearly choked her yet Krysta was compelled to say them for they were as stones that had weighed her down far too long.

"She *was called* into the sea," Raven protested. "That is entirely different."

"So you have always said. What am I to believe then? That she became a creature such as Dragon spoke of or Sven thought to prattle about? Or that she was a woman as I am a woman, and that life became more than she could bear? So much so that not even her own child's arms could hold her?"

"She loved you! And wanted to stay with you."

"Then *why* didn't she? How could she leave me?" A glistening drop appeared on Krysta's hand. Another followed. She stared, surprised, until she felt the dampness of her cheeks and knew she was crying. Never had she spoken of such things, rarely had she ever even allowed herself to think about them. But they were out now, raw and ugly, beyond recall.

Her chest hurt yet she forced herself to speak. "I'm sorry, you did not deserve this. I know you have always done your best for me, you and Thorgold both."

"We did as your mother wished, as she would have done had she been able to remain with you." Gently, Raven touched Krysta's cheek, catching the tears. "You share your mother's gift, to call those of us from the other world into this one. But always have I told you, there is another side to that gift. *You* can be called into the other world. That is what happened to your mother when her unhappiness in this world became too much for her to bear."

Krysta sighed deeply. For just a moment, she wished to hide herself against Raven as she had so many times when very young, be covered by the black wing of her gown, and remain still and safe. Then had Raven called her fondly "my little chick" and they had both laughed over that. But she was a child no longer. Raven was right, every flight brought risk, yet the wide world beckoned still.

"Go and find him," Raven said softly. "He is not a man of deception. If it is too soon to know what is in his heart, see what is in his eyes."

Krysta nodded. She remained a moment longer close to Raven, gazing out at the sea. Then she gathered up her courage and her dreams, and went.

H AWK WATCHED HER COMING TO HIM ACROSS THE training field. With the day so still, he had tied a band around his forehead to catch the sweat that would otherwise sting his eyes. Shirtless, wearing only breeches, he lowered his sword and waved off the lieutenant with whom he had been sparring.

She looked much more at ease than she had the evening before, but he still sensed a strain in her. Her usually winsome smile seemed forced. All the same, he appreciated the quick, all-encompassing glance she swept him, followed by the darkening of her cheeks. That she was aware of him as a man was good.

"I hope you don't mind," she said, and her voice was soft as the breeze that just then began to ruffle the tops of the trees. "The day is so warm, I thought you would like a drink." She turned slightly, gesturing to the servants who followed her. Two young girls stepped forward with horn goblets and skins glistening with droplets of cool water drawn from deep wells.

Hawk sheathed his sword. His eyes never left Krysta as he smiled in turn. "This is most welcome. Thank you for it."

Her flush deepened. Such a simple gesture, bringing cold water to laboring men, but it was the first domestic task she had performed at Hawkforte. Cautious yet of her status, wary of Daria, she had treaded lightly. Yet when she asked the servants to come with her and told them what was needed, they had sprung to obey with smiles that suggested she might not have so difficult a time to win them over as she had feared. Their master, however, was another matter.

Hesitantly, she met his gaze. As always, the light blue clarity of his eyes startled her. She felt as though she were staring into the heights of the sky at the peak of day. Her hands shook slightly as she filled a drinking horn and gave it to him. She watched with helpless fascination as he tipped his head back and drank, the powerful muscles of his throat working. With a smile, he returned the horn to her.

"If you wouldn't mind . . ."

She filled it again quickly, happy to have pleased him. She also felt relieved, for she saw no hint that her earlier worry had any foundation. Perhaps Raven was right and the Lord Dragon had merely spun a tale plucked by chance from the sea of his imagination.

The serving girls moved on to fill horns for the men. Hawk and Krysta were left alone. She was too self-conscious to speak, he too distracted. The breeze riffled her hair, pulling curls from the loose braid hanging down her back. Her brow was sun kissed. Freckles marched across her nose. Her mouth was very full, soft, and inviting. Too easily, he remembered how it had felt beneath his own.

"Dragon said he would take messages from you back with him. Did you speak with him?"

She shook her head. "It was kind of him to offer but I truly had nothing to say."

He nodded, unsurprised. Already he knew she and her half-brother were not close. From what Dragon had told him of Sven, he was glad of it.

"You seem to be settling in well. If Daria disturbs you, tell me."

Krysta was caught by surprise and uncertain how to respond. His willingness to help her with Daria warmed her, yet she was reluctant to involve him in family strife. "Thank you," she murmured noncommittally.

Silence drew out between them again. Hawk broke it. "How do you think it's going?"

"How what is going?"

"Getting to know each other." He made it sound like a task to be gotten through.

"Oh, that. I suppose it's going well enough."

He looked relieved to hear it. "I think so, too. I know you like to swim, don't eat meat, can read, and like hair ribbons."

"How do you know that last part?"

"Thorgold told me. I've been meaning to get some for you. What have you learned?"

"Well, I don't know exactly. . . . You read, you value peace, you are a strong leader . . . you think getting to know each other is easier than it really is."

The words were out before she could stop them. Krysta groaned, stung by her own candor.

"I . . . what?"

"Your pardon, lord. I should not be so blunt."

"No, that's all right. I prefer honesty to deception." Yet he spoke coolly, making her think she was not the only one stinging.

"I only meant that perhaps men are so unaccustomed

to knowing women that even a little knowledge seems like a lot."

She had a point. He did think he knew her well on only short acquaintance. But in truth, he seemed to have learned more about her than she had about him.

"I read," he said. "So much everyone here knows. I value peace. That, too, is obvious as it is the very foundation of our betrothal. I am a strong leader. True enough, but I could chalk that up to simple flattery. So tell me, lady, what else have you learned of me?"

Krysta was silent for a long moment. She knew he issued a challenge to her and she was torn whether to accept. To do so would be to bare at least a portion of her soul, were he astute enough to realize it. Yet pride drove her to make her point.

Slowly, she said, "You have a deep, rich laugh that seems to startle people, as though they were not used to hearing it so often. I wonder if it startles you, too. You like to skip rocks and are good at it. You are careful of children and do not wish to frighten them. You are not ruled by emotion. You did not like it when you thought me a servant yet desired me. You fought against that just as you fought against your anger when you discovered how I had tricked you. You drink only moderately, again I think because you do not like to lose control. You came of age in a time of brutal chaos, and as a result, order is very important to you. You love this land and these people with fierce strength. You would die for them and think the price worth paying. When you are tired, a tiny pulse beats above your right eye. Shall I go on?"

"No need, my lady," Hawk said quickly. "I am humbled." In truth, he was embarrassed and at the same time obscurely pleased. Never had he thought anyone could notice so much about him. It made him wonder what else he had inadvertently revealed.

He was looking at her, wondering simultaneously ex-

actly how many freckles she had and whether he should
invite her to go riding again, when a sudden gust of wind
distracted him. He glanced up, his eyes narrowing. The
sky looked little different than it had a few hours before,
white with high clouds, but he felt a sense of foreboding.
He went very still, breathing slowly and deeply. The air
smelled ripe and heavy. The morning had been so still,
hardly a breath of air, then the sudden breeze, now a gust,
followed soon by another, carrying that strange, torpid
smell he'd encountered only once before.

Fate had called him to be a leader and a warrior, but
he was a sailor to the bone. He knew the ways of wind and
water, knew the sudden turning of the weather, knew by
smell and touch and simple instinct what lay over the
horizon.

"I need to speak with Edvard," he said. "Come
with me."

T HE HARVEST IS GOING WELL, MY LORD," THE STEW-
ard said. He appeared puzzled to be summoned at
such an hour when normally the Hawk was occupied with
other matters, but, as always, he had his facts and figures
ready to hand. "I estimate half the oat and barley crops
have been brought in, as well as most of the apples. Work
is proceeding smoothly. We should be finished by the end
of the week."

"I am pleased to hear that, but the end of the week
will not do. The harvest must be completed by tomorrow."

Edvard gaped at him. "Tomorrow? But, lord, how is
that possible? Except for the garrison itself, everyone is
working from dawn to dark in the fields as it is."

"We will take torches into the fields. The watch will
be kept as always but the rest of the garrison will put their
swords aside to pick up scythes. By tomorrow nightfall, I

want to see bare fields. Moreover, the oat and barley is not to be stacked in the fields to dry but is to be brought inside wherever it can be stored." He gestured around the room where they stood. "If you have to fill this very hall, do it."

"Lord . . . the sheaves will rot."

"They won't be here long, only a day perhaps. Put the children to gathering the rest of the apples." He turned to Krysta. "Will you go with them? Help them to manage?"

"Yes, of course, but what is wrong that there should be such hurry?"

"Perhaps nothing, but we may be in for an unusually bad storm. If that happens, we could lose everything still in the fields."

Edvard paled at the thought. He clutched his accounts tightly. "That cannot be allowed. Such waste would be abominable."

"My point exactly," Hawk said. There was comfort in knowing that it was only waste they would face, not disaster. So wealthy was Hawkforte that it could withstand even the loss of half its crops without threat of starvation. Yet he was determined there would be no such loss, or at least no more of it than he could prevent.

Edvard rushed off to spread the word as Krysta hurried to assemble the children. She went to Edythe first, rightly judging that the little girl would have her friends organized. In short order, they were all trooping off toward the orchards.

On the way they passed one of the fields gold with high, feathery-topped stalks of oat waving in the breeze. Hawk and his men were already there. The soldiers of the garrison and Hawk's lieutenants had, indeed, put aside their swords and taken up scythes. It would have been a startling scene were it not for the master of Hawkforte himself cutting through sheaves of oat as though he had been born to the task. The peasants and townsfolk who were also working the field were astonished. The sheer impact of so unlikely a spectacle reminded them of how extremely serious the situation was and they fell to with a will.

As did the children who scampered up the heavily laden branches of the apple trees to shake the fruit into waiting blankets held out by their fellows. They shortly had so many baskets filled that a wagon was needed to haul the bounty back to Hawkforte. While they waited for it to return, Krysta insisted they sit down under the trees and rest.

"Why does Lord Hawk think a bad storm is coming?" Edythe asked as she finished drinking and passed the water skin to Krysta.

Never had water tasted so good as it did after the hot work in the orchard. Several of the children were flopped on their backs, already dozing. Others clustered nearby, listening quietly.

"I don't know," Krysta admitted, "but I am sure he has good reason."

"The day seems little different from any other," Edythe persisted.

"It does smell a bit odd though, don't you think?" Krysta had noticed that only as they were working. Mingling with the perfume of the apples was a deeper, heavier odor she couldn't identify.

Edythe took a sniff and frowned. "Yes, it does but it's not a bad smell. I wonder where it's coming from."

"I warrant you wonder about a great many things," Krysta said with a smile.

The little girl shrugged. "That's true. Mama says I ask too many questions but she always tries to answer them just the same. Papa says if I wag my tongue so much, it will come loose and fall off."

"I wouldn't worry about that happening."

"Oh, I don't, that's just Papa wanting a bit of quiet

after working all day. Besides, Aelfgyth, says it's good to wonder about the world, otherwise how would we ever learn anything?"

"Aelfgyth? Is she your sister?"

Edythe nodded. "She is and she's desperately glad to be your maid. She was surprised, at first, when Dreadful Daria sent her to you because she's never gotten along with her, but then she realized—" The little girl broke off abruptly, taking a sudden interest in the blades of grass she was plucking.

"It's all right," Krysta said. "Not that I would encourage disrespect, but I understand people have feelings they can't always contain."

Edythe nodded gratefully but did not continue. Krysta hesitated, reluctant to gossip, yet too curious to let the matter drop. "What did Aelfgyth realize?"

"That Lady Daria wasn't looking for the best maid in the world for you. She was always complaining about Aelfgyth's work so she obviously didn't think much of it, which is what made her choose Aelfgyth for you."

Krysta laughed and shook her head ruefully. "I'm surprised I didn't end up with a dozen or more maids, for I have the impression Daria thinks very little of anyone's work."

"Oh, that's the truth! There's absolutely no pleasing her so everyone has given up trying. If you do something exactly the way she said she wanted it done so it's perfect, she'll turn around and claim she wanted it done differently."

"How tiresome of her," Krysta said, even as she wondered at how the high-handed woman had managed to avoid outright rebellion among the servants. No doubt it was their respect for Hawk and their gratitude for the safety he provided that kept them at work.

"Perhaps things will change now," Edythe said with a sidelong glance.

"Perhaps they will," Krysta said but made no promises. She was not eager to tangle with Daria despite Hawk's assurances that she could bring any problems to him. But beyond that, she could not even begin to assert herself as Hawkforte's mistress before she was wed to its master.

The apple gathering resumed a short time later. By dusk, the children were done. Krysta led them back to the fields where torches were being set up, as Hawk had ordered, but they might not be so needed now for the sky was clearing, the rising wind pushing the clouds away. An almost full moon cast a brilliant ribbon of silver over the land.

Food was brought out to the fields. The people ate quickly, making do with chunks of bread and cheese and mugs of cider. Everyone looked bedraggled and tired, but determined. Krysta left the children with their mothers and went off to find Hawk. He was working with a group of men bundling sheaves of oat and throwing the bundles into wagons for transport. For a few moments, she stood off to one side watching him. He was taller than the peasants and townspeople, and much more heavily muscled, but beyond that there was nothing to set him apart from the others, no visible sign of his rank or authority. Yet was there no mistaking that he was the leader even as he worked right alongside the others, doing as they did. He spared himself no task and nothing missed his eye. If a man needed help hefting bundles into the wagon, Hawk was there to offer a quick, encouraging word and lend his own strength. When water was passed around, and offered to Hawk first, he shook his head and let it go by until all the rest had drunk. Only then did he ease his own thirst. Even as he told the other men to rest for a few minutes, he continued to work, pausing only once to glance up at the sky.

He paused again when Krysta joined him. He tossed

another bundle of sheaves into the wagon, wiped his arm across his forehead, and nodded to her. "Are you finished in the orchards?"

"We are. I've sent the children to their mothers. They'll sleep beside the field while the grown-ups work." On her walk from the orchards, she had seen how much had been accomplished in only a few short hours. Yet there was much more still to be done. "Are you still convinced there will be a storm?"

Hawk shrugged broad, bare shoulders begrimed by hours of hard labor. Bits of oat stuck to his hair and skin. Krysta had to resist the urge to remove them one by one. "If we are fortunate, it will skip to one side of us or the other. If it comes at us directly, it will be a storm such as I have seen only once before."

"Where was that?"

"At Winchester. I was there with the king. It was five summers ago. The day before had been very still, as this one began, then the wind picked up slowly, bringing with it the smell of lands far distant from here. By morning, when Alfred and I went out sailing, the wind was heavy but we thought little of it for the sky remained clear. We were out only a few hours when the storm came up over the horizon. A wall of clouds charged at us, thunderheads grayer than any I have ever seen. Ahead of them, the sky turned yellow. Within minutes, the water churned so fiercely that we almost capsized. As it was, we barely made it into a sheltered bay before howling winds and sea battered our boat to pieces. We had to swim the last few hundred yards and it took all our strength to do so. To our great good fortune, we were able to wait out the storm inside a cave, but when we emerged the world looked transformed. Trees were knocked down, the beach had vanished, the grass was flattened, and all the peasants' huts were destroyed with many killed. Even the timber roof of the church was ripped off."

Krysta's eyes had widened during this telling. She had known bad storms before, snow that fell so thickly no one could stir from indoors for weeks, lashes of ice that bent full-grown trees to the ground. But never anything such as Hawk described. "You think that will come here?"

"I think there is a possibility and that is enough. However, there is nothing for you to worry about. Hawkforte's walls can withstand any blast." He glanced toward the men, who were on their feet again, ready to resume work. To Krysta, he said gently, "Go now and rest. You have done enough."

"Rest? But everyone else will be working through the night." Everyone, she thought, save Daria and the priest, Father Elbert, for she had seen nothing of either of them.

"I certainly don't expect you to do that," Hawk said. "You have already done more than most ladies would."

Just how was she to take that, Krysta wondered. Had she shown herself to be less than a lady by the work she had done? Or did he simply presume she was of such delicate sensibility as to be incapable of doing more? Reluctantly, she remembered Daria's claim that he had wanted to marry a "lady of true nobility."

"I am glad to help," she ventured tentatively.

"There is no reason. All is proceeding very well. Go get some rest." He gave her a little pat on the back to speed her on her way.

Hesitantly, Krysta went. She did not wish to gainsay him, much less present herself as less than a proper lady. Still, she glanced back several times over her shoulder, thinking he might relent. He was too busy to notice her, heaving huge bundles up onto the wagons with rhythmic ease that made her vividly aware of his strength and will.

Trudging down the road back to Hawkforte, she felt her gown sticking to her back. She glanced down at her hands, seeing them stained with dirt. Her face felt suspiciously as though it might be in the same condition.

Wincing at the thought of the picture she must have presented to him, Krysta plodded on. She was tired and the thought of sitting down in a cool, stone room was almost irresistible. Yet she loathed the notion. Everyone save Daria and her pet priest was hard at work. As she passed by one group on their way to yet another field, she glimpsed Raven perched on a bundle of sacks with Thorgold crouched beside her. They were chatting amicably with several of the townsfolk who seemed puzzled by them but still glad to have their help.

The littlest children were asleep already in the cool shadows at the edge of the fields where their parents were working, but those even a few years older were still scampering about, doing their best to gather up fallen sheaves. They could continue to contribute to the effort but Krysta was supposed to absent herself, being too refined a lady to possibly continue.

What hogwash! She was nothing of the sort and if Hawk wished otherwise, he was in for a keen disappointment. With a glance over her shoulder, she confirmed that she was out of his view. Resolve filled her. He might be angry later but that was a risk she was willing to take. She couldn't bear the thought of acting like such a weakling that she would take her ease while others labored through the night.

Coming upon a group of women bundling sheaves, Krysta saw her chance. She slipped in among them and began doing as they did without a word to anyone. For quite some time, no one noticed her. She was just one more pair of welcome hands—hands that were quickly sore and aching. The small of her back throbbed and her shoulders felt as though they were being wrenched from their sockets, but she persisted. Gather . . . tie . . . gather . . . tie . . . over and over until she lost all track of the passing hours. She could only be grateful that there were men to lift the bundles into wagons. The piles of oats waiting to be bundled seemed never to lessen, for others were going before them, scything through the field. As one filled wagon pulled away, another appeared.

Night came and still they worked. The torches did help but it was the moon that lit their way, turning the world to brilliant silver and casting long shadows across the fields. Were it not for the bleaching out of all color, it might have been day. From time to time, a woman would break off to check on the children. All of them were now fast asleep and still the adults labored. The night was warm but the wind was increasing. Even knowing what it might portend, Krysta was glad of the faint relief it offered.

It was well after midnight, by the position of the moon, when a woman came up beside her, began gathering more sheaves, and suddenly stopped.

"*My lady?*" Aelfgyth stared at her in shock. Like Krysta, she was sweat-stained, grubby, and exhausted. Her hair hung in tatters, as did Krysta's. Her face was smudged with grime, as was Krysta's. And her hands bled from a hundred tiny pricks of the oat sheaves, as did her mistress's.

"My lady, you cannot possibly be here!"

So tired was she, so numbed by the endless hours of exhausting toil, that Krysta could do nothing but laugh. "Then this must be a dream. What a relief! Obviously, I'm asleep in bed."

Aelfgyth continued to gape at her, as though she were an apparition previously unimagined. "Surely his lordship did not tell you to remain here?" In the stark white light of the moon, even her pretty face looked wan and weary.

"Well, no, of course he didn't, but neither did he tell me I had to leave . . . not precisely."

The maid shook her head. "You do not have to be here. Why are you?"

"Why do I not have to? Will I not eat of this oat just as everyone else does? Through the winter to come, will it not help to sustain me even as it does you?"

Aelfgyth blinked, so tired she could scarcely follow but trying all the same. "Yes . . . I suppose . . . but no one expects you to do this."

"I see no harm in doing what is not expected."

And so they returned to work, mistress and maid together, as the night aged and with aching slowness, dawn came.

And still the fields were not yet emptied.

Sometime in the depths of night when the moon had set and only stars whirled overhead, Krysta fell asleep. Aelfgyth was beside her. So exhausted were they that neither could have stayed on her feet a moment longer. They slumbered only a few hours while all around them weary men and women dropped where they stood and did the same. Before the cock's crow, the laborers stirred and stumbled to their feet, rubbing bleary eyes. It was the wind that woke them for it had increased significantly.

As Krysta helped Aelfgyth up, both their skirts whipped around their legs. Scattered blankets suddenly freed from the weight of sleepers began to billow across the fields. Children raced after them and after the empty baskets that also went tumbling. Yet still the sky was clear.

"Perhaps we'll just have a blow and it will be done," Aelfgyth suggested.

Krysta nodded but she was unconvinced. There was still that strange, heavy smell, all the more pronounced now.

Wearily, aching in every bone, they returned to their tasks. Krysta's arms felt so heavy she marveled that she could still lift them. The pain between her shoulder blades had become a burning ache. After a night spent on the ground, her whole body felt bruised. Yet as she gazed out over the fields, she was astonished to see how much had been accomplished. Whole swathes of land she had last seen still covered by uncut stalks were now bare. She blinked, thinking she must be imagining it for surely it had seemed to her that all the workers had gotten at least some sleep.

All save for the bands of men still moving through the fields, still scything and gathering, still hoisting the bundles into the wagons. Schooled to the stamina of battle, led by the unrelenting Hawk, the garrison had worked through the night without pause. Men who under ordinary circumstances would never have deigned to do such humble labor had put aside class, pride, and every other consideration, at their leader's bidding.

As a group of them approached down the road, accompanied by half-a-dozen wagons, the peasants Krysta was among stopped. As one, the men pulled off their caps in deference to the weary warriors. In their midst, helping to push one of the wagons over a deep rut, was Hawk himself. There were dark shadows beneath his eyes and deep lines etched around his mouth. Yet he flashed a grin as the wagon came free and continued on its way. A moment later, his gaze fell on Krysta.

He stopped as the others continued on and stared at her. She fought the urge to try to fade back into the little group. Those around her became aware of the focus of their lord's attention and found sudden, pressing matters to see to elsewhere. Aelfgyth lingered, but as the Hawk shook off his stunned stupor and advanced toward them, she shot Krysta a sympathetic look and vanished.

"It's you," he said slowly. He lowered the scythe he was carrying to the ground and leaned on it as he studied her. So tired was he that he seemed not quite sure of what he was seeing. "Didn't I tell you to go back to the manor?"

"You told me I *could* go back to the manor," Krysta said softly. "It didn't sound to me as though you were saying that I *had* to go back."

He was shaking his head before she had finished. "You know perfectly well I expected you to return to the manor. Why didn't you?"

Krysta took a breath, willing herself to be calm. He didn't look angry, just surprised. He was also very tired. Her heart twisted as she thought of him laboring through the night. The possibility of adding to his travails by disappointing or displeasing him wrenched at her.

Softly, she said, "I really wanted to help, to be part of this. Hawkforte is to be my home and these my people. It did not seem right to me that I should sit at leisure while everyone else was laboring so hard."

He blinked at her once, twice, and leaned a little harder on the scythe. "You look worn out and you're very dirty."

"Well, I'm sorry," she said with some asperity, "but you might want to take a look at yourself."

"That's different."

"Why?"

He shot her a skeptical look, as though she couldn't possibly be so obtuse. "Because I'm not a lady."

That anything so blatantly obvious needed to be pointed out made Krysta laugh despite her fatigue. "Well, I guess not." She was silent for a moment before she said quietly, "Perhaps I'm not either. Or at least not your idea of a lady."

Tired though he was, Hawk's battle senses were not dulled. He realized at once that this was important. It was just that his poor, fogged brain couldn't figure out why. Loath though he would be to admit it, he was dog tired. It would be many a day, if not forever, before he looked at peasants scything a field with anything less than utter respect.

"I guess you're not," he said slowly. His sister, Cymbra, was a lady but Cymbra was so unusual that she wasn't a useful standard to set anyone beside. Daria too was a lady, and he shuddered at the thought of more of the same. His first wife had been a lady and the less he dwelled on her, the better. Perhaps then being a lady, whatever that meant, was not so important after all. Perhaps it was the woman herself who mattered.

Krysta looked upset but he had no idea why. He could barely remember what he'd just said to her and besides, he had no more time for standing around chatting. Weary though he was, he was also well aware that the wind was strengthening.

"We'll be finished in a few hours," he said, "and just as well. At least promise me you won't dawdle in the fields. Get back to the manor promptly as soon as we're done."

She nodded but said nothing, leaving him to wonder why she was so quiet suddenly. She wasn't a quiet sort of woman. He definitely could add that to his list of things he knew about her. Hell, he didn't think he'd had a quiet moment since she'd arrived—strange servants, outrageous disguise and all. A weary smile lifted the corners of his mouth. Quiet was not so desirable. Perhaps even order was overrated. There was much to be said for a fey Norse beauty, freckles and all.

His smile deepened. He felt less tired suddenly than he had done. They were going to win; the crops would be gathered before the storm hit. It was a small victory in the overall scheme of such things but it was his own and he savored it.

When this was over, he decided, he was going to buckle down to the business of getting to know Krysta. And to start with, he would satisfy his curiosity about an aspect of her that had been tantalizing him from the first.

Exactly how many freckles *did* she have?

Chapter

NINE

DAWDLE. KRYSTA HAD NEVER DAWDLED IN her life. And she most certainly hadn't been dawdling the past day as she'd worked herself to exhaustion helping to save *his* oats and *his* apples and . . . No, that wasn't fair. Hawk was working harder than anyone else and he hadn't expected her to do anything. He had even asked if she would supervise the children instead of telling her to do so.

But he did not think her a lady, that much was clear, and the knowing of it hurt especially when her mind wandered yet again to the damnable "lady of true worth." Granted, they had gotten off to a poor start but her motives were pure and he might have forgiven her, indeed she thought he had. She should have known better. It was all well and good to dress up in her mother's beautiful clothes and have a maid for the first time in her life, but none of that made her a lady.

Ladies were not sweat-stained, dirt-splattered, grimy wretches with bleeding hands and the aroma of a day's worth of hard labor clinging to them. They did not tumble into water and come up laughing, or confess to never having ridden a horse before, or kiss back.

That was probably where she'd gone wrong, right there in the stable when Hawk had kissed her and instead of protesting as a proper lady no doubt would, or merely passively assenting, she had actually kissed him, too. Her wantonness had shocked him, he'd made that clear, but she'd been foolish enough to think it was because he believed her a servant disloyal to her mistress. Now, looking back, she saw her folly and with it every misstep she had taken.

Mortification gripped her. She had told him—no, shouted at him—that she did not want him in the beds of other women. She had tried to chase off the redhead. She danced with the children and went grubbing about on the beach when she should probably have been—

What was it ladies did?

Daria seemed to do nothing but order people about and complain that they did nothing right. Likely, she was not the best example to consider. But Krysta knew no others, knew nothing at all about being a lady save the few bits and pieces she had managed to glean about the fabled Lady Cymbra, sister of the Hawk, wife of the Wolf, gifted healer, possessor of strange powers, and utterly devoted to the cause of peace. Surely no one could hope to live up to the standards of such a paragon.

The problem ate at her as she rejoined Aelfgyth and the others. She had no good model of ladylike behavior, no method for proceeding. Never had she felt so lost and uncertain. Were she not already sweating so much, she would have suspected the tang of salt striking her lips was from tears. But she knew better. She was not crying. *She was not.*

Gather and tie . . . gather and tie . . : over and over while the pain of her weary body dissolved into the anguish of her heart. Until at long last, as she bent over to scoop up yet another bundle of oats, Aelfgyth laid a hand on her arm.

"Lady, we are done."

She straightened up as much as her back would let her and glanced around. The fields were bare. As far as her eyes could see, not a single stalk was still standing. Which was all to the good, for as she turned around and looked to the south, Krysta gasped. Dark thunderheads were moving toward them. Already the sky was a sickly yellow, and the wind groaned in the trees.

"Come," Aelfgyth said, "we must go."

They and everyone else still in the fields went in a rush, pressing their exhausted bodies to the limit as they made haste to reach Hawkforte. The children had already been sent on ahead, only the garrison force lingered, making sure everyone was safely on the way. Last within the manor walls was the Hawk himself, who came switching the backsides of the oxen pulling the final wagon filled to brimming with golden sheaves.

With her last bit of strength, Krysta drew two bucketfuls of water from the deep well inside the stronghold. Aelfgyth offered to help, then looked tearfully relieved when Krysta sent her on her way. She was just beginning to drag the buckets up the stairs to her tower when Daria stepped out of the shadows near the bottom of the stairs.

"Oh, my," Daria said, "what have we here?" She lifted the hem of her wide sleeve and placed it delicately before her nose. "Have you been rolling about with the pigs, Krysta? You certainly smell as though you have been." Small, dark eyes gleamed. "You would be funny, really, if you weren't so pathetic. You haven't done a single thing right since you got here. Poor Hawk! He must be frantic, trying to figure out how to break the betrothal he never wanted."

Krysta's head throbbed. She was wearier than she had

ever been in her life and Daria was the last person she wanted to see just then.

It wasn't so much the reminder that she was less than a lady but the malicious smile of satisfaction that accompanied it that undid Krysta. She could have simply gone on her way but pride would not allow it. Grimly, she said, "I smell the way almost everyone else here smells because the only people who have not been working desperately hard since yesterday morning are you and your pet priest. Apparently, you two think yourself too good to labor saving the crops, but I warrant you'll be happy enough to be eating them come winter."

"How dare you—!"

"I dare nothing but the truth. As for the rest—" She looked Daria up and down coldly. "You may call me pathetic but it is you I feel sorry for. I would not wish to be in your position."

"My position? I am the lady of this manor. I say what is to be done. People obey me and they always will!"

"They don't obey you," Krysta said. "They serve Lord Hawk. As for you being lady here, you know perfectly well that is soon to change." She spoke with far greater confidence than she felt, mindful that she was not the lady Hawk wanted, but not for a moment would she let Daria see her doubts.

Scarcely had the words left Krysta's lips than Daria turned a bright, mottled red. Her eyes glowed with fury. *"Nothing will change! Nothing!* You vile little upstart! If you seriously believe for one moment that you will ever be lady here, you are stupider even than you appear! These are *my* lands, *my* manor. *I will always rule here!"*

Before such fury, Krysta could only stare dumbstruck. She had no idea what to say to Daria, much less how to calm her. Yet that such calming was necessary could not be questioned. The woman appeared about to burst out of her own skin.

"And not only that," Daria shrieked. "That is only the smaller part of it. Before this is done, you will see what it means to defy me, to—"

"My lady." It was Father Elbert, appearing suddenly from around a corner and hurrying to Daria's side, his black robes swirling around his legs. "My lady," he said again, "you are troubled. Come with me. We will pray over this and you will be easier in your mind."

She started and stared at him, unseeing. He laid a hand on her arm as though to both coax and control her. "Do not distress yourself, my lady. All will be as you wish. But come, let us unburden our hearts before the Lord. He knows the righteous and the just. He will never forsake you."

"Yes . . ." Daria said slowly. She blinked once, twice, as though awakening from slumber. "Unburden . . . I do carry so very many burdens."

"But you need not carry them alone. Trust me, my lady. The Almighty knows of your endeavors. He sanctifies your faithfulness. He will never fail you."

"So many have," Daria murmured, her voice high and weak. "So very many have failed me. There have been so many disappointments."

"I know," Father Elbert said. He spared a quick, knife-sharp glance at Krysta before leading Daria away.

Shock faded, leaving Krysta wearier than ever. She had known Daria was unpleasant and difficult but she had not expected the depths of the woman's rage or insanity. Krysta couldn't concentrate on that now. It was all she could do to resume her climb up the stairs carrying the buckets of water.

Once in her tower room, she stripped off her filthy clothes, wondering vaguely if it would be possible to get them really clean again. For the moment, all that mattered was washing away the dirt and sweat still clinging to herself. Never had she enjoyed a bath more, for all that it had to be taken standing up. She even managed to wash her hair and was toweling it dry when she looked out the window.

Heeding the Hawk's warning, the ship captains who had vessels in port had sailed them into the bay to ride out the approaching storm. Already, the wind was blowing a thick mist off the water, making the dark hulls barely visible. They appeared and disappeared like ghost ships. The sturdy houses of the town were closed up tight, every shutter fastened, everything movable brought inside. Guards still manned their posts on the walls but she hoped they would seek shelter soon.

Krysta's hair was still damp but her arms ached too much to continue drying it. She let the towel drop to the floor, something she would normally never have done, and glanced longingly at the huge bed. Slowly, it came to her that she knew no reason why she should not lie down. A low groan of relief broke from her as she eased her weary body beneath the covers. Between one breath and the next, sleep snatched her.

ASSURED THAT ALL HAD BEEN DEALT WITH PROPERLY, Hawk joined his lieutenants in the sauna. Though he would perish before admitting it, he hurt more than he could ever remember doing after a battle. Working in the fields had been a revelation to him, one he didn't expect to soon forget. He suspected the other men felt the same though none was any more inclined to speak of it than was Hawk himself. They contented themselves with a few grunts and groans as they scraped away the dirt of their labors.

Before they could fall asleep where they sat, they dragged themselves back outside and emptied buckets of cold water over their heads. That helped but not all that much. Telling his men to seek their rest, Hawk dropped a clean tunic over his head and went to speak with the guards still on duty. He instructed them to withdraw to the safety of the watchtowers before the wind grew stronger. That the watch would be maintained even in the throes of a savage storm struck no one as odd. There were always curious eyes about to take note of such things, and wagging tongues to report them later.

Edvard had managed to get all the oats stored without resort to stacking them in the great hall but he could have done so without it being in anyone's way. At an hour when several hundred would have been gathering there for the evening meal, the hall was deserted. Everyone was simply too exhausted to eat. As was Hawk himself. His body cried out for rest but before he could consider it, there was one more thing he had to do. Aching in every bone, he climbed the stairs to Krysta's tower.

She was asleep. He saw that the moment he stepped into the room. Although it was far from sunset, the light had faded to an eerie yellow-gray. Rain had begun to slash through the windows, which, he noted, she had left uncovered. With a shake of his head, he pulled the heavy wooden shutters secure. Immediately, the wail of the rising wind lessened. The storm was building rapidly but the worst was not yet upon them. He judged that it would be soon, though, and hoped Krysta would not be frightened.

Cautiously, so as not to disturb her, he approached the bed. She lay on her side, the covers pulled up over her shoulders and her glorious hair spread out all around her. Her riot of curls brought a smile to his face. Hardly aware that he did so, he reached down and plucked a golden strand, letting it drift silken smooth through his fingers.

She smelled of lavender soap, he realized, mingling with the salt tang of the air from the sea, reminding him of summer days spent racing off shore, close enough to catch the scents of wildflowers. How many times had he actually done that? Once, just recently, but before then? How many moments had he taken just for himself?

He couldn't remember and he had no idea why he was wondering. Indeed, he was so tired that some time passed before he realized that he was just standing there staring at her without a thought in his head. He ought to go. He should get some rest in case anything went wrong and he was needed . . .

Rest . . . right now, right there . . . with her.

He was so close he could touch the bed. That wonderful, huge, welcoming bed. So very tired . . . After battles, he had never needed more than a quick nap to feel revived. It would be the same now, he would only stay a little while. In so large a bed, he wouldn't even touch her. That being the case, he might as well be comfortable. Without further thought, he kicked off his sandals, pulled his tunic over his head, and slid beneath the covers. The sheer pleasure of lying down after so long wrung a groan from him. He must have been this exhausted some other time in his life but before he could remember when, he was snoring.

The wind rattled Krysta's dreams. She murmured in her sleep and turned over, flinging out a slender arm. It hit what she thought was a rock, and she grumbled to herself but did not come near to waking. Some time later she heard a monstrous shriek. She ran through a field of wildflowers that were being slammed to the ground by some unseen force. Up ahead, a mighty oak loomed. As she watched in frozen horror, a huge beast ripped a limb from it and sent it hurtling at her. Stunned, almost paralyzed, she could do nothing but moan.

She was snatched away just in time, gathered into warmth and strength. Safe, she murmured a little sigh of relief and knew nothing else.

The storm struck in all its fury yet did Hawkforte

hold fast. A few tiles flew off some of the roofs and went careening down the lanes but the stone walls Hawk had insisted on for every cottage, shop, and workman's hut in order to prevent fire proved their worth against this cataclysm of nature as well. Snug within them, men and women listened to the fury of the wind and gave thanks for the foresight of their lord. Close by them, the children slept undisturbed.

Not so Krysta, who woke suddenly to darkness and the piercing knowledge that she had forgotten something vital. She sat up, struggling to throw off the fog of sleep, and stumbled from the bed. Outside, she could hear the wind howling and with it the tearing fingers of fiercely driven rain smashing against the . . .

. . . Shutters. The shutters were closed. She had no memory of doing so yet she must have been so tired that she saw to them without thought. Greatly relieved, she returned to the bed and was about to get back into it when a soft, rumbling sound froze her. It was very dark in the room for no braziers had been lit. She found one of the tall iron basins set on a tripod almost by touch and struck flint to tinder to raise a faint glow of flame. Even so, it was difficult to see. She peered through the dimness, her eyes widening in disbelief as she beheld the outline of another's form smack in the middle of the huge bed. Her hand pressed to her mouth to keep from crying out, Krysta just then remembered that she was unclothed. After bathing, she had not bothered with a night robe. Trembling in her haste, she snatched up a fur cover pushed to the foot of the bed and wrapped it around herself. Creeping a little closer, she tried to see who the intruder was. Raven, perhaps, upset by the storm . . . or even Aelfgyth, similarly affrighted? But no, the form was far too large to be either of them. Indeed, there was only one person she could think of who possessed such height and, now that she looked more closely, such span of shoulders and chest visible above the covers pushed down to his narrow waist.

Hawk. In her bed. Without a word to her, much less a by-your-leave. Did he assume then that since they were betrothed, he had such right? If that, why had he not exercised it before now? Or did he simply think that it was no matter to her as she was not a proper lady? Any one of whom would probably be shrieking her dainty little head off by now.

Krysta did not make a sound. She edged a little nearer, peering down at him. He really was a magnificent man, perfectly formed and so very different from herself. Those differences were fascinating . . . tantalizing, really. It was all she could do to remember that he shouldn't be there.

The wind intensified, hammering against the shutters. Krysta shivered. In the ebbs between blasts of wind, she could hear the roar of breakers pounding against the beach. Never had she known such a storm. Not even the wild, wind-driven blizzards that descended on Vestfold in the winter were a match for this. She lingered a moment longer beside the bed, trying to decide what to do. She was still very tired. It was, after all, her bed.

Cautiously, she eased back the covers, then stopped when she realized she was still wrapped in the fur throw. That would be much too hot to sleep in. She should find a shift. On the other hand, if she didn't and if Hawk awoke . . . She blushed at the thought but maidenly modesty proved poor competition for the passions he aroused in her. She told herself she was merely being practical, when was she not? They were betrothed and supposedly getting to know each other. Didn't that knowing involve this, too, this so-tempting intimacy of bed and body? This haven of safety that seemed to beckon to her? Ever sensible, yet trembling slightly, Krysta dropped the fur and got back into bed.

• • •

HAWK WOKE WHEN THE WIND DIED, THE SUDDEN SI-
lence jarring him from sleep so deep as to seem
dreamless. He sat up, instantly alert, and listened closely.
No wind. The rain continued but the fury of the storm
seemed spent. Remembering the storm he had experienced five years before near Winchester, he was not fooled
and he hoped his people would not be either for he had
spread word of what this meant. Soon the wind would
shriek again, pounding against their walls. Only when it
fell silent for a second time would the danger truly be over.

He was about to lie down again when memory thun-
dered back. Sitting up abruptly, he stared at the woman
asleep beside him. Disbelief gave way to astonishment.
What imp of mischief had possessed him to climb into
bed with Krysta? Had exhaustion truly so clouded his
mind as to banish any shred of reason? Or had he merely
yielded to temptation and done as he secretly wished? As
though in answer to that question, his body stirred. He
cursed under his breath, and began to rise from the bed,
only to stop when Krysta cried out softly.

The stillness was gone, the wind was pounding once
again, and the sound of it must have frightened her. He
hesitated, truly torn, but the low whimper she made decided him. Glancing up in the general direction of heaven,
in the hope some help might be forthcoming, he got back
into bed. Carefully, so as not to wake her, he drew her to
him. Only then did he discover that his betrothed slept
unclothed. A deep, shuddering breath escaped Hawk.
Her skin was warm and so soft it seemed at odds with the
strength he had seen in her. Her limbs were slender, perfectly formed, and her breasts . . . She moved slightly and
fire darted through him. Thinking to set her aside and
make a prudent escape, he stopped when he realized she
had relaxed, her fear gone. Hawk closed his eyes, praying

for patience, willing restraint, and stayed where he was, propped up against the pillows, holding his Norse bride-to-be in his arms through the remainder of that very long, acutely chaste night.

At first light, he finally slipped away. The storm was over, he was certain Krysta would awaken soon, and he did not wish her to be frightened or upset by his presence. Nor did he care to test his self-control a moment longer. She had slept so deeply as he held her that he was confident she had no idea he had been there. It was his wish that she remain in ignorance, and not only out of thoughtfulness for her feelings. That he had spent the night in the bed of a beautiful woman and not possessed her was something he preferred to keep entirely to himself.

Descending the tower steps, he was relieved to find the great hall empty. It was still very early and few were stirring. Outside, he went first to the watchtowers where the guards manning them reported that the night had been quiet. That wrung a grin from Hawk but he took their meaning. By the standards of those who had fought the Danes, even so fierce a tempest was no more than mild inconvenience. Leaving the stronghold behind, Hawk descended into the town and was relieved to find few signs of damage. The streets were muddy and everywhere heaps of sand blown in by the wind could be seen, but there was little debris. When he returned to the great hall, shutters were being flung open and men and women were emerging. As expected, Edvard awaited him. The steward looked rumpled and still sleepy but also well pleased.

"But for your prudent warning, lord, fully half our crops would have been lost. As it is, damage is minor. One of the docks was ripped loose but that will be easily repaired. What looks to be the trunk of a tree is lodged in the wheel of the mill, but I have men on that right now and it should be removed forthwith."

"Were there any injuries?"

"Only one, lord. Alwin, the fellow who helps the tanner, needed to relieve himself in the night and for unknown reasons thought a pot wasn't good enough. He went outside instead, was knocked over and blown a fair distance, but he landed up against the baker's door and Wilhelm took him in. He's all right except for a bump on the head and some bruises."

"And I suppose by this time tomorrow, he'll be gifted with at least half-a-dozen pots to remind him not to repeat the experience," Hawk said with a smile.

"No doubt, lord. At any rate, we must count ourselves very fortunate."

"We are that," Hawk agreed.

In Edvard's company, Hawk rode out to survey the fields. The damage to them was as great as he had anticipated. Anything left in them would have been flattened. Dismounting, he handed his reins to Edvard and went down on one knee. The soil was very wet, as was to be expected after such a rain. He touched his fingers to it, then raised them to his nose and inhaled.

As he remounted, he said, "It will be a day or more before the ground is dry enough to stack the oat. In the meantime, send out men to remove the top few inches. Tell them to dump it into the sea."

Edvard's brow furrowed. "I will, lord, of course, but may I ask why?"

"It smells of salt. The rain was not pure but was mixed with spray from the sea. If it is not removed, next year's crops will be stunted."

"Your pardon, lord, but if I may say, you think like a farmer."

Hawk laughed and remembered suddenly what Krysta had said about him being startled by the sound of his own laughter. He was finding it impossible not to think of her at the oddest moments. "Am I supposed to be insulted by that, Edvard?"

"No, lord! Such was not my meaning, I assure you. It is only that I find it surprising a warrior would know so much about the land."

"I fought for this land," Hawk said quietly. "That would have been a damn foolish thing to do if I didn't know how to take proper care of it once I had it."

The young steward nodded thoughtfully. They continued back to Hawkforte.

W HERE KRYSTA WAITED, HAVING AWAKENED SUDdenly not long after the Hawk flew from her bed. She opened her eyes surprised to find it a fair morning and stunned to find him gone. Gone without word or touch. Gone as though he had never been.

Had she imagined him? Had her exhausted mind somehow conjured his presence from no more than wisps of longing? Barely had such a tentative notion sprung up within her than Krysta quashed it firmly. No, by heaven, she had not. He had shared her bed and the lingering warmth on the sheets proved it. Not to mention the depression of a head on the pillow next to hers.

She stared at that pillow as she dressed and made some scant order of her unruly hair. Far in the back of her mind, a memory stirred of safety and warmth, of being held against hard, smooth skin, in arms at once gentle and strong.

A light flush stained her cheeks. She nibbled at her lower lip and wondered how she was to face him.

He had not wanted her. That much was evident, for all too clearly she recalled her audacity at slipping back between the covers naked. He had been kind to her, true enough, but it was not kindness she sought. Or at least not entirely. Humiliation stung her. Her one and only effort to tempt a man had failed spectacularly. She could not think how she was to go on.

But go on she must and as though naught had occurred, for her pride would allow nothing else. Yet was she tormented by the growing fear that Daria was right: Hawk wanted a different bride, the "lady of true worth" who so held his heart he could lie naked in bed beside another woman, even hold her for the sake of kindness, and remain immune to passion's lure.

Damnable woman! What did she possess that Krysta did not? No doubt her voice sounded like lark song or something equally insipid. Her hands would be lily white, and should a drop of blood ever appear on them, the cause would be an embroidery needle, tool of that gentle art with which Krysta had no experience. She would not have freckles earned by gamboling in the sun. She would never speak above a murmur. Never challenge her lord or disagree with him. Never labor like a peasant to save his crops . . . or dye her hair and pretend to be a serving girl or—

The fact remained, their promised marriage was the pledge of peace. They were both of them trapped in a promise they could not break lest they plunge thousands into untold suffering.

With such thoughts at her back, she descended to the hall and from there went outside to see what the storm had wrought. Her mood lightened when she saw how little damage had been done. Yet did she still glance around anxiously, wondering where Hawk was and hoping she would not have to face him anytime soon. It was a coward's wish and she despised it, but try as she might, Krysta could not help but wonder what hope there was for their future together.

She was trying hard not to think of that when Aelfgyth found her. The young maid looked entirely recovered from the past day's labors and in high spirits. "My lady, there you are! What a relief to have that over and how lucky we are to have escaped all but unscathed." Her smile faded as she surveyed Krysta. "Are you still tired, my lady? Perhaps you did not sleep with all the noise last night?"

"Oh, no, I slept well enough," Krysta said. She was anxious to put that subject behind her as quickly as possible.

"Good, then perhaps we could get started? There is much to do."

"Started on what?" Surely, after all they had just done, there couldn't possibly be much of anything left. Could there?

"Why, preparing for the harvest celebration, of course. Is that not the custom in Vestfold?"

"Celebration? Yes, of course. But are you certain I should be—"

"Lady Daria never has anything to do with it. She says only prayers of thanksgiving are appropriate and the rest is pagan." Aelfgyth wrinkled her nose but a moment later she laughed. "Fortunately, the Hawk feels differently. Edvard has seen to most of the preparations in recent years, but this time he thought you should be involved. He told me so last night—I mean . . . yesterday." A blush suffused Aelfgyth's cheeks.

"I see," Krysta said with a smile. "In that case, I would be delighted. Where do we begin?"

It soon became clear that the food was most important because everyone would expect a great deal. There were hundreds of sweet pasties to be made, stuffed with raisins and honey, and as many loaves of fine bread from the first-ground grain. Fruits had to be stewed, cider pressed, milk churned for butter and curds, and wood gathered for the outdoor fires that would roast entire sides of beef. All the servants helped but so did the townsfolk and the peasants from the surrounding farms. Hawk and his men hunted each day while the fishermen plied their curraghs along the coast, bringing in nets bursting with eel, mackerel, and herring. Young men were preparing themselves for the ritual dances beneath the encouraging eyes of young women. Everyone was happily busy save for Daria and Father Elbert, who went about scowling, muttering of damnation, and praying ostentatiously for the souls of those they called blasphemers.

Krysta noted they were careful never to do so when Hawk was about, waiting instead until he rode out each day and ceasing their efforts when he returned. As he remained ignorant of their doings, so did others simply ignore them.

"Since you are here, my lady," Aelfgyth said, "folk are happy to harken to what you say and heed not the shrill harpings of one who has never meant us any good."

Pleased though she was by such acceptance, Krysta felt driven to caution against disregarding Daria too much. "It would be as well to remember that I am not yet Lord Hawk's wife."

Aelfgyth laughed as though this was a source of much amusement, but Krysta did not share in the joke. She still stung from the night of the storm and was well aware that her betrothed seemed disinclined to seek out her company. In the three days since she had awakened to find her bed empty, they had said scarcely a word to each other and those no more than courtesy required.

To be fair, everyone was well occupied from earliest morn to after dusk. That he was too busy to seek her out was no consolation for Krysta. She caught herself looking for him at odd moments of the day, listening for the sound of his voice, and trying in vain to think of some way to seize his attention as they sat side by side each evening in the great hall. But her tongue felt tied in knots and her mind seemed a hopeless blank.

Raven suspected as much and scoffed but could not hide her worry. Thorgold muttered into his ale and frowned at Hawk each time their paths crossed. The day of the feast, Hawk caught him at it and paused on his way to the stable to rub down his stallion. He handed the horse's reins to a groom instead and gestured to Thorgold.

"What ails you?" Hawk asked when the troll-like man shuffled over.

Thorgold peered at him from beneath bushy brows. "Me? Nothing ails me. It's not me ye need to be worrying about."

Hawk glanced around, saw that they were alone, and nodded. "All right then. What ails her?" He could not hide a certain plaintive note that surprised Thorgold and wrung a reluctant grin from him.

"Got ye flummoxed, has she?"

"Say so if it pleases you, but answer my question: Is she ill?"

"Of course not! Girl's healthy as a grass-fed colt. What makes ye think she's ailing?"

"She scarcely speaks to me, for one, nor will she meet my eye. I haven't seen her smile since I can't remember when, before the storm for certain. Is she angry about all the work she did? Is that the problem? Or is it all the work she has been doing to prepare for the harvest festival? That hasn't escaped my notice, old man, in case you think it has. But I didn't ask her to take on either task and she needn't think her life here will require such work."

Thorgold was silent for a moment, twirling the ends of his great black beard. When he looked at Hawk again, his eyes were sparkling. "Tell me, lord, are ye prone to misdirection? When yer off sailing that fine boat of yers do ye have a tendency to lose track of where ye are? Or when yer riding, is it up to that great beast of a horse to find the way home for ye?"

"Of course not. What puts that in your mind?"

"Think about it, lord. If there's one thing the Lady Krysta has never shirked, it's hard work. Why, when she was just a little slip of a girl, she'd be out in the fields with the rest of us doing anything and everything she could to help. Her father was still alive then and he wouldn't have wanted her wearying herself, but she thrived on it and hated to be idle."

"Then it's me. I've done something to upset her." Hawk looked at the old man cautiously. It had been in his mind these days that perhaps he was wrong and Krysta did know he had come to her bed. She would have every right to be angry at him yet he still hoped she had not complained of it to her servants.

"I don't see what," Thorgold said. "Seems to me ye haven't been half-bad for a mor—that is, for a Saxon."

Hawk's mood eased a little. He even managed a wry smile. "I thank you for the vote of confidence but I would still know how to lighten her spirit."

"I told ye about the hair ribbons, didn't I?"

"You did but I don't really think—"

"Trouble is you think too much," Thorgold interrupted. "Get yerself a nice fistful of hair ribbons and go talk to the girl. Better yet, get her off someplace where she can't be rushing about doing this or that."

Hawk knew good advice when he heard it even from so unlikely a source as a fellow who bore an uncanny resemblance to a troll. He went down into the town, paid a visit to a happy merchant, and left with what he had sought. But there was no time to seek out Krysta, for the harvest celebration was about to begin.

The sun was drifting westward but the sky was still well lit as all the residents of Hawkforte and the surrounding area gathered in the large field closest to the stronghold. There, tables had been cobbled together from trestles and planks of wood, covered with cloths, and loaded down with the bounty of all their efforts. Large fires begun much earlier in the day were being tended by young boys under the stern eye of the manor cook, who saw to it that the sides of beef and the whole pigs were kept well turned and basted. Aromas to make the stomach sing greeted the celebrants. Barrels of mead and ale were tapped, and eagerly attended. Children ran about under-foot, drawing indulgent smiles from all.

Coming out onto the field, Krysta paused and looked around anxiously. So far as she could see, everything was as it should be but as she had never participated in so large a celebration, she was yet unsure. Aelfgyth had stayed to help her dress in a gown of mauve and violet that looked woven from the last whispers of the setting sun, then had gone off at Krysta's bidding to see to her own prepara-tions. She was in the crowd somewhere, no doubt with Edvard. Those two seemed destined to make a happy match. Krysta was glad for them even as she wondered what chance there was for her to do the same.

The answer to that lay with the tall, powerful man who stood near the center of the field, chatting amicably with all and sundry and looking as though he had not a care in the world. Resentment tugged at her as she beheld his ease but it faded quickly before the rush of emotions at once tender and fierce. He was dressed with simplicity in a plain black tunic embroidered with gold. Around his taut waist was a belt of gold links that held the bejeweled scab-bard of his sword. The thick curls of his chestnut hair framed his face bronzed by wind and sea and in which his light blue eyes shone brilliantly. He towered head and shoulders above most of the other people, and as she watched she saw him stoop to meet the eyes of an elderly woman who seemed bent on teasing him about some-thing. They both laughed and the woman went away smiling.

He was straightening up when he saw Krysta. At once, his smile faded. Her stomach plummeted to see it go. For a moment she considered trying to lose herself in the crowd, but pride made her hesitate and then it was too late. Hawk walked to her with deliberate speed. As though he had sensed her intention, he put a hand to her elbow before he spoke.

"My lady," he said gravely, "my thanks for all you have done. I can't remember a more splendid harvest feast."

To her dismay, Krysta found herself blushing and unable to meet his eyes. "It is Edvard you should thank, my lord, and all the others. I did little but help."

"That is not what Edvard and the others say." His manner was lightening now that he was reasonably assured she would not elude him. He tucked her arm into the crook of his and led her deeper into the crowd before she could object. Quickly, they were surrounded by townsfolk and peasants alike, who smiled to see them together and in apparent harmony.

He led Krysta to the high table and seated her before taking his place beside her. Their arrival was the signal for the feasting to begin. Amid the parade of dishes, the flow of ale and mead, and the clamor of the guests, Krysta struggled to get her bearings. Everyone wanted to speak with Hawk and did so unhindered, calling out to him from other tables. He was involved in several conversations at once, juggling them all with gracious ease. High good humor abounded, and any barriers of formality that might usually exist dissolved in the spirit of the moment.

Cheers erupted as a young man and woman from the town came forward shyly to present Hawk and Krysta with poppets made from the last gleanings of the harvest. This was a custom with which she was not familiar and she was uncertain what to do until Hawk rose, taking her hand, and led her to an old oak tree that stood at the edge of the field. Following him, she placed her poppet together with his high on a branch of the tree as the watch-

ing crowd cheered. The sun was setting and torches had
been lit. By their dancing flames, the world seemed cast in
ancient shadows.

"King and queen of the harvest," he explained, gesturing to the poppets. "Some folk still believe honoring
them assures the fertility of the land."

"Do you believe it?" she asked quietly.

He shrugged. "I don't see that it does any harm."

Holding her hand high in his, he led her back to the
table. As they resumed their seats, a line of young men
garbed all in white with their faces blackened ran out into
the open space before the diners. From their costumes
dangled hundreds of brightly polished bits of metal that
reflected the firelight over and over, making them seem as
though they moved in the midst of tiny suns. They carried
sticks that they began to bang together rhythmically as
they moved in the patterns of a dance so old it seemed
etched in their blood and sinew.

Krysta watched with delight, she who loved to dance,
for here at last was something familiar. She had seen such
dances, performed by Vestfold folk.

Hawk watched her watching the dancers and smiled
to see her greater ease. He still had no notion of what troubled her but he was determined to set it to rights, whatever it might be. The business of getting to know each
other had surely gone on long enough. He meant to tell
her so but not here, not now in the midst of such revelry.
It needed a private moment, that rarest of gifts but one he
intended to give them both, soon.

He looked out toward the sea and smiled, knowing
what the morrow would bring.

Chapter

TEN

K RYSTA PAUSED AND LOOKED AROUND CAU-
tiously before descending the last few steps
into the hall. There was no sign of either Daria
or Father Elbert, for which she gave silent
thanks. She had no doubt that having been made to endure the spectacle of the harvest feast, albeit from the distance of her quarters, Daria would be in even worse
humor this day than was usual. She would be looking to
take back her own in any and all ways available to her,
with Krysta her most likely target. Therefore was it
Krysta's notion to see what she could do to absent herself
for at least some little time. She was thinking over that,
and munching on an apple, when Hawk strode into the
hall, saw her, and smiled.

"I was in search of you, my lady. Did you sleep well?"

How she had or, more to the point, had not slept was
not a subject she cared to discuss with him. Toward the
end of the harvest feast, when ale and mead flowed in
abundance, couples took to going off hand-in-hand to
find their pleasure. Even staid Edvard was nowhere to be
seen by the time the feast was over, nor was Aelfgyth.

Envy was a petty emotion yet Krysta could not elude it. It had kept her restless throughout the night.

"Why in search, my lord?" she asked, dodging the question.

"I wondered if you might like to go sailing."

"Sailing . . . with you?"

"I was not suggesting you go alone." He spoke with gentle chiding.

"No, of course not, I only meant . . ." Flustered, she took a breath and tried again despite the sudden racing of her heart. "Yes, thank you, I would like to go sailing."

He grinned at her formality but looked relieved in the bargain. "Come then, before a host of well-intentioned folk appear with dozens of matters requiring our immediate attention."

Our. A sudden carefree spirit seized her. She laughed and took the hand he offered. They slipped away down back lanes to the pier where Hawk kept his boat. He helped her into it, untied the mooring rope, and jumped down to join her. A cat prowling among barrels of salted fish watched them go.

Hawk raised the single mast and unfurled the sail. The wind filled it, skimming them lightly over the water. He put a hand to the rudder and guided the boat out into the bay. Seated beside him in the stern, Krysta breathed deeply of the salt air and turned her face toward the sun. She had been too long without this and had missed it sorely. With each moment, she felt her emotions become less frayed. She looked out toward the white-gold curve of the shore and smiled.

"Your lands looked marvelous from the back of a horse, my lord, but I must tell you, they look even more beautiful seen this way."

He laughed, pleased by her spirit. "Should I conclude you prefer sailing to riding?"

"You would be safe thinking so."

"Then perhaps you would like to try your hand at it."
The day was clear, the wind mild. He saw no harm in letting her take the rudder.

She glanced at him in surprise. "You would not
mind?"

"So long as you don't capsize us," he said with a
smile. "Here, let me show you how—"

As he spoke, Krysta took hold of the rudder. She
laughed with sheer delight to feel the power of the wind
and sea in her hair. Without hesitation, she turned the
boat so that the wind was directly astern. In response,
they seemed to leap forward. At Hawk's startled look, she
grinned, tacked smoothly to port, and brought them
across the wind so that their speed slowed.

"You know how to sail," he said, looking just a little
grumpy about it.

"When I wasn't swimming, I was doing this," Krysta
confessed. She wondered if she had overstepped herself
but as she made to turn the rudder over to Hawk, he
shook his head.

"Oh, no, my lady, if you can sail, then by all means do
so. I'll sit back and enjoy myself."

She glanced at him doubtfully but he insisted, going
so far as to lean back with his arms stretched out on either
side along the boat railing, looking as though he had not a
care in the world. He even made a show of closing his eyes
although she noticed he opened them frequently to check
on her progress.

"There are rocks over that way," he said finally, a moment before Krysta spotted the telltale roiling of water
over submerged stone. She steered easily around them
and continued north along the coast. It was dotted with
bays and inlets, all smaller than Vestfold's, but lovely just
the same. Beyond them came mainly dense forest almost
to the water's edge, although here and there she saw clear-
ings that spoke of human habitation. She considered how

greatly this soft landscape contrasted to the ruggedness of Vestfold and realized for the first time that she could not remember when she had last thought of the place that had been her home.

"What troubles you?" Hawk asked suddenly.

Drawn back to the moment, she looked at him in surprise. "Nothing. I was just thinking how different this is from Vestfold."

He hesistated, as though tempted to drop the subject, but instead said, "I didn't mean just now. I meant these last few days. Since Dragon was here, something has made you unhappy."

She stared at him, so startled that he had made such a connection that she had no idea of what to say.

"Are you homesick?" Hawk asked. "Did his coming here remind you of the home you left?"

"No! That is, I truly did not think of it. I am not homesick."

He sighed deeply and ran a hand through thick curls. So distracted was she by the glint of sun off them that she almost missed what he said next. "Then it is this betrothal that saddens you."

Krysta shook her head in bewilderment. She could not fathom his thoughts, perhaps because the mere fact that he had been thinking about her feelings astounded her. That he had, in the process, come to a stunningly wrong conclusion only added to her perplexity.

"I am not sad about our betrothal. I thought you regretted it."

It was Hawk's turn to be surprised. "Me? How did you come to think that?"

She could not meet his eyes. As he watched, her cheeks darkened. He glanced down at her slender hands on the rudder and saw that the knuckles shone white against the honey tones of her skin. Such very lovely, soft skin . . .

Abruptly, a memory rose. Waking the night of the storm, seeing Krysta beside him . . . seeing her clearly despite the darkness. Seeing because a brazier glowed beside the bed. A brazier that had not been lit when first he came into the room.

She knew.

"I see . . ." he said slowly. "Obviously, an apology is owed you. I should not have done as I did."

She looked at him for all the world as though he spoke in a tongue she could not comprehend. "Do we speak of the same thing? The night of the storm, you . . ."

"I shared your bed. But I did you no harm and if you were frightened or offended, I am truly sorry." He fell silent for a moment, remembering. The lit brazier. She must have done that and in the doing, seen him. Why then had she returned to the bed . . . unclad? A possibility teased at the edge of his mind, tempting him. Gently, going very carefully, he asked, "*Were* you frightened or offended, Krysta? Or did you by chance have other feelings I didn't recognize?"

She answered so softly that he had to strain to hear her over the song of the wind. "A lady of true worth would not have such feelings."

The back of his neck prickled, the same way it would do on a battlefield when someone right behind him was about to split his head open with an ax. Then the appropriate response was simple and straightforward—if necessarily brutal. Now he had to go much more cautiously.

"You think a lady shouldn't have feelings?"

She darted a quick look at him before turning away. "Proper feelings, certainly, at the proper time and place. She should be . . . restrained."

He thought of how she had kissed him in the stable and spared a moment's fervent thanks that such restraint was foreign to her nature.

"I think you have an odd idea of what makes a lady."

He was beginning to smile broadly at the realization that her chagrin came not from what he had done but from what he had not. What a fool he had been not to think of that sooner, and how much more pleasant these last few days would have been for both of them if he had. But done was done. It was now that mattered.

"A lady is merely a woman of property and position," he said. "Nothing more or less. To be a lady says naught about what is in a woman's heart." He leaned closer and put his hand over hers on the rudder. "Nor does it say what *should* be in her heart. That is for her to decide."

Her eyes as they met his were doe-wide. She did not protest when he turned them downwind. The sail billowed, snapping in the stiff offshore breeze. They raced over the water glinting with the captured treasure of sunlight. Gulls circled overhead and a startled porpoise raised its head to watch. Krysta gasped when she saw a small island coming up swiftly directly ahead, but Hawk's hand tightened on hers and they deftly steered around it with almost no loss of speed. The wind changed direction slightly but he seemed to sense it before it happened and maneuvered so adroitly that the sail never sagged. Quickly, she realized that he close-hauled with steely skill, something she rarely dared to do. Sailing so close to the wind brought special challenges and dangers, but he clearly thrived on both. With a start, she realized that just perhaps she did, too, for never had she enjoyed a sail more.

"Does anyone ever race you?" she asked, vividly conscious of the warmth and strength of his hand over hers.

Hawk laughed and she felt the movement of his chest against her back. "Wolf and Dragon will, no one else. They win half the time, too." He sounded pleased, as though he relished true competition.

"What about you?" he asked. "How did you learn to sail?"

"My father taught me. We used to go out together whenever he came to visit."

"Was that often?"

"As often as he could. Between his visits, I would go out by myself. He didn't know that, though. I think he would have worried."

The thought of her as a child sailing alone along a coast the Danes had been known to raid before the Wolf of Sciringesheal established his iron hold over it made Hawk frown. "Did no one even try to rein you in?"

She turned her head to look at him and was startled to discover how very near he was. So near that she could see the fine etching of lines around his light blue eyes and at the corners of his firm mouth. His skin was sun burnished and smoothly shaven. He smelled of soap and the sea. Her mouth was suddenly very dry.

"I am not a mare, my lord," she said softly. "There are no reins on me."

He reached around and took the rudder with both hands. She was effectively trapped within the circle of his arms. His breath was warm on her cheek, sending a delicate shiver down her back. "Then I suppose I'll have to resort to persuasion," he said and caught her mouth with his.

His kiss was swift and hard, leaving her breathless. He broke off abruptly and gave his attention to the boat. Several moments passed before Krysta realized that she had sagged back against him. She tried to straighten up but he stopped her with the light pressure of his arms. Belatedly, she realized she had no desire to move.

They turned in toward a golden strand of shore fronting an isolated bay. Hawk lowered the sail, stepped into the water and pulled the boat up onto the sand. Krysta was about to get out when he caught her around the waist, lifting her easily, and drew her close. The touch of his body all along the length of hers made her tremble.

Slowly, he slid her down until her feet brushed the sand. She thought he meant to kiss her again, and was awaiting just that with more eagerness than she cared to admit, when he let go of her suddenly and reached into the boat.

"Are you hungry?" he asked, hefting a small sack.

Was she? She had absolutely no idea. "I suppose . . ." Where had the food come from? She hadn't noticed him carrying anything when they went down to the boat.

He saw the question in her eyes and grinned abashedly. "I asked Aelfgyth to tuck something away for us."

His thoughtfulness touched her even if it did mean that by now everyone at Hawkforte likely knew of their excursion. After living amid so few for so long, she was beginning to realize how precious privacy really was.

Hawk shook out a blanket, placed it on the sand, and set the sack on it. Straightening, he glanced at Krysta where she still stood, watching him. Gently, he said, "I don't bite, you know."

Her cheeks warmed. She supposed she looked very silly to him but her sudden self-consciousness was almost as uncomfortable as her overwhelming awareness of him. He was so tall, so perfectly formed, so male . . . so *everything*. He seemed to leave her scant room even to draw breath.

"Would you like to go swimming?" he asked.

It came to her then that he was seeking some way to put her at ease. How many men would go to such trouble? How many would spend a day away from the pressing demands of their duty to calm a fractious betrothed? Her heart warmed and she found herself smiling.

"Do you see that rock over there?" she asked, pointing to a large boulder jutting above the water several hundred yards beyond the shore. When he nodded, she reached for the laces of her gown. "I'll bet I get there first."

He stared at her in astonishment for a moment before

his face split in a broad grin. "I'll take that bet. We can discuss the stakes later."

She laughed and tugged off her gown, feeling perfectly well covered in her shift. It did not occur to her that the angle of the sun shining through it rendered the fine linen all but transparent. Such did not escape the attention of the Hawk. He was sufficiently distracted to still be tugging off his boots when Krysta dived neatly into the water. She surfaced a good twenty yards off shore, pausing just long enough to glance back at him before heading for her objective.

He followed swiftly, hesitating only a moment before tossing off his tunic. Best she become accustomed to him. Having seen her swim before, he knew better than to give any quarter. Even so, he only just managed to reach her while she was yet a few yards from winning. His longer and more powerful legs gave him the advantage and he touched the rock scant moments before she did.

"You could have won," he said, treading water and grinning at her chagrined expression. He gestured to the cloth floating about her. "That weighed you down."

"What about your tunic?" Belatedly, she realized her mistake. He laughed at her sudden flush and followed as she turned back to shore. She was almost there and about to stand up when she stopped abruptly and sank back down into the water.

Hawk stopped, too, in water that came to his waist. "Is something wrong?"

"No! That is, everything's fine. I just don't want to come out yet."

A suspicion formed in his mind and with it came a smile. She had her back to him but even so, he could glimpse the rosy smoothness of her skin through the linen made transparent by the water. He drew a little closer so that he could see her in profile. Judging by her expression, she was prepared to remain right where she was until she froze.

Hawk sighed. He spared a fond thought for the days when his relationships with women were simple, then put such memory aside for good and waded out of the water. He heard Krysta give a quick gulp but didn't look in her direction. The easier and more natural he was about all this, the sooner he thought she was likely to adjust.

Without bothering to dry himself off, for the air was warm, he picked up the blanket and returned to the water's edge. "Come on, now," he said gently and held the blanket open for her to step into.

Slowly, not taking her eyes from him, she rose. Her arms were crossed in front of her breasts and her hair hung like a sleek mane over her shoulders. She took a step toward him and another. Only a few more and he would be able to enfold her in the blanket. What he would do after that, he wasn't absolutely sure. He had little experience with virgins. Unlike some men, he never sought them out. His first wife had left him with a marked preference for women who had long since shed their innocence without regret. But Krysta was . . . different. Or he had become different, he wasn't sure which it was. She aroused an odd mixture of feelings—desire, to be sure, but tenderness as well. There had been so little room in his life for gentler emotions that he wasn't sure how to cope with them. He could only try.

And in the trying, he waited patiently for her to come to him, to cover herself, to leave him with the problem of how to soothe her fears, calm her natural nervousness, coax her to trust him. She did not. Instead, she took a deep breath and dropped her arms. Her gaze never left his as she reached up and took hold of the top of the blanket. He thought she meant to wrap it around herself but she surprised him . . . yet again. He would have to become accustomed to that, he thought faintly, too absorbed in the watching of her to think much of anything at all. Her motions were spare and elegant, her expression grave as she neatly folded the blanket and handed it back to him. A soft flush stained her cheeks but she still did not look away. Bending down slightly, she lifted the hem of her shift and in a swift, graceful move, drew it over her head. It dangled from her hand as she tossed back her magnificent hair, took another breath, and said, "You were right. I would have won without this."

"You have won," Hawk said gruffly and gathered her to him. Her courage moved him as much as did her beauty. But more than anything, it was her honesty that struck to his core. Honesty to face her fears and admit her desires. He could do no less.

S HE WAS SHAKING WHEN HE LAID HER ON THE BLAN-
ket and told herself it was from the chill of the water. But she knew better, knew she trembled with a mixture of excitement and nervousness at facing the mystery of a man. Yet was he truly so mysterious? Her eyes swept over him in the moment before he lowered himself to her and a wave of heat moved through her. Driven by a sudden impulse she could not deny, she reached up to him, cradling him in her arms.

He sighed deeply as skin touched skin, bringing a strange sense of homecoming, she thought, and sighed with him. Their breaths mingled, lips touching, mouths joining. She tasted and was tasted, relishing the discovery even more than she had in those moments in the storm-lit stable. He surrounded her with warmth and care, holding his weight above her until she tightened her arms, drawing him nearer, needing to feel the strength and power of him.

He ran a hand down the length of her, seeking, learning, over the full curve of her breasts, the indentation of her waist, the chalice of her hips to her smooth flanks and back again, his thumb teasing her nipple until she made a low sound deep in her throat and arched against him.

Hawk shuddered with pleasure at her response. To hold such a woman in his arms, and she a virgin given to him as his betrothed, was more than he had ever imagined. Distant memories of disappointment and sorrow echoed one last time before they dissolved beneath the sheer impact of his relief. He took her mouth, drinking of her deeply. It was in his mind to go slowly, to do everything possible to assure her pleasure, but his mind wasn't working very well just then. Restraint eroded swiftly. If she would only be still . . . but no, he didn't want that and she wouldn't. She moved beneath him, her hips arching to his, her hands stroking, and made soft keening noises deep in her throat.

His spirit leaped in response yet he slowed all the same, finding himself driven to savor her. Her breasts were high and full, perfectly fitted to his hands. Beneath them, faint shadows traced along her rib cage. His mouth drifted down over the smoothness of her belly. She whimpered and yanked hard on his hair, wringing a laugh that turned to a groan when he tasted the essence of her. She went rigid in his arms and for a moment her hands pushed hard against his shoulders, struggling to unseat him. An instant later she melted, crying out softly as she fell back against the blanket.

Krysta opened her eyes to the cloudless helmet of heaven but did not see it. She could only hear the thudding of her own heart and feel the reverberations of ecstasy she had never known existed. Hawk moved above her and where she had not seen sun or sky, she saw him. Saw the man, solid and real, fierce and tender, so powerful that he could overwhelm her without effort, yet waiting . . . his eyes meeting hers, questioning.

A moment more she hesitated, her head tilting back, savoring the echoes of virgin pleasure taken without price. It was not enough. She reached out, her touch lingering over the contours of his massive shoulders and chest to his flat abdomen and beyond. Gently, she cupped him, feeling his heat and strength. Deep within her, joy stirred. She bent her legs, making a place for him, and felt him fit it perfectly.

"Krysta . . ." He lingered over her name as he lingered over her, going slowly, watching her every moment. His gaze never lessened, nor did hers, as he penetrated the virgin barrier, wincing as he did so as though the pain was his. She saw that and her heart opened with her body. Clasping her to him, cradling his head against her breasts, she rushed toward the power unfolding within her and took him with her.

I T WAS AN INTERESTING THING, HAWK THOUGHT, TO get this far in a life filled with challenge and adventure, and realize he hadn't ever suspected what he was actually capable of experiencing. Pleasure certainly, he was no stranger to that, yet pleasure was but a faint taste of the soul-shattering ecstasy from which he was only slowly emerging. Interesting, too, to think at all, since for very long moments he was quite sure he had been capable of doing nothing of the sort. He turned his head, mildly surprised he could manage that as well, and saw Krysta lying beside him. Her eyes were closed, her mouth curved in a gentle smile. She looked well pleased with herself . . . and with him. He leaned on his side and stroked a finger along the damask curve of her cheek. Her eyes fluttered open.

"I've got something for you," he said. She looked surprised. He reached into the sack he'd brought along but kept what he withdrew from it concealed in his hand. "Close your eyes," he directed. She did so but promptly tried to peer from beneath her lashes. "No peeking," he chided and waited until she obliged.

Something teased at her nose. Krysta tried to wiggle it away but it was back in an instant. She flicked her hand at it, wondering what was taking so long. The gift itself mattered not at all, it was the notion that he had thought of such a thing. Added to all that had just happened, it heaped upon her dazed senses so much gladness as scarcely to be borne.

What *was* that tickling her nose? She forgot her promise, opened her eyes, and found herself staring at . . .

Her breath caught. A hair ribbon danced before her, a length of brushed velvet the exact shade of green as she knew her eyes to be. "Oh, Hawk . . ."

The way she said his name, that aching whisper of sheer delight, made his throat tighten. He wondered when the last time was anyone had given her a gift and felt a surge of gladness that he was the man to do it. As she twined the ribbon through her fingers, staring at it as though it were the loveliest thing she had ever seen, he reached back into the sack and drew out handfuls of hair ribbons, ribbons in every possible color, ribbons of velvet and rarest silk, embroidered ribbons and bejeweled ribbons showering down upon her like fragments of a rainbow.

She gasped and laughed, all at once, trying to catch them as they fell over her breasts and belly, over the sleek smoothness of her thighs, into her hair, and all around her. She fell back against the blanket, gazing up at him, a look in her eyes as though he had given her the world. Just then, he felt he could.

They lingered on the beach, enjoying the repast Aelfgyth had packed, then swam again. Heartbeat to heartbeat, they surrendered to their need for constant, small touches, the brush of lips, the stroke of fingertips, skin touching skin, a language words could not equal.

They teased and laughed, stared at each other for long moments, and laughed suddenly once more. Gulls swooped to catch the bread they tossed and sandpipers raced among them, claiming their share of the bounty. Coming out of the water, they spied a clump of blackberries and ate them greedily until their kisses tasted of sweet, summer-poignant juice.

"I have never known such a day," Krysta said at last. She lay above Hawk, her body draped over his, her head resting on his broad chest, soft whorls of hair pillowing her cheek. Her heart ached with the beauty of it all. "I wish for a golden rope to catch the sun and hold it fast in the sky so that it may never descend."

"But night has its own gifts," he said softly, and thought of her in his big bed with all the long hours of darkness to savor her.

They sailed back to Hawkforte on the late afternoon tide. The wind was high but they tacked slowly, drawing out the time that was theirs alone. When they finally came within sight of the piers stretching out into the water, torches were already lit and the first faint stars could be seen.

So, too, could they see the vessel in dock, a Viking ship by the look of the curved prow but much battered, its sail hanging tattered and torn from a mast that appeared not quite steady.

"Someone ran into trouble," Hawk said. "Likely the storm that blew through here did damage farther north."

"Perhaps . . ." Krysta hardly knew she spoke. All her attention was on the vessel. As they drew nearer, the ominous sense grew within her that she had seen it before. Something in the carving of the dragon's head on the prow, looking too large and top-heavy, jogged her memory. "I'm not sure but . . ."

She never finished what she was about to say for just then they drew up alongside the pier and she saw the man standing there. He was of middle height with thin, stooped shoulders, lank hair of a nondescript hue, and a pale face. With one hand he clutched a cloak tightly around himself as with the other he gestured wildly to Edvard, who appeared to be trying to soothe him.

As Hawk jumped out to secure the mooring rope, the man caught sight of him. He brushed off the steward and hurried forward, armored in self-importance, oblivious to the scornful stares from everyone else on the dock including his own crew.

"There you are!," he exclaimed. "And about time, too. I dare the worst storm in a century, I almost drown getting here, and then I have to listen to your man tell me he has no idea where you've gone off to."

Hawk looked the interloper over and raised an eyebrow. "You have a name, I assume?"

The fellow stared at him blankly. Before he could speak, Krysta stepped out of the boat and stood beside Hawk. Quietly, she said, "My lord, this is my half-brother, Sven."

Scarcely had she spoken than Sven flushed darkly. His eyes lit on her with stark hatred. He took a step toward her, the cloak tangling around his legs. Stumbling, he yelled, "You bitch! Humiliating our family, threatening everything! I'll teach you—"

In a single motion, Hawk stepped in front of Krysta and lifted Sven off the ground. He held him, feet kicking in midair, his face turning a mottled red as the neck of his tunic tightened, slowly strangling him. "Do you realize who you are addressing, cretin?"

Sven stared at Hawk with a mixture of terror and righteous indignation. His feet beat all the harder. In a frantic squeak, he said, "I know exactly who she is! It's you who don't!"

Chapter

ELEVEN

H E'S A FOOL," HAWK SAID HE WAS STRETCHED out on the bed in Krysta's tower, having absolutely refused to leave her after the scene on the dock. His hands were folded behind his head and he looked at his ease, save for the murderous glint in his eyes. Krysta was behind a screen, changing for supper after giving up the battle to get him to leave. To be truthful, she hadn't tried all that hard, and that worried him. She seemed deflated somehow, her usually resilient spirit dampened. All thanks to that cursed halfbrother of hers. For a few moments, Hawk entertained himself with thoughts of various ways the idiot could die. It solved nothing but did make him feel slightly better.

"Dragon called him a slug and a dullard, and he was right," Hawk added. "His own men have been busy telling anyone who will listen that it was the smallest of squalls they hit, not some great storm, and that it was only the stupidity of Lord Slug that led them into harm." This he knew from Aelfgyth, who had whispered it as she left, after bringing hot water, honey cakes, and a fierce hug for her mistress. Edvard was going to marry that girl and soon, Hawk had decided, for she deserved nothing less.

Krysta emerged from behind the screen. She had changed into a simple gown in a dull shade of brown, far plainer than the elegant garb she usually wore in the evenings. Her hair was dragged into two tight braids that hung over her shoulders. He winced to see it so confined. She appeared tense, downcast, and clearly filled with dread. Hawk cursed inwardly but took pains to appear unconcerned. "Look, sweetheart, it's not your fault he's family. I've got Daria to cope with. I'm the last person to cast stones because someone else has an unpleasant relative."

"It's not that," she said softly yet offered nothing more.

He got off the bed and went to her, putting his hands on her shoulders to stop her when she tried to turn away. "Then for pity's sake, what is it? Do you not want him here when we wed? Fine, he'll be gone on the next tide. He simply isn't important, Krysta. I don't understand why he has you worried so."

"Did you not hear what he said, that he knew who I was and you did not?"

"I heard it . . . it means nothing. Unless you are to tell me you are not the Lady Krysta of Vestfold." A sudden thought flooded his mind. "Mercy of heaven, you aren't really her servant, are you?" He was scrabbling to think how he would smooth over the inevitable problems that would occur with his insistence on wedding the maid rather than her mistress, when she put that to rest.

"No, of course not. I am Krysta of Vestfold. But I don't think you can simply discount what brings Sven here. He never bestirs himself if he can possibly avoid it, yet he came all this way. For what purpose?"

"Did he give evidence of having half a brain, I would say to wish us well. However . . ."

"Exactly. After our father's death, Sven summoned me to his manor." She shuddered at the memory. "He left no doubt that he loathed our father for marrying again and that he despised me. Truly, I have no idea what he would have done eventually had the jarl of Sciringesheal not chosen me as your bride. Not even Sven is stupid enough to go against the Wolf but I fear he has some other plan in mind now. For all that he lacks intelligence, he can still do great harm."

"You are mistaken. He can do naught to hurt you."

He saw her eyes glisten with unshed tears and cursed again but inwardly. Gently, with great care, he took hold of one of her braids where it fell across her breast. She offered no resistance. Slowly, meticulously, he unwound first one braid, then the other, and ran his fingers through the curls of gold. When her hair tumbled free, he found the most heavily bejeweled ribbons and handed them to her.

"If you would, wear these to please me."

She did and, understanding his intent, returned behind the screen to change the drab gown for the one of spun sunlight and sea foam she had worn first on the night she assumed her true identity. The impulse to dress herself so plainly had faded almost as quickly as it had come. Her mother's gown gave her strength, and the look in Hawk's eyes when she emerged again offered her even more.

Thus garbed, Krysta steeled herself for what she suspected was to come. She walked beside Hawk into the great hall with her head high and the sorrow of her heart well hidden. The rustling of all those gathered there died away, replaced by an expectant silence.

Scarcely had Hawk and Krysta taken their seats than Sven appeared from the guest quarters. Daria was at his side, her thin face unusually avid with excitement. With them was Father Elbert, who strove without success to maintain his usual guise of aloof piety. The effort was too much for him and he sported twin spots of color on his pallid cheeks.

In violation of all the canons of hospitality, Hawk did not rise to greet his "guest." Neither did Edvard spring forward to offer the usual seat at the high table or summon the servants to attend the lordling. Rather, the steward remained standing just behind Hawk's high-backed chair, arms folded across his chest, his expression grim.

"You have recovered yourself?" Hawk asked coldly.

His tone brought Sven up short. He stopped where he was, several yards in front of the high table, and set his features in an expression of long-suffering. His high-pitched voice grated. "Well enough, I suppose, given the ordeal I have endured. First called to account to the jarl for this one's disappearance, then finding out she had come here disguised as a servant. I see you made fast work of that, my lord, and I salute you, but I fail to understand why she sits in the place of honor at your side."

"Because she is my betrothed?" Hawk spoke as though to a dullard child. Around the hall, people sniggered at this blunt assessment of the lordling's intelligence.

For his part, Sven remained undeterred. "Was, Hawk of Essex, only *was*. The shame she has brought upon our family renders her unfit to be any man's bride."

"You left behind whatever passes for your brain when you departed for these shores."

There were men in Winchester, powerful men around the king, who quaked when they heard the Hawk speak in that tone. They were wise enough to sense his anger rising and know the savage danger it represented. Sven was unburdened by any such awareness. He merely shrugged his narrow shoulders. "Insult me all you like, it makes no difference. Mind you, you should be thanking me for what I have saved you from but I don't expect you realize it yet." He paused, then with a dramatic wave of his arm toward Krysta announced, "She is a changeling." As one, those assembled in the hall gasped and quickly positioned themselves for a better view of the violence they were certain was about to follow.

Belatedly, and still only dimly aware that he had transgressed the bounds of courtesy, Sven added, "Before you think to deny what I say, hear the rest. Her mother was a witch who seduced my poor benighted father and bore him a changeling child. He near died from the shame, hiding her away as best he could. Out of respect for him, we kept the secret. Never did I imagine she would come to the notice of one such as the Wolf and that he would intend her to be the honored bride of so great a noble as yourself. But he had heard rumors that I had a half-sister and insisted on meeting her. Scarcely did he do so than he decided she was the one for you. I tried to tell him otherwise but all he would talk of was the dowry. The great dowry he insists is your due. . . . But never mind, it is not an issue now. None of our father's property is rightly hers, she deserves nothing, and her behavior of late cannot leave doubt of that in the mind of any man. But do not fret, lord, another will be found for you. Although not," the miserly fool hastened to add, "any of my true sisters. They are . . . indisposed to wed."

He glanced at Daria. "A lady of true worth is needed to honor your bed and name." He turned his gaze to Krysta. "And bear you children of a human ilk, not changeling creatures of the sea."

"God's blood!" Hawk roared and rose from his seat.

Finally alarmed, Sven scampered back behind Daria and Father Elbert. "Oh, yes, you may curse me now but time will prove me right. Look at her. She is no lady nor will she ever be. I disown her and deny she is any part of my family! There will be no dowry for her. She deserves to be just what she cast herself, a servant . . . nay, a slave!"

"Hold your tongue! Are you so lackwit as to give no thought even to your own life? I swear—" Hawk's hand went to his sword.

"No," Krysta cried. She put her hand over his. "Kill him and kill the hope of peace! If a Norse noble dies in your hall, what chance any other will give you his sister or daughter?"

"I want no other woman! This buffoon thinks to save himself the coin of your dowry, nothing more. He concocts a tale to be told to credulous children and expects me to believe it!"

"It is no tale," Sven said with stiff affront. "Not even one such as she will deny the truth of it." To Krysta, he said, "Give no thought to returning with me. Never again will you set foot in the lands of my father. Nay, keep her, lord, or dispose of her as you will. I give her to you and gladly. Knowing what you know now, no doubt you will want to punish her for her effrontery, and that is as it should be. You should lose no time chastising her."

"The only person I have any interest in chastising is you, you insufferable prig. As you value your skin, get you from my sight!"

Finally Sven realized that he had gone too far. Or perhaps it was Daria and the priest tugging at his sleeves that alerted him to danger. They swept him from the hall, still with an expression of incredulous affront because the Hawk of Essex had not received his news with humble gratitude.

To Edvard, Hawk directed, "Get that crawling excuse for a man from my shores."

"The tide turns at dawn, lord. He will be gone." The steward paused delicately. "Leastways, he will be if a crew can be found to man his ship. It seems few who came with him are eager to continue in his service."

"Give them coin enough to make it worth their while and chains to clap him into if he causes them any trouble, but get him gone from here!"

Edvard smiled then and hastened to do Hawk's bidding. That done, the master of all he surveyed slumped back in his chair for a moment and looked at the woman beside him. Krysta was pale and drawn, her mouth trembled, and she plucked at the arm of her chair with nervous fingers.

He signaled to the servants to bring forth supper and turned to her. Leaning close, his voice for her ears only, he said, "Forget him, he is nothing. We will be wed on the morrow."

She turned startled eyes to him. "We cannot. You heard what he said, I have no dowry."

"I care not. Your dowry is the peace our marriage will help to bring. Naught else matters."

"How can you say that? You told me yourself that a lady is a woman of property and position. I have neither and you cannot marry other than a lady, peace or not."

"I can marry anyone I please," Hawk declared. He bit the words out and glared at her as though daring her to disagree.

"You say that now but how will you feel later?"

"Vindicated. Have you given a moment's thought to what will happen to your father's weak-minded whelp when Wolf gets wind of this? He will have the news by fast ship to Sciringesheal, I promise you, and when he does there will be no more talk of mere dowry. Fully half and more of what your father left will pour out to you in recompense for this insult."

"You assume the jarl will still think this marriage desirable. Why would he do that when he hears what Sven has to say?"

"What he has to say? You mean that changeling tale? You can't think Wolf foolish enough to believe it."

"What if it is true? Have you thought what that would mean for you . . . and for the children I bear you?"

Though they spoke in low murmurs, her words resounded through him with the force of a thunderclap. He looked at her narrowly. "You're not serious? Perhaps your ears were filled with some tale as a child, but you are a woman now and you must know it to be false."

"You weren't certain the tale Dragon told was false. You thought it a strange story, true enough, but you did not dismiss it."

"It was an amusement told around the fire, nothing more! Dragon is an entertaining fellow, leastways unless you're trying to best him on the training field. But he makes no claim that his stories are fact."

She turned her head, looking off to the side. Raven was there, dark and shining, gazing at her with unblinking eyes. Thorgold would be somewhere nearby, unless he had crept off beneath his favorite bridge to nurse his ale and his worry.

"You have seen my servants."

"A loyal pair. What of them?"

"Don't you find them . . . unusual?"

"There have been times when the sun coming up of a morning strikes me as unusual, mainly because I didn't expect to live to see it. Living without fighting is unusual, waking in the morn with nothing more to do than see to my lands and people is still unusual though I have been doing it for years now." He leaned yet nearer and his voice was a caress. "Lying with a woman who makes me believe all things are possible is unusual, to say the least. So what care have I for your servants, whoever they may be?"

Krysta's throat was so tight she doubted she could speak, yet she tried. He was so far beyond her dreams, so much more than she could ever have hoped for. She loved him with all her heart and soul, and with that love she could do naught else but set him free.

"I will not marry you."

He paled, he who had faced screaming hordes of
Danes without flinching, and slammed his goblet against
the table. Silence fell in the hall yet he did not notice it, so
swept was he by . . . what? Anger, disappointment . . .
fear. Not fear! He was a man and a warrior, no woman
could make him afraid. But he had touched something
with her, glimpsed it in those hours on the beach, and now
it was being snatched away. And he was afraid.

"Damn you."

The words reverberated through the hall and straight
through Krysta. She sucked in her breath and gripped the
sides of her chair as though the sheer force of his anger
might hurl her from it. A wave of coldness swept over her.
In its path, she felt clammy and sick, gripped by a fever of
the soul.

"I am sorry." So weak and inadequate but there was
nothing else she could say. She was sorry for it all—her
mother, herself, her foolish hopes and dreams. Sorry for
everything except the stolen hours on the beach. Those
she would treasure forever.

"I will go." She hardly knew what she said as she rose
from her chair on legs that threatened not to hold her.
Desperately, she glanced around for Raven but she was
gone. How could she be, she who was ever faithful? Yet
gone she was and there was no sign of Thorgold. Krysta
stood alone before the eyes of the enraged Hawk and all
his people.

Edvard had come back to the hall, his mission to dis-
patch Sven accomplished. Hapless Edvard, who knew not
what he walked into. Hawk pinned him with his gaze. The
steward came forward swiftly.

Hawk stood. He loomed over Krysta, a dark and
powerful presence like night on a storm-tossed sea. "You
will go nowhere," he said, and gestured to Edvard. "Take
the Lady Krysta to her quarters and secure her there."

"L-lord?" Edvard stammered, he who had seen the tender regard his master had for this lady.

"You heard me. She goes nowhere. In time, this will all sort itself out. Meanwhile, what love and honor cannot bind, a solid iron lock will keep."

"You cannot. . . . !" Krysta cried, but Edvard's hand was on her arm and already he was drawing her away. Hawk's lieutenants were on their feet, cold and stern-faced men who would obey his commands in a heartbeat, and all the others in the hall were watching her with somber, disappointed gaze.

All save Aelfgyth, who looked upon Krysta with shocked sympathy and touched the hem of her sleeve to tear-filled eyes.

E DVARD LINGERED IN THE TOWER ROOM, SENDING servants for more coal for the braziers and water for the ewers, fussing over the shutters across the windows, inquiring as to whether there were enough bedcovers, enough oil for the lamps, enough of this and that and everything.

"You have not eaten," he said at length when all else was done and he had no other reason to tarry.

"I cannot," Krysta said, moving her lips with effort.

"Oh, well, as to that, you must." He looked with relief to Aelfgyth, who was at the door that stood, for the moment, open.

"You must eat, my lady," Aelfgyth agreed. "Look at what I have brought you." She held forth a tray. "The tenderest greens plucked fresh this eve with the vinegar you like the best to season them, a round of your favorite cheese, loaves of bread warm from the oven, raspberries from the bushes by the cove—you know they are the best—and smoked herring that Cook swears you will like above all else." She set the tray on the table and smiled encouragingly. "How could you say no to this? Oh, and cider kept lowered down the well until scant minutes ago so that it is crisp and chill." She paused for a moment, looking at Krysta, and her smile crumbled. "Please, my lady, you truly must eat."

"Later," Krysta said, because she did not want to hurt her friends as they still seemed to be, despite all. "I will eat later. Now, if you don't mind, I would as soon rest."

They left with backward glances and admonitions that she must take care of herself. After the door closed, she heard the iron lock clang into place and thought that she heard Edvard sigh as he obeyed his master's order.

Then there was nothing left to do save stand for a while in the center of the room, not moving and scarcely breathing, as she struggled to understand all that had happened. In the space of hours to go from virgin to woman, betrothed to . . . what? . . . was more than she could encompass. What was she now? Hawk still insisted on their marriage but she knew better. He would have time to think and in that time he would come to realize he could not take the risk of marrying one such as she . . . whoever and whatever she was. He would be glad, when all was said and done, to have turned away from her.

But he was a stubborn man, she reminded herself, and his pride was hurt. He would not give in easily. She walked to the door and tried to turn the handle, so as to leave no hope in her mind that she was other than a captive, the room her prison.

For a moment, her spirit rebelled like the wings of a bird beating frantically against its cage. She desperately needed to be free, to feel the wind and sea, to run and dive and leap, to vanish far from this life. As her mother had needed to do, in the end when she had known that love was not to be.

Krysta walked over to the windows. There were many of them around the curved walls of the tower, most looking out toward the sea. Edvard had closed the shutters but she opened a pair now and gazed out. The night was moonless and the water very dark. She leaned out the window and looked at the stars blazing overhead. Long ago, her father had taught her about their shapes. She knew how to pick out the huntsman and the bear, among others, and she could reckon by the star that never moved, always showing the way north. The way barred to her now by Sven's decree. He was head of the family and he had the right to disown her. No one would dispute that, whatever Hawk believed. As for the dowry, she knew not what the Wolf would do but it scarcely mattered. Sven had forced her to confront what she had tried so desperately to deny, that the mystery of her past threw a shadow over her entire life and made it impossible for her to nurture the hopes and dreams common to ordinary women.

Her throat was very tight and she knew she was perilously close to tears. The long, tumultuous day had left her exhausted. She went to the table and managed to eat a very small amount of what Aelfgyth had brought. Not wishing to worry her maid, she crumbled up the bread and threw it out the window for the birds to find in the morning. Wondering again where Raven was, Krysta lay down on the bed, in the place where Hawk had been. Weeping, she slept, and sleeping, she wept. The two entwined in dreams of loss that haunted her throughout the night.

Aelfgyth came in the morning with fresh water, more food, frowns of concern, wobbly smiles and—wonder of wonders—several books. She herself carried the books, unwilling to trust them to the lesser servants who had brought yet more food and water as well as their own curious, worried glances. When they had departed, Aelfgyth set the books on the table with tremendous care, then breathed a sigh of relief as she stepped back.

"His lordship handed them to me just as I was on my way up the stairs, otherwise I would have gotten Edvard to carry them. I never thought to touch a book in my life and heaven knows I don't ever want to do so again. What if I bent a page somehow or left a smudge? But there his lordship was, pressing them into my hands and telling me to bring them up to you." Aelfgyth shook her head somberly. "I must say, the poor man doesn't look well. I warrant he didn't sleep a wink." She peered at her mistress to see how this news was received but Krysta was too distracted by the books.

He had sent her books. After damning her and locking her away, he had sent her objects more valuable to her than jewels, and apparently trusted her to look after them properly. She turned away quickly lest the finely turned leather covers be stained by her tears.

"Oh, there, now," Aelfgyth clucked. "Everything will be all right, you'll see. The Hawk's not one to stay angry and he's good to his word. If you look out the window, you'll see the fastest ship he has setting sail for Sciringesheal. Your half-brother is leaving, too, but I don't think he's going to enjoy the trip. Word is his crew has already put him in irons, judging Lord Wolf will only reward them for it."

"Do you really think that will matter?" Krysta asked.

The question surprised Aelfgyth. "How not? The dowry must be paid, it's only proper, and Lord Wolf will see to that. Lord Hawk doesn't blame you for the delay, not really, or he never would have sent the books."

"But the dowry is only part of it," Krysta said slowly. "What of the story my half-brother told?"

"About you being a changeling?" Aelfgyth blushed at her boldness. "It's true everyone is talking about that. All agree he isn't anywhere near as good a teller of tales as the Lord Dragon. Why, I believed *his* story about the Irish lord and his bride from the sea. So did most folks. Sends a shiver down your back, doesn't it, to think such a thing could be? But no one actually expects to meet someone like that, not in real life."

"You mean . . . it couldn't have to do with me?"

"Of course not." Aelfgyth grinned at the thought. "Although Dreadful Daria is tearing about, moaning about demons and all manner of nonsense. The more she spouts it, the less anyone believes."

So because the people of Hawkforte knew her, and because they both knew and despised Daria, Krysta was rendered innocent. Even as she marveled at that, Aelfgyth went on. "It's only natural to be nervous about marrying, or so I'm told. And of course you don't want to go to your husband without a dowry, what woman would? But it will all sort itself out, as Lord Hawk said."

For a brief moment, Krysta thought of confiding the truth—that the story might not be false, that there was more to the "real" world than Aelfgyth wanted to believe, that it might be fundamentally wrong for her to marry Lord Hawk for reasons that had nothing to do with the missing dowry. But she kept silent, unwilling to burden the young woman and to expose so deep and painful a part of herself.

Aelfgyth went away a short time later, trailing behind her reminders to eat, to rest, and not to worry. She would be back in just a few hours, she could stay with Krysta if she was lonely and wanted company, she could bring more amusements. When the door finally closed behind her, Krysta breathed a small sigh of relief. Much as she appreciated Aelfgyth's concern, the strain of concealing her true fears was difficult to bear. Alone, she did not have to conceal anything, including how touched she was that Hawk had sent the books.

She did not open them at once but sat at the table, running her fingers over the leather covers. Without the books, the long hours would quickly grow torturous. But with them . . . For the first time in her life, she had nothing to do but read. No people to care for, no responsibilities to carry out, no duties to fulfill. How very odd that she should find such freedom only in captivity.

Through all that day and the next, Krysta read. Given her choice, she would have stopped only when her sight grew so blurred and her head so heavy that she had no alternative but to sleep. But Aelfgyth came with food, spotted an untouched tray, and sternly stood over Krysta until she was satisfied her mistress had eaten. She came again with hot water, the effort of heating and carrying it up the stairs being more than Krysta could ignore. The bath was welcome and she felt the better for it, but she sped back to the books as soon as she was dry. She read the psalms, delighting in the beauty of their poetry, savoring the stories they revealed, wondering at the men who had first written them. She plowed through Augustine, struggling to understand him, going back over and over to dwell on passages that eluded her. And Boethius—Hawk had even sent the book he himself had been reading. In it were notes carefully written in the margins giving Alfred's thoughts on the work he had translated. On and on she read as the second day blended into the third. Morning had turned to afternoon when she heard through the open windows the peal of a signal horn announcing the arrival of noble guests. Carefully setting down her book, she went to see who they might be. Her tower perch was too high for her to do more than make out the royal insignia waving from the banners carried by the equerries. But that was enough to shatter the strange peace of the last several days and remind her that the problems of the world were never to be denied for very long.

Day had fled when Hawk came. She heard his step outside the tower door before the iron lock opened. He stood for a moment at the threshold, garbed in black shot through with gold, gold again at his neck and on the powerful muscles of his upper arms, gold in the glint of his hair shining in the light of the braziers. Krysta sat curled on the bed, wearing only a shift for she had expected no visitor save faithful Aelfgyth. She started when she saw him but resisted the urge to reach for a cover.

He turned, closed the door behind him, turned again to face her. She heard him clear his throat. "You are well?"

Despite the books, she had braced herself for some admonishment. His concern surprised her. "Fine, thank you, and thank you also for the books. That was very kind."

He looked a little embarrassed. "You are not accustomed to doing nothing. I thought it best if you had some activity."

"It is true, the days would be very long without diversion."

He nodded, standing with his hands tucked behind his back. Silence drew out between them. Before it became unbearable, Hawk's gaze lit on the table where the latest tray Aelfgyth had brought stood barely touched.

"Your maid says you aren't eating."

Was that why he had come? Krysta wondered. Silently, she chided Aelfgyth for having said such a thing and for planting such worry in Hawk's mind.

"I most certainly am eating. If it appears I'm not, it's because my maid insists on bringing me meals five and six times a day. If I ate even half of what she sets before me, I'd look like the Christmas goose in short order."

He started to laugh, caught himself and stopped, and continued to look at her sternly. "Be that as it may, you still aren't eating meat."

"I've never eaten meat," Krysta corrected.

"I would you do so. You cannot be healthy without it."

"Do you think me sickly and a weakling? I assure you I am not."

"Not now, but you will be if you do not eat properly. A good slab of beef, that's what you need, nice and rare, plenty of juice to strengthen your blood. I'll tell Aelfgyth to—"

"Nay, do not! I swear I could not swallow such a thing. If you try to compel me, I will be ill."

"You exaggerate, but if you must be so finicky, I'll tell her to see it is cooked more, although that is a waste of good beef. Even so, you will eat it."

"Hawk, truly I cannot! Please believe me."

"Such a fuss over a little beef . . ." He paused, eyeing her. "I suppose I might be persuaded to relent."

She was aware suddenly of her heart beating very fast. "How . . . persuaded?"

"I have been summoned to court. Come with me."

Her mind stumbled over that. Surely he did not mean . . . "To Alfred's court?"

"It is the only one of consequence. You will enjoy it. There are more books, interesting people, all manner of diversions."

He was there before her, looking utterly solid and real, yet the words he spoke made no sense. Bewildered, she shook her head. "How can I possibly come with all that stands between us?"

He ran a hand through his hair, unsettling it. She wished she could smooth it back and had to stop herself from doing so. "Nothing stands between us but what you have put there," he declared. "There is naught but your own imaginings." He looked at her closely. "Unless you merely seek some excuse to prevent this marriage."

"No! How can you accuse me of that? It is only your

own good I look to. You must marry a lady and one without any taint of . . . of anything."

"Of magick. Say it, Krysta, do not deny the word for
it is of that you speak. Of magick and all the nonsense
swirling around it, of pixies and elves and little people, of
shape changers and changeling babies and even skelkies,
that's what they're called, isn't it? Granted, you swim ad-
mirably well, but I have lain with you and you are as
purely natural as I could ever hope a woman to be."

She straightened up on the bed, on her knees, heedless of how her movement drew the shift more tightly
around her. Her hair tumbled in glistening disarray down
her back. Green fire like that caught in emeralds burned
in her eyes. "You need not remind me of what passed between us! I remember it all too well. Indeed, the memory
taunts me, for now I know the full extent of what can
never be, even if you will not accept it. How is it I have a
greater care for your honor and well-being than you do
yourself? Have you thought of that? In your wisdom,
great Hawk of Essex, do you know the reason for that?"

He shrugged broad shoulders and a flash of tenderness passed over his rugged features. "I suppose because
you love me."

She choked, struggled to breathe, emerged from a
moment of panic to stare at him aghast. "I do not!"

"Krysta, delude yourself with tales of fantasy if you
must, but do not lie."

"I'm not, I'm not!" Hot tears flowed down her
cheeks, "Oh, God, I am! Curse you. I love you! I should
not, cannot, but it does not matter. I lost my mother, my
father, my home. I can lose you and survive."

He took a step nearer to the bed, even held out a hand
to her, but he caught himself and let it fall. He was there
to challenge, not to comfort. To win rather than console.
"And beyond that, more than mere survival, can you do
that, too?"

"Damn you!"

"As I damned you in the hall when you said we would not wed. But, sweet lady, it is not for you to decide. You will come with me to Winchester, to the king, and we will see what fate holds for both of us."

"And if I will not?"

"Your half-brother gave you to me as servant, slave, whatever I desire. You *will* come, Krysta. As I stand before you, so shall it be."

Never, Hawk of Essex!

The words remained unspoken. He could compel her, as she knew full well. He could take her to Winchester as he had sent Sven to Vestfold, in irons if necessary. Her pride rebelled and her curiosity was caught, a potent combination made more potent still by her simple longing to be with him.

To Winchester and the king. The scholar-king of books and learning. The valiant warrior against the Danes and all the ravages they represented. The hope of peace . . . and love.

To Winchester then and fate be damned.

TWELVE

WIND FILLED THE SAILS OF THE LONG-
ships passing through the strait to the
south of the port of Hamtun. There where
the rivers Test and Itchen joined, just opposite the diamond-shaped island with the ridge of chalk
running like a backbone along its breadth, the water took
on a hard chop. For once, Krysta had no wish to be at the
rudder, glad simply to watch Hawk as he expertly maneuvered their vessel between the pebbly shore of the main-
land and the chalky cliffs of the nearby island. Sunlight
glinted off the thick mane of his hair. When he smiled, his
teeth flashed brightly against his burnished skin. He was
shirtless, wearing only breeches for even out on the water
the late summer afternoon was pleasantly warm.

For three days they had sailed on fair winds, anchor-
ing only at night. For three days she had watched the
passing countryside with its verdant valleys, plentiful
rivers, and rolling chalk downs. For three days she had
done her utmost not to think of the man who was never far
from her side. Not once had he mentioned her confession
of loving him, nor had he spoken again of her belief that

they could not wed. He seemed intent on ignoring both, yet she wondered if what seemed to be lack of concern or interest wasn't instead the workings of a master strategist.

He touched her, never carnally or romantically, but lightly and even seeming impersonally, the strength of his hand on her arm to steady her when the boat rocked, the quick stroke of his finger along her cheek to brush away spray, the pressure of his leg against hers as they sat together, on and on through each day in myriad tiny contacts that kept her constantly on edge and aware of him. And then there were the nights . . . Hawk insisted on sleeping beside her, pointing out that there was very little sleeping space on the vessel and what there was, everyone had to share. He made her concern sound silly, as though there could be no conceivable reason why she would object. To be fair, he did not touch her at night, but each morning she woke mortified to find herself curled against him, saved from humiliation only because he slept deeply and seemed unaware of her weakness.

And weakness it was, of that she had no doubt, like sweet wine flowing through her veins and fogging her mind. A hundred times, nay a thousand, she caught herself staring at him. The beauty of land and sea, great as it was, could not hold her, but the beauty of the man proved a compulsion she could not resist. He was so perfectly formed, so ideally male, so innately graceful. It was all so easy to remember how he felt in her arms and in her body. . . .

Krysta groaned and turned her head away but not before Hawk heard her. "Something wrong?" he asked pleasantly. She murmured in the negative but that did not satisfy him. "Are you sure? The water's gotten rough. You're not feeling nauseated, are you?"

His cheerful solicitude made her frown. "I don't get seasick."

"Anyone can, you know. I did myself one time when

we hit a squall somewhere way the hell off the coast of
Gaul. There wasn't a man on board who wasn't emptying
up his guts. Why, the deck was slippery with it, and the
smell— Oh, I'm sorry, that's probably not the best story
to tell right now when you aren't feeling well."

"I'm feeling perfectly fine! Or I was until you chose to
share your charming reminiscences."

He adopted an expression of such blatantly false repentance that it would not have gulled a newborn lamb.
"Forgive me, I'm not used to having a woman on board
ship. It's too easy to forget."

"You *forgot* I am a woman?" If she gave him a really
hard shove, was there a chance she could knock him over-
board?

"Not forgot exactly. It's just that you fit in so well.
You don't talk a lot or complain about the food. You do
not need any special treatment. Believe me," he added
hastily, "I mean that as a compliment."

"And to think people laud the Dragon of Landsende
for his way with women. I'm amazed it isn't you they go
on about instead."

"Well, that's nice of you to say but . . ."

"I wasn't saying it!"

"Now don't get upset. Just because I won't let you
steer right now—"

"I don't want to steer!"

"You're getting emotional. It's probably from being
cooped up. You'll feel better when we get to Winchester.
You'll be in the company of other women, you can sit
around and do needlework, gossip, that sort of thing."

"You know, I'd be willing to bet one of these oars
could put a really big dent in your skull."

He raised an eyebrow. "You think so? I wouldn't be
so sure. It's pretty thick." He allowed her several moments to struggle against uttering the obvious response,
then burst out laughing. The look he gave her was boldly

male and sent a shiver straight down to her toes. "On top
of everything else, you're fun to tease."

"Everything else?" Disgruntled, she couldn't help
adding, "You mean besides being just like one of your
men?"

Hawk grinned. He leaned over and dropped his voice
to a gravelly murmur. "Sweetheart, if that's what you
think, we need to find another nice, secluded beach. Or
better yet a large bed someplace where no one will disturb
us for a very long time."

The fiery red of her cheeks was due to the sun, Krysta
told herself, nothing more. He did not have the power to
make her blush with just a few well-chosen words. She
was not some callow maiden overawed by the great Lord
Hawk. No, she was some callow *former* maiden overawed
by . . . She sighed and gave her attention to the sea. He
watched her for a few moments, then chuckled and did
the same.

T HEY RODE INTO WINCHESTER AS THE SUN WAS SET-
ting, their horses having come ashore from the long-
boat that accompanied them bearing the animals and
more men from Hawk's personal guard. Krysta's first
glimpse of the royal city stole her breath. Hawk had told
her it was far larger than his own burgh but she hadn't really imagined what that meant. Now riding up the broad-
est, straightest road she had ever seen toward massive
stone walls surrounded by a vast double ditch into which
it looked whole armies of men could vanish, she struggled
to absorb what she was seeing. By the fading glow of the
sun added to the light of high torches set every few yards,
everything appeared new or almost new, the stone of the
walls still showing the sharp white marks of chisels, the
heavy oak gates bearing the pale sheen of young wood.

"Alfred rebuilt Winchester," Hawk said. He rode by

her side, garbed in black, adorned with gold, a figure of undoubted power and authority. Behind him, the men of his guard rode in strict formation, the hawk-emblazoned banners flying from their upright spears. "The Danes sacked the town during the reign of his father. It was left no more than a burned-out shell."

"He has done a great deal of building, hasn't he? Or inspired it."

"Alfred has many faces. War leader, to be sure, and king above all. But he loves to build, is fascinated by even the smallest details. He has a rare gift for organization and it shows in all he does."

A moment later, as they passed through the main gate, Krysta saw what Hawk meant. The city was laid out as though on a grid, with a long wide street running from the central gate all the way to the far end and the king's own residence. Along that road were side streets leading off in opposite directions. Around the inside of the great wall was another broad road linking all the gates. Everywhere she looked, she saw houses, some grand and some much simpler, jostled together along with shops of every description and stalls selling all manner of goods. Despite all this, it was the people who surprised her most. Even at that hour, there were so many of them out and about, thronging the roads, hurrying in and out of the houses and shops, haggling with the stall keepers. In a single glance, she saw men and woman of nobility as well as peasants, scholars, priests, and monks. Along with their animals, they created a din, not to mention an odor, unlike any she had ever encountered before.

Hawk glimpsed her wrinkled nose and laughed. "You'll get used to it. Besides, Alfred's residence is generally downwind from the worst of this."

"I hope so," Krysta murmured. Courtesy forbade her from saying more but privately she already longed for the fresh sea breezes of Hawkforte. Which was a foolish thing to do since she had no idea what would happen to her or where she would go when she finally convinced Hawk that they could not wed. She had no doubt that he would ultimately see the implacable sense of that, for she believed no man who had fought so valiantly, endured so determinedly, and achieved so greatly would be willing to risk all for a tainted wife. And if he did not come to see what must not be, she would have to be strong enough to see it for them both, no matter that the seeing shattered her heart.

If she continued with such thoughts she would weep, and she determinedly cleared her head of worry as they approached the very threshold of the royal court. Hawk dismounted, came around to her horse, and held out his arms for her. He lifted her from the saddle before she could demur, took her hand in his, and led her up the steps to the mead hall of the king.

Torchlight reflected off the hundreds of hammered shields hung along the walls, rendering vivid the hues of battle banners descending from the high-timbered ceiling, and revealing the curious faces of the lords and ladies who turned to see the new arrivals. Belatedly, Krysta realized they had come at such an hour when the royal court was gathered to sup. She was suddenly very glad that her hand was in Hawk's and that it was he who walked beside her, for elsewise she doubted she could muster the courage to enter so august a company. Never had she seen folk more lavishly dressed. Even the young pages serving at the long tables were garbed in velvet. But it was not the raiment that struck her most. Rather it was the swift, all-encompassing, and knowing glances of men and women more worldly and sophisticated than any she had ever met before.

At the center of that court—and at the center of the high table—sat the man responsible for it all, the king already called Alfred the Great. Krysta was surprised to see a man of seemingly ordinary appearance, his height no more than moderate, his hair brown and worn to his shoulders, a neatly trimmed beard obscuring the lower part of his face. It was only as she drew closer that she spied the keen intelligence in his eyes and saw to her great relief the ready smile that curved an unexpectedly sensual mouth.

"Hawk!" The king rose from his seat, went around the table, and embraced the man who was clearly his friend as well as his subject. "You must have had good winds to get here so quickly."

"I assumed you commanded them, my lord," Hawk said lightly.

Alfred laughed and turned his gaze to Krysta. "And this lovely lady must be . . ."

"The Lady Krysta of Vestfold." Hawk squeezed her hand rather more firmly than was absolutely necessary. "My betrothed."

"Of course, how good of you to bring her. You are most welcome, my dear. I had hoped for an opportunity to meet you. Your journey here was pleasant, I trust?"

As he spoke, Alfred took her hand from Hawk's and with great courtesy led her to the high table. Already servants had hastened to bring forth additional chairs and place them on either side of the king's and that of his queen, a plump and pleasant woman named Eahlswith, with whom he was said to be well content, not in the least because she had brought him peace with the Mercians. Acutely aware that she was the target of all eyes, Krysta was deeply grateful for the queen's kind smile. She sank into the chair beside Eahlswith, wishing she could as easily have sunk into the floor.

That was not to be. Even as she struggled to respond to the queen's quiet remarks and engage in the conversation that was obviously expected of her, Krysta dared a glance at Hawk. He looked very much at his ease seated beside the king and in high good humor as well. He was entirely at home in such surroundings, hardly surprising since she knew he visited Winchester often. . . . Certainly often enough to have realized that the timing of their arrival would place them foursquare before the court and destroy any chance for Krysta to remain anonymous. Although she managed to maintain her smile and nod courteously at whatever it was the queen was saying, inwardly she felt the pull of despair. Once again, he had arranged matters to his own liking but it was she who would have to deal with the consequences.

That dark thought weighed her down, yet the excitement of her surroundings made it impossible for her to sink into gloom. As minstrels sang and strummed their lyres, and witty sallies darted around the table, a parade of exquisitely fashioned dishes passed before her. Perhaps sensing her unease, Eahlswith quietly suggested several Krysta might find appealing and showed no particular surprise upon hearing her soft admission that she did not eat meat. The queen had five living children, as she told Krysta, and she was by nature motherly. Before very long, Krysta found herself relaxing at least enough to draw her first easy breath since entering the great hall.

But her relative ease did not last long for as her gaze drifted over the glittering assembly, she met the stone-hard stare of a beautiful woman seated not far from the high table. The lady was perhaps a year or two older than Krysta, magnificently garbed in velvet emblazoned with jewels, and endowed with hair so light it appeared spun of moonbeams. Her face was oval, her features dainty and perfectly formed, and her skin as smooth as fresh milk. Seeing Krysta looking at her, the lady tilted her head slightly to one side with poised grace and stared down her pretty, freckleless nose.

Her obvious disdain embarrassed Krysta, who felt as though she had been caught gawking. She looked away quickly but not before noting the men seated to either side of the lady. They, too, looked at Krysta with unmistakable contempt.

"Lord Udell," the queen said quietly as she took note of the silent exchange. "And Lord Wolscroft. That is Udell's sister, Lady Esa, between them." Eahlswith hesitated a moment before she offered gentle counsel. "You must not be troubled by Udell and Esa. Whatever they may wish people to believe, there was never any clear understanding of a marriage."

"Marriage?" The word emerged as little more than a croak, so startled was Krysta.

"Oh, dear," Eahlswith murmured, "perhaps I should not have said anything. Or perhaps it is best you know after all. Not that there is anything to know, really. Only that Udell and Esa would have liked to make an alliance with Lord Hawk. Esa fancied he would marry her but there has never been any indication Hawk himself really considered it."

Despite the queen's reassurances, Krysta's heart plunged. She glanced again at the lovely Esa and knew in an instant she must be looking at the woman Daria had described as a lady of true nobility and worth whom Hawk had wanted to marry. She was as beautiful as any woman could ever hope to be, as well as graceful, elegant, and poised. No doubt she also had a respectable dowry and a family proud to claim her. No wonder Esa looked upon her with contempt. She must regard her as having stolen her own proper position.

Crestfallen, she stole a quick look at Hawk but he was deep in conversation with the king and a priest who sat at Hawk's other side. They were talking animatedly about something or other. So far as Krysta could tell, Hawk appeared unconcerned by the presence of the woman who had expected to marry him. Nor did it appear that he gave her any notice throughout the evening. Instead, it seemed to be Krysta who drew his attention for just as she realized how tired she was, Hawk said a quiet word to the king, who spoke in turn to the queen, who summoned several servants.

"Forgive me, my dear," Eahlswith said, "I have so enjoyed talking with you that I've overlooked how weary you must be from your journey. Quarters have been prepared for you. Do get a good rest." She gave Krysta an affectionate smile. "I believe my husband has plans for an excursion tomorrow and you are invited along."

Hardly hearing that last part, Krysta murmured her thanks. Hawk rose as she did and accompanied her from the hall. At the foot of the stairs leading to the guest quarters, he took her hand and touched it lightly to his lips. His eyes, meeting hers, were watchful. "Sleep well."

She nodded although she believed there was very little chance of that. She hardly noticed that the room to which she was shown was as luxurious as that which she occupied at Hawkforte. A smiling young maid did her best to make up for the absence of Aelfgyth, who had remained gratefully at home with her Edvard. When Krysta had bathed and donned a shift, the maid brushed out her hair, then took her leave. Left alone, Krysta sat at the window for a few minutes, listening to the sounds of revelry still floating up from the great hall. But before long, they began to lessen. Her head felt very heavy. She made her way to bed scant moments before sleep claimed her.

IN THE DEPTH OF THE NIGHT, KRYSTA AWOKE. TURNING over in the bed, instinctively reaching for the warmth and strength to which she had become accustomed, she encountered only emptiness. It was enough to drive her from her dreams. She sat upright, looking around with some confusion until she remembered where she was. Realized, too, why she had awakened. With a small sigh at her own indiscretion, she hugged her knees and tried to convince herself that she could go back to sleep. Her effort failed. Instead, she left the bed and padded back to the windows from which she could look out over the town below. As at Hawkforte, the walls were manned. Torches blazed along them and she could see the guards walking back and forth. Otherwise, it seemed as though everyone slumbered save herself. The lamps were extinguished in the houses and shops, the cooking fires well banked.

Yearning for some distraction, she looked around the room. The stone floor was covered with woven rush mats instead of the more usual loose rushes. The walls were paneled with wood set in intricate designs. Along one wall hung a tapestry depicting huntsmen pursuing a wild boar. As she was admiring it, Krysta noticed a door set in the wood paneling that she had overlooked previously. Surprised, she tried the latch and was yet further startled when the door swung out into an adjoining room.

Hawk heard the door open and went very still. Under ordinary circumstances, even here in the residence of the king, his hand would have sought the sword never far from his side. But he knew who had been given the adjoining room because Alfred's steward, spiritual kin to the redoubtable Edvard, had told him so. The man had mentioned it matter-of-factly as Hawk was retiring for the night, thereby giving evidence of the skill and discretion he brought to his position. That such thoughtfulness had been shown him did not surprise Hawk. Alfred, for all his genuine piety, was a man who had struggled in his youth with what he regarded as excessive love of women. In marriage he found the reconciling of passion and piety, and was a happy man for it but he had not forgotten how hot the blood could run.

Unmoving, eyes shut, he listened to Krysta's soft footsteps as she crossed the room. She came hesitantly, pausing several times, and once she seemed to turn back, only to reverse herself. At the side of the bed, he heard the sudden agitation of her breath and had to fight against a smile. The night was warm, he slept nude and without covers. The knowledge that she was looking at him swiftly began to have the predictable effect and he wondered how long he would be able to maintain the pretense of sleep. A soft sigh escaped her and it tugged at his heart. He knew that the seduction he contemplated was reprehensible, but he told himself it was all for an honorable end—that she should marry him—and besides, he had never hesitated to take advantage of any weakness in battle. That this was combat of a sort he did not doubt. He merely salved his conscience with the thought that he intended neither of them to lose.

Even so, he found himself hard-pressed to remain unmoving as he felt the whisper touch of her fingers gently easing aside a lock of hair that had fallen across his brow. She sighed again and this time there was a little catch to her voice that sounded suspiciously like a sob. He clenched his hands into the mattress to keep from reaching out for her and hoped she would not notice.

Krysta did not, engulfed as she was in a riptide of emotion. Not even she could swim against so strong a current as seized her the moment she saw him lying on the bed, his splendid body fully revealed to her. That current had drawn her into the room, to his very side, and even to touch him against all her better sense. She had to leave. *Had to.* Yet there she stood as though frozen, fighting the urge to touch him yet again. To let drop her shift and ease onto the bed beside him. To trace the chiseled line of his mouth with her fingers and twist within them the silken curls of his hair. To run her hands over his powerful shoulders and along the contours of his heavily muscled chest, over all that taut, burnished skin. To twine her legs around his and tease her toes down his sinewy calves. To move between his thighs and gently cup him in her palms, to taste him as he had tasted her . . .

Krysta lifted the heavy mane of her hair with both hands, baring her neck as she stretched languorously. It was very hot in the room. She could scarcely bear even the light brush of her shift against her taut nipples. If only she could flee into deep, cool water, there would be some hope of taming the unruly impulses of her body. As it was, to stay longer was sheer folly. Not daring to look at him again, knowing that if she did she would have no prayer of caution, Krysta took one step from the bed. Her shift jerked taut and she could move no farther. Her eyes widened as she saw the hand twined around the delicate fabric, tethering her. Startled, her gaze flew to Hawk's face. A slumberous smile curved the mouth she knew too well.

"Don't go," he said, just that, no more. Yet he kept close hold of her as desire warred with prudence.

"I should not have come . . ."

He sat up slightly and her helpless gaze strayed down the length of his body. He was fully aroused, hard and thick.

"You slept curled against me these past three nights. Why sleep alone now?"

"You weren't supposed to know about that! I thought you asleep each morning when I woke—"

"I sleep very lightly, the legacy of too many battles." He let go of her shift and seized her hand instead. His conscience stirred one last time and was firmly pushed aside. Little experience that he had wooing women, somehow with her it did not seem so difficult. "Sweet Krysta, don't leave me now. Who knows how much time we may have together. The world is so uncertain, life itself but a moment." He brushed a kiss over her fingers even as he wrapped an arm around her hips and drew her to him. She pressed her hands to his broad shoulders in a halfhearted effort to break away but he was already pulling up her shift, baring her long, lithe legs, and she felt his mouth against her belly, his breath blowing softly, melting away all resistance.

Time was fleeting; he was right about that. The past was gone, the future she yearned for could not be, nothing existed save the present. Was it so terribly wrong of her to seize just a small measure of happiness? She had a sudden flashing image of Lady Esa and her cool, disdainful beauty. Would she be the one Hawk married finally, the lady of true nobility and worth chosen to sit at his side? Perhaps, for she was very lovely and, even to Krysta's inexperienced eyes, very determined.

If it came to that, one thing only she wanted so fiercely that it tore like barbs at her heart: Let him not forget her. When he was a very old man, as she prayed he would live to be, let him still remember the touch and taste, the sound and feel of her. Let the memory of what they shared make bright his dreams forever . . . and her own.

He felt the moment when she yielded and the triumph of it was bittersweet. He had won unscrupulously to be sure but he could not, would not, let that matter. Swiftly, he stripped her shift over her head and tossed it to the floor. Her skin glowed like cool alabaster but her heat matched his own. He drew her down, draping her over him, stroking her slender back and firmly rounded bottom. His long fingers delved between her thighs as his mouth took hers in a searing kiss. Ravenously, he tasted her, his tongue stroking deep and hard, mating with her own. His need for her was insatiable, made all the more so by three days and nights of incessant, unsatisfied desire. He could think of nothing but to ease her beneath him and make her his when Krysta twisted suddenly in his arms. With the provocative smile of an innocent imp, she sat up, straddling him, and tossed the glorious riot of her hair over her shoulders, baring her breasts to his bedazzled gaze. Her eyes filled with tender yearning, she stroked her hands lightly down his chest. Her voice no more than a soft, embarrassed whisper, she murmured, "Please . . . I would so like to . . ."

With a groan, Hawk fell back onto the bed. Already he was painfully aroused and if the look in her eyes was any indication, his torment had only just begun. Her innocent passion tantalized him even as he doubted how much more he could endure.

Yet he tried as his heart hammered savagely in his chest and his blood ran thick and hot. She was an artless temptress, delighted by her own boldness, glorying in his response. She explored him with light, flickering touches of her hands and mouth, with leisurely caresses and hungry kisses, with every part of her body and every inch of her warm, silken skin. Nor was she silent. Soft little sounds of pleasure escaped her, surprised exclamations of delight that filled him with bemused pride and mocked the control he maintained by no more than the most slender of threads.

Beads of sweat shone on his forehead when she rose above him, a sweetly seductive smile curving her lush mouth and a shy question in her eyes. He saw it, clasped her hips, and gently guided her onto him. Her stunned surprise gave way to a moan of delight. Slowly, tantalizingly, she drew him within her. When he was fully seated, his fingers entwined with hers as with innate grace she began to move. He watched, enthralled, as her skin flushed with the intensity of her arousal, her nipples firm buds beckoning to his mouth.

To her pleasure-drenched senses, this was almost too much. Krysta cried out as he suckled her, waves of ecstasy coiling within her, tighter and tighter still until they exploded suddenly in an incandescent burst that seemed to last forever. She fell against him, limp and gasping. The world revolved suddenly and she found herself beneath him. His chiseled features were tautly drawn, his eyes shining as he loomed above her. He drove himself within her harder and faster, over and over. Without reprieve, she was hurled again into dark, swirling release. A moment later, he joined her, clasping her tightly to him as though he meant never to let her go.

It was not enough. They woke again before dawn already entwined, hands and lips seeking, and made love more slowly this time, drawing out their pleasure. Afterward, they fell into sleep so deep that not even the usual morning noises of the royal residence bestirred them. Only when the full din of the busy town, all the clatter and creaking, calling and haggling, the sharp-barked orders of guardsmen and the merry song of minstrels floated through their windows did they finally return groggily and reluctantly to the world.

Even then only the sternest discipline enabled them to rise without yielding to the temptation of scattered touches and long looks. Even as Krysta stumbled into her own room, wrapped in a sheet, the maid who had served her the night before knocked once perfunctorily, then entered. Her eyes widened and her cheeks were suddenly rosier than they had been a moment before, but she said nothing. Setting down the tray she had brought, she bobbed a curtsy and swiftly drew out garments appropriate for the day. When a shirtless Hawk, his jaw festooned with soap and a shaving blade in his hand, stuck his head in a few minutes later to remind Krysta they were going with the king, the maid turned a fiery red and so overpoured the milk that it flowed right out of the bowl, across the table, and down onto the floor. Krysta sighed and knelt to help her clean it up despite her protests, knowing all too well how easy it was to be utterly unsettled by the Hawk of Essex.

For certain, she had been, and worse yet, she could not find it in herself to mind. Indeed, it was proving most difficult not to smile at every moment. She was giddily happy, beyond care, and quite besotted with the world and the man.

She was dressed and had even managed to eat a little before it occurred to her to wonder what Alfred had planned. That the great king was no more than an afterthought made her all the more mindful of her precarious state, and caused her to resolve that come what may, she must find some way to conceal it. She was still mulling over how that might be accomplished when Hawk came to get her. He swept a quick, all-encompassing glance over her, the look of a man well pleased with what he sees, and combined it with the heart-stopping grin of a boy.

"We're shamefully late," he said, with a quick nod to the flustered maid. "Fortunately, there's always something for Alfred to do so I doubt he'll mind."

He swept her out of the room and down the stairs before she could even begin to gather her thoughts. The great hall was empty save for a few servants, reminding her again that much of the morning was already gone. Outside, the day was brilliant, a fresh breeze swaying the branches of the young trees within the royal compound. Hawk led her briskly to a stone building set a little apart, surrounded by a pleasant garden that bestowed an air of serenity unusual in bustling Winchester. A quick glance through the open double doors confirmed Krysta's guess that this was a church. They followed a path around a corner of the building and the scene changed suddenly. Where there had been serenity suddenly there was activity. Several dozen monks sat outside at tables positioned beside linen screens cleverly set to block the wind and any dust or dirt that might blow with it. Thus sheltered, they had the blessing of bright sunlight to do their work. And what work it was. Krysta gasped softly when she realized that the monks were inscribing *books*. As young acolytes scrambled about to fill orders for more ink, more nubs, more parchment, or sat in a circle beneath a tree being instructed in the finer points of calligraphy by a master of the art, precious books were being created.

"Alfred believes he will be most remembered for restoring learning to this land," Hawk said quietly. "He says this is so because the peace he has brought will not survive without learning, so it is that which is most important in the end." He gestured toward a complex of buildings some little distance from the scriptorium. "Our nobles vie to foster their sons with the king even though he requires that they spend a portion of each day in study. There are many still who do not see the sense of that or who think it somehow unmanly, yet they will not gainsay Alfred. The most cloddish of them leaves here with at least a smattering of Latin and more knowledge of the world than he would otherwise ever hope to have."

Krysta felt a moment's envy at the thought of what it must be like to dwell within such a place, to have at her fingertips all manner of books and people to explain them. Surely that was a touch of paradise. She looked up into Hawk's blue eyes and fought again to hold on to reason. "Dare I ask if women are also permitted to learn?"

"How did I know you would ask that?" he teased. "Some feel learned women are inclined to be discontented, unwilling to accept the authority of their fathers and husbands. Mayhap there is some justice to that, for I have not noticed you to be overly compliant."

"Mayhap you value compliance overmuch," Krysta answered. A moment later she regretted the words for they sounded like a challenge. He was a warrior and a leader. Of course, he would expect to be obeyed.

Quietly, he said, "I have accepted more disobedience from you than from anyone I can remember. Do you wonder why that is, Krysta?"

She had no time to answer for just then Alfred emerged from the scriptorium accompanied by the priest he and Hawk had been conversing with the preceding evening. Catching sight of the newly arrived couple, they came over to them.

"There you are," Alfred said. He appeared in good humor and more, all but bubbling over with enthusiasm that belied the gravity of his position. "My dear," he said to Krysta, "I don't believe you have met my good friend, Father Asser, the long-suffering soul who undertook to instruct me in Latin."

The priest smiled and inclined his head to Krysta. "My lady, well met. I assure you, however, that the task was not so onerous as our king would have you believe."

"He flatters me," Alfred said. "It's because I built this scriptorium and others like it around the land. He plans to flood Wessex with books and I am his willing accomplice."

"I would flood the world with books if I could find a way to do it," the priest acknowledged. "Indeed, I have lately turned my own poor hand to writing a history of the present reign."

Alfred sighed good-naturedly. "So now I must be especially good to him, as all anyone is likely to know of me in years hence is what he deigns to write."

"I rather think people will remember one or two other things, my lord," Hawk said dryly.

Father Asser laughed. "Listen to him, my lord. He is young and vigorous, and much more attuned to the ways of the world than an old penitent such as myself."

"Don't wrap your years around you too closely quite yet," Alfred cautioned. "I have much use for you, my friend. You have only begun to do your work."

"May it please Lord God that is so," the priest said matter-of-factly. He turned to Krysta and surveyed her with frank interest. "Lord Hawk tells me you can read."

Alfred, too, appeared to find this curious but not displeasing. "How did you learn?" he asked pleasantly.

In the presence of the priest, Krysta hesitated to answer, but she realized she could hardly decline to do so. "When I was very small, a monk came to my father's holding in Vestfold. He asked permission to speak of Christ to the people there. My father was disquieted by this, he thought it might bring trouble, but on the other hand he did not want to offend the monk in case it came to be that his god truly was powerful. So he sent the monk to me. Brother Malcolm stayed with us some ten years. He preached the gospel to great effect and he also taught me to read." She hesitated again, seeing how this was taken. When it appeared that neither king nor priest was disturbed by the tale, she added, "As he believed I had some aptitude, he decided I should also learn to write and to cipher." When this, too, did not seem to shock more than a little, she finished. "He also taught me Latin."

"Latin?" Alfred exclaimed. Now he truly did look at her as though she were some species of being he had never before encountered. "You read Latin?"

"I am fortunate to be able to do so. Brother Malcolm was a very kind and patient teacher. When he died, we all mourned him deeply."

"Did your people heed the word of the Christ?" Father Asser asked.

Krysta nodded. "We all did, and so have many others in the years since. Even my father, toward the end of his life, saw it was not something to be afraid of but rather the hope of a better world."

"Then Brother Malcolm's years were well spent," Alfred said. "He must have been an unusual man to see the possibilities of instructing a young girl. I have always believed that a man of sound judgment builds on a modest foundation and gradually proceeds to greater things. Perhaps it would be possible to offer some simple instruction to the daughters of some of our lords and see if they are inclined to go further."

"An excellent idea, my lord," Hawk said at once and won a surprised but thoroughly approving look from Krysta. He saw it and grinned as he added, "Provided, of course, they do not shirk their womanly duties."

"We could have none of that," the king agreed. "Still, it might be possible—" He broke off, considered the matter for a few moments, then smiled apologetically. "You must forgive me. My mind always runs to how I might better accomplish the earthly tasks to which I have been set. At any rate, my dear, the first copy of a new book has just been finished, a treatise on the organization of government. I have come to view it and when I invited Hawk to accompany me, he said he thought you might like to do the same."

This was the excursion the king had in mind? How extraordinary and how telling of the man. And how kind of Hawk that he would think to include her. Just one more of his many virtues to haunt her in that arid wilderness beyond the present day, but she would not dwell on that. Greatly excited at the prospect of seeing any new book, let alone being one of the very first to see it, Krysta smiled warmly. "I would love to do that, my lord. Until I came to Hawkforte, I had seen only a very few books. Now it seems that I cannot get enough of them."

"An admirable affliction, my dear," the king said and kindly offered his arm. Hawk and Father Asser were left to follow as Alfred escorted her into the scriptorium.

It was, Krysta quickly decided, every bit as wonderful a place as she could ever have imagined. First, there were the smells. The crisp aroma of fresh parchment, the acrid scent of glue, the rich and heady fragrance of fine leather mingled with the sea-sour whiff of ink, the metallic tang of gold, and the pungent odors of ground rocks and plants mixed to make paints. She closed her eyes for a moment and breathed deeply, knowing that forever after she could be put down anywhere, smell that unique blend of essences, and know precisely where she stood.

Yet was that only the beginning. On tall wooden desks, books stood open, some in the process of being created, others completed and being read. Their colors leaped out at her, brilliant gold, blue, red, green, and black entwined in the serpentine forms of letters and also in the delicate, complex illustrations scattered throughout each work.

She was staring enraptured at a capital A constructed of intricately intertwining vines in which myriad birds perched when Hawk cleared his throat, recapturing her attention. Alfred and the priest had moved on to a table at the far end of the room where an elderly monk stood guard over the precious new book. "You have charmed the king," Hawk said lightly. "That is no small feat but I expected no less of you."

His praise warmed her but it also left her flustered. "I know nothing of charm, my lord," she said honestly. "It was not covered in my education."

"True charm cannot be taught, my lady. Perhaps it comes from an open heart and a gentle spirit."

She looked at him in frank surprise, then burst out laughing. "Forgive me, my lord, but for you of all men to call my spirit gentle . . . Did I not just yesterday suggest your skull would be the better for being dented by an oar?"

Hawk laughed as well but his eyes on her suddenly held a shadow of concern. "Better you speak your mind clearly than you bestow false smiles and hide ill-thought behind them. *That* is all too common here where power gathers, and you would do well to remember it."

His warning sobered her for already she had some sense of what he meant. The undisguised contempt of Lord Udell and his sister was not forgotten. She wondered if there were others who would resent her as readily and shivered inwardly at the thought.

Hawk's hand closed warm and strong on hers. Without further delay, they rejoined the king and Father Asser.

Chapter

THIRTEEN

THE QUEEN'S SOLAR OCCUPIED THE MIDDLE floor on the eastern side of the royal residence. It was a bright and cheery room, well suited for the constant work of weaving, sewing, and embroidering, to which even the most noble ladies were expected to devote themselves. Krysta made her way there with the help of a maid after her visit to the scriptorium. She understood that the king and Hawk had much to discuss, and though she would have liked to hear what they said, she was not surprised to find herself gently but firmly dismissed. Her natural inclination to go off alone was thwarted when Hawk excused himself for a few minutes to escort her back to the residence, and found a maid to assure him she would get where he clearly expected her to go. His reward was a bemused frown that turned into a gaze of pure longing the moment his back was turned.

As soon as Krysta stepped inside the solar, she was certain she had made a dire mistake. Several dozen ladies were gathered there, of all ages but alike in the sumptuousness of their dress. They reminded her of the glorious birds sitting on the vines of the A, each garbed in magnificent plumage and seemingly interested only in what went on beneath their noses. At the moment, that meant Krysta. Before she could draw a breath, she was pierced by gazes both curious and knowing. They froze her in place and for an awful instant she thought she would not be able to move. Then Eahlswith, that wise queen and gentle mother, saw her. The queen's smile seemed a rope thrown into a storm-tossed sea. Krysta went to her gratefully and took the seat she indicated directly beside her.

"I was hoping you would come," Eahlswith said. "You must tell us all about your visit. Is the new book everything my husband hoped?"

Several of the nearby ladies adopted expressions of polite interest but one did not. Lady Esa continued to give all her attention to the exquisite bit of embroidery she was stitching. Only the slight, sardonic curve of her lovely mouth hinted at her thoughts.

"The book is wonderful, my lady," Krysta said, ignoring Esa determinedly. "It is very well organized and clearly written, setting forth those laws King Alfred believes are essential to the good ordering of the kingdom. It is divided into three sections, the laws as they pertain to men who pray, men who work, and men who fight. The script itself is in a very able hand, much easier to read than some I have seen, and the book as a whole is magnificently illustrated with each first capital on a page done in gold and many beautiful pictures drawn throughout."

"How relieved I am to hear it," Eahlswith said, "for I vow, my dear husband cares almost as much for his books as he does for his children, and that is saying a great deal indeed."

The ladies smiled kindly, all save Esa, who rolled her eyes slightly.

Either the queen did not see her or she chose to ignore

such behavior. Krysta suspected the latter for she had already surmised that Alfred's queen was as wise in her own way as he was in his.

"What did you think of the scriptorium?" Eahlswith asked.

"I think it the most wonderful place I have ever seen," Krysta said candidly. "We were there long enough for me to read parts of several books, and the king was so kind as to say that I could borrow one."

"How wonderful that you read," the queen said. "I have thought from time to time of trying to learn, but with the children and all, I have rarely had a free moment."

Krysta nodded, imagining how very difficult it would be even for a queen to steal time from her "wifely duties."

"I was fortunate to be taught as a child."

"Fortunate?" Esa's voice was soft but carried far. Several of those in attendance perked up their ears as though this was what they had been waiting for. The lady smiled winsomely. "I would hardly call it fortunate to be raised without parents on the far edge of nowhere. From what I hear, Vestfold is a terrible place, barren and savage. No wonder you were so anxious to get here that you disguised yourself as a servant to make the trip." She looked down her lovely nose at Krysta and inquired sweetly, "That is why you adopted such an outrageous pretense, isn't it, my dear?"

Before Eahlswith could intervene, Krysta said, "No, that is not why I did it. Vestfold is far from barren. It holds a haunting beauty all its own and I was in no way anxious to leave."

"I see," Esa said, her expression making it clear she did not. "Then did you merely think it . . . *fun* to pretend to be a servant and fool the Lord Hawk?"

The other ladies tittered. This was rare entertainment and it was clear they relished it. Again, the queen looked about to break it off but Krysta forestalled her. She was not about to leave the impression that she was unable to stand up for herself.

"My reasons are my own, lady, and not to be paraded before such as you."

Esa's eyes narrowed. Her lovely mouth looked petulant. "A poor parade it would be, I am sure." She paused, giving her followers time to voice their further amusement with the same light scattering of swallowed laughter and looks of furtive humor.

"Pray excuse this," Eahlswith said. "Gossip travels on the wind and is about as useful as any chaff that does so. Unfortunately"—she pinned her gaze on Esa—"there are those among us without wit to ignore it."

At once, Esa adopted an expression of repentance. "Oh, my lady, if I have given offense I am most sorry. It is only that I am like most everyone else here, so in awe of the Lord Hawk, so appreciative of all he has done, that the mere hint of insult to him rouses me to . . . well, I would say anger were it not such an unwomanly emotion."

Krysta was having no trouble feeling that emotion herself. Her fingers twitched as she fought the urge to pick up one of the ewers of cool water standing nearby and upend it over the smirking face of the Lady Esa.

Eahlswith set aside the tunic she was stitching for her royal husband. Quietly but firmly, she said, "Lady Krysta is betrothed to Lord Hawk, their marriage a vital cornerstone of the peace our king builds between Norse and Saxon to protect us from the ravages of the Dane. Let us remember that Our Savior blessed the marriage at Cana *and* He told us that peacemakers are blessed. Therefore must we conclude that this union will be doubly worthy in His eyes."

Krysta's throat tightened. She wanted to cry out to the queen that she was wrong, there was no blessing to be had, and that Hawk must marry elsewhere for his own honor and well-being. But thankfully, no words could

escape her. She remained mute while Esa pouted rebel-
liously and resumed her embroidery with short, stabbing
pokes of the needle that seemed to add nothing whatso-
ever to the design.

When the moment had passed and the ladies returned to their sewing, Eahlswith summoned a maid. She
gave her a softly worded instruction, then resumed her
stitching. A short time later, a young monk came in nervously, clearly unaccustomed to being in the exclusive
company of women. He carried with him a book.

"If you would not mind, my dear," the queen said to
Krysta, "I thought perhaps you might read to us as we
sew. I am certain whatever may be contained within these
pages is far more elevating than mere chatter."

The monk hesitated, but under the steady stare of the
queen he reluctantly turned the book over to Krysta. She
examined it cautiously, delighted to discover that it was a
volume of the tales of a fabled Greek called Aesop.

"I have heard of these but have never read them.
They are said to be wonderful."

Eahlswith smiled encouragingly and picked up her
sewing. With great care, Krysta opened the book and began to read.

T HE REMAINDER OF THE AFTERNOON FLOWED
smoothly, at least in part because Lady Esa pleaded a
headache and departed, taking her followers with her.
With them gone, the mood in the solar seemed to ease although Krysta wasn't sure whether she only imagined
that. Certainly, she was far more relaxed.

With the men busy elsewhere, the ladies took their
midday meal together. For the first time, Krysta found
herself enjoying the company of women. She remembered
how Hawk had teased that she would feel better when she

could "sit around, do needlework, gossip . . ." and how annoyed she had been, only now to find the experience very different. Over the meal, the ladies talked about the stories Krysta had read, drawing parallels to their own lives and laughing as they did so. Some of the women were nicer than others, some wittier, but she could see something to like in each of them . . . now that Lady Esa was no longer among them.

But she would be back and no doubt she would continue to make herself as unpleasant as possible. The thought of Hawk marrying such a woman filled Krysta with dread. He deserved so much better, truly he should have nothing less than the perfect wife. Once she had foolishly hoped to be that, and would still, had love not placed such a burden upon her conscience. But surely she would not make so wrenching a sacrifice only to see him wed to a cold, hard woman unlikely to ever love anyone save herself.

Yet again, Krysta caught herself on the verge of tears. All her emotions seemed heightened, pain and pleasure vying equally, and she seemed fated to swing between one and the other. No wonder she felt vaguely nauseated, as though the meal she had eaten did not sit comfortably on her stomach. Eahlswith looked at her just then and frowned.

"My dear, are you not well?"

"I am . . . that is, I thought I was." A wave of dizziness swept over her. She shut her eyes for a moment, hoping that might help, but it did not. The queen leaned over and put her hand on Krysta's, a mother's touch, gentle but firm. "Your skin is clammy. Did you eat anything else today besides what we just had?"

Krysta shook her head. "There was no time. I slept late and then—"

Several ladies giggled suddenly and looked abashed.

A few even blushed. The queen sent them a sharp, admonishing glance but it was too late, the damage done. Krysta paled.

"You really do not look well, my dear," the queen said. She stood up and signaled to several of the maids. "Come now, you are going back to your quarters and we will see what can be done to make you more comfortable. I'm sure there is nothing to be concerned about but this is the season when such upsets are more common."

Grateful for any excuse to leave, Krysta stood up and was instantly assaulted by a fresh wave of dizziness. Still, she managed to walk with a little help from the maids. "Please don't disturb yourself," she entreated Eahlswith. "I will be perfectly fine."

"Of course you will be, my dear," the queen said. "But I am coming with you all the same."

Brushing aside any further objections, Eahlswith accompanied Krysta back to her quarters, saw her comfortably settled in bed, and insisted that she sip an infusion of chamomile. Krysta did so simply as a courtesy, but within a few minutes she had to admit she was feeling better.

"I can't imagine what came over me," she said with an apologetic smile. "I am never ill."

"I would say you have had a great deal to cope with of late. That can be unsettling."

The queen's sympathetic understanding touched Krysta greatly. She who had never known the love of a mother realized that Eahlswith must be a very good one.

"Your children are very fortunate to have you to care for them, my lady. As is your husband."

Eahlswith looked surprised by the compliment and very pleased. "Thank you, my dear. I have sometimes felt that I do not keep up well enough with all the grand and exciting doings here at court but then I console myself that my family is well and happy."

"I can think of no greater accomplishment than that," Krysta said honestly.

"One I am sure you will shortly know."

She was overly tired and still feeling ill. Her mind spun in confusion and her heart felt near to breaking. Perhaps that was why she could not repress the soft sob that broke from her as she turned her face into the pillows.

At once, Eahlsworth clucked in alarm. She gave a quick order, sending the maids from the room. When the door closed behind them, she held out her arms. Krysta went into them without a second thought.

"There, there," the queen said gently. "My poor child, you must tell me what distresses you so. I will do everything in my power to see it put to rights."

Deeply embarrassed by her display of emotion and at the same time grateful for the queen's kindness, Krysta shook her head helplessly. "I thank you, my lady, but truly I don't believe there is anything you can do."

"Oh, no?" Eahlswith gave her a very womanly smile. "I have always been a good and obedient wife. Anyone will tell you that I have never failed to defer to my husband in all matters. However, you should not think for a moment that means Alfred does not hear my views."

She sat back, gave Krysta a warm smile, and said, "Now let us see if we can get to the root of this problem. First, are you homesick?"

"Why does everyone ask me that? Or at least Hawk did. I am not homesick. My home was gone the moment I left it. My half-brother rules there now and I knew I would never want to return even presuming he would allow me, which he has made clear he will not."

"He told you that? What a dreadful thing to say. What manner of man is he that he should be so unkind?"

"An angry and resentful man who never forgave our father for taking a second wife, my mother. But in all fairness, I have to say there were . . . complications with that union."

"I am sorry to hear it but these things happen. Many men remarry after being widowed. If you are not homesick, then are you unhappy about your betrothal to Lord Hawk? It is only natural for a young girl to be concerned when she is sent to wed a stranger. I well remember my own concern when that happened to me. But truly, you have nothing to fear from Lord Hawk. He is an exemplary man."

"I know that," Krysta said. "Believe me, I hold him in the highest esteem. But it is for that very reason that I . . ." She was well aware of the import of what she was about to say. But the queen looked so kindly and understanding, and Krysta so badly needed to confide in another. "I cannot marry him."

Eahlswith stared at her for a long moment as though trying to interpret words she must certainly have misunderstood. Slowly, it dawned on her that she had not. Her eyes widened in alarm. "You cannot marry him? But child, think what that means! Your marriage is the hope for peace between our peoples. It was arranged by the king himself and the great jarl of Sciringesheal, Hawk's own brother-in-law. Believe me, I understand the burden of being wed in such a way for so was I, but you must put aside whatever fears you carry and do what is right. Far too much depends on it."

"It is because I must do what is right that I cannot marry him. Too much hinges on this marriage to take the risk that—"

"That what? Child, this is gravely serious. You must tell me everything that is in your mind that I may have some hope of understanding how you could possibly have come to such a dire conclusion."

"I may as well tell you," Krysta said, her voice very low. "Sven told everyone at Hawkforte so I suppose word of it will reach here soon enough." Quietly, without looking at the queen, she related the story of her mother. As she did so, she was certain that Eahlswith must be greatly shocked and even repelled, for surely such a tale would dismay any Christian woman.

But when she had finished, the older woman only sighed deeply and shook her head. "My poor child, what a dreadful weight to bear upon your young shoulders. But whatever the truth of it, and I would not presume to judge that, you have no reason to think you are other than a mortal woman." She put a finger beneath Krysta's chin and tilted her head up so that she had to meet her gaze. "Do you?"

Krysta thought of Raven and Thorgold, and of the glimpses she sometimes had of a world other folk did not seem to see. Softly, she said, "In all honesty, there are circumstances in my life that sometimes have made me wonder." She took a deep breath, feeling strangely calm all of a sudden with all the strength drained out of her. Wearily, she said, "I came thinking somehow I could make everything all right but I realize now how foolish that was. Hawk deserves better. Even more than that, do you truly believe any union so shadowed can be pleasing in the eyes of God, enough so to be the basis for lasting peace?"

The queen was an honest woman; she could not say what she truly did not believe. Her gentle face looked somber. "I think there are more things in God's Creation than we know and that they all serve some higher purpose. But as to the present situation, I do see now why you are so concerned. However, I counsel you to make no hasty decisions or take any intemperate action. This requires deep thought."

"I fear I have no more to give it," Krysta said and laid her head back against the pillows. Yet the queen's injunction relieved her somewhat. Though she despised herself for so weak a thought, she could not help but hope for just a little more time before she and Hawk parted.

Eahlswith's mind seemed to be running in a similar direction, for she asked, "If you believe you cannot marry and you know you cannot return to your family's lands, what then did you think to do?"

"I didn't think," Krysta admitted, "at least not until today." She took another breath, certain she was about to shock the queen yet again. Though the very thought of leaving Hawk was as a dagger in her heart, standing in the scriptorium that day a fleeting wish had come to her that if she must survive without him, she might at least be able to give her life to some useful work. It would be no consolation for the pain certain to assail her but it might at least give purpose to her otherwise empty days. "I wonder if there might be someplace for a woman who is interested in learning. Men with such an inclination may enter the priesthood or become monks. Is there anything like that for women?"

Eahlswith hesitated, clearly uncertain of how much she should say. But once more, innate honesty compelled her. "There are abbeys for women, under the rule of abbesses who often are themselves devoted to learning. So far, there are only a few such places but I have founded one myself and mean to found others." She looked at Krysta closely. "Entry to such a place would require you to take holy orders. Do you believe you could do that?"

"I don't know," Krysta said candidly, "nor do I know if any abbey would consider accepting one such as me."

"My own dear sister is abbess of the foundation I endowed. She is a most sensible woman who also possesses a kind heart. However, we leap ahead. It is far too soon to be considering any such thing." The queen paused, looking at Krysta closely. "I would counsel you to think long and hard, my dear. It is no small matter to reject marriage with a great lord and seek the sanctuary of holy orders instead. Such a step, once taken, could never be renounced."

A short while later, the queen departed with admonitions that Krysta should rest. She lay for a little time listening to the sounds of the town floating up through the windows. The light breeze was very pleasant and the room smelled prettily of dried flowers gathered in bouquets. A starling lit on the windowsill and peered at her for a moment before darting off. She was drifting in a state halfway between consciousness and dreams when the door was flung open. Hawk strode into the chamber, went directly to the bed, and grabbed hold of her. He gave her a little shake as he stared at her with stark concern.

"What's the matter with you? What's wrong?"

So startled was she by his sudden appearance that Krysta needed a moment to get her breath. "I'm fine, really. I just felt a little ill, that's all, but it was nothing—"

"What do you mean 'a little ill'? Do you have a fever?" He landed a hand on her brow. "No, you don't. What's wrong then? Does something hurt?"

Astounded by his obvious worry, Krysta strove to reassure him. "My stomach was upset, that's all." No need to mention that she was also dizzy; the man was flustered enough as it was and wasn't that amazing? Who would ever have imagined the great Hawk of Essex worried because she had a stomachache?

He shook his head, let her go abruptly, and began pacing back and forth beside the bed, all the while glowering down at her with mingled relief and exasperation. "It's because you don't eat right."

"It is not! And don't start that again. I just felt a little queasy, that's all." She almost added that having to deal with Lady Esa might have had something to do with making her nauseated.

"How did you find out I wasn't well?"

"One of the maids told me." He looked at her a little more calmly. "Are you sure you're feeling better? Alfred has excellent doctors here. Perhaps one of them should see to you."

"The queen has already seen to me and very kindly so. I'm actually quite embarrassed to have caused such trouble." A horrible thought occurred to her. "You weren't still with the king when the maid found you?"

He shrugged, yet further astounding her. "It makes no matter. But I am relieved that you are better."

"Indeed I am and I should be getting up. It is slothful to lie about in bed during the day."

"Oh, really?" He sat down again on the edge of the bed and looked at her challengingly. "Have you so much experience with lying about that you can judge the worth of it? I rather thought you were always working. Certainly that is what I saw at Hawkforte."

He was very close, his hand lying so near to hers that their fingers brushed. It was such a slight contact, yet did Krysta feel it acutely. In the bright light of day, her weakness of the previous night returned with a vengeance. She looked ahead into the lonely years to come and knew that no matter what work she might find, her heart would never heal.

"How long do you think to stay in Winchester?" she asked without looking at him.

"A week perhaps—" He broke off and she felt him staring at her. "Why do you ask?"

"I merely wondered . . ." A coward's response. She caught herself and tried again. "I think you know why I ask. Because things must be settled between us."

He got up and walked to the side of the room. Abruptly, he turned to face her. Gone was the kind and tender man concerned about her well-being. In his place was the Lord Hawk, powerful and ruthless, holding fast to that which was his. "Things *are* settled between us and you would do well to accept that. I will allow no fancy of your mind to interfere with what must be."

"You will allow——?" Pride flared and with it prudence fled. "Think you the matter of our marriage is entirely yours to settle? How can that be when this is a marriage of state? The individuals are of no account when the welfare of so many others must be considered."

"Yet supposedly it is for my own welfare that you would set yourself aside."

"Not supposedly but truly. How I wish you could see that!" Her voice broke and she rose quickly from the bed, thinking only that she must get away from him, somewhere off by herself where she would not have to hide her torment and her shame. But Hawk would have none of it. He caught her to him with gentle but implacable strength and refused to let her go when she struggled to be free.

"Krysta, sweetheart," he pleaded, "you upset yourself over nothing. Whatever stories you were told, they matter not."

"They matter to me." Her voice crumbled. Lacking any other place to do it, she hid her face in the shelter of his broad chest.

Hawk sighed deeply. He put his arms around her, holding her close with no more thought than to keep her from crying. She was such a strong, spirited woman that it was easy for him to forget how her pride had been devastated by the contemptible action of her dullard half-brother, may he rot in hell for all eternity. It would all be put right, Hawk remained convinced of that, but it would take time. That being the case, he would just as soon spend it doing something pleasant.

"Sweetheart," he murmured again and lowered his head, nuzzling her neck. A delicate shiver raced through her. He bent down slightly and scooped her up into his arms. Beside the bed, he paused and said softly, "If you truly don't want this to happen, say no now."

She looked at him with such anguish in her eyes that for a moment he was afraid she really would say it. All his self-control was needed to keep him from crushing her mouth with his, and silencing her words. But instead she reached out and gently, lingeringly stroked his face, as though memorizing him with her fingertips. He groaned with sheer relief and swiftly rising passion, and lay her down on the bed.

Chapter

FOURTEEN

HAWK WAS GONE WHEN KRYSTA AWOKE
the following morning. That was just as
well, for barely had she lifted her head from
the pillow than she was assailed by a fresh
round of the nausea that had troubled her the day before.
This time it followed to its natural conclusion and left her
gasping as she staggered back to bed. Her maid came
shortly thereafter and Krysta did her utmost to look perfectly well. She had no thought of breakfast but the young
girl brought a tray and set it directly on the bed.

"The queen said you were to eat as much as possible,
my lady. She promises it will make you feel better."

Wondering how Eahlswith had guessed her stomach
would still be disordered, Krysta tried to imagine how she
could politely decline the food. But a glance at the tray reassured her. There was nothing save another cup of the infusion of chamomile that had helped her yesterday and
several dry husks of bread. Ordinarily, such a meal would
hold no appeal for her but she suddenly found herself
tempted to try it.

And after she had, she felt noticeably better. Enough

so that she was able to rise and dress without either dizziness or nausea. Delighted by her swift recovery, Krysta thanked the maid and left her chamber. She was making her way in the direction of the queen's solar when Esa intercepted her.

Gloriously dressed and exquisitely beautiful, with absolutely no sign that *she* had woken up nauseous, Esa smiled coldly.

"Why, it's the little servant girl. Of course, if you were a servant in my household, I would insist you dress better and do something with that awful hair of yours."

Krysta thought she was perfectly well dressed in a simple but attractive gown of forest green. She had let her hair down, tied back loosely along its length by several of the ribbons Hawk had given to her. Yet she had to admit she looked far less elegant than Esa.

"Let me pass," Krysta said and tried to go around the lady, but Esa merely laughed and rolled her eyes, setting off titters of amusement from her followers. Did she never go anywhere alone?

"In such a hurry to get to the queen, are you? Poor, sweet Eahlswith is gulled by you now but that won't last long. Soon enough even she will realize how utterly unsuited you are to marry a lord who stands so high in the estimation of the king. I'm surprised Hawk even brought you here, but perhaps he intends for Alfred to see just how unworthy you are to be his wife."

"I have no wish for conflict with you," Krysta said with dignity. Again she tried to continue on her way but the passage was small and Esa was able to block her.

"You could not survive conflict with me," the lady said bluntly. "You would do well to remember that. Since you are clearly as ignorant as you are inept, I will tell you that my brother, the Lord Udell, is first among the lords of Mercia. Oh, it is true that the family of the queen still imagines that honor is their own, and even that fool

Wolscroft thinks himself important, but they are quite mistaken. My brother now outstrips them all in the number of his shieldbearers and the acreage of his lands. He will bear no slight to me. Alfred knows this well. Were it not for the importuning of that Viking savage Hawk's poor, benighted sister wed, none of this would have happened."

"And yet it has happened," Krysta said, looking at her more closely. Did she have no thought for matters beyond her own immediate wishes? "The people want peace. What can you do to bring it about?"

The challenge so startled Esa that she was at a loss for words, if only for a moment. "You would do better to ask what I can do to prevent it. Have you any notion what would happen to Alfred's stand against the Danes if he could no longer hold together the alliance of the Saxon kingdoms?"

Krysta really had very little idea of that since she knew almost nothing about how Alfred had put together the alliance to begin with. But obviously, it would not be anything good. "Why," she asked, "would the Saxons be so foolish as to rebel against the leader who has brought them unity and peace?"

Esa shrugged. "You really are quite simple, aren't you? They will do it because they are men. Men always like to fight and strive against each other. The moment one gains any supremacy, all the others are discontent. Alfred is no longer young. He has worn himself out in the struggle against the Danes. Besides, there are many who find his preoccupation with learning to be weak and foolish. Who needs such things when all that really matters is power?"

As much as Krysta truly wanted to believe that Esa was merely being provocative, she had a sinking feeling that the lady was entirely serious. Looking into her clear gray eyes, she saw nothing but sharp ambition and contempt.

"Lord Hawk values learning," Krysta said. "He owns books and he reads them."

"What of it? Such is the fashion today."

"It is not fashion with him. He has a keen mind and the will to use it."

"Oh, does he?" How strange it was that Esa could even sneer prettily. "You know him so well? And, of course, it is his *mind* that interests you. What do you do when you are alone, sit around and have long discussions?"

Her ladies laughed openly, egging her on. Krysta felt anger rise within her and tried to contain it but could not entirely. "You concern yourself where you should not. How well I know Lord Hawk is none of your affair."

"Is it not?" Color flooded the lady's delicate cheeks but not a mottled color, rather a smooth, rosy hue that only made her look lovelier even as her mouth thinned angrily. "I know him far better than you do for I have known him far longer," she paused, smiled coldly, and added, "although by no means so intimately, for unlike you, I am not a fool."

She took a step closer to Krysta, filling the air with her perfume of lavender and honeysuckle. A rather overpowering odor, Krysta thought, which put her in mind suddenly of the flowers scattered over the dead.

"He's already had you so there is no longer any mystery to you. You are just like any other woman he has lain with except that you—an irresponsible creature foolish enough to shame him by tricking him into believing you were a servant *and* immoral enough to lie with him without the bonds of marriage—you are somehow supposed to help bring about peace with the Norse. How utterly idiotic. Hawk has never cared for anything except his lands. He dispenses with anything that does not serve his power and once he sees that you do not—" Esa shrugged and looked at her with contemptuous pity. "I warrant you will be gone before the moon turns."

Sickness crept over Krysta, not of the body as she had experienced earlier but of the spirit. Beneath her superficial beauty, Esa was a despicable woman, driven only by the selfish lust for power and position. Yet none of that prevented her from being right, and even more right than she realized for the shadow of Krysta's birth was as yet unknown to her. Of that Krysta was certain, elsewise Esa would have thrown it up to her along with everything else. That was small consolation and did nothing to ease the hollow sense of helplessness that swept over her.

Esa seemed to realize that she had done sufficient damage, for the moment. With yet another pitying smile, she stood aside and let Krysta pass. But just as she did so, the lady called out, "Run to the queen now, little servant girl. Let Eahlswith console you while she may. But remember, she has no power. I and my brother do and we will not hesitate to use it."

Krysta did not look back as she hastened from the passageway but Esa's parting words lingered in her mind. Was the lady truly so foolish as to promise war with Mercia if she did not get her way? And was there any real chance of that coming to pass? Thoughts of her own future slipped aside as Krysta contemplated the possibility that Esa's threats might be more than idle. But how to find out? She was still mulling this over as she entered the queen's solar. Eahlswith was there with her ladies. She smiled when she saw Krysta.

"Come and sit down, my dear. How are you feeling?"

Somewhat self-conscious after what she had revealed to the queen the day before, Krysta was glad of her matter-of-fact welcome. "Very well, thank you, my lady, and thank you also for your kind care. I am most grateful for it."

"Not at all, I was happy to help. Do you feel well enough to read to us again?"

Krysta could not imagine circumstances in which she would not wish to read. She took up the book of Aesop's stories and began where she had left off. Yet did the problem of Esa and the Mercians linger in her mind. She was wondering if she might have a chance to speak of it when at midday Eahlswith laid down her sewing, dismissed her ladies, and suggested that Krysta join her in her garden.

Surrounded by walls and accessible only through a doorway from the bottom of the stairs that led to the queen's solar, the garden was a sanctuary of quiet. In the center stood a small pool where birds drank. Nearby, an ancient oak spread its arms generously to shade a stone bench. Late-blooming asters and daisies still raised their heads in the carefully tended flowerbeds. So, too, did a few hearty herbs yet waiting to be plucked. Eahlswith bent to remove a stray weed and looked about her with wistful pleasure.

"Alfred had this garden made after the birth of our first child. He wanted me to have a quiet place to which I could withdraw when the bustle of the court became too much." She gestured to the bench. "I used to sit on that bench and watch our children play. Sometimes I can still see myself there just as I was years ago, and see the children as they were, throwing their balls and rolling their hoops. I must admit there are times when I miss them terribly." Eahlswith sighed, then drew herself up and shrugged apologetically. "Forgive me, my dear. I had a letter this morning from my daughter, the eldest of my children, Athelflad. She is married to the Ealdorman Athelred of Mercia. Athelflad is a dear girl and we remain close despite the distance separating us. Yet we are little alike for she has always taken after her father. Now she writes to say she and Athelred are beginning construction of more fortified burghs."

"This concerns you?" Krysta asked softly.

"I suppose it should not. Towns where people feel well protected are good for trade and that alone is reason to build them. Yet I wonder if Athelflad and her husband have more than just that in mind."

As she spoke, the queen walked to the bench and sat down. Krysta followed her. Together, they looked out over the protected garden where the turmoil of the world seemed kept at bay.

"Mercia is at peace, is it not?" Krysta asked. Mindful of kind Eahlswith's feelings, she thought to go very carefully. But the queen had inadvertently given her a chance she could not resist.

"What is left of Mercia is at peace," Eahlswith corrected gently. "Fully half the land was lost to the Danes years ago. Indeed, I suspect all of Mercia would be in Danish hands today had not Alfred's father, who was then King of Wessex, come to its defense."

"Was that when you and Alfred were married?"

"Yes, after the battle at Nottingham where the house of Wessex turned back the Danes. Alfred was only a younger son then and none thought he would be king one day. But so it came to pass and Mercia has benefited from it. He has been a kind and just . . . adviser."

"Adviser? To the King of Mercia?"

"There is no king of Mercia. The last one was a client of the Danes. When he died, the ealdormen and bishops of English Mercia declined to name a successor. Instead, they gave many of the powers of the king to one of their own, Ealdorman Athelred, my daughter's husband."

So Mercia lacked a king but did have a ruler of sorts, married to the strong-willed daughter of King Alfred of Wessex. No doubt that suited the royal house of Wessex well, but Krysta could not help but wonder if it also suited the noble families of Mercia, including Esa's.

Carefully, she asked, "Are there many Mercians at court?"

"They come and go, although Athelflad is not able to visit as often as I would like. Others are here rather more often than I would prefer, but I understand that my husband wishes to keep them close."

"Is there anyone in particular he wishes to . . . keep close?"

Eahlswith looked at her shrewdly. "Are you thinking of Lord Udell and the Lady Esa?"

"They are the only Mercian nobles I know," Krysta admitted.

"Esa has made herself unpleasant, as usual, but I hope you will pay her no mind."

"I do not wish to give her any importance at all but I did wonder . . . what is Mercia's role in King Alfred's efforts against the Danes?"

"The ealdormen and the bishops of Mercia provide men, arms, and taxes to support the army, as do those of Kent, Essex, and many other lands. They also lend their wisdom to the resolving of disputes and the judging of legal cases. All this is important to the king."

"Since your own daughter is married to the Ealdorman of Mercia, I thought perhaps they were most important."

"Not most, I would not say that. But Mercia is a rich land. I am certain Alfred counts on their support."

"Then did he ever consider other marriages to assure the loyalty of the Mercians?"

Eahlswith sat back on the bench and looked at Krysta carefully. "He may have, but if you are asking me whether he encouraged Lord Hawk to look with favor upon marriage to the Lady Esa, no, he did not."

"May I ask why not?"

The queen hesitated but then she clearly came to a decision. "Alfred is a very practical man—he has had to be in order to preserve the kingdom. But he is also deeply loyal to those he believes deserving of it. That combination of practicality and loyalty would make it impossible for him to urge such a marriage upon one who has served him as valiantly as Lord Hawk has done."

After a moment's thought, Krysta realized that the queen had just told her that marriage to Esa would be a poor reward for Hawk's endeavors on behalf of the crown. She could scarcely agree more, yet did she wonder what Alfred's opinion would be if he learned of her own shadowed past, assuming he had not already.

"There is one thing I am curious about," Eahlswith said. "You told me that you came to England believing that despite your past, you would be able to make your marriage a success. What happened to change your mind?"

Krysta did not answer at once. The rustling of the old oak's leaves seemed to whisper of time's fleeting passage. She thought of the queen sitting on the same bench, watching her children play, and years later still seeing the shadows of those they had been, now forever beyond her reach.

Softly, she said, "Love is a cursed blessing."

"Or a blessed curse. I have never been able to decide which." She put her hand over Krysta's, squeezing gently. "I thought that might be it."

They sat a little while longer until the slanting rays of the sun reminded them of the passage of time and the ever-present duties that could not long be shirked. Then they returned inside, the daughter whose mother had fled into the sea and the mother whose children had flown into the great world. Just before they stepped inside, Eahlswith plucked a last rose tucked away in the shelter of the wall and handed it to Krysta.

"I invite very few into this garden," the queen said. "But you, Krysta of Vestfold, are always welcome here."

HAWK LEFT THE SMALL, PRIVATE CHAMBER WHERE he had been speaking with Alfred. He passed several nobles of his acquaintance but without seeing them. Those worthies were left to wonder what so preoccupied the great Hawk of Essex that he neglected even the simple courtesies.

He was outside in the courtyard before he became aware of his surroundings and even then he did not stop until he was beyond the walls of the town itself, surrounded by no more than trees and the gurgle of the passing river. There he stopped, and without an instant's thought slammed his fist repeatedly into the trunk of an impassive oak.

Damn her! How could he have thought her such a gentle, if misguided, woman? How had he imagined she would be malleable to his hand? His for the persuading and the winning. He had even thought to woo her! What a mockery on the poor benighted fool twice tricked by that scheming vixen of the northlands.

She had gone to the queen. Without a word to him, without a hint of what she intended, she had laid her case at Eahlswith's feet and somehow persuaded that good woman to take up her cause.

And now—what was it Alfred had said? *Perhaps she would be better suited to an abbey.* A place where she could put to use her love of learning and do good works. One marriage of disappointment, why risk another? There were other maidens in Vestfold worthy to be his wife. A word to the Wolf to set it right and then . . .

No, by God! A thousand times *No!* She was his, given to him by her wastrel brother, and he was damned if he would ever let her go. No one, not even the king, could take from him that which was his. Never had he spoken to his lord in such a way, never had Alfred known the heat of his rage. The king had borne it well, even smiling after a small start of surprise. But Alfred had not relented. Indeed, he had gone on to say a great deal more. *Not worth the risk. Too much at stake. Why take the chance if the lady herself is unwilling?*

The lady would damn well do as she was told. She had lain with him, held him in her arms, welcomed him into her body, matched his passion with her own and in the process given him a glimpse of paradise he did not think to relinquish. And all the while she had plotted to end their betrothal. Incredible.

He slumped against the abused tree, rubbing his forehead into the rough bark, and tried to think how a warrior and leader of his experience had been so gulled. He was no untried boy when it came to women. Always they had come to him eagerly and he had treated them well, within limits. Limits *he* set. Perhaps some had hoped for more from him and been disappointed, but he had never given any cause for such hope. Yet he had a sudden sense of how a woman might feel when she finally and irrevocably realized that he was slipping from her.

As Krysta thought to slip from him, for whatever reason, that nonsense about her mother, some natural fear of marriage in a far land, whatever. He cared not, it made no difference. She would not leave him! But, an inner voice whispered, she could do just that with the support of the king. She could vanish into an abbey, surrounded by her beloved books, no doubt rising one day to a position of authority, and he would be powerless to stop her.

It was that revelation of his inability to control events that struck him to the core and brought a fresh surge of anger. Not since tenderest childhood in the midst of savage war had he felt so unable to control his destiny. Was it for this that he had fought and striven, sacrificed and endured? To have snatched from him the one thing he had ever wanted purely for himself?

Damn her! How much better if she had never come, never tantalized him with a glimpse of a future he should have been too wise to believe could ever be, never stirred his heart to fierce tenderness.

Fine then, let her go into an abbey. Let her wrap her spinsterhood about herself, wear out her eyes and bow her shoulders, dry up her passion and let her youth become no more than flecks of parchment vanished on the wind.

He would forget her, take another woman to wife, sire a dozen sons, and never wake of a night yearning for the soft sound of her breathing close beside him. Oh, yes, and as easily would he sprout wings and fly like the ravens who clustered in the nearby trees, cawing their raucous song.

Damn birds.

He turned to go with no clear idea of exactly where and almost stumbled over the squat fellow sitting on his haunches near where the river turned. Thorgold looked up, sighed, and shook his head.

"Yer in a rare state."

Of an instant, Hawk reached down, grabbed hold of him, and yanked him off the ground. "Just who I was looking for before I left Hawkforte," he snarled, "you and your black-garbed friend. Where the hell were you?"

Thorgold looked in no way disconcerted to be dangling several feet in the air. He picked a stray bit of something or other from between his teeth, and said, "Making ourselves scarce, of course, leastways till your anger cooled."

"Then you've picked the wrong moment to reappear because my anger is hotter than ever. God's blood, man, do you have any idea what she's done?"

"She told ye she couldn't marry ye."

"How do you know that? Where were you lurking when I locked her away?"

"Ye've a very nice bridge 'bout half a mile outside of town but never mind about that. Didn't keep her locked away long, did ye?"

"I was summoned here. I could hardly leave her where she was."

"Aye, ye could have. She wasn't goin' anywhere locked away like that. Ye just didn't want t'be parted from her."

Hawk didn't even try to deny that. He set Thorgold down and took a deep breath, seeking to calm himself and finding only regret instead. "More fool me for it."

"Love turns any mortal into a fool."

"Who said I was in love with her?"

"I'll warrant ye haven't said it, least not to her, and why not I'd like t'know."

"Place a weapon like that in her hands? Are you mad, man? It's bad enough I've got this . . . temporary disordering of my thoughts. I've no intention of making it worse."

Thorgold made no effort to hide his reaction. He hooted with laughter. The ravens cawed right along. Slapping his knees, he grinned broadly. "Now there's a way to describe it, temporary disordering of yer thoughts. I'll have to remember that one."

"It's no joke," Hawk protested. "She went to the queen and enlisted her aid. I could actually lose her." He heard himself and scowled. "And why not? Good riddance to her. Who needs a wife who causes so much trouble?"

"You do," Thorgold said flatly. "But ye'll have to work that out for yerself." He turned as though to go.

Hawk caught him by the scruff of his leather vest and noticed absently the odd little bits hanging from it—

several brooches, a couple of belt buckles, colored bangles and beads, pins of all sizes, glittering crystals hanging in woven bags, feathers, all swaying right along with their owner.

"You told Krysta those half-wit stories about her mother, didn't you? You and the old woman. Why did you do it?"

"Half-wit? Is that what ye think? Well, then what should we have told her?"

"The truth."

Released, Thorgold turned his neck this way and that, making it crack loudly. "Which truth is that?"

"*The* truth. There's only one."

"Is there now? What a simple world ye live in. Must be nice sometimes . . . but I don't know, chances are I'd get bored right quick."

"Stop nattering and just tell me, what really happened to her mother?"

"She was called to the sea."

Hawk paled. Suicide was anathema to the Church, utterly forbidden. If Krysta's mother had taken her own life . . . "What are you saying?"

"I'm saying she was called to the sea."

"What does that mean? She . . . took her own life?"

Thorgold sighed very loudly. "The sea abounds with life. Ye sail it enough to know that."

"For God's sake, you know perfectly well what I mean! No mortal woman can live in the sea."

Thorgold peered at him from beneath bushy brows. "Suppose she was a mortal woman but one with a rare gift, that of calling into this world beings from the other realm. But suppose the gift had another side to it, that *she* could be called from this world if the unhappiness she found here became too much for her to bear."

Hawk was silent for a long moment. He knew something about women with rare gifts who could suffer because of them. Yes, by God, he did know about that. Even so, he said, "People cannot go and live in the sea, no matter how much they might want to."

"Ah, but they don't want to, there's the thing, because they believe they cannot. They carry their bodies about with them from the day they're born an' they get to thinking there is nothing else fer them. But life . . ." Thorgold gestured to the surrounding trees thick with leaves soon to fall, to the river rushing by so swiftly no droplet of water could be seen for more than an instant, to the sudden shower of seeds borne on milk-white clouds that wafted past them and vanished as though it had not been.

"Life is always transforming itself," Thorgold said. "That's what life does, nothing more and nothing less. The trick is noticing."

Hawk's mind turned that over, turning and turning, getting nowhere. It was important somehow, he knew that, but the notion was like gossamer, uncatchable.

"You spun this tale to make Krysta feel better," he tried. It was logical, even compassionate. He couldn't blame the odd pair too much if that was what they'd done.

"If you like."

"I don't like! But I think I understand. If she suspected the truth—"

"Whose truth, what truth, truth's truth? Open yer mind, Hawk of Essex. It has wings ye've yet to unfurl."

And with that, Thorgold was gone. One moment he was standing there and the next he was not. Hawk looked around swiftly in all directions but not so much of a glimmer of the little man remained to be seen. However, listening closely, Hawk thought he caught the jangle of brooches and buckles, bangles and beads dancing on the air.

FIFTEEN

D EEP IN THOUGHT, KRYSTA TOOK A WRONG turn after leaving the queen and found herself in a wing of the royal residence she had not seen before. It seemed set aside for servants' quarters and at this hour of the day it was deserted. She wandered for some time, trying to retrace her steps through a labyrinth of corridors, before finally finding a door that led out into a courtyard. There she spied a boy hurrying about some errand and managed to stop him long enough to ask her way back to the great hall. From there, she assumed she could find her quarters.

"Through there," he told her, scarcely slowing down, "turn left then left again, go straight away and take the second—no, the third right. It'll still be a bit but you'll get there."

On that less than helpful note, he sped off, leaving Krysta struggling to remember what he had said.

"Left . . ." she murmured as she followed his directions. A while later, "And left again, then straight—"

She came to a long corridor lined with doors on one side and windows on the other looking out over yet another courtyard. From behind the doors, she heard voices reciting in Latin. One door stood partly open and through it she made out the scratch of pens on parchment and caught a glimpse of young men with their heads bent in study.

From that she concluded that somehow she had worked her way around to where the royal school joined the king's residence. Which meant, if she was right, that she should be able to see the scriptorium from the windows up ahead.

But no, she couldn't, and she felt exasperated. Perhaps if she turned around and went the other way? She was about to do so when a man emerged suddenly from a side passage. He was tall, well built, with dark hair to his shoulders and a narrow face. Despite the warmth of the day, he wore velvet and was adorned with much gaudy gold in the form of a heavy chain around his neck and thick, jewel-studded bands at both his wrists. Seeing her, he stopped abruptly.

Krysta's heart sank. She recognized him all too well and wondered at the unkind hand of fate that had her not merely lost but face-to-face with Lord Udell.

"My lady," he said and bowed mockingly. "What a surprise to find you here. I thought you always at the ear of the queen."

Ignoring his provocation, Krysta said, "I was on my way to my quarters and took a wrong turn. If you would excuse me—"

"Oh, by all means." He moved just as she did, blocking her way. When she tried to go around him, he moved again with the same result.

Frustrated, Krysta stopped and shook her head. Udell stood grinning, hands on his hips, waiting to see what she did next. But his smile faded abruptly when she simply turned on her heel and walked away from him. She got so far as to open a door and step out into the courtyard, but just then he caught up to her and grabbed her arm. As Krysta tried to pull free, he pushed her up against an outer wall of the building and, still keeping hold of her, said, "Even for a Norse, your manners are poor. It isn't done to show your betters disrespect."

Krysta bit back the impulse to tell him she saw no betters and instead tried again to twist free. She had not thought he would lay hands on her and was shocked that he had done so. Although there were rooms nearby and people in them, she felt acutely vulnerable alone with him in the courtyard. He loomed very large over her, not so large as Hawk to be sure but threatening nonetheless. His grip on her arm hurt and she suspected he was bruising her.

Yet she was not so foolish as to let him see her alarm. Calmly, she said, "Why do this, Lord Udell? There is nothing for you to gain."

He stared at her in surprise for a moment, then laughed sharply. "Do you always think that way, in terms of gain or loss?"

She did not, but she kept that to herself. "It is a sensible enough way to think and by all reports you are a sensible man."

In fact, she had no idea whether anyone thought Lord Udell even remotely sensible but the notion seemed to please him. He eased his hold on her yet did not let go. "You have been speaking of me?"

"Your sister speaks of you. She praises your power. And of course it is impossible to be at court even a short time without being aware of your stature."

This flattered him greatly. "Perhaps you are not as foolish as I thought if you have wit to perceive that."

Deliberately, she looked at his hand still fastened to her arm. "I also have wit to wonder why you do this. Why give the Hawk any excuse to come against you?"

"Are you so certain that he would? You were not his choice, but rather chosen for him."

"It matters not. Would you allow another to take your property simply because you had not selected it for yourself?"

"No, of course not, but—" He shook his head. "What a hardheaded creature you are, quite unlike most women. I wonder if Hawk has the sense to appreciate that." Udell moved closer to her, his fingers caressing the skin he had bruised. "You have a wild look to you, that mass of hair I suppose, and those eyes. Is that deceptive? Or is there truly passion in you?" He bent his head, his lips brushing the curve of her cheek.

Krysta suppressed a shiver of pure revulsion. She turned away, schooling her features to utter calm. To her dismay, Udell chuckled. "A valiant try, my lady." He laid his hand just below her breast. "But I can feel how frantically your heart beats."

That he was so vain as to believe it beat with desire for him astounded Krysta but she took some comfort in knowing he did not sense her fear. That comfort fled in the next instant as Udell said huskily, "You are wasted in Essex. Hawk will never be anything but a mere retainer to the king. Surely, one so practical as yourself"—He lowered his head again and put his mouth to the slender column of her throat—"and so tempting can aspire to something higher."

The nausea she had experienced earlier in the day was returning with a vengeance. Krysta fought to contain it and to keep herself safe at the same time. "What is higher than a marriage to bring peace between two peoples?"

Udell leaned back and looked at her. His eyes shone as though the two of them were sharing a joke. "Oh, to be sure, peace is to be sought above all else." He caught a handful of her curls and crushed them in his fist. "But think, my lady, why should the Norse only make peace with Alfred, an aging king whose victories are in the past? Why should they not seek alliance with younger, more vigorous leaders?"

"What leaders are equal in stature to Alfred who is king and whose son will be king after him? I hear of no others."

"Then you must learn to listen more carefully." He dropped her hair but did not move away from her. Almost to himself, he said, "You really are oddly interesting. There's something about you. . . ."

Krysta had a very good sense that the "something" Udell found so intriguing was simply that she belonged to the Hawk, a man so far above him as to be the inevitable target of his bitter resentment and envy. But she was also vividly aware that whatever the cause, he was becoming aroused. Repugnance clawed at her and she made an instinctive effort to put distance between them.

Udell caught her chin, twisting her face so that she had no choice but to look at him. "Don't be coy. It doesn't become you. Peace with the Norse has much to recommend it to any king, including of Mercia."

Through stiffened lips, Krysta said, "There is no king of Mercia."

He flushed slightly, his eyes gleaming. "Today there is not. Tomorrow—" He shoved her hard against the wall and put his hands to her gown, pulling up her skirts to bare her legs.

"Wouldn't you rather be a queen than a mere lady?" he murmured as he ground himself against her.

Her stomach truly was going to rebel, and wouldn't that be a surprise for the despicable Lord Udell? Tempted though she was to let it happen, Krysta remembered suddenly what Thorgold had told her.

"There's men with black hearts, girl," he had said in his gruff but loving way, "who care the earth for their own

wants and pig spit for anyone else's. Do you meet one like
that, ye keep yer wits about ye good, an' when they least
expect it, ye—"

Krysta took a deep breath, closed her eyes, and followed Thorgold's instructions precisely. The howl that
erupted from Udell made the starlings nesting in the eaves
flee into the sky.

Doubled over, his face turning purple, he gasped,
"You bitch! How dare you! I'll—" Belatedly, she realized
that he was, for all his posturing, a warrior and as such
well accustomed to pain. He lunged after her and she only
just managed to elude his grip, but the door back into the
corridor stuck as she tried to open it and for a horrible moment she thought she was undone.

Until a blur of shining black and a raucous caw made
her hope otherwise. A raven swooped into the courtyard,
followed by another and another. Within moments, the
air seemed filled with them as they dived and darted about
Udell, pecking at him mercilessly. He screamed and tried
to cover his head but to no avail. Rivulets of blood ran
down his face and still the attack continued.

Krysta stood frozen in horror for a moment before her
own peril drove her on. This time, the door yielded and
she tumbled into the corridor even as Udell fell to the
ground in the courtyard, writhing desperately in his efforts to keep the ravens from his eyes. His screams disturbed the hushed sanctity of the royal school. Doors
began to open up and down the corridor as students and
masters alike emerged to see what was happening.

Krysta did not wait to be seen by them but lifted her
skirts and ran swift as the wind. She kept going until she
came skittering around a corner and into the great hall.
There she stopped abruptly for although it was not yet
time to dine, there were people present. As curious eyes
turned in her direction, she struggled to appear calm and
composed.

To her immense relief, Hawk was there. She almost sobbed to see him and hurried to his side without thought, only to be shocked when he took a step back and stared at her coldly. "I was looking for you," he said. "Come with me."

He strode from the hall and into the well of the stairs leading to the guest quarters. Krysta trailed after him. Glad though she was to be away from the scrutiny of others, she found no comfort in the harsh gaze he turned on her the moment they were alone.

"You went to the queen."

There was no mistaking that as anything other than an accusation. Still dazed by Udell's attack, she scrambled to defend herself. "I did not go to her. I was ill and Eahlswith kindly cared for me. It was the impulse of the moment to tell her what was in my heart, that is all."

"I am to believe you did not think she would tell the king and he tell me?"

"Believe as you will, but no, I did not consider what she would do. Perhaps I should have."

"Without doubt you should have. Does it please you, lady, to know that now Alfred thinks you may be better suited to an abbey than to marriage with me? Does your heart rejoice at news that he has spoken to me of finding another bride?"

In truth, her heart felt near to breaking but she tried valiantly to shore it up. This was what she had known must be. Why then did it shock so deeply that her very soul cried out in protest?

"There is no joy in this, my lord. If you believe otherwise, you are sorely mistaken." She turned away, determined he would not see her anguish. Hawk reached out to stop her and gripped the same arm Udell had bruised. Krysta cried out and an instant later found herself free.

"Is my touch now so repugnant to you?" he demanded, his face hard with anger and something else that looked very much like grief.

She truly had not thought of the consequences when she spilled her thoughts to Eahlswith and that was not a mistake Krysta would make again. If she told what had happened with Udell, she had no doubt that Hawk would go after him, his anger at her notwithstanding. Could she prevent it, she would not be the cause of any such confrontation.

"I am merely tired," she said and knew it for the weak response it was.

He looked at her for a long moment, his features taut and his eyes so shadowed she could not see into them. When the silence had drawn bow-tight between them, he turned and without another word walked away from her.

THREE DAYS PASSED. DAYS OF SILENT MISERY FOR Krysta in which each moment seemed to hang endlessly before sinking, one more drop, into the ever-widening pool of her unhappiness. The door between her room and Hawk's remained closed. Though they sat near each other at the high table each evening, they retired separately and without a word to each other.

Udell did not approach her again although several times she caught him looking at her with such deadly intent as to make the fine hairs at the nape of her neck rise in warning. She had made an enemy there and knew she might well live to regret it.

Eahlswith, however, remained a friend. Each morning, the queen sent a tray with a dry husk of bread and an infusion of chamomile, which soothed Krysta's troubled stomach due, no doubt, to her anguish over Hawk. She was quite certain he was the cause but she did not blame him for it. Indeed, she could blame him for nothing, for it was her own relentless conscience that had plunged them into such conflict.

Raven and Thorgold were about, and she caught glimpses of them from time to time, but neither came near. How dearly she would have welcomed their company for never in her life had Krysta felt so alone. In the midst of the crowded court, always with the queen and her ladies, she felt as though she existed in a hollowed-out world that held only herself.

And perhaps also Esa, who could not contain her good cheer and who seemed to be everywhere at once. She was a figure of such relentless gaiety that people began to look at her with some wonderment as they speculated about the cause. By the third day, Krysta realized that such discussions broke off whenever she approached. She was the recipient of quick, sympathetic looks that set her teeth on edge.

To her disgust, she began to look for times when Esa and Hawk were together and quickly wished she had not, for such occurrences were all too frequent. When the court rode out to hunt, Esa maneuvered her mount next to Hawk's. Later, when Hawk and his men joined some of Alfred's on the training field beyond the town, Esa took her ladies and went to picnic nearby. Krysta caught sight of them from the queen's solar and rolled her eyes at the thought of fighting men being the object of such frivolous attention. But perhaps they liked it, for did not all men have a soft spot for flattery? Miserable at the thought that Hawk might actually enjoy Esa's simpering presence, Krysta withdrew and spent the rest of the afternoon sunk in sorry thoughts. That evening, in the great hall before they took their seats, Esa approached Hawk and engaged him in conversation. It seemed one-sided to be sure, for he appeared to respond in monosyllables, but she laughed gaily nonetheless, as though they were of one lighthearted mind.

Krysta put on a brave face until the meal was winding

down and she gratefully took her leave. She slept poorly that night and woke the next morning determined to speak with Hawk. That he believed she had in some way betrayed him was no longer to be borne.

Finding him proved difficult as she was unwilling to go about asking if anyone knew his whereabouts. There was already far too much fodder for the gossip mill. She was walking toward the stables, thinking to see if his favorite stallion was there, when the frantic yelping of a dog brought her up short. As the animal's cries of pain increased, she turned in the direction of the sound and quickly found its cause.

One of the hunting dogs had been taken out of its pen and was being severely beaten with a stick. The sight shocked her, for she had never permitted any mistreatment of the animals on her lands. The very thought that a helpless creature would be so abused horrified her. The pitiful animal crouched low, whimpering for mercy in between blows. Krysta started forward without thought, anxious to stop the cruelty, only to realize suddenly that the enraged man wielding the stick was none other than Lord Udell. His face shone dark red and a twisted sneer distorted his features. He seemed completely out of control as he struck the dog furiously, again and again.

"Stop!" Heedless of her own safety, Krysta darted forward. She was convinced he would beat the animal to death.

"Stop it! You're going to kill him!"

Taken by surprise, Udell made to shove her aside. When he recognized her, his eyes dilated wildly. "Bitch! Get the hell away from me or—"

The threat was never uttered, for the dog, no longer cringing beneath blows, sank his teeth into his tormentor's ankle. As Udell howled and tried to kick the animal away, the stick came loose in his hands. Krysta was wrenching it from him when it slipped between her fingers and slashed across Udell's face.

At that, everything seemed to happen at once. Udell screamed, trying to stem the flow of blood from the wound that ran from his forehead down his left cheek and just missed his eye, while hopping about on his one unin-jured ankle. The dog disappeared around a corner of the stable. Several grooms ran out to see what was happening. Hard on their heels, a group of nobles returned from a ride, among them Lady Esa. She took one look at the scene and commenced shrieking.

"*Murderers!* Someone has tried to kill Lord Udell! Merciful God, what infamy! In the very house of the king! Help! Help!"

She flung herself off her horse and at her brother, knocking him to the ground where he lay, groaning and bleeding. Others clustered around, the ladies adding to the cacophony with their own shrieks as the lords drew their daggers and shouted orders to one another to defend against the imagined assailant.

Krysta observed all this with blank astonishment. Granted, Udell had been injured but he was hardly in threat of his life. Moreover, although she'd had no inten-tion of hurting him, she rather thought he deserved it for his treatment of the dog. Assuming that eventually some-one among the dozen or so people clustered about him would decide to stop shouting and render him aid, she turned to go. But just as she did, Udell surged to his feet, a blood-drenched hand still clutching his face, and yelled, "She did it! That's the bitch! Stop her!"

At once, several of the lords advanced on Krysta, not touching her for they were yet mindful that she was the betrothed of the Hawk, but preventing her from escaping. One reached over and yanked the stick from her hand, grinning with satisfaction as he brandished it. "She is caught with the very weapon she used still in her hand!"

"She attacked me!" Udell declared with an air of as-tounded affront. "I had trouble with my dog and while I was seeing to him, she leaped upon me with that stick. It is true what they say, all Vikings are savages."

"You were beating your dog!" Krysta exclaimed. "I merely tried to stop you and you were struck by the same stick you were wielding against that poor animal."

Udell straightened, letting his hand fall to reveal the jagged wound on his face. He looked around at the assembled lords and ladies, all hanging eagerly on his every word. "A man has not the right to chastise his own dog? What a strange tale she weaves to try to excuse herself."

Remembering what had passed between her and Udell four days before, and well aware that he held more against her than the wound to his face, Krysta belatedly recognized her peril. Lords and ladies of Mercia, all no doubt loyal to Udell, surrounded her. No one else was about save for the grooms clustered off to one side and she did not expect they would risk the rage of such powerful nobles for her sake.

"It is a crime to strike a lord," Udell said. He advanced on Krysta with an ugly smile. "You will find my wergild is among the highest in the land. I do hope your dowry is large enough to cover it. Of course, if it isn't, Hawk will have to pay the difference." The thought made him laugh with relish and the others quickly joined in, all save Esa, who pushed her way to the front of the group. She glared at Krysta with gloating malice.

"But, my brother, what is this you say? Only the nobility can pay the prescribed fine for such an offense. Servants and slaves pay an altogether different kind of penalty."

Udell looked genuinely surprised, as did everyone else save Krysta, who knew in a horrified heartbeat that somehow Esa already had news of what Sven had said at Hawkforte. A moment later, the lady confirmed it.

Pointing to Krysta, she said, "This one's own half-brother came all the way from Vestfold to denounce her."

She paused dramatically. "He proclaimed her the unnatural child of his poor benighted father and a creature of the sea." Before the shocked gasps died away, Esa continued. "Oh, yes, I know, it is too horrible to contemplate, but he swore it was true. He disowned her, declaring she has no family and no dowry. Indeed, he refused to let her return to his lands and instead gave her to Lord Hawk as *servant or slave!* This he did declare before all the folk of Hawkforte."

Far from pleased with this news, Udell appeared dumbfounded. "How do you know this?" he demanded suspiciously.

Esa shrugged as though the answer should be obvious. "Would news like this stay in Hawkforte? Just this morning I heard it from a merchant who has my custom. But I warrant before nightfall it will be known through all of Winchester and by tomorrow there will not be a mewling babe in Wessex who does not know it."

"That won't mean the knowing is worth anything," Udell said. He turned on Krysta, his face dark and hate-filled. "Is this true, woman? Are you not lady but servant, say even slave?"

It did not occur to Krysta to lie. Neither her pride nor her innate honesty would have allowed her to do so despite the obvious peril. Head high, the pain of her heart well concealed, she said quietly, "So he who was my half-brother has named me."

A curse broke from Udell that should have shriveled the leaves on the trees. Hard on it, he advanced on Krysta. "God's blood! You dared to refuse me and worse! You who are *nothing*? Never have I borne such insult and I will not now!" He looked around wildly for some way to release his rage.

Seizing the moment, Esa said, "A servant or slave who strikes a lord is flogged. That is the law."

The other lords around Udell started at this but

quickly they cast hard, speculative looks at Krysta. The ladies tittered, aroused by shock. Udell was breathing hard. He paced back and forth, his fists opening and closing, staring at Krysta as though he still could not believe the offense she had done him. He looked away only to gaze fixedly at his sister, as what she had just said slowly penetrated the fog of rage clouding his mind.

"By God, that is true! The law speaks clearly. I will be satisfied with nothing less!"

One of the Mercian lords, a man of Udell's years but seemingly more cautious temperament, looked uneasy. "But, lord, the Hawk . . . ?"

Udell whirled on him, eyes bulging. "Matters not! Do you hear me? *He matters not!* The law is the law. There is nothing more precious to Alfred, is there? Always he has insisted we live within it, and the illustrious"—his voice dripped scorn—"Hawk of Essex is always at his right hand ready to enforce the royal dictates. Well, now, let him live with this! Let him see the law in action as it is meant to be!"

Before anyone else could raise objection, Udell pointed to a nearby post. "By God, I will have justice and without delay! Tie her there!"

Hard hands seized Krysta. She cried out and struggled to free herself. "Do not! I am on the king's lands! Only Alfred can pronounce judgment!" In fact, she did not know if this was true but such was the custom in Vestfold and she had to pray it held in Wessex as well.

"Alfred will know better than to gainsay me on this," Udell declared. "If he does so, Mercia will rise against him!"

Before she could speak again, Krysta's arms were yanked around the post and swiftly secured by a rope. Esa herself darted into the stables and returned with a whip, which she handed to Udell. As a last step in all she had set in motion, she seized the dagger of a lord standing nearby before he could think to stop her, strode to Krysta, and slashed open the back of her gown.

As it fell open to reveal the slender line of her bare back, so too did silence fall. Krysta heard the frantic beating of her heart as well as the hastily in-drawn breaths of those gathered around her. Hear, as well, the crack of the whip as Udell struck it against the ground. Getting the feel of it, she supposed in a far corner of her mind, before using it to tear open her back and avenge himself for the humiliations she had cast upon him.

There was no one to stop him; even the ravens were gone. Later, if Hawk was angry or Alfred displeased, the damage would be done. Desperately afraid, she closed her eyes and prayed for strength. Above all, she did not want to shame herself. She was concentrating very hard on that, her body braced for the blow she was sure was coming, when a well-familiar voice broke the stillness.

"Hold."

Krysta jerked her head around and saw Hawk, who stood calm and impassive, his arms crossed over his broad chest, not even looking at her. Beside him panted the stable boy who had run to alert him to what was happening.

Udell's mouth worked. He cracked the whip again and gazed at Hawk in challenge. "Your *slave* has broken the law. She struck me and for that she will be flogged."

Hawk studied the wound on Udell's face without comment. He glanced at Esa for a moment as she fairly bounced with excitement. His gaze on her was contemptuous but it went blank again as he turned his attention to Krysta. He walked to where she stood tied to the post and slowly looked her over. Not a hint of his thoughts escaped him as he said, "Did you put that mark on him?"

She swallowed hard against the bile rising in her throat and nodded. "He was beating his dog. I tried to stop him. We struggled over the stick and it slipped."

Hawk heard her out but when she was done he said,

"It makes no matter why it happened. A servant cannot strike a noble."

Though he called her servant instead of slave, it too made no difference. He had publicly acknowledged what there was no point in denying. Sven had disowned her. She had no family and no position. In the eyes of the law, she was no better than any other landless peasant.

Shame filled Krysta. Through its crawling pain, she heard Hawk say, "Your wergild is high, Udell. Wouldn't you rather have that?"

"Are you offering to pay it?" the Mercian shot back. He sounded in high good humor, as though he had never enjoyed himself more, as well he might for surely he had never before had a man of the Hawk's stature in such a position.

Yet was Hawk silent for a moment, as though thinking the matter over. Finally, he said, "I will pay it."

Udell chuckled. He waved a hand around to his attentive audience. "What a magnanimous gesture. I am almost tempted to accept and indeed I might were I not so fervently devoted to the rule of law. After all, has the king not impressed upon us the sacred nature of the law, that only it stands between us and anarchy? How then can I put my own personal gain above obedience to such vital rule?" He sighed long and loud at the sacrifice he was making. "No, I must insist. Only a flogging will do."

Still without expression, Hawk said, "The law specifies twenty lashes for such an offense."

Krysta cringed inwardly, wondering how she could possibly withstand such punishment.

"Twenty lashes will leave her too damaged to be of further use to me," Hawk went on. "I will pay twice the wergild."

The crowd gasped, for this was a truly impressive sum. Only a very few lords of the land could afford to pay it, and the receipt of such bounty would make Udell an even more potent force to be reckoned with. The Mercian understood that full well. His expression left no doubt that he was sorely tempted. But whether it was the reminder of the blow she had delivered to him in the courtyard four days before or the still-throbbing wound to his face that would likely leave him scarred for life, Udell would not relent.

"No," he snarled. "My honor demands that she suffer the whip."

"I grow tired of haggling," Hawk said. He reached over, pulled together the back of Krysta's gown, and said, "A master is responsible for the actions of his servants, therefore this fault is ultimately mine. Twenty lashes are nothing to me. I will take the whipping for her."

Chapter

SIXTEEN

AWK SPOKE SO CASUALLY THAT HE
might have been discussing nothing more
than the most minor inconvenience. But
those who heard him thought differently.
As one, they gasped and immediately began to mutter
among themselves. Twenty lashes were no small matter
even for the strongest among them. What manner of man
would offer to take such punishment to spare a woman?

Krysta could not bear the thought of Hawk hurt and
far preferred to bear the pain herself.

"No!" she cried out, struggling against the ropes.

Trying his damnedest to control anger so great that it
threatened to overwhelm him, Hawk came very close to
slamming his hand over her mouth. And why not when
every time she opened it, she made things worse? First to
the queen, now to the insufferable Udell. Was there no
end to her impulsiveness? Or to the proud courage of her
nature that forbade her to take the easy way out of any situation?

He couldn't let himself think like that. Indeed, it
would be far better if he thought of nothing at all except

how to get her away from Udell and the Mercian crowd in the fastest, safest way possible. After that . . . He allowed himself a scant moment to consider what he would do once Krysta was beyond harm, then returned his attention to Udell.

"Surely you don't expect me to wait all day? Agree and let's be done."

Udell sucked in his breath. Hawk watched impassively the struggle playing out on the Mercian's scowling features. He had already rejected the payment of wergild, even twice the normal amount. To go back now and try to take it would make him appear ridiculous, and that, above all, so vainglorious a braggart could not bear. In his rage, no doubt he had savored the thought of making Krysta suffer but without seeing the trap into which the Hawk had led him. Hawk was, by law, her master. He had, by law, the right to inflict punishment on her. But he also, by law, had the right to take such punishment on himself when she had transgressed against another. Such was never done yet the law supported it. Alfred's law. The very law Udell claimed to uphold.

"Well?" Hawk said. He looked faintly bored, as though he had better things to do and would get on with them as soon as this small annoyance was sorted out.

"Piss on you, Hawk of Essex!" Udell snarled. "You think I won't flog you because of who you are? You think you can make such an offer to me and I will be afraid to take it?"

Hawk let the insult go by with a mere shrug of his broad shoulders. He flicked a bit of dust from the sleeve of his tunic. "Whatever you're going to do, I wish you'd make up your mind." He glanced over to the side as though just noticing the man who had arrived minutes before.

"My lord," Hawk called to him, "will you confirm that I am within my rights? As I am unwilling to have my property damaged but am willing to take the punishment upon myself, he must release her."

There was a quick inhalation of breath as Alfred stepped into the circle of lords and ladies. The bolder among them dared to show frowns of disapproval yet they all gave way before him, falling back as rats do before the master catcher.

The king surveyed the scene with a thoughtful air. His gaze lingered a moment on Udell's mutilated cheek, then passed on. Calmly, he said, "The Lord of Essex has the right of it. The girl must be released."

Even as he spoke, he gestured to the men-at-arms who just then came running around the corner of the stable. Their sergeant moved forward and with a quick nod of approval from Hawk, cut the ropes that held Krysta. Holding the back of her gown closed with one hand, she laid the other on Hawk's strong arm. Just then she needed contact with him more than anything else. He did not look at her but he did put his hand over hers, completely covering and protecting it.

"Well?" he asked again, raising an eyebrow at Udell.

The Mercian stared from Hawk to the king and from them both to the swiftly expanding circle of armed men gathering around them. Alfred's men some of them, but now pouring in from all sides the men of the Hawk. They were coming from every corner, every direction, some off the training fields, others from their leisure. All armed, all with the keen-eyed readiness of the most superb fighting force in all of England, renowned even above the army of Alfred himself. Men bloodied in battle, spoken of as legends, whispered to have followed their lord into the very maw of hell. Men who would die for him without hesitation but who were far more likely to kill without a second thought.

"You know damn well I cannot flog you!" Udell protested. "I would not live to take two steps!"

Hawk did not bother to deny it. Indeed, the notion amused him. Cheerfully, as though offering a friendly suggestion, he said, "We could try single combat. If I fall to you, my men are honor bound not to take vengeance."

Udell's mouth twisted convulsively. Single combat against the Hawk. There were men who had done that. Of course, none of them happened to be alive. "Are you challenging me?" the Mercian demanded, and his voice broke on the brittle edge of fear.

Hawk's smile deepened. Seeing it, Krysta shivered and even Alfred paled slightly. The Lord of Essex, vanquisher of the Danes, champion of his people, the most feared warrior in all of Britain, glanced around at the watching lords and ladies who had thought to rise to ever greater power on the ambitions of the man who now stood before him cringing in the face of certain death. Slowly, he returned his attention to Udell. In a voice that carried to the far reaches of the circle, he said, "Not yet."

The words still reverberated on the air when the Mercians dispersed. They went swiftly, the ladies tripping over their gowns and the lords elbowing them out of the way in their haste to be gone. Udell went too, but not without difficulty. Esa gripped his arm, struggling to hold him back. In the rush to be away, her coif had been knocked to one side and there was a rip in the sleeve of her under tunic.

"He has insulted you!" she cried out. "And *she* has done even worse! You cannot let them go unpunished!"

"What would you have me do?" her brother demanded. He spared one more look at Hawk and scowled at Esa. "Die? Would that satisfy you, you greedy, grasping harridan?"

At her outraged shriek, Udell raised his hand and cuffed her so hard that she fell back into a pile of offal deposited by the horses. He went on without another look, disappearing around a corner of the stable. Krysta took a step toward the filthy, stunned woman only to be stopped by Hawk, who simply lifted her off the ground so that her feet moved to no effect.

"If you would excuse us, my lord," Hawk said courteously, "we have troubled you long enough."

Alfred worked hard to confine a grin but failed entirely. He laughed outright when Hawk tossed a shocked and protesting Krysta over his shoulder. Her objections were drowned out by Hawk's own men joining in the relieved merriment. Guffaws and helpful suggestions to their lord trailed off behind them as Hawk strode back to the royal residence.

"Put me down!" Krysta demanded before they had passed through the double doors to the great hall.

Hawk ignored her and kept right on going. Passing startled servants, surprised priests, amused lords, and, it seemed to Krysta, most of the population of Winchester, he stopped finally at the entrance to his own quarters, shoved the door open with his foot, and walked into the chamber. Without pause, he went straight to the bed and dumped her on it. She came up quickly on her elbows in time to see him stride back to the door and drop the heavy wooden bar across it. Assured they would not be interrupted, Hawk returned his attention to his wayward betrothed.

Standing beside the bed, he began removing his boots. Half bent over, tugging them off, he said matter-of-factly, "You are the most infuriating woman I have ever known."

Krysta looked at him cautiously. He didn't sound angry and he certainly didn't look it but she knew him far too well to be misled by that. Udell had walked the keen edge of death only a short time before because of Hawk's concealed rage. That it was so little in evidence meant nothing.

"What are you doing?"

He looked up at her, as though surprised she had to ask. "Taking my boots off."

"W-why?" She wasn't nervous, absolutely not. Nor did she feel the deep thrumming of desire stirring within her. She was merely curious, that was all.

"Because," Hawk said as he straightened and unclinched the sword belt around his waist, "they're heavy and I wouldn't want you getting walloped at a crucial moment."

If her mouth continued to open and close like that, she would be mistaken for a fish. This was really carrying matter-of-factness too far. If he thought she was just going to lie there and accept what he intended after almost four days of scarcely a word between them, not to mention everything that *was* hanging between them, then he—

—Had been willing to be whipped in her place.

What possible chance did she have to resist such tender valor? The man had absolutely no sense of fairness at all. But, oh, lord, he surely did have a beautiful chest, all rippling muscle and burnished skin, and her hands just begged to be run over it. Propping herself up a little higher, Krysta tossed her hair out of the way—no sense obstructing her view—and said, "Do you understand I'm only doing this because I want to have beautiful memories of the time we had together?"

About to strip off his breeches, he stopped and stared at her. "When you're in the abbey, bent over your parchments, all hunch-shouldered and bleary-eyed?"

"Don't joke. You'll be an old man then, too." It was impossible to imagine him old. He would always be young to her no matter how many years passed.

He pulled off the breeches, tossed them aside, and joined her on the bed. Catching glistening strands of her hair around his fingers, he said, "According to Thorgold, I'll still be buying you hair ribbons. Now do you honestly believe that stubborn old troll is wrong?"

His hands were on her breasts, caressing them
through the fine linen of her gown. His bare, heavily muscled thigh was pushing between hers. His mouth was hot
along her throat. So very hot . . . as though she were about
to go up in flames at any moment. Yet she shoved her
hands against his shoulders and forced enough space between them so that she could look at him.

"What did you call Thorgold?"

Reluctantly, he gave up sweetly tormenting the hollow at the base of her throat and said, "A stubborn old
troll. Would you describe him differently?"

Her heart sputtered, started again at double speed.
"You think Thorgold is a troll?"

Hawk shrugged those massive shoulders she was unconsciously stroking. "He disappeared on me just the
other morning. One minute we were talking and the next
he was gone. Who does that kind of thing?"

"Trolls . . . ?"

"I'm no expert but it seems to fit. Before he went he
told me my mind has wings I have yet to unfurl."

"Thorgold is a poet."

"So it seems. Notice I'm not asking about Raven.
Best I leave that alone, I think. Is it my imagination or did
Udell have a pecked look to him?"

Krysta sighed deeply and felt the tight coil of sorrow
that had existed within her these many days loosen a
notch. "Udell and I had an . . . encounter four days past.
Somehow it must have disturbed the ravens and they attacked him."

To her regret, he gave off caressing her and sat up.
The tender, playful lover yielded to the outraged lord.
"You will tell me what happened."

Because she always tried to obey him—surely no one
thought it her fault that it seldom worked out—Krysta
did as she was told. She kept the telling very short. When
she finished, she hoped they would get back to the

business at hand. Hawk had other ideas. He rose from the bed and reached for his tunic.

"I'm going to kill him now."

"Wait! What? You aren't!"

"I'll be back in no time. Don't go anywhere."

"No!" Krysta hurled herself at him, grabbing the tunic he had half on and ripping it from his hands. "What are you talking about? Killing Udell? Are you mad? If he dies, Mercia will rebel."

"You have it the wrong way around. If he lives, Mercia will rebel."

He knew. What she had merely feared and wanted to believe was deluded bragging was real. Horror clawed at her but with it came swift hope. Grace of God, Hawk knew, which meant Alfred must know as well.

"Why do you think I was summoned to Winchester?"

She stared at him in shock. "Because of Udell?"

"Do you think Alfred has united a splintered kingdom, ignited the light of learning where there was only darkness, and become the hope of his people for generations to come without having a keen eye for everything that goes on around him?"

"But then . . . something must be done."

"Yes, which is why—"

He was going to kill Udell. If not right then, sometime very soon. He had known that when he stood amidst the Mercians and offered him twice his wergild, money to buy an army and march against a throne, knowing Udell would never live to collect it. When he had been willing to be flogged, knowing the hand that wielded the whip would soon be in the grave.

"Not now." Krysta spoke emphatically but she didn't count on words alone. She hurled his tunic into a far corner of the room and promptly discarded her torn gown, shimmying it right up over her hips and breasts, freeing the glorious mass of her hair and tossing the garment somewhere over her head. As naked as he, she faced him proudly. "You aren't upset about Thorgold?"

He ran his eyes over her with frank pleasure. "No, it's Udell I'm going to kill."

"I understand that. But if you wanted to shed blood in the house of the king, he would be dead already."

The corners of his mouth were twitching. "You're infuriating to be sure but you have a good head on your shoulders."

Very clearly, because she had to do this while she had the courage, she said, "I am part of your world and part of something more. All my life I have fought against it. When I came here, I feared only sorrow lay ahead. Was I wrong to do so?"

Her heart was beating so hard she thought it must surely burst. She was terrified to speak so frankly, terrified of how he would respond, terrified of being terrified as though she would never be anything but if he should turn from her and leave her bereft in the cold.

And she did feel cold, so much so that she began to tremble. She wanted to wrap her arms around herself but could not lift them. Indeed, she could do nothing but stare at him with all her longing in her eyes.

"You are a foolish woman." He spoke with gruff tenderness and yanked her to him, engulfing her in his arms, warming her with his strength. They tumbled back across the bed, limbs entwining, mouths seeking.

Hawk tried, he truly did, but four days without her had left him ravenous. Even as he struggled to go slowly, to assure her readiness and draw out her pleasure, his need mounted unbearably. Groaning, he cupped her breasts, squeezing them together, his mouth moving from one to the other. Beneath his tongue, her nipples were hard and full. He suckled her urgently as he thrust a steel-hard leg between hers, opening her to him. Her arms closed around him in fierce embrace as though never to let him

go. The soft, curly apex of her thighs brushed his en-
gorged manhood as her hips arched.

"Please," she whispered tautly, less entreaty than de-
mand.

He took her mouth, his tongue plunging deep, and
felt her guide him just a little within her. He went slowly,
beads of sweat showing on his forehead, as he struggled to
give her all the time she needed to adjust to him. Even
then, he held himself very still, not moving except at the
very tip, stroking the hot, silken sheath that held him so
snugly. Darkness swirled behind his eyes as a wall of sensation struck him with such force that he was robbed of
breath. Gasping, he raised his head and watched in fascination her own surprise at the swiftness of her climax. In
the distant regions of his mind still capable of thought, he
realized he was not the only one who had found four solitary days to be exquisite torment. When pleasure ebbed a
little, she lay beneath him, panting softly, her hands moving over his back with tender strength.

Hawk rose above her, taking his weight on his knees
and arms. He gave her a moment to recover, no more, before driving into her hard and deep. The exquisite milking
sensation of his own release seized him and he erupted in
surging bliss that seemed to go on forever.

From the crest of pleasure to which he had so swiftly
taken her, Krysta soared yet higher. Wave after wave of
ecstasy rushed through her seemingly without end. She
sobbed, crying out his name, and clung to Hawk as the
world flew apart and she with it.

THEY WOKE SOME HOURS LATER TO THE DISTANT
sounds of revelry in the king's hall, where their absence no doubt sparked amusement. It did not matter.
They came together again more slowly, drawing out their
pleasure and slipped seamlessly from it back into gentle

sleep, only to be awakened again a short time later by the tantalizing aroma of fresh baked bread. It drew them to the tray left in Krysta's room, no doubt by her thoughtful maid. With childlike glee, they carried the repast back to bed and fed each other choice morsels until such intimacy had its inevitable result. They finally slept deeply and without dreams, not stirring again until the full light of dawn flowed through the high windows and over their entwined forms.

"I must see the king," Hawk murmured, scarcely awake as he kissed the sweet curve of Krysta's breast. He moved his hand over her belly and between her thighs, stroking her, and was rewarded by a soft whimper of pleasure. His lean cheeks roughened by a night's growth of whiskers teased her skin primed to exquisite sensitivity. She arched against him, tangling her fingers in his hair, and traced the hard curve of his mouth with the tip of her tongue. "Later." Whatever reply he might have made was lost in the quicksilver flare of his own response. The king would have to wait.

As he did until well into midmorning when Hawk finally slipped from the bed. He stood beside it, gazing down at the woman turned on her side facing him, her hands tucked under her chin and an expression of utter innocence upon her lovely face. A deep, contented sigh escaped him. The world felt completely right and Hawk himself so utterly at peace that if he ran into Udell right then, he decided he would kill him quickly instead of drawing it out as he had thought to do when learning that the Mercian traitor had dared to put his hands on Krysta. Moved to mercy in his present mood, he would be content merely to lop off his head. Such was the astounding effect of a good woman, he mused, as he looked around for whatever it was he had thought to find.

Clothes, that was it, and some water to wash with. He could shave later. Alfred had seen him in far scruffier condition when they sloughed through days and weeks of chasing the Danes from battlefield to battlefield. He was buckling on his sword as he left the chamber, spied a serving girl, and learned the king's whereabouts. Alfred was in the stables visiting with a colt born just that morning to his favorite mare. The king looked up as Hawk entered, assayed his disheveled condition, and shook his head ruefully.

"A restless night, Lord of Essex?"

Hawk grinned. "Actually quite a refreshing one, sire." He bent down to admire the colt. "May he be as steady as his dam and as fast as his sire."

Alfred nodded. "They make a good combination." He got to his feet and dusted off his hands. "Udell left in the night."

"Good. I assume Athelred awaits him at the border."

"He does, although he had some difficulty convincing my daughter to remain behind." The king could not suppress a proud smile. "Athelflad thought to ride with him."

"A true daughter of your house, my lord." Wise enough to have sniffed out Udell's perfidy and sent her royal father swift warning of it. "Udell should have ample time by now to grow careless. I ride within the hour. Between us, Athelred and I will squeeze the life from his traitor's bones."

"Ordinarily, I'd suggest bringing him back to stand trial but—"

Alfred did not have to go further for Hawk understood full well. The king focused his attention where it belonged, on the Danes. It was only by so doing that he had forged and kept the peace. Udell would not be allowed to distract him from it.

Hawk took his leave a short while later. He went around to the barracks where his men were housed. His lieutenants awaited him. Keen-eyed men long skilled in intrigue, they had known full well what the outcome with

Udell would be. Their horses were saddled and waiting. Behind them, drawn up rank upon rank, Hawk's personal guard, the most feared army in all of England, was mounted and ready. Sooner even than Hawk had promised, the force rode out through the gates of the royal residence and down the long road heading north out of Winchester. Hawk turned once in the saddle, eyeing the room where Krysta slept as it faded into the distance.

He supposed she would be concerned when she found him gone. Perhaps she would think he should have awakened her. But there had been too many farewells in his life; he had a keen dislike of them. Besides, he would be back within scant days and all would be well between them. Reassured that he had taken the proper course, Hawk continued on his way, his mind clear and untroubled, filled with pleasant thoughts of killing Udell.

H E'S GONE WHERE?" KRYSTA ASKED. SHE STARED AT Eahlswith in bewilderment. What was this the queen had just told her? Hawk gone after Udell and without a word to her? That could not be.

"He left at midday," Eahlswith repeated. She looked at Krysta sympathetically. "I know you are surprised but this is how men are. I cannot count the number of times Alfred marched to battle without saying a word to me."

She must still be asleep and dreaming, Krysta thought. That had to be it. Whatever the king had done, Hawk would not leave her like this. He would at least tell her he was going, reassure her all would be well, kiss away her fears and—

Oh, lord, no wonder the man preferred to sneak off. How could he possibly want to be saddled with her worry when he needed to turn his mind to the task at hand?

Yet she was still shocked by his sudden absence, and vaguely hurt. Her resentment faded as the day wore on and she was left with only worry. She was well aware of Eahlswith doing her best to draw her into the circle of ladies and so distract her that she would not think overmuch of Hawk. Not more than with every other heartbeat, rather than with each and every one. A hundred or more times she told herself he was the most feared warrior in all of England, leader of the most renowned army, his skills long honed in battle and fortified by keen intelligence. Beside him, Udell was no more than vermin. But even vermin could get lucky. Victory came as much by chance as by strength.

When she could no longer contain herself, she murmured apologies and slipped away to the little church near the scriptorium. There she went on her knees to pray long and earnestly that God in His mercy would shine His light on Hawk and cast his enemies into darkness. She prayed heedless of the young priests who moved about quietly, lighting the tall candles and singing the offices of the day. Only when she realized that they were singing complines did she return to any sense of passing time. She had come at nones when the sun was high above the tops of the trees, and it was now the hour before sleep. In between, the soaring peace of vespers had slipped past without her notice. Slowly, she rose on legs that seemed scarcely able to hold her. Her body was stiff and sore from her vigil but the balm of peace had flowed over her heart. For that, she was deeply grateful.

Outside in the cool night air, Krysta paused for a few moments to look at the stars. Was it merely a fancy of her mind to wonder if Hawk might be looking at them, too? How desperately she wished that she might reach out and touch one of the sparkling lights against the deep velvet black sky and in the doing, touch him as well.

She was sighing, wondering how she would ever sleep alone, when a shadow moved around the corner of the church. She had only a moment to wonder who it might be before a hand slammed down hard over her mouth and a powerful arm closed around her waist, yanking her off her feet.

"Bitch," the voice hissed in her ear. "Did you truly think you could challenge me and not pay?"

Terror roared through Krysta. She kicked out frantically and tried to sink her teeth into the hand over her mouth. For her trouble, she was hurled to the ground so hard that the air was knocked from her. Her arms were pulled behind her and roughly tied. As she tried to regain her feet, she was flung down again and her ankles roped together.

"Quickly," Udell ordered, his voice thick and harsh. Hard hands lifted her. She was carried away into darkness.

SEVENTEEN

H AWK TURNED HIS MOUNT IN A TIGHT
circle, carefully examining the marks on the
moist ground and the signs told by broken
branches. A large group on horses had
passed that way just hours before and done so in great
haste. Not far away, near where the road forked, a bundle
lay dropped as though fallen from a saddle. One of his
lieutenants opened it and with a laugh, drew out a lady's
mantle. He shook it free and held it up for all to see. The
back was elaborately embroidered with a garishly large
butterfly done almost entirely in gold.

"I never thought I'd say this," Hawk declared, "but
I'm glad of the Lady Esa's unique taste in garments."

Thus assured, they continued on the right track, the
force moved quickly. Within the hour, Hawk was certain
they were closing in on the Mercians. The droppings left
by their horses were that fresh. He nodded grimly as he
saw they were heading directly into the trap set by Alfred.
Just as they crossed the border into Mercia, when they
imagined themselves to be safe, they would be caught in a
pincer between Athelred and Hawk himself. The women

would likely survive for no one would seek their deaths, although Athelflad might have something to say later about Esa's fate.

Yet as the prints left by the horses became clearer, Hawk's easy mood began to darken. He had taken the measure of the Mercians at court and knew their numbers. It seemed to him there were fewer mounted than he would have expected. Concerned, he called a halt and got down to look at a clear stretch of the prints more closely.

"Is there a problem, lord?" one of his lieutenants asked. He waited nearby, astride his mount and holding the reins of Hawk's stallion.

Slowly, Hawk straightened. He continued to stare at the prints as he said, "I make this a dozen or so short."

Hearing him, the men closest by glanced at one another in surprise.

"The ground is very soft, lord," the lieutenant ventured. "Some of it looks rode twice over."

"Possibly," Hawk agreed, yet he was unconvinced. The thought began to form in the back of his mind that perhaps the Mercians had not all stayed together. In their panic to get away, some might have struck off on their own. That *was* possible, yet it was also possible that there was something more at work. Something vastly more threatening.

Udell was a vain, treacherous, venal bastard. But he wasn't stupid. No man actually could be stupid and survive any length of years in the cauldron that was English politics.

Hawk was mulling that over, on his haunches beside the hoof prints, when he looked up suddenly and noticed the ravens clustered in the trees overhead. They had not been there minutes before, of that he was quite sure. But then he had learned the hard way to pay much more attention to such matters than ever he had before.

"Ravens," he muttered and his lieutenant frowned, struggling to discover what concerned his lord.

"They are only birds," he said.

"Absolutely, only birds. You did not hear me say otherwise. Birds, that's all."

One of them, the largest of the bunch, with a shrewd glint in her eyes, cawed loudly. At once, Hawk heard a rustling in the nearby brush. He was on his feet, hand on the hilt of his sword, when a dog bounded forward. The animal ran right at him, jumped up on its hind legs, laid its paws against Hawk's broad chest, and dragged a wet tongue over his bemused face.

"He likes ye," Thorgold chuckled. The little man stepped out onto the road and whistled for the dog, who gave off licking Hawk and loped over to Thorgold's side, where he sat on his haunches, panting happily.

"He's a good dog, he is," Thorgold said, gently petting the animal, who waved his tail even more vigorously.

Looking more closely, Hawk saw the signs of a beating he suspected was recent but that seemed to be healing with unusual—he wasn't going to think "unnatural"—speed.

"Is that—?"

Thorgold nodded. "That's him."

"I'm glad he landed on his feet," Hawk said with a grin. "All four of them."

"Aye, he did an' ye can be gladder of it than ye know. He has the scent of Udell an' can follow that bastard over stone."

"That's why he's here, because you're trailing Udell?"

"Nay, because ye aren't. Yer fetchin' up a dry gulch, lad."

Hawk stared at the old troll as the confirmation of what he had seen in the hoofprints settled over him. His hand tightened on the hilt of his sword, the knuckles glowing white. The curse that broke from him sent the ravens into the air.

Thorgold waited until the leaves stopped shaking before he spoke the words he knew would plunge the Hawk into white-hot fury. Then he prudently stood back as with lightning speed the Lord of Essex divided his force. He chose with unerring precision the deadliest killers among his men. At his orders, they handed over to the others all weight that might conceivably slow them down. What was left was a war band honed to single purpose and lethal will.

An extra horse was brought. Thorgold bounded onto it and whistled for the dog, who leaped onto the saddle before him. Hawk spared a single glance to be sure they were well seated, spurred his stallion to a flat-out gallop, and raced back down the road toward Winchester. Only one thought drove him on, to find the woman he loved while she lived.

L YING WHERE SHE HAD BEEN THROWN IN THE BOW OF a boat, her arms and legs still cruelly tied and a gag biting into her mouth, Krysta fought the twin demons of nausea and terror. Her prayer that they would be stopped leaving Winchester had not been answered. On foot, hidden by shadows, Udell and his men had evaded the guards. What an enemy army could not have done, they managed. Once beyond the city, they moved quickly to a boat waiting for them on the River Itchen. Rowing throughout the night, they put many miles between them and the royal fortress before sunrise.

From time to time throughout the long hours of darkness, Udell called out, telling her what he would do to her. He described his plans in loving detail, dwelling on exactly how she would suffer and the measures that would be taken to assure she did not die too quickly. His voice became a kind of torture itself, reminding her of how very far she was from hope or help.

Yet through it all, as he ranted on and on, she refused to give in to her fear. When at last the boat turned in toward shore, she closed her eyes briefly, prayed deeply, and gathered her courage to face whatever was to come.

Given the horrible threats Udell had been spewing, the reality was anticlimactic. He was in far too much of a hurry to pause long enough to do anything to her. Horses awaited them in the small clearing beside the river's edge, brought there apparently by prior arrangement. Several furtive men looked around anxiously, accepted a pouch heavy with coin, and vanished back into the forest. In the gray light of pre-dawn, the Mercians hurried to mount and be gone. Still bound, Krysta was about to be thrown up across a saddle when her frantic protests finally drew Udell's attention.

"Jesu, you squeal loud enough to wake the dead! Perhaps I'll just smother you now and be done with it."

During the long hours in the boat, Krysta had ample time to think and she had come to her own conclusions about why Udell would have taken the risk of stealing her from beneath the very nose of the king's guard. She doubted very much that he had done it only for vengeance.

Even so, she was daring greatly as she stared at Udell with frank disbelief. Refusing to be silent, she continued her protests until finally, in exasperated fury, he yanked off the gag.

"By God, I swear I'll kill you right now!"

"No, you won't." Though her mouth was so sore that it hurt badly to talk, Krysta forced herself to continue. She straightened up as far as her knees, all she could manage with her ankles still tied, and said, "You need me as a hostage."

"I *need* to kill you."

"Maybe eventually but not yet. You know Hawk is coming after you."

Udell stared at her for a long moment, his mouth working. Finally, he said, "He's far from here and headed in the wrong direction. By the time he realizes, I'll be in Mercia and you'll be dead."

"You won't kill me just because you reach Mercia. You're not such a fool. You know perfectly well no border will stop the Hawk."

Udell laughed but uneasily. He stood with his hands on his hips, looking down at her with such utter hatred that it was all Krysta could do not to cringe. Instead, she kept her back straight and her head high, ignoring the burning pain in her limbs. Not for a moment did she allow her gaze to waver.

"Then he will come," Udell said and shrugged. "On my own lands, in my own stronghold, I can defeat him easily. With the Hawk dead, all of Mercia will rally to me. I will take Wessex and the throne."

So he had worked it all out in his disordered mind and so he truly believed it could happen, for the moment. Soon enough, Krysta suspected, he would begin to remember the many battles of the Hawk, the enemy armies destroyed, the mighty fortresses laid waste. Fear would eat at him and his actions would become unpredictable. But for some length of time yet, she could turn his insane confidence to her own ends.

"Thus the sooner you reach Mercia, the better for you. Why am I still tied then? Surely you don't believe I can escape from you and a dozen armed men?"

When Udell said nothing but only continued to stare at her, Krysta said, "My weight and yours on one horse will slow you down. Let me ride."

He hesitated and for a moment she was certain he would refuse. But speed was uppermost in his mind and he could not deny the truth of what she said. Besides, how could one lone woman escape a band of armed men?

Udell barked an order. Krysta's bonds were cut. She stifled a groan of sheer relief as she tried swiftly to rub some circulation back into her muscles. As Udell turned away to throw a saddlebag over his mount, she said, "Give me a moment to see to my needs."

He turned and glared at her. "Why the hell should I?"

Struggling to her feet, Krysta said, "Because you are not afraid of me. You don't wonder why the ravens attacked you. You aren't concerned that the story my half-brother told might be true. And surely you aren't puzzled why the most powerful warlord in England will march through hell to reach me. For after all, I am only a mere woman."

Even in the gray light, she saw his face pale. He looked around hastily to see if any of his men had heard. Reassured they had not, he hissed at her, "Do it then and be quick! But by God, if you try witchwork on me, I'll see you burn!"

Krysta made haste before he could reconsider. She was not so foolish as to try to escape where she had no hope of getting away, but the temptation was strong all the same. Every ounce of her courage and determination was needed to mount the horse beside Udell's. The reins had been removed and a rope tied to the horse's bridle. Udell had hold of the other end. Krysta clung to the pommel as the horses set off at a gallop.

They rode for hours without once slackening their pace. By afternoon, Krysta was close to despair. They would have to stop for the night at some time, that or run their horses into the ground. But once they halted, no doubt she would be bound again. The thought of what the long hours of darkness in the company of a hate-filled, vengeful man could mean made her blood run cold. Perhaps it would be better simply to take her chances and hope she could get away into the forest somehow. But to elude Udell and his men on foot would be impossible.

She was searching frantically for some faint ray of hope when she glanced to one side and noticed through the thick-leafed branches the glint of fast-running water. From time to time during the long hours she had caught a glimpse of the river, enough to realize that the road they were on must roughly parallel it. But now it seemed unusually close and the road appeared to be turning in its direction.

A few moments later, her suspicions were confirmed when she realized they would have to cross a low wooden bridge that joined the two parts of the road on opposite sides of the river. As they approached the bridge, she saw that the water beneath it was turbulent, breaking against submerged rocks and sending up froths of spray that showered rainbows of light to either side. Under other circumstances the beauty of such a display would have struck her, but now all she could think of was that day was fast fleeing and taking hope with it.

In the lead, Udell slowed his horse to a walk. The hooves of the animals resounded sharply against the wooden planks. They were about to ride out onto the bridge when Udell stopped suddenly. A long pole attached to a trestle had been lowered across the entrance, blocking their way.

"What the hell is this?" Udell demanded.

Barely had he spoken than a little man bustled forward from somewhere beneath the bridge. He was quite short but powerfully built, with long black hair that merged into the beard that hung halfway down his barrel chest. There was an air of importance about him as he confronted Udell and the others.

"Pay the toll, cross the bridge," he announced in a low, rumbling voice.

"Toll?" Udell looked at him incredulously. "What

are you talking about? There's never been any toll on this bridge."

"There is today," the little man said. Boldly, as though it concerned him not at all to be facing a band of armed warriors, he held out his hand. "Cross my palm with gold and cross the bridge. Elsewise, turn back or—" His eyes, hidden beneath great bushy brows, gleamed. "Or would you rather swim? River's running hard though. Only a truly good swimmer would have any chance of making it to the other side, much less downstream."

"What're you prattling about?" Udell demanded. His hand went to the hilt of his sword. "Get out of my way, old man, or by God I'll cleave you in two."

Far from being alarmed by this threat, the little man merely shrugged. "Are ye a good swimmer then, Lord of Mercia? Feel up to takin' yer chance in the water, do ye?"

Udell looked at him in disbelief, then threw back his head and laughed. "By God, the fellow's addled. He knows who I am and he's still doing this!"

The men behind Udell also laughed but they sounded distinctly less amused. Krysta scarcely heard them. She was staring at the water through the dancing rainbows of light, thinking about what the little man had said. The river was running hard and there were the rocks, not to mention the rapids she had glimpsed just north of where they had left the boat. The current would take her at once and she would have very little chance of fighting it. But if she could catch hold of a fallen log and keep her head up enough to get air—

Udell would not be delayed much longer. Already he was drawing his sword.

"Get out of the way, old man."

Krysta pressed her heel into the side of her horse, urging him over near the edge of the bridge.

"And move that damn pole."

All in the space of a heartbeat, she breathed deeply, raised her hand in thanks to the little man, swung her leg over the horse, and jumped. The current took her with stunning force. There was no time to think or breathe or even try to swim. Behind her, she could hear Udell shouting and managed to turn her head just enough to catch a glimpse of him frantically gesturing to his men. Then bridge, Mercians, and all else vanished from sight as the current pulled her under.

Just beneath the surface, the river looked far calmer. Dappled light illuminated forests of waving fronds that grew out of the gravelly riverbed. Swirls of mud rose in eddies, momentarily obscuring Krysta's vision until she was thrust clear of them. Rocks flew past, some small, others the size of huts. Of a sudden, she found herself staring directly into the eyes of a fish, a salmon she thought. Then it, too, was gone and the current flowed on.

It was very peaceful really for all its speed. She was vaguely surprised to have no sense of danger. Indeed, she felt nothing but relief to be free of Udell and all the turbulence above. The river rounded a bend and she was suddenly thrust again into the sun. She surfaced gasping, terrified for an instant that she could not breathe, and had no time to think of the absurdity of that before her starved lungs drew in air.

Her clothes dragged at her and she was pulled under again. This time, she fought her way back into the open and found herself cast into a quiet pool that flowed off to one side of the river. On hands and knees, she crawled onto the mossy bank and collapsed in an exhausted stupor.

Some while later, she had no sense of how long, she raised her head and looked around. She had no idea how far she was from the bridge but all her instincts told her to keep moving. Udell would not be willing to lose the hostage who stood between him and certain death. He would come after her if only to recover her body, for if Hawk was hunting them and he found her dead, he would attack without mercy.

Staggering to her feet, Krysta struggled to decide what to do. If she tried to follow the river road back the way she had come, Udell would have a far easier time of finding her. But if she abandoned the road, she might easily become lost in an area where there were few settlements and many natural dangers. That left the river.

She stared at it hesitantly. The current was still flowing fast. Ordinarily, to trust herself to it would be madness. And yet it had not killed her when by all rights it should have. She was weary and a little bruised but that was as nothing against what might well have happened. Somewhere up ahead were rapids. She was quite sure she had not come upon them yet and that she would not survive doing so. But if she could keep aware and leave the river before the rapids, she just might have a chance.

The pool lay in the shadow of several old oak trees. One of them was dying. A long arm of a fallen branch lay on the bank, almost in the water. Tentatively, Krysta pushed it into the pool. She watched until she saw it float. Quickly, before she could think better of it, she stripped off most of the clothes that had so weighed her down. Wearing only her shift, she waded back into the water, grabbed hold of the tree limb, and kicked toward the river.

HAWK DREW REIN AT THE EDGE OF THE CLEARING. He took note of the boat drawn up on the shore and of the marks left in the soft earth. A wave of his hand brought Thorgold to his side.

"Let the dog have a go at this."

Scarcely had the animal been set down than he began to race around the clearing, nose to the ground. He did this faster and faster, narrowing his search area, until within minutes he was back on the forest trail and trotting north. Half a mile on, where the road forked, he moved left unerringly.

"Good dog," Thorgold said and whistled him back up into the saddle.

"How did you know about the clearing?" Thorgold asked as they rode on.

"I've used it myself," Hawk replied. "Just beyond are rapids. You either portage around them or go on by horse. It's the second of the main routes into Mercia. I thought there were too many of them fleeing court to go this way and it seems most didn't. But Udell had other ideas."

His face was grim as he spoke. They had ridden relentlessly since earliest day. It was now afternoon but no hint of fatigue marked the Hawk or any of his men. Nor could they afford to let any creep over them. Udell had far too great a lead. To catch him they would have to press themselves to the limits of endurance and beyond. Or they would have to get very lucky.

The dog was luck, Hawk thought. Without him, they would not have known for certain that they were on the right road and they could not afford to go wrong again. But it would take more. Much more.

They continued on upriver. Long ago, when his life had seemed to consist of nothing but battles, Hawk had learned the trick of falling into a watchful reverie. It allowed his weary mind and body some measure of rest while keeping him alert to danger. Now he sought that state purely for release from the anguish that had tormented him from the moment he learned that Krysta was in Udell's hands, but he did not find it.

A thousand times he berated himself for not anticipating what the Mercian might do. He had been too confident of being able to defeat Udell, too certain the traitor would fall neatly into the trap set for him. And perhaps he

would have if Krysta had not been at court to draw his eye
and spark his rage. She should have been left safe at home
in Hawkforte, even if he'd had to keep her locked up to do
it. But no, he had put his own belief that confronted by
king and court she would give up any notion of rejecting
their betrothal above all other regard.

And now she could die.

He inhaled sharply, stabbed through by a thought
more painful than any blow he had ever taken in his life of
battles. He could not lose her! By God, he could not!
Please God, he would do anything, bargain with anything, promise anything.

Hawk had rarely prayed. He saw little point in it since
it was not his observation that God favored any side
in battle. He had seen men he would have given his life
for die in an instant while others escaped death time
and time again. His own continued life he credited to
his skill, to luck, and to whatever fate might have planned
for him. He found some pleasure in the mass, if only
for the brief respite it offered from worldly concerns,
but he did not consider the recitation of prayers to be
prayer itself.

Now he prayed as he had not known he could do,
prayed with all his heart and soul while the long miles
passed and time inched by. If God would spare her, he
would do anything, even give her up if that was what was
needed. He could live without her, however barren that
life would be, if only he knew she yet lived somewhere in
the world. To imagine a world without Krysta was more
than he could bear.

The dog barked.

Hawk returned from his bleak reverie to see Thorgold
struggling to contain the animal, who was trying to leap
out of the saddle. "Something's spooked him," Thorgold
said. He gave up trying to hold the dog and let him down.

Barely had he done so than the animal began rushing in circles, seeking a scent.

Hope flared in Hawk. Mayhap they were closer than he had thought. If something had happened to delay Udell—

The dog continued in circles, nose to the ground, but without success. He grew increasingly agitated as he failed to find what he sought. Thorgold dismounted and went to him. "What's the trouble, boy?"

The dog lifted his head and whined softly. His tail drooped.

"Have we lost him?" Hawk asked. He could not imagine how. Udell would have no greater goal than to reach Mercia and his stronghold. Leaving the road would slow him down tremendously, and he could not return to the river because he had left his boat below the rapids. Unless he had arranged for another boat, but there was no sign of that, no clearing where boats could be brought ashore, no indication of horses milling about as riders dismounted.

"Nay," Thorgold said, "he's been this way all right but the scent isn't fresh. Still, something got this fellow going." He patted the dog's head reassuringly and made to return to his horse. At once the animal stiffened, looking toward the river. He raised a front paw, stretching out both nose and tail.

"He was trained for hunting," Hawk said. All his senses were suddenly, keenly alert. He too looked toward where the glint of fast-running water shone through the trees. "Could Udell have doubled back for some reason?"

Scarcely had he uttered the question than hope rippled through him. Krysta was a woman of uncommon strength and courage. If she could have found any way to escape, she would have seized it. Quickly, Hawk urged his mount off the road and through the brush toward the river. His men followed, as did Thorgold and the dog. Barely had they reached the edge of the water than the animal began to bark again. He ran back and forth between the bank and the watching men. Finally, he sat down on his haunches, tongue lolling, and stared directly at Hawk.

"Damn if he isn't trying to tell me something."

Hawk dismounted and walked down the bank until the water lapped at his boots. He stared up and down the river. In the quiet of late afternoon, the only sounds were the creak of saddles, the faint rustle of birds in the trees overhead, the hum of insects, and the low snorts of the horses. The silver gleam of a trout flashed by in the water.

A few miles south the river would smash into rapids but here it ran wide and deep. There was only a scattering of rocks to be seen and a handful of dead tree limbs being moved along by the current. One of the limbs seemed to be dragging something—

Hawk looked a moment longer but already he knew, for the dog was barking again and his own heart was soaring even as it tripped with dread. He went into the water in an instant and was swimming swiftly toward what he had seen before his men knew what he was about. Against the current, all his strength was needed to bring him quickly to the log. Before he was there, he knew he was right. Krysta was clinging to the wood, soaked and bedraggled, her face very pale, but when she saw him an exhausted smile lifted the corners of her mouth. Hawk redoubled his efforts, his mighty chest and arms straining. He reached her within moments and got an arm around her.

"Are you all right?" he demanded gruffly, all the fear and dread of the past hours stark in his voice.

She nodded but did not try to speak, saving what was left of her strength. For so long she had fought the current as it threatened to smash her into rocks or drag her under again that it was all she could do to cling to consciousness. Her body was weak but her spirit soared at the sight of Hawk.

With rough tenderness, he said, "You have to let go now. Hold on to me."

She nodded again to show she understood but her cramped hands could scarcely move. Gently, he eased her off the log and into his arms. She clung to him as he battled his way against the current and back to the bank of the river. Before they reached it, his men were in the water, surrounding them and helping bring them ashore.

Hawk carried Krysta out of the river and laid her carefully on the bank. Her eyes were closed and her breathing was ragged. Thorgold hurried over with a cloak. Hawk wrapped her in it and began briskly rubbing her arms and back. For long moments she did not move, but finally she lifted her head, met his frantic gaze, and touched a gentle hand to his roughened cheek.

"You need to shave."

He stared at her, momentarily unable to make sense of her words. When he did, he laughed in relief, in thanks, and in sheer, unbridled joy. "Woman, if you can notice that, you must be all right."

"I'm fine," Krysta assured him, then ruined it by wincing as she tried to sit up. Instantly, Hawk urged her back down. "Don't move. You're bruised from head to toe. That you're even alive is a miracle. You do realize that after this I'll be hard-pressed not to keep you locked up?"

Krysta muttered something he couldn't quite catch. When he bent nearer, she repeated it. His eyes widened slightly before he grinned. "I'd consider it. Being locked up with you isn't the worst fate I can imagine."

Before she could remark on that, he lifted her again and carried her to his horse. As he placed her gently on the mount and swung into the saddle behind her, Krysta warned, "Udell may be after me."

Hawk took hold of the reins with one hand, wrapped a steely arm around her, and said, "I'm counting on it."

Signaling to his men, he turned back toward the road in the direction from which they had come. His intent was to get Krysta to safety before hunting down Udell. But he was well aware that such might be the Mercian's desperation that he would overtake them quickly. Within the hour, that suspicion was confirmed when the dog barked again. Swiftly, Hawk guided his horse from the road and into the surrounding trees. His men and Thorgold did the same. After his initial warning, the dog fell silent, watching alertly as the men dismounted and deployed.

"Stay with her," Hawk told Thorgold. The old troll nodded and guided Krysta farther into the woods. She began to protest but he hushed her firmly. Hawk spared a glance to be sure the pair had vanished, then gave his full attention to the road.

He did not have long to wait. The pounding of hooves galloping toward them signaled Udell's approach. Long ago, Hawk had worked out a system of hand gestures so that he could issue orders to his men in silence when necessary. He had found it useful more than once and now he did so again.

Udell and his Mercians never saw the rope strung across the road that stopped the horses in the lead. As the animals reared, panicky, their riders were thrown. Udell landed hard but regained his feet quickly, coming up with his sword drawn. Instantly, Hawk was upon him. As his men engaged the others, he cut Udell off from any help and closed in on him remorselessly. The Mercian paled at the sight of the warrior facing him, but he too was blooded in battle and knew his only hope lay in attack. He came in swiftly, slashing with the broadsword he held clasped in both hands. Hawk merely let him come, easily blocking every blow, all but overwhelmed by the urge to draw out Udell's death. The temptation was great but the thought of Krysta stopped him. She needed care and rest without delay.

As Hawk raised his sword yet again, he found himself suddenly swept clean of all sense of hate or lust for revenge. In his heart and mind, in the essence of his spirit, there was only gratitude that Krysta lived. Beside that nothing else mattered. For the first time since learning she had been taken, he drew a breath that felt pure and free. Deep within him a single shining thought unfolded: *By thy will, Lord.*

Chapter

EIGHTEEN

UDELL FROZE, HIS EYES WIDE AND STARing fixedly beyond Hawk. Whatever he saw appeared to fill him with horror but he had little time to contemplate it. The blade of finely honed steel wielded in the hand of a master slashed through air and man together. The Mercian died in an instant, his head severed from his body. His blood drained into the rich earth of the land he had thought to usurp from its anointed king.

Hawk lowered his sword and looked around. He saw that Udell did not go alone to his fate. The other Mercians were falling to the men Hawk had handpicked for the task. Within minutes, there was only stillness.

Until the ravens cawed.

Hawk wiped his sword clean on Udell's cloak. He signaled to two of his men.

"There's a village about an hour east of the clearing. Get together some of the peasants and see this lot buried."

He would not leave even traitors to the ravens and the wolves. But neither would he give them any further thought. Quickly, he sought out Krysta, finding her a short distance into the forest. She was still wrapped within his cloak, her hair hanging in a sodden mass down her back, and her face so white he swore he could count every freckle. When she saw him, she sprang up, glared at him, and flung herself into his arms.

"You had better be all right, you had just better!" she yelled, striking her fists against his chest. The blows were so soft he could scarcely feel them but he knew better than to let her see that.

"Ouch! Stop that, woman! Udell did not cause me such discomfort as you now inflict."

"Is he—?"

"Of course he is. Now put him from your mind. Thorgold, did you never think to teach this wench manners? Look at her, beating me when all I've done is pull her out of a river and get rid of a nuisance."

"I'll leave the manners to ye, lord," Thorgold said with a chuckle. He whistled for the dog and headed back to the road.

"I do have manners," Krysta said plaintively. "Truly I do, it's just that you bring out the worst in me. I cannot think when I am around you. Every time I try to do so, I stumble over feelings that overwhelm me."

Her reward for this befuddled confession was a heart-stopping grin that stole her breath. She had yet to recover it when Hawk swept her into his arms, carried her back to his horse, and set off for Winchester, which he intended to reach with absolutely no further delay.

They entered the city shortly after nightfall. Every torch was lit and watch fires blazed from the guard towers. Alerted to Udell's treason, crowds were gathered in the streets. They cheered mightily as Hawk and his men rode by. Alfred himself came out to greet them in the courtyard of the royal residence.

"My dear friends!" the king exclaimed. "You have ever been in our thoughts and prayers. Praise God for restoring you to us."

Krysta was received into gentle hands, but the moment Hawk dismounted he reclaimed her. Holding her high against his chest, he said, "I thank you, my lord. Udell is dead. Now if you don't mind, I would like to make arrangements to return to Hawkforte."

Looking at the exhausted woman asleep in the Hawk's arms, Alfred said apologetically, "I don't mind at all. However, I'm not the one you have to convince."

Even as he spoke, Eahlswith descended the steps to stand at her lord's side. She glanced at Hawk, peered at Krysta, and clucked. "That poor dear child. Bring her inside at once. She needs a bath, rest, good food, and care."

"Of course she does," Hawk agreed. "But quickly, my lady, if you wouldn't mind. We start for Hawkforte at dawn."

The gentle queen, loving mother, and mild-mannered helpmate, gazed at the mighty Hawk, who towered above her, unshaven, blood-splattered, and as fearsome a sight as to dwell in the nightmares of any man. She frowned. "*You* may start whenever you wish, my lord. But your lady remains here until I say she is fit to travel."

Hawk looked to Alfred in surprise but the king merely shrugged. "I would just give in if I were you," he said quietly. "It's so much simpler in the end."

Thus blessed with new understanding of the inner workings of the royal marriage, Hawk trudged up the steps in Eahlswith's wake. The queen's ladies met them at the top and promptly clustered about, chirping with concern. He was allowed to go as far as Krysta's chamber and even to deposit her on the bed. That done, he was dismissed. Scarcely did he realize what was happening than the door was closed firmly in his face.

It remained closed through that night and into the

next day, as did the door connecting the two chambers. Whenever Hawk knocked, as he did regularly, he was met by one of any number of sweet-faced, gentle-voiced ladies who told him flatly he could not come in. Krysta was asleep, he was informed. She needed her rest. She would be fine. He would be told when he could see her.

He appealed to Alfred, who shrugged again and suggested they go hunting. This they did, but upon returning late in the afternoon only to be barred yet again from Krysta's door, Hawk rebelled. He insisted on being admitted, which threw the gentle ladies into a flutter and caused the queen to be summoned. To Eahlswith, he pleaded his case.

"I only want to see her for a moment," he said, feeling ridiculous, for when had he ever pleaded with a woman for anything? Yet he was so grateful that Krysta lived and that she was being properly cared for that he could do nothing but entreat.

Eahlswith took pity. She allowed him to come into the room and stand beside the bed but with a caution to remain quiet. Just as he had been told, Krysta was deeply asleep. She lay on her back, her glorious hair shining clean and neatly braided, the top of a chaste white shift peering from above the covers. A great surge of relief went through him as he finally saw her but it was gone in an instant, replaced by shock.

A livid purple and blue bruise covered most of her right cheek. On the other side, her forehead was badly scraped and swollen. Her wrists were bandaged. He turned to Eahlswith, who said softly, "She was tied for a time. The ropes cut her wrists and ankles. We must be grateful that was the only harm Udell did to her directly. The rest came in the river. She is bruised from head to toe but no bones are broken and—and no other damage was done. She will recover but she cannot possibly go anywhere for some time yet."

Hawk shook his head numbly. "I didn't realize . . . riding back here, she was asleep most of the time and I was just so glad to have her alive that I didn't think—"

Eahlswith laid a hand on his arm gently. "You know as well as I that bruises take time to show. Getting her here quickly was the best thing you could have done."

His face was anguished as he looked at the pale, still figure lying in the bed. "She must be in pain."

"She was when she awoke this morning although she tried her best to conceal it. I gave her a soothing draft and she slipped back to sleep. Nothing will heal her as quickly as sleep will do."

And he'd been banging on the door, demanding to be admitted.

Eahlswith saw the look in his eyes and correctly interpreted it. "Listen to me. I will tell you exactly what I would tell either of my own sons. You are not to blame for this in any way, and even more important, you saved her. She is here, she will recover, the two of you will be together again. Give thanks for that and let the rest go."

Hawk nodded, not trusting himself to speak. His eyes burned and his vision was blurred. He knelt beside the bed and took Krysta's hand very gently in his. Holding on to her, he bowed his head.

Later, leaving the chamber, he still felt deeply shocked and subdued. But by the time he stepped out into the brilliant sun of a fading summer day, anger was surging within him. Even as he fought to control it he wished Udell might yet be alive if only so that he could kill him again. But the Mercian was gone beyond his reach and Athelred would deal ably with the others. Lacking any outlet for his rage, Hawk sought some way to distract himself. He walked aimlessly until he found himself outside the scriptorium. After hesitating briefly, he went inside. The priest Asser was there, looking over another copy of Alfred's law book that was nearing completion.

Seeing Hawk, he took his leave of the scribe. Together, they walked back outside.

"There is something I can do for you, my lord?" Asser asked.

Hawk nodded. He had not known what he intended when he entered the scriptorium but it was clear to him now. "I wish to commission a book."

The priest looked surprised. "You have scribes of your own at Hawkforte?"

"Able men but not so skilled as some here. I want this to be a special book."

"And the subject . . . ?"

Hawk thought for a moment. "Birds, something to do with that. Real information about them, not just the tales people tell. With illustrations that make them seem to come alive."

"A laudable idea, my lord, but if you will forgive me, I had not realized your great interest in this area."

"I have none," Hawk admitted. "But the Lady Krysta does. I intend this as a gift for her."

The priest looked at him for a moment, then smiled. If he thought it strange to give a book to a woman, he did not show it. "I see. Well, then, we must find the best hand for this. There is a young monk here who daily feeds the birds in the garden. I have noticed him observing them and making sketches. I think he might do."

"I leave it to you then."

"Be assured I will see to it. Is there anything else I might help with, my lord?"

Hawk thought for a moment and grinned. "Not unless you happen to know where in Winchester I could find hair ribbons."

Asser admitted he did not but a dairymaid bringing fresh milk to the scriptorium did and she was delighted to tell Hawk. He went off realizing that the quickest way past his anger was to think of Krysta and what would be likely to please her. He spent the rest of the day doing just that and was a happy man for it.

PROPPED UP AGAINST THE PILLOWS, KRYSTA LOOKED out over the expanse of the bed to the cluttered room beyond. To no one in particular, she said, "Someone has to stop him."

Several of the ladies giggled. Seated nearby on a chair from which she had removed several bolts of cloth, Eahlswith smiled. "I think it's terribly sweet."

"Oh, it is," Krysta agreed bemusedly. She looked at the swirls of color lying on the bed, indeed taking up a great deal of it. "But if this goes on much longer, any woman in all of England who wants a hair ribbon will have to get it from me. Not to mention the most beautiful perfumes, the rarest fruits, more silk and velvet than I could ever imagine using in a lifetime." She continued to scan the room, shaking her head. "And all those jewels. What am I ever going to do with them?"

"Wear them?" one of the ladies suggested. She spoke kindly but with the same dazed amazement as had characterized all the ladies since Hawk's gifts began arriving late the previous day. With the morning, Krysta had awakened to find her chamber transformed into a treasure room and still the gifts continued to appear.

She was having difficulty coming to terms with it because with her return to consciousness had come a return of the nausea that had plagued her since shortly after her arrival in Winchester. The queen's remedy of dry husk and chamomile had worked once again, but Krysta was still stiff and sore from all the bruises. A hot bath did make her feel much better, especially since it was scented with some of the rare oils Hawk had sent. But a look in the mirror as her hair was being brushed made her shudder. She could not bear the thought of him seeing her like that.

When he came by later in the day, she pleaded fatigue but sent out a message thanking him for the gifts. No doubt he would be content with that, for what man wanted to be in a sickroom?

Hawk was there the next morning when she awoke. He was seated beside the bed in the chair previously occupied by the queen, who hovered in the background with her ladies. He had an extremely firm look on his face, as though it would take nothing short of an act of God to move him. When he saw that she was awake, he smiled. Leaning forward, he said gently, "Good morning. How are you feeling?"

Krysta began to sit up, meaning to tell him that she was fine, but before she could speak the damned nausea hit her yet again. Mortified, she groaned and pressed her hand to her mouth. Instantly, Hawk was on his feet, bending over her at the same time as he demanded of the queen, "What's wrong with her? She's ill. What's the matter?"

Eahlswith bustled to Krysta's side, helped her to sit up just a little, and handed her the cup of chamomile that was already prepared. As she sipped it slowly, Eahlswith said, "She's been queasy every morning when she awakens for more than a week now." Her eyes met Hawk's. "I was concerned that might no longer be the case after the battering she took in the river, but happily nothing has changed."

Krysta heard her as though from a distance and with bewilderment. Why on earth would Eahlswith be happy that she was still nauseated every morning? That made no sense at all. And why was Hawk staring at her like that, as though the ground had just dropped out from under his feet? He actually looked pale, and what was that he was saying?

"Sweetheart, I'm sorry."

Sorry? Why would he be sorry?

She shook her head, giving up trying to figure out any of it. Still scarcely half-awake, she said, "There's no reason for you to apologize. It's hardly your fault I have an upset stomach."

Hawk and the queen looked at each other. She raised an eyebrow. He reddened. "My dear," Eahlswith said gently, "I know you did not have the benefit of a mother's guidance when you were young, but there were other women who helped to raise you, were there not?"

What a very odd subject for the queen to want to discuss just then. All the same, Krysta did her best to respond. "I was raised by two faithful servants, Raven and Thorgold. But yes, there were women on my lands."

"And did they talk to you about . . . things?"

"Of course. We always talked about the harvest, the weather, how people were faring and so on."

"I see . . . What about this—Raven, you said her name is? Does she have children of her own?"

Krysta hesitated. She truly had no idea what Raven did when she went off. "I don't know . . . she might. We've never talked of that."

Eahlswith patted Krysta's hand, sent a sharp look in Hawk's direction, and ushered her ladies out of the room. When they were alone, he sat down again slowly, without taking his eyes from Krysta. The loudest sound was her chewing of the husk, which she tried to make as quiet as possible before she gave up and stuffed it under the bed-covers. After a moment, he cleared his throat. "Well, then . . . that is . . . basically you're all right . . . which is wonderful really, a tremendous relief . . . and that stuff you're drinking, it helps?" He gestured to the cup she still held.

She brushed away a few crumbs with her free hand and said, "It's very good and the queen has been very kind. If you won't mind my saying, you don't look entirely well yourself. Perhaps Eahlswith could suggest something that would make you feel better."

Really, if he kept staring at her so oddly, she would think something truly was wrong with him. Without warning he smiled, a big flashing grin. "I don't think I really could feel any better. Well, no, that's not true, there is one thing that would help."

Krysta looked a little alarmed. He didn't mean buying her more gifts, did he? Cautiously she asked, "What's that?"

He took the cup from her and set it on the table, then took both her hands in his very gently, looked deeply into her eyes, and said earnestly, "Getting married, right here in Winchester, as soon as you're able. Father Asser can do the honors, Alfred and Eahlswith will be delighted, and we can return to Hawkforte as man and wife."

Krysta's heart skipped. She felt cold, then hot, then nothing at all, so consumed was she by the sudden vision of her future thrust before her. Yet old fears lingered. "My mother—"

"Was a fine woman, I'm sure. If she were here, I have no doubt she would tell you we should be married without any further delay."

He spoke emphatically, with unshakable certainty. The lure of his confidence was all but irresistible. Only honesty prevented Krysta from succumbing at once.

"Hawk . . . there's something I have to tell you."

"Something else?" He looked surprised, then alarmed. Her servants . . . her mother . . . what *else* could there possibly be? "It's not anything about your father, is it?"

"Oh, no, he was a perfectly normal man. But that's the problem, you see."

He tried, he truly did, but failed. "What's wrong with him being normal?"

Krysta took a deep breath and held on to his hands.

"He was a normal man and men don't always seem to feel the same emotions that women do. Perhaps it's because you're raised as warriors. My mother loved him but he wasn't able to love her in return. She couldn't stay here in this world without the bond of love to hold her. Just as she could call beings from the other realm into this one, she in turn was called there."

Hawk frowned and she could see he was struggling to understand. Quickly, before she could think better of it, she said, "I didn't tell you the truth about why I came to Hawkforte disguised as a servant, or at least not the whole truth. I did think that if I could get to know you first I could be a better wife, but I wanted to be the best wife possible so that you would fall in love with me." Her voice dropped, becoming little more than a whisper. "That way, I wouldn't have to worry about suffering the same fate as my mother."

Slowly, Hawk nodded. "And now this troubles you because . . . ?"

Really, was the man so dense? If he couldn't see that she yearned for his—

"I don't believe it!" Hawk jumped up, paced a few yards from the bed, whirled, and glared at her. "I absolutely don't believe it! After all that's happened, you can lie there and claim you don't know that I love you? God's blood, woman, are you deaf, dumb, and blind? You have turned my life upside down, made me doubt my own reason, yet I accepted all without complaint. I asked you days ago if you wondered why that was. Did you have no thought to what I meant when you yourself had said you had more care for my honor than I did because you loved me? Did you not think for even a moment that I would have more care for you *for the same damned reason?*"

As romantic declarations went, it lacked poetry. Yet Krysta heard him out with heart pounding and eyes aglow. He loved her? He loved her! How could she have been so foolish? Surely, had he not loved her, he would have wrung her neck by now.

She gave a little shriek of joy, scrambled off the bed, and launched herself into his arms. Hawk caught her with a look of horror.

"What are you doing? You're bruised from head to toe. Why are you jumping out of bed? For God's sake, woman, you'll turn my hair white before my time." With great tenderness, he laid her back down but continued to hold her. Krysta snuggled against him, overwhelmed with happiness. She could think of nothing but the storms they had weathered, born of her own conscience and Udell's lack of one. But now they had come to safe harbor, they were together, and the future lay before them golden with promise.

With a contented sigh, she turned in his arms. Her hand lay against his broad chest. She loved the strength of him, so different from her own strength yet complementing it perfectly. How she had missed him, longed for him, needed him. Unconsciously, she moved her hand over the granite bone and muscle lightly covered by fine linen. How easily that could be cast aside. How readily they could be together without hindrance. It had been so very long . . .

"Oh, no!" Hawk sat up with unconcealed alarm. He looked at her darkly. "I swear I will not last out a year before you drive me truly mad. What do you think to do here? Do you think I can lie like that, with you in my arms, breathing your scent and being touched by you without needing to make you mine? You who are so bruised and battered, yet by the grace of God still——" He shook his head as though to clear it.

"Still what?" Krysta asked. She propped herself up on her elbows, the better to look at him as he got off the bed and stared at her . . . nervously? Was that it? How curious, but perhaps men got like that when they were in love.

"Never mind. Go to sleep."

"I have slept a day and more. I cannot possibly sleep more now."

"I will tell Eahlswith to drug you again."

"Fie on you for such a thought! I will not drink it. Nay, do not go. I need amusement."

"Amusement?" He looked torn between anger and laughter. "You toy with me?"

She sat up further, smiling. The shoulder of her gown slipped away, revealing the creamy swell of her breast. "Aye, I will if you will permit it."

He was tempted, so tempted. She watched the battle raging within him, saw the moment when his sterner self won, and sighed with disappointment. "Go then." Mutinously, she flopped back against the pillows. "I will be fine."

"You will be," he agreed as he strode to the door. Over his shoulder, he said, "But I will send you amusement, lady, as is fitting for a bride."

Such was Krysta's lingering innocence that she did not take that for the dire threat she shortly discovered it to be.

K RYSTA WINCED, TRIED TO MOVE, WINCED AGAIN, and stared at the queen beseechingly. Eahlswith smiled. "You look absolutely lovely, my dear. It's coming along very well."

Mindful of the seamstress directly beside her, wielding what must be the sharpest pins in the world, Krysta chose her words with care. "Is it done?"

"Almost," Eahlswith replied. "What do you think, Martha, another hour or so?"

"Hmmmpf."

Thus having signaled her agreement, perhaps, the seamstress continued with her devilish work. Krysta closed her eyes and prayed for patience. Three days had passed since the queen had judged her fit to leave her bed. Three days of endless toil in preparation for what was apparently intended to be the largest wedding held in Winchester since the marriage of the royal couple's daughter. Indeed, Athelflad and her husband were only two among the hundreds of guests invited for the occasion. They were streaming in from all over England, eager to do the renowned Hawk honor. And no doubt curious to get a look at his Norse bride.

Already the celebrations had begun. Nightly in the great hall, mummers, jugglers, minstrels, acrobats, and the like performed their arts for the amusement of the ever growing assembly. Outside in the courtyards and spilling over into the town, common folks joined in the festivities. A wedding at the end of summer when the harvest was in, and in the aftermath of Udell's defeat, gave everyone the perfect excuse to cast ordinary life aside and celebrate. From highest to lowest, youngest to oldest, all the residents of Winchester went about smiling and carefree, save perhaps the seamstresses and the cooks who would have their own rest when the deed was finally done.

If it ever was, as Krysta had truly begun to wonder for it seemed to her that day passed day and her gown came no nearer to being finished. Yet, within the hour, while still she avoided gazing into the vast mirror of polished bronze brought from the queen's own quarters, the redoubtable Martha straightened her back, rose laboriously to her feet, and proclaimed, "There."

The ladies clustered around, clasping their hands and exclaiming. Krysta gathered her courage and dared a peek such as she had avoided through all the long, laborious process. There was a goddess in the mirror, deep within the glowing sheen of the bronze. Adorned in rich silk and velvet the hues of a summer forest bathed in shafts of sunlight, the cloth studded with pearls and costly gems, a cascade of golden hair spilling over her shoulders, she gazed back impassively at the mere mortal staring at her.

Gaping, really, for Krysta could not contain her astonishment. That could not possibly be her. She was . . . freckled, disheveled, often wet. She laughed and groaned, sweated and sighed just like all mortals. But not like the creature in the mirror, who smiled suddenly, a winsome smile of piercing sweetness as though beckoning her into a mystery.

"Oh, my." A sigh of sound, nothing more, but it was enough to make Martha snort.

"Oh, my, indeed." She dusted off her hands and looked at Krysta of the mirror with satisfaction. " 'Twas worth every moment though I doubt my poor eyes will recover. Never again will I make such a gown." She glanced around at the array of fabrics still filling the room, fruit of Hawk's unbridled gift giving. "Unless, of course, your ladyship wants another."

"Oh, no!" The very thought dismayed her although she knew something would have to be done with the fabrics if only because Hawk obviously intended that to happen. She was beginning to understand that he was extremely good at getting his own way. "That is, not just now."

As it was, other seamstresses were already at work on lesser but still luxurious gowns, shifts, and all the rest that Eahlswith insisted had to be made. Moreover, just that morning the queen had announced that the wedding gifts were arriving. General hilarity among the ladies greeted Krysta's dismay. Hawkforte was a large keep, true enough, but surely there was a limit to how many gold plates and cups, finely woven wall hangings, chests of spices, furs, and the like that any one place could accommodate.

Yet still the tribute to Hawk poured in. That was how she thought of it, tribute to the man who stood at Alfred's right hand, who had slain Udell and who married as a pledge of peace between Norse and Saxon. He deserved every bit of it, she had no quibble with that. She was just feeling a little overwhelmed, that was all.

"Perhaps you should sit down now, dear," Eahlswith said. She gestured to Martha and her helpers. The magnificent gown was deftly removed, leaving Krysta in her shift. A stool was set beneath her and a cool drink pressed into her hand.

"Even dear Athelflad," the queen said, "who is rarely discomposed by anything, found the preparations for her wedding tiring and we had half-a-year for that, not a mere fortnight."

Privately, Krysta could not imagine undergoing such rigors for six months but she did not say so. She was deeply grateful to Eahlswith for all that the good woman was doing, and that she did say.

"You have been so kind, I will never be able to adequately thank you."

The queen smiled and actually looked a little embarrassed. "No thanks are needed, my dear. I'm enjoying myself thoroughly."

Krysta thought it fortunate that somebody was, but by the time the sun rose on her wedding day, her own spirits had improved greatly. For one thing, she was no longer nauseated. Indeed, she felt filled with energy and health. Slipping out of bed as the first rays of light filtered through her windows, Krysta stood for a few minutes gazing out at the town. So crowded was it with noble guests and their servants that there were people sleeping outside on pallets thrown down wherever there was room. Fortunately, the weather could not have been better. Fall had come with rich, dappled warmth. Insects still buzzed in the bushes and scarcely a leaf had changed color. The only real indication of the season were the splashes of gold and red to be glimpsed here and there in the surrounding wood. That and the shortening days that brought night on more speedily than weeks before.

The thought of night made Krysta feel suddenly flustered, and wasn't that foolish? She did not go to her bridal bed a virgin and was deeply glad of it. Imagine trying to cope with all the guests, the ceremony and the rest, while worrying about the coming night in the arms of a stranger. Hawk was dearly known to her, no stranger but the man she loved and trusted above all else in the world. She closed her eyes for a moment and whispered the hope that night would come on swift wings and overtake the laggard day. For laggard it was, each moment seeming to stretch out intolerably.

The queen and her ladies came while she was yet at the window. They brought food, bath water, and welcome chatter. Glad though she was of the distraction, Krysta still wished for something, anything that would speed up time. Each moment passed with aching slowness but despite that, when the bells heralding sext rang out, she was surprised. Midday already and the ceremony scheduled for nones. Suddenly there was not so much time left after all. Three scant hours for preparations that seemed endless. She laughed when her nails were buffed, both fingers and toes, but had to admit the pearly glow that resulted was very pretty. She suffered through the endless brushing of her hair, upon which the ladies insisted even when she warned them it would only make her tresses even more wild. Some small degree of order was achieved with hair ribbons so weighted down with jewels that she had to remember not to tilt her head back.

And then, surprising her by its sudden arrival, came the moment to dress. Clad in a shift of linen so finely woven as to feel weightless, wearing silk hose gartered at the knees, Krysta held out her arms as three ladies lowered the gown over her head. The bodice was entirely of forest-green velvet embroidered with gold thread and pearls interspersed with jewels. The wide sleeves gathered at her wrists and the skirt were gored and inset with tawny silk visible only when she moved. Intricate patterns of gold thread and jewels coiled along the square neckline and the hem of the skirt. The gown was laced at the sides beneath her arms, drawn snugly enough to emphasize the high fullness of her breasts and her slender waist. Heavy gold brooches set with rubies secured the cloak of amber silk that hung from her shoulders down her back and for several yards beyond. Her tawny hair, each riotous curl perfumed and gleaming, spilled over her shoulders, held back from her face by a circlet of gold and gems that matched the brooches.

When all was done, the ladies stepped back and afforded her a look in the mirror. Only by carefully tipping her head first to one side and then to the other did Krysta manage to convince herself that what she saw reflected in the polished bronze was truly . . . herself.

"Astonishing," she murmured, watching as the remarkable creature's lips moved just as her own did.

Eahlswith smiled. "You would look lovely in anything, my dear, but the gown suits you very well. No bride has ever been more beautiful."

Krysta turned to the queen and took her hands in hers. With all her heart, she said, "I will never forget your many kindnesses and I hope I will always prove worthy of them."

Tears shone in Eahlswith's eyes. "You will, child, of that I have absolutely no doubt. Now go to your marriage with joy for it is truly blessed."

Barely had the queen spoken than the bells began to ring, their clear voices calling out the summons to prayer at the ninth hour after sunrise, the hour at which Hawk and Krysta would be consecrated to each other in marriage.

Suddenly, time sped up and there seemed scarcely a moment to draw breath. The door was thrown open, she was ushered out, ladies holding high the train of her cloak. She sped down the stairs, aware of, yet untouched by, the hundreds of eyes turned toward her. A white mare waited in the courtyard. She mounted and was led by children past cheering crowds to the royal chapel. The sun was very bright.

Her heart was pounding. She could not draw a breath. And suddenly it was all right because Hawk was there, coming toward her, garbed in black velvet and gold. He held out his arms and she went into them. His strength made her feel feather-light as he settled her so gently beside him.

Father Asser awaited them at the entrance to the chapel. Nearby, Alfred and Eahlswith beamed.

"Why come you here?" the priest asked.

"For the blessing Our Lord gave at Cana," Hawk replied.

Thus did the ritual begin. The prayers were read over them and they were escorted into the chapel. There at the altar they knelt to receive from the hand of the priest the bread and wine of the mass. For Krysta, it was a time of peace stolen from the turbulent world. She bowed her head in thankful prayer where previously she had prayed in desperation for Hawk's safety. The chants of the monks resounded through the hallowed space, incense perfumed the air, and always she was vividly aware of the vital presence of the man kneeling close beside her.

They rose at Asser's bidding and Hawk slipped onto her finger a simple band of gold, symbol of their union for all time. With her hand clasped firmly in his, they left the chapel to receive the good wishes of the assembled crowd.

Krysta blinked in the light, momentarily blinded and felt the unwinding of the coil of fear that had existed in her from the day she learned of her fate to wed a stranger in a far land. It spun away on the cheers of the people and her own light heart, fading faster and faster until it was gone but for the faint wisp of mere memory. In its place was joy so great she thought if she just stepped a little more firmly, pushed a little harder against the restraining earth, she would soar right into the clouds. To prevent that, and simply because it felt so very good, she kept tight hold of Hawk. Escorted by the jovial throng, they walked the short distance to the great hall of the king, where they were engulfed in celebration.

Chapter

NINETEEN

S O NOW THEY WERE WED. THAT WAS FINE,
just as he'd wanted it. A bit more complicated in
the doing than he had imagined but done all the
same. The second time for him but he wouldn't
think of that. No memories would taint this union.

Hawk ran a hand over his jaw, reassured himself it
was still sufficiently smooth, and reached for the towel to
dry his face. He was alone in the room he had occupied
since coming to Winchester. Through the adjoining door,
closed at the moment, he heard the laughter and fussing
of the women who had escorted Krysta to her chamber.
That he was alone was a feat of maneuvering in which he
took just pride. With Alfred's connivance, he had slipped
away from the bridal feast shortly after the bride herself
took her leave surrounded by the ladies and flushing
slightly from the ribald jokes that rose on air well scented
with mead and ale. He wondered just then if she had reddened because the jokes embarrassed her or because she
was restraining her laughter. With Krysta, he suspected
the latter and was damned glad of it.

His worthy lieutenants had held off the pack that

tried to follow him and Hawk had made good his escape. Now he had nothing to do save wait. He glanced at the closed door and wondered how long. There was a flurry of sound and movement in the next room. The door to the passage opened, then closed. Quiet descended.

The ladies were gone. That was good. Krysta no doubt awaited him. Also good, indeed he was profoundly relieved to be married to a woman he knew would not shirk the marriage bed. He'd just take a few more minutes to make sure he had himself under control. She was with child, after all. Never mind the burst of pride he felt at getting her that way so soon, he was still in a quandary about whether or not to tell her. On the chance that she had any fear of childbirth, he preferred to wait as long as possible. But she was an intelligent woman and she was likely to figure it out for herself. Whether she did or not, he was resolved to treat her with the utmost gentleness. It was astonishing that she and the baby both had survived the battering in the river, and he wanted no more chances taken with either.

So he'd just wait. They had all the rest of their lives together. There was no point being in any hurry. . . .

The adjoining door flew open. Krysta stood there, barefoot, clad in a translucent shift of pure white silk, her glorious riot of hair tumbling over her shoulders, beaming the same winsome smile that never failed to make his heart catch. She looked like a very beautiful and very naughty pixie.

"They're gone," she exclaimed and flung herself into his arms. On tiptoe, dropping kisses along the curve of his jaw and at the corners of his mouth, she chanted, "Gone, gone, gone. We're alone!" Drawing back slightly, she bubbled on. "Wasn't the ceremony wonderful and the feast, I never imagined it would be so much fun. The jugglers were amazing and the acrobats, incredible! I'll never be able to thank Alfred and Eahlswith enough. And

Athelflad, to tell you the truth, I was a little intimidated at the idea of meeting her but she turned out to be so sweet. She says we must come and visit when we can. Her husband thinks the world of you, he goes on and on about how brilliant your campaigns have been. He was a little jealous that you got to kill Udell but he's over it now."

"Over it . . . ?" Surprised, and powerfully aroused by her nearness, Hawk struggled to grasp the torrent of words, failed, and promptly gave up. She was happy, that was enough. She was also tugging at his hand, leading him to the other room.

"You have to see what they did. It's so lovely."

He paused at the threshold. The chamber was filled with candles, each flame a miniature sun gleaming in the softly shadowed darkness. Flowers were strewn across the floor so thickly that each footstep released their scent. The bed was hung with gossamer curtains that fluttered lightly in the soft breeze admitted through the windows that stood open to the night sky. Sprinklings of petals adorned the bed linens and pillows. Into that feminine bower he stumbled, a thoroughly masculine and befuddled presence.

He had been that way since first catching sight of her as she came to him on the white mare, the horse garlanded in ribbons held by laughing children. For just a moment, she had looked like a glorious idol adorned with jewels and gold, a distant creature beyond the touch of any man. But then she had seen him, and the look in her eyes . . . Ah, that look. He would carry the memory of it into the world beyond.

Now she was here, adorned in little more than her satiny skin. His hand looked very large and dark against the slender curve of her shoulder. Slowly, he drew her to him. The bruises were faded but he thought of how recently she had been hurt, and hesitated.

"Oh, dear," she murmured.

He yanked his hand away as though burned. "What?"

She looked up at him through the thick fringe of her lashes and he saw the laughter dancing in her eyes. "Marriage hasn't turned you bashful, has it, my lord?"

Bashful? There were men who would fall over holding their sides, rolling around on the floor at the thought of the Hawk of Essex being bashful. There were women, not all that many but a fair enough number, who would be equally amused.

Yet even as he thought that he felt a dull flush creeping up over his face and realized she wasn't entirely wrong.

"I wouldn't say bashful . . . exactly. But you've been through a lot and I wouldn't want to hurt you."

"Oh, Hawk." So tenderly did she speak his name that it lingered like a caress. He was still savoring it when she sat down on the bed, took his hand in hers, and drew him to her. "Never could you hurt me. Only your absence can do that."

That clinched it. There was only so much a man could stand and he had reached his limit. Teetered right over it, really, for he could do naught but join her on the bed, gathering her to him, running his hands over her as though he could not quite believe she was really there with him. *His wife.*

Hesitation vanished as easily as did their garments. They came together hungrily, rejoicing in each other. Yet for all that Hawk went very slowly, drawing out her pleasure until she was mindless with need for him. Even then he lingered over her, passion pierced by tenderness and lit by wonder that her exquisite body held within it such mystery. When his mouth drifted over her hips and soft belly where their child slept, he knew joy so fierce as to eclipse all else. With the greatest care, he entered her but kept the rhythm of their lovemaking gentle. Her release when it came so enthralled him that his own struck

without warning. It went on and on, seeming without
end, until with a vast groan he slumped against her. With
the last of his strength, he rolled over to protect her from
his weight. She curled close, her head on his chest, panting softly. Long moments passed before her eyes drifted
open.

And when they did, she laughed.

Hawk just managed to lift his head and look down at
her, then at himself. He would have chuckled too, but it
required too much effort. It was enough to fall back
against the pillow and give fervent thanks that none of his
enemies could see him as he was just then, bedewed with
the labor of love and covered with clinging flower petals.

T HEY LINGERED A WEEK IN WINCHESTER. FOR THE
first three days, they did not stir from the bower.
Food, wine, water, every conceivable need was brought to
them. They slept, fed each other delicacies, made love,
took playful baths together, and slept again. Time passed
too swiftly.

On the fourth day, Hawk emerged to take part in the
games held in honor of the marriage. He received the
usual good-natured ribbing about his absence along with
the predictable suggestions that with his strength so
sapped, he would be a less than formidable adversary.
This he took in mellow humor before going out onto the
field to defeat the half-dozen opponents foolish enough to
face off against him. These worthies departed limping and
wiser.

He enjoyed himself tremendously. Seated beside
Eahlswith in the reviewing stand, Krysta endeavored to
do the same. Through the first of his matches, she scarcely
breathed and held so tightly to the arms of her chair that
her nails left marks in the wood. By the third match,
her hands were folded in her lap and her neck no longer

felt so tense that it might snap off. By the fifth match, she even managed to cheer. At the end of the sixth, when no further opponents presented themselves, she whooped with joy, ran out onto the field, and right there in front of everyone kissed her sweaty, begrimed, contented warrior.

When the time came at last to leave, Krysta could not hold back her tears as she parted from Eahlswith.

"No mother has treated a daughter more kindly than you have me. I will never forget it."

There were tears in the good queen's eyes as well. "I will miss you, my dear, as I miss my own daughters. You have reminded me that love is the source of all true strength and courage."

"We will be back," Hawk said gently as he saw the women's distress. "I come often to Winchester and Krysta will come with me."

There was comfort in that, but even so, Krysta turned twice in the saddle to wave farewell to the woman who had filled a hole in her life she truly had not wanted to admit existed.

They were some little way still from the port of Hamtun when Hawk glimpsed something down the road that made him draw rein. Krysta did the same, as did the men riding behind them. A moment later, she saw what Hawk's keen eyes had glimpsed first. Thorgold came riding toward them on a shaggy pony, the dog Udell had beaten loping along happily at his side.

"I wondered where you'd gotten to," Hawk said. He greeted Thorgold with obvious pleasure that warmed Krysta. So, too, was she delighted to see the dog, who ran circles around her horse, frantically wagging his tail.

"He's well again! How wonderful. Are you keeping him, Thorgold?"

"It's more a matter of him keepin' me, lass. But we seem to make a good pair."

"I'd say you do," Hawk agreed. "We missed you at the wedding."

"Ah, well, now I was there, don't ye know. I'm not one to let pass a fine feast and that was the finest I've ever known. I just prefer to keep a bit to the shadows. But it's right glad I am to see ye got the job done, lad."

They rode on, Thorgold beside them. It was not long before Hawk noticed ravens swooping from tree to tree along their route but he said nothing about that. Nor did he comment when one raven in particular followed them all the way into Hamtun. There were just some things a wise man did not remark upon.

Their ships awaited them. While the horses were being loaded, Krysta sat on a bale of hay and watched. Although the animals were superbly trained, including for travel by ship, the process was still dangerous and had to be done with care. One wrong step and a horse could go into the water, possibly being injured in the process. If an animal panicked and bolted, the men around him could likewise be hurt. Hawk saw to the boarding of his own mount as well as Krysta's, then helped with the others. Last aboard was Thorgold's shaggy pony, who clip-clopped up the gangway as though born to do so.

They sailed on the tide into a day so brilliantly clear as to sting the eyes. As Hamtun and the road to Winchester faded from sight, Krysta felt swept by regret, but her mood improved when Hawk left the rudder to one of his lieutenants and came to sit beside her in the prow.

"We will be back soon, sweetheart," he said as he drew her into the circle of warmth beneath his cloak. It was brisk out on the water and she was glad of his care. "It is my preference to keep Christmas at Hawkforte but Alfred may visit us before then and bring Eahlswith along."

"That would be wonderful. Perhaps we can also visit them in the spring."

Hawk did not answer, thinking that come spring she would be in no condition to travel. Yet no doubt she would still expect to be swimming, sailing, and all the rest. He would have to watch her carefully. The thought did not trouble him overly much, indeed he felt an unexpected sense of pleasure. There were worse things by far for a man to do.

Mindful of all she had been through so recently, Hawk resolved to make this journey as easy for her as possible. By late afternoon of the first day, he signaled the ships to put in to shore. When Krysta expressed her surprise, he said, "It is better for the horses to have some exercise."

"You did not put in on the way to Winchester."

"Udell's plotting made the journey urgent."

She nodded and he turned away lest she catch him rolling his eyes. The nonsense about the horses prevented the argument he was sure would happen if she thought he was coddling her.

They made camp on a sandy shore close to a swift-running brook. While some of the men formed a perimeter guard and others went out to hunt, Hawk enjoyed a rare moment of tranquility with his bride. Beneath the star-draped sky, they supped, laughed over tales Thorgold told, and finally withdrew a little away to sleep until the first faint light of dawn drew them back to their journey. Thus did they proceed until on the afternoon of the fourth day, the cliffs near Hawkforte came into view.

Standing in the bow, his arm around Krysta's shoulders, Hawk looked out toward the fair, green land lazing in the early fall sun and knew a sweetly piercing contentment. Krysta felt it too, for she looked up at him just then and said softly, "I will miss Winchester, my lord, but it is very good to be home."

Home. His and hers together. Hawk's arm tightened around her. His pleasure in the moment was boundless.

"Truly, sweetheart, I am so glad to get you back here safely that I swear, I'll even be glad to see Daria."

Krysta gasped a little at his bluntness but she smiled. No doubt or worry hovered over them as the ships turned toward the quays and the crowd already gathering there.

T HEY WERE BACK, HER OVERWEENING HALF-BROTHER and the Norse whore who should by all rights be dead or at the very least dismissed. Inexplicably, she was neither. The fierce pleasure of the moment when that Viking fool stood in Hawk's own hall and denounced the stupid bitch, even calling her a creature of unnatural union, was no more than cherished memory. The dark joy of what should have followed—Hawk outraged at the insult done him, the alliance of Norse and Saxon shattered beyond repair, the land torn by violence that would destroy the hated Alfred and bring the honors and riches so long overdue—was still denied. So cruel and perfidious was fate that defeat seemed snatched from certain victory.

Almost but not quite, for she was not done yet. She had come too far, endured too much to give up. Besides, it would be easier now. They would imagine themselves secure and would drop their guard. She would hide herself behind false humility and bide the moment she was sure must be coming. Then would she strike, the instrument of righteous justice, and all the poisoned torment of her twisted heart would be satisfied at last.

God of vengeance, let that moment come quickly. Let the sins committed against her through all the years of slight and derision be washed away in blood.

"Let me not wait long, Lord, that I may do thy bidding."

"Lady?" Beside her, Father Elbert turned with that look of concern in his eyes she saw far too often. Abruptly, Daria realized she had spoken out loud.

Her thin face hurt with the effort to smile. "A prayer, nothing more, Father. Surely that is permitted?"

"Most certainly. I only wonder if this is the best moment."

She frowned at the implication of criticism, however mild, but swiftly hid her thoughts.

When Hawk stepped onto the pier, habit causing him to sweep his keen gaze over the assembled crowd, he saw nothing to cause him any concern. Turning, he held out his arms to Krysta and lifted her from the ship. The moment he did so, the crowd erupted in wild cheers and pressed forward to greet them.

Edvard and Aelfgyth were right in front. Even as the steward struggled to control a grin that proved uncontainable, Aelfgyth said, "Oh, my lady, welcome home! We were all so thrilled to hear the tidings of your marriage! Rumor has it yours was one of the grandest weddings ever seen in Winchester. Do say you will tell us all about it."

"Every little bit," Krysta promised with a grin. "I shall so bore you with details that you will never want to hear tell of any wedding again."

"Oh, I doubt that, my lady. Indeed . . ." She shot a shy glance at Edvard. "I could do with much advice in the planning of mine."

Which set off a round of squeals and hugs that made the men sigh patiently as Hawk thumped Edvard on the back and congratulated him for being smart enough to snare the girl.

Only then did he take note of Daria and Father Elbert standing a little way to one side. They each looked sour as usual but at least they were present. He nodded to them but there was no opportunity to speak as the crowd closed around the newlyweds. Hawk and Krysta's horses were brought. He ignored hers and lifted her into the saddle with him. That inspired yet more cheers that accompanied them all the way through the thronged streets to the stronghold itself.

People called out their good wishes as flowers rained down upon them. Children ran up to the horse to hand bouquets of posies to Krysta, who soon had a lap heaped with blossoms. She shone with joy, waving to all and bestowing a warm smile of thanks on each child.

Hawk's pride in her knew no bounds, nor did his happiness. Yet even as he saw Krysta settled into his quarters, now theirs, and went off to receive Edvard's report of all that had occurred during their absence, a niggling sense of doubt teased at him. He had heard Edvard out and was seeking a few minutes to himself in the sauna before the source of his concern finally surfaced in his mind.

Love had come to him when he had never expected to experience it. Love shining and glorious, giving meaning to life and even, he dared to think, understanding of God's purpose. Yet had it come so easily when all was said and done. That should have pleased him and perhaps it would have were it not for the harsh instruction of experience.

Nothing he valued had ever come to him easily. For the land he loved, he had fought, bled, and come very close to dying many times over. For the woman he loved, he had needed patience and to kill an enemy, nothing more.

Too easy.

He shook his head. It was folly to think that. Life was uncertain and fraught with peril, yet he had Krysta safe and by his side. Was he becoming like an old man to fret over shadows?

But there was one shadow and honesty forced him to admit it. A thin, ugly shadow cast by his half-sister. Daria had run his household for more years than he cared to remember. Now she would have to yield that authority to his bride. A woman of ordinary temperament might well resent such change. Daria was likely to loathe it.

He had fought Danes with more relish than he contemplated the action he must take and yet he was unwilling to put it off. Something Cymbra had said to him once in passing, having to do with difficulty establishing herself in her husband's household, encouraged him to settle the matter quickly. He rose from the sauna, doused himself with cold water, dressed, and went in search of Daria.

He found her in the chapel. For a moment, entering that hallowed precinct of filtered light and scented air, he had the sudden perception that she had meant him to find her like that. Her head was bent, her hands clasped in reverent prayer. She looked the very image of a righteous woman.

Daria gave no sign of knowing he was there yet he was certain that she did. His own senses were too keen to credit her unawareness. The thought drifted through his mind that he did her a disservice—that for all her unpleasantness perhaps Daria was truly devoted in her faith. He let go the notion as quickly as it came to him for it made no difference. It was her behavior that mattered and he had always in the private places of his heart thought her conduct distinctly unchristian.

She stirred then as though awakening from a trance, blinked several times, and turned her head slowly. At first she appeared not to see him, and when she did, finally, she mustered an apologetic smile.

"Brother, have I kept you waiting? I ask your pardon."

Hawk had little patience with pretense and he showed none now. "Ask pardon for being at prayer? I do not think so, lady. Had I been kept waiting too long, I would have left."

She frowned and he was glad to see it for he thought it

the first honest response from her since he had entered the chapel. Slowly she rose as though made stiff by her devotions. Always she had made a show of such things, nurturing ills she was too noble to disclose. He had no patience with that either.

Yet he must find some, for he truly wanted to deal with her gently.

"You will always have a home here." It was not the most tactful way to put it but he wanted her to know that he had no thought of abandoning her. She was his half-sister, they were bound by blood; whatever his personal thoughts about her and whatever the changes that occurred in his life, he would provide for her.

"Home," she said and looked at him quizzically. He thought of his own pleasure in what that word represented and wondered if she felt anything approaching the same.

He plunged on. "But the Lady Krysta is now my wife and she must have the ordering of the household. Therefore, you will turn over your keys to her."

Something moved behind Daria's eyes. He was too skilled a warrior not to catch it yet was it gone in a moment, replaced by a swift nod.

"Yes, of course, I had planned to do that without delay. Naturally, I will be happy to assist her in any way I can."

He had an argument prepared, a speech for persuading her to comply. So swift was her agreement that the words remained unspoken. Yet they hovered on his tongue, for he was that surprised to have such easy victory.

Too easy?

The same thought again, niggling at him. He dismissed it impatiently.

"Good, then all will be as it should."

Daria said nothing more but only stood there in the

scented chapel, her arms across her thin chest, the hands
hidden in her sleeves. Hawk did not see that they were
clenched.

Father Elbert delivered the keys to Krysta. He
brought them to her in the kitchens where she had gone
with Aelfgyth, little Edythe trailing after them. Her first
day back, a feast in the works, she thought it right to be
there even as she wondered at Daria's absence. The priest
explained it in his fashion.

"I am instructed to give these to you," he said and
contrived to hand over the keys in such way as to take no
risk of touching Krysta, a woman, a suspected pagan for
all her claims otherwise, twice unclean.

He looked torn, relieved of his burden and wanting to
be gone yet driven all the same to instruct her from his
lofty heights. "The Lady Daria has set a very high standard in the keeping of this manor. I hope you will en-
deavor to do the same."

Privately, Krysta did not think Daria's standards high
at all, at least not in the matter of treating people with
proper regard. But it would have been ungracious to say
so. "I will do my best," she said, and sighed with relief
when he left, scowling as he had come.

Scarcely was he gone than Aelfgyth could not contain
herself. She bounced up and down, grinning hugely. "Oh,
my lady, I hardly dare believe it! You're mistress here now
and praise God that is so."

Mistress, Krysta thought, and tried to return her
friend's bright smile but apprehension tugged at her.
Never had she had the running of any place as grand as
Hawkforte. By comparison, her lost home in Vestfold was
small and simple. How was she to manage with so many
hundreds of people looking to her to do what was right,
expecting it of her really, and she dreading the thought
that she might let her husband down?

"None of that," Aelfgyth said sternly, correctly

divining what was going through Krysta's mind. "You'll do splendidly. We'll see to it, won't we, Edythe?"

"Of course we will," her little sister agreed. "Besides, there's no reason for you to be worried. Mother says the Lord Hawk is so far gone in love with you that you could serve him brine for supper for a month before he'd notice."

"Edythe!" Aelfgyth looked aghast at such candor even as she struggled not to smile. "I'm sorry, my lady. This one has yet to learn how to curb her tongue."

"I don't see why I shouldn't say that," Edythe protested. "Everyone knows it's true. Why, just this morning I heard the baker's wife say that if she'd ever seen a man better satisfied than his lordship, he lacked strength to walk. I'm not sure what she meant exactly but—"

"That is quite enough of that," Aelfgyth said. She was trying her hardest to look stern but could not avoid a hint of a smile.

For her part, Krysta's cheeks were very warm, yet she was glad that Hawk's people knew he was happy. In the sum total of all things, that mattered a great deal more than whatever problems she might have assuming her new duties.

They feasted that night in the hall of the Lord Hawk and spilled out well beyond the hall, down into the town through every lane, in every house, and even to the ships docked in harbor or riding at anchor just beyond. Torches gleamed like a sea of stars reflected in the water and in the tendrils of mist that rose from it with the cooling of the day. Long after the hour when all sensible men and women should have been abed, the revelry continued. Hawkforte resounded with song and laughter, the beat of drums and the high, haunting music of pipes. Dancers swirled in the torchlight, children ran about giddy with excitement until they subsided beneath gently sheltering trees and slept as fairy children do with music in their dreams. Barrel after barrel of mead and ale was cracked open to hearty cheers. Food there was in abundance, greater even than at the harvest feast. When the full moon rose over the beach below Hawkforte, men went down to the strand with their seines, tossed them out into the silvery water, and pulled them back filled with the bounty of mackerel that were roasted on spits over open fires.

Late in the night, perched on a stone wall overlooking the beach, Krysta licked bits of honey cake from her fingers and leaned her head against Hawk's strong shoulder. "Did you ever wonder when the priests speak of heaven if they mean a place like this?"

"Some say hell can be found on earth and I have been places where I believe that is true. It seems only fair that heaven should also be glimpsed."

He tightened his arm around her as the thought pierced him that he would be content and more to go through eternity gazing out at the moon-garbed sea so long as she was at his side. But his fey pixie had other ideas. Laughing, she fed him bits of cake until all were gone, then bestowed upon him lingering, honeyed kisses of sweet ardor that ran hot in his veins.

Which is how it came to pass that the Lord of Hawkforte made love to his bride on the sand beneath the high walls of his fortress, finding for them a secluded spot deep in the shadows where they lingered until gentle darkness yielded to a new morning. A few valiant stars still shone when they finally made their way back inside, laughing like guilty children and stepping over the bodies of exhausted revelers who slumbered where they had fallen.

A visitor to Hawkforte that day might have thought it a strangely enchanted place whose inhabitants had been put to sleep by a charm. Scarcely anyone stirred in the town. Yet did the guard still keep watch, stern men uncomplaining in their duty. They were not alone. After seeing Krysta to bed and satisfying himself that she would stay there, Hawk joined them. It was good to be among his men, receiving their silent nods and exchanging a few words with his lieutenants. The crisp breeze from the sea banished the wisps of sleep and made him feel rejuvenated. He walked the walls, looking out over his domain, and felt within himself the fierce will to protect what was his rising stronger even than ever before. Yet he kept his gaze steadfastly outward, with no thought for the possibility that the danger was already within.

"DID YOU NOTICE THE MOON LAST NIGHT?" Aelfgyth asked. They were in the weaving shed, counting the lengths of cloth that would be made into winter garments for the servants. The air was filled with little tufts of flax and wool that made them sneeze.

"This place needs to be aired out," Krysta said. She looked around critically at the narrow windows covered with wooden shutters that appeared nailed closed. "And how can anyone work in so little light?"

"The Lady Daria believed too much light and air was distracting for the weavers. She thought it would cause them to shirk their duties."

Krysta's eyebrows shot up but she said nothing. There were too many opportunities to confront what Daria had thought and what she had imposed on people. To yield once to that temptation would be to bring on a deluge. Instead, she kept her views to herself and said, "Tell the carpenters to take off these shutters and expand the windows. Also, when the weather is fair the women should be weaving outside."

"They will be pleased to hear that. In truth, there has been trouble getting enough women to weave because the conditions were so poor."

Krysta understood that Aelfgyth had this from Edvard. Already the two were working together as a pair and their wedding still a fortnight off. It pleased her greatly to see that.

"I did see the moon," Krysta went on. She smiled to herself as she remembered the circumstances. If there was a sight more beautiful than her husband's powerful, sculpted body bathed in moonlight, she did not know it. Truly, they should make a habit of visiting the beach together. Was it really only a little more than a month since they had first made love, and then, too, by the water's edge? A lifetime seemed to have passed, yet when Krysta considered, she realized it was scarcely two months since she had first come to Hawkforte. So much had happened since then that she was not surprised it seemed longer. The moon had been full when she came, full again when she first lay in Hawk's arms, and shone full once more with her now his wife. Three courses of the moon marking the ancient rhythms of time . . .

Marking, too, the rhythms of her body.

So much had happened yet one thing had not. Krysta had not bled since shortly after coming to Hawkforte.

A shock went through her. She paused in the midst of counting cloth and thought deeply. With all the tumult of events, she could not fault herself for failing to notice, yet was she startled nonetheless. Her courses had always been so regular. But mayhap it was not odd after all for there had been such tumult. If only she knew more about these things, had someone she could talk with about such matters.

She thought of Aelfgyth for a moment but decided not. Perhaps women were accustomed to discussing such things among themselves but she had never had such a luxury. Besides, nature would likely correct the oversight soon enough. It was not as though she was . . .

She could not be, *could she*? Swiftly she counted and almost laughed at herself. She would have had to conceive when she and Hawk first lay together. Even she, ignorant though she was, knew the unlikelihood of that.

Unlikely but not impossible. There was a chance, however slim. She really could be . . .

"My lady, is something wrong?"

Krysta looked up, startled to find Aelfgyth studying her with concern. Swiftly, she said, "No, nothing at all. Everything is fine. Shall we go on to the dairy? I'd like to take a look at the cheese stores."

In truth, she had no interest at all in cheese or anything else just then save for the incredible, amazing possibility that had occurred to her. Could it truly be that she was with child? The very idea made her want to hug herself, jump up and down for joy, seek out Hawk, smother him with kisses, tease him about his impending fatherhood, and do all manner of other silly, wonderful things. But she restrained herself, for the idea was still so new and fragile that she feared her joy would vanish if examined too closely. Yet she was a happy woman as she lingered in the aging room beside the dairy, smiling broadly over each fragrant golden round until Aelfgyth could hardly be faulted for believing that her mistress was extraordinarily fond of cheese.

Krysta's good humor lasted past midday and no doubt could have gone on long after that had she not encountered Daria. Her sister-in-law was emerging from the chapel when their paths crossed. Aelfgyth had gone off to help her mother sew her bridal gown and Krysta was alone. She stiffened at the sight of Daria but the older woman merely blinked at her, as though her eyes were having difficulty adjusting to the brilliance of the day. She appeared disinclined to speak, but Krysta, cherishing her tentative hope and mindful of all her blessings, did not think it right to let her husband's half-sister pass without the courtesy of speech.

"Good day, my lady. I trust you are well?"

Daria blinked again and for a moment it seemed she would not respond, but suddenly her face transformed and she smiled with what could almost be thought of as warmth. So unexpected was that, and so oddly unnerving, that Krysta had no notion what to make of it. She had little chance to ponder the matter, for Daria said swiftly, "Oh, I am very well, my dear. Indeed, I cannot remember the last time I felt so at peace and unburdened. But I will confess to just a little worry. I do hope the responsibility of Hawkforte will not weigh too heavily on your young shoulders. If I can do anything to help, anything at all, you will tell me, won't you? For such time as I am still here, I would be happy to assist you however I can."

So great was this seeming transformation, so unexpected this generosity, that Krysta was at a loss as to how to respond. Finally, she said, "Thank you . . . I appreciate this greatly. But forgive me, what do you mean 'while you are still here'?"

Daria smiled again and dropped her voice a notch, confidingly. "I haven't spoken to Hawk about this yet but it is in my mind to seek the joyful serenity of holy vows. Long have I felt drawn to the cloister but I could not leave off my duties here. Now that you and Hawk are wed, it is finally possible for me to follow my heart."

She sounded so sincere that Krysta did not think to doubt her. Here then must be the explanation for Daria's sour temperament—a thwarted calling to the convent. How sad that she had postponed her yearning for so long, but how fortunate that she could leave Hawkforte happily.

And what a change that knowledge had brought to her. Why, she was being positively pleasant.

"It is most kind of you to offer your help," Krysta said.

"Oh, it is the least I can do. After all, Hawk gave me a home here all these years since my poor husband's unfortunate demise. Perhaps before I leave, I could show you around myself, point out one or two things that might be of interest to you?"

Although Krysta thought she had already been shown around Hawkforte more than amply, first by Edvard and most recently by Aelfgyth, she would not be so discourteous as to say that. Instead, she said, "I would be happy to go with you. Only say when."

"Soon," Daria said and smiled. "But one thing, dear, if you wouldn't mind, pray say nothing to anyone of my plans. I fear Hawk would hear of it and think I was absenting myself for the wrong reasons. He might feel badly over that and all for no cause. Before I speak with him, I would prefer to have everything arranged."

"Of course I will say nothing, but I do not think you need make haste."

"That is kind of you but I confess to a certain sense of urgency." Daria's smile deepened. Her eyes were very bright. "I have already waited so long."

Krysta was about to suggest they look around the manor the following morning when she heard a sudden shout from the watchtowers. She bade Daria excuse her and scrambled up the stone steps to the top of the wall. There she peered out toward the sea. Her startled gaze beheld no fewer than three dragon-prowed vessels entering the harbor. Two appeared so heavily laden she thought they must be merchant ships. The other was unmistakably a vessel of war, but the sight of it did not trouble her for she recognized the insignia emblazoned on the sail.

A soft laugh broke from her as she considered how very pleased the redhead would be.

D RAGON SWUNG ONTO THE PIER, CLASPED HANDS with Hawk, who awaited him there, and gestured to the fat merchant ships he had brought with him. With a broad grin, he said, "Sven had a change of heart."

Hawk nodded slowly, surveying the vessels. One he would have expected, but two? "I didn't realize Sven was such a generous fellow. To think I sent him from here with nothing but a set of chains."

"Wolf liked that touch."

"What did he do with him?" Hawk asked with mild curiosity as they began walking up the pier.

"Banishment. Which freed up all his property, by the way. His two charming sisters are being married to men who will know how to manage Sven's former lands. Sven himself was last seen moping off in the direction of Jerusalem, complaining every step of the way. No doubt he'll give the Deity an earful. I bring you his coin, plate, furs, and the like as dowry for the charming Lady Krysta, whom I hope you have had the good sense to wed by now."

"A fortnight past at Winchester."

This prompted much pounding on the back and good wishes that continued up to the moment the pair walked past the guard towers and Dragon spotted Krysta. He didn't hesitate but swooped her up in his arms, gave her a big hug, and kissed her—chastely on the forehead. Even so, Hawk was scowling when her feet next touched the ground and Dragon could not contain his laughter at the sight.

"Is that an imp of jealousy I see on your shoulder, my lord? You who were so loath to marry?"

"He was loath?" Krysta asked. Surprise loosened her tongue. "But I was the one who said we shouldn't wed."

"You what?" Dragon asked with such obvious intent to cajole the story from her that the outcome was inevitable. Hawk groaned and ushered them quickly into the hall, where he wasted no time calling for ale.

Krysta stumbled over her response, trying to be discreet, but Dragon was soon roaring with laughter and casting chiding looks at Hawk. "It took you how long? Two weeks, and you had to drag her to Winchester to get it done?" He shook his head in amazement. "All for a tale spun by that half-wit Sven?"

"That's right," Hawk said firmly before Krysta could reply. "A half-wit's tale, but my wife is a sensitive sort and she took it to heart. By the way, sweetheart, your dowry so overloads two merchant ships that they look in danger of foundering."

"My dowry? But I have none. Sven said—"

"Sven has decided the climate in the Holy Land suits him better than that of Vestfold," Dragon said smoothly. "His lands are given to the husbands of his sisters, the rest of his possessions are yours."

Her eyes widened. She thought to ask what had caused so sudden a change in her half-brother but decided she would rather not know. "My father was a skilled warrior and even more able at trading. He left Sven very well off."

"Left *you* very well off," Dragon corrected. He glanced around. "Good thing Hawkforte's as large as it is. You're going to need the room."

Krysta thought of all the wedding presents she had only just managed to find places for and groaned. That set off a fresh round of amusement between the men. They remained in high good spirits through supper, during which Dragon renewed his acquaintance with the redhead, who blithely shoved aside anyone else trying to serve him and took that task entirely upon herself.

Watching her, Krysta remembered her own brush with jealousy and reddened. Her cheeks warmed yet further when Hawk leaned over and suggested they retire early since their guest obviously planned to do the same.

Making love under the stars was thrilling but there was also a great deal to be said for their big bed high up in Hawk's tower room. He was in a mood to be indulgent and gave her free rein to explore the body so very different from her own and so very tantalizing. She lingered over him, her hands and mouth drifting languidly across his broad, heavily muscled chest, following the arrow of fine golden hair that ran down his abdomen and thickened at his groin. She could not get enough of him. When he groaned, his hands clenching into the mattress in the struggle not to seize her and be done with it, she finally took pity. Tossing back the tangled mane of her hair, she lowered herself slowly onto him. He grasped her hips, guiding her even more cautiously, and remained still within her despite the effort that so dearly cost him. His features were taut, sweat beading his forehead, when Krysta began to move.

Even then he would not allow her complete freedom but controlled the pace of their lovemaking until she thought she could not possibly bear any more. Her head dropped onto his chest and her back bowed as he continued to move within her slowly, lingeringly, an exquisite torture that ended finally in an explosion of release that made her oblivious to all the world.

When she returned to full awareness, she was still lying atop Hawk and he was gently stroking her back. She raised her head and looked at him chidingly.

"That was very unfair."

He raised an eyebrow and said, "But effective, you can't deny that."

Krysta was well aware of her unbridled response. "I have no restraint where you are concerned," she admitted. The smile he gave her was boldly male, prompting her to add, "And sometimes you have too much."

He said nothing but only drew her closer, turning onto his side and tucking her into the curve of his body in a gesture that was oddly protective. "Go to sleep," he murmured and promptly did the same.

I T WAS LATE THE FOLLOWING DAY WHEN KRYSTA RE-membered Daria's wish to show her around Hawkforte. She would have thought of it sooner but scarcely had she appeared than Aelfgyth found her. Her maid looked flustered, her soft brown hair in tangles around her face, her cheeks flushed.

"Oh, my lady, thank heavens! Edvard, that clodhead, finally saw fit to mention that Lord Hawk has decided to honor our wedding with a feast. The gown my mother and I were making is far too simple and neither of us has any idea what to do. I should have considered all this when I agreed to wed a man of Edvard's stature but now I'm afraid he will be ashamed of me and . . ." She looked close to tears.

"Now, now," Krysta said reassuringly as she hugged the young woman, "everything will work out fine. You've seen the bolts and bolts of cloth we brought back from Winchester. We'll just pick out whatever you like best and get to work on it right away."

Aelfgyth looked tempted but shook her head. "I cannot ask you to—"

"You needn't ask at all. I'm simply saying that is what we will do. Come along and dry those eyes. You don't want Edvard to see you like that, do you? He'll think you're having second thoughts about marrying him and you'll find yourself whisked off to Winchester!"

The absurdity of that made Aelfgyth laugh. The two young women climbed to the tower room Krysta thought to make into a solar modeled on Queen Eahlswith's. The chamber looked east and south with wonderful light for sewing. It had been used to store weapons but Hawk had graciously agreed to remove them. That had yet to be done completely, with the result that bolts of glorious fabrics, embroidery frames, and the like shared space with swords, lances, and shields.

Krysta moved a particularly large shield out of the way and reached for a length of azure-blue silk that was strewn with tiny stars. She held it up eagerly. "What do you think of this? It matches your eyes and I think it would go very well with your coloring."

Aelfgyth looked from the fabric fit for a queen to her mistress and back again. Stunned, she said, "My lady, I cannot possibly take anything like that."

"Cannot ask, cannot take." Krysta rolled her eyes. "We shall be here all day at this rate." As though suddenly speaking to herself, she went on, "What can I say to convince her? Shall I mention how overwhelmed Edvard will be when she comes to him so garbed? How he will forget every other woman who has ever crossed his path and give thanks for the great good fortune that makes Aelfgyth his wife? Or should I point out that she should begin as she means to go on and to be the wife of such a man is no small thing?" Turning her gaze back to her bemused friend, she said, "Think grandly, Aelfgyth! Transform yourself. I became a maid that I might be a wife. Surely you can become a lady for the same good purpose."

Looking again at the fabric, Aelfgyth let out her breath slowly. "I have scarcely slept since he asked me. I said yes so quickly after so many months of longing for him. But I didn't let myself think at all."

"Thinking is highly overrated," Krysta said briskly. "I certainly did far too much of it. Come now, let us find your mother, who I happen to know has a wonderful hand with a needle, and get to work."

The morning sped by but before it was through, the women were interrupted by the shouts of men rising from the yard below the soon-to-be solar. Krysta glanced out a window and her heart sank. "They must be unloading the ships."

Aelfgyth and her mother joined her at the window, both exclaiming in amazement. Several dozen burly Vikings were dragging chest after chest, crate after crate, and bale after bale up the road from the harbor. Truly, there seemed no end to the procession. A raven flew overhead, seeming to supervise the operation.

With a heavy sigh, Krysta put aside her sewing and went down to the great hall, followed by both women. Hawk and Dragon were there. As each chest or crate or bale was brought in, it was opened for their inspection.

"Furs," Dragon said, waving a hand at what to Krysta looked like a mountain of them. "Gold, much in plate and ornaments but much more in coin . . . spices, several years' supply I think . . . salt—apparently Sven put a very high value on salt for he had an extraordinary amount of it. You should never have to buy any again."

He went on, pointing out intricately carved chests of wood and beaten gold, vividly colored pottery dishes, goblets inlaid with jewels, and then as though that were not enough, a parade of weapons, some of which Krysta recognized from her father's visits. His sword was there, a mighty blade with a hilt that held a large ruby, and his shield scarred in many battles.

Seeing her expression, Hawk picked up the shield and held it carefully. "This will always have a place of honor in my hall. It will be mounted beside my father's shield."

As she smiled her thanks, Dragon said as though in passing, "By the way, the ships that carried all this are also the Lady Krysta's."

Hawk looked startled for a moment, then laughed out loud. Krysta was too overcome to react at all. From the belief that she came to her husband without family or fortune to discover that she was instead an heiress of great wealth was more than she could contemplate. She decided not to try, but she did store away in her heart an especially grateful thought for the Lord Dragon and his fearsome brother, the Wolf, whom she suspected had plotted together to restore her honor.

When the crates, chests, and bales had been stored away and good progress made on Aelfgyth's gown, it was time for supper. This proved a jovial affair with Dragon spinning his tales once again, drink flowing freely, and Saxon and Norse affirming the peace between them in good fellowship. It was only when Krysta saw Daria coming into the hall accompanied by Father Elbert that she remembered her intent to tour Hawkforte with her sister-in-law. But just as she was about to speak to Daria about it, Dragon began another story and the thought fled her mind once more.

She did remember it again but that was much later, just as she was drifting off to sleep in Hawk's arms. Morning came in a rush, Hawk announcing that he was taking Dragon hunting, Aelfgyth and her mother appearing early and bubbling with yet more thanks for the gown they all three continued working on, and toward midday the happy news that the tanner's wife had birthed healthy twin girls, which turned Krysta's thoughts again to the possibility that she was with child. The sun seemed to speed across the sky and it was night again before she thought of Daria, too late once more to do anything about it.

So did most of a week pass. Krysta found herself occupied from dawn to dusk with her new duties as Lady of Hawkforte and from dusk to dawn with the pleasures accompanying that high estate. She existed in a haze of happiness that was at once sensual and more. With a swiftness she could scarcely credit, Hawkforte had become her home. For the first time in her life, she was part of a community that accepted her simply and entirely as a normal woman. The story Sven had told was forgotten, dismissed as the rantings of a dullard. She was met with warm smiles everywhere she went, honored as the wife of the lord but also appreciated just for herself. Deep inside her in a place she had never really wanted to think about, she finally felt whole.

Which was not to say that her past was entirely wiped away. Raven came often during the day, appearing suddenly in the solar, and even struck up a friendship with Aelfgyth and her mother, both of whom could not get over Raven's skill at plaiting baskets.

"Try doing it without hands," Raven snorted as she deftly twisted long strands of cane. "This way will forever seem easy."

If that struck the women as an odd remark, they were far too polite to say so.

Thorgold too visited regularly and was introduced to Dragon, who seemed already to know him.

"Have we met somewhere?" the Viking lord asked the first evening they sat at supper together. He looked at the small, darkly bearded man closely. "In Vestfold . . . I think. Somewhere near a bridge . . . ?"

Thorgold coughed into his ale and shook his head. "Nay, lord, I doubt that. Very little time I spend around bridges, very little indeed." He cast a quick look in Krysta's direction as she frowned.

"No, I'm sure it was a bridge. You challenged me to pay your toll and I said I'd trade you a story instead of a coin. We ended up drinking the night away, swapping tales. You had some damn good ones. Trouble was, come morning I couldn't really remember them and you were gone."

"Ah, well, that's the way of it. Joyful nights, sorrowful mornings." Thorgold shrugged abashedly and gestured to a serving boy. "I'll have a bit more of that ale, if you don't mind."

Hawk changed the subject just then but Dragon continued to look puzzled off and on throughout supper. Still, it didn't seem to hinder his enjoyment. Indeed, everyone was in high good spirits save for Daria and Father Elbert, who remained present yet aloof. They reminded Krysta of gray ghosts flitting about the manor, disconnected from the life of the place yet unable to leave it.

And for that she felt responsible, for surely once Daria had completed what she thought was her duty, she would be free to do as she wished and take holy vows. That she seemed an unlikely candidate for the convent made no difference and surely it was not Krysta's place to judge her but rather God's.

A week after Dragon's arrival, when all the dowry goods had finally been put away and Aelfgyth's gown was well in hand, Krysta went in search of Daria. It was late afternoon. Hawk and Dragon had gone hunting again and had not yet returned. Aelfgyth and Edvard were stealing a little time together. The day was warm for early fall. Bees still buzzed among the last flowers clinging to sheltered spots near the walls. It was that quiet time when much of the labor of the day was done but people had not yet begun their preparations for supper. Even the port was quiet.

Daria was in the chapel. Krysta hesitated to disturb her as she knelt at prayer, her thin back rigidly straight, her face concealed by her bowed head. Such reverence was admirable, no doubt, yet it made Krysta uneasy somehow. She shook that off and resolved to wait patiently, but scarcely had she begun to do so than Daria raised her head and saw her. For a moment, the shadows of the chapel concealed the older woman's expression. When she moved, her face fell into light and she was smiling.

"My dear, at last. Dare I hope you have a few spare moments?"

"As many as you need. I am sorry to have taken so long. Every time I turn around, there seems to be something to do."

"Isn't that the way of it?" Daria rose and came to where Krysta was standing near the door.

"You are so good to help your maid prepare for her wedding," Daria went on. "And to give her such cloth as you have done. Very few would be so generous."

The words were kind enough, yet Krysta somehow received the impression that Daria did not approve of what she had done. Perhaps she had been more giving than was usual, but Hawk had expressed pleasure at her actions.

"I hope you will be here for Edvard and Aelfgyth's wedding," Krysta said courteously.

They had just stepped outside the chapel. Daria stopped and looked at her closely. "Have you said anything to Hawk of my plans?"

In truth, it had not occurred to Krysta to do so simply because she had been so busy. But upon reflection, she realized she would not have said anything to him even had she not given her word to Daria. He was likely to be relieved if not delighted by his half-sister's impending departure, and Krysta was loath to raise his hopes until it was certain they would not be dashed. But that was an unkind thought and she put it from her mind.

"No, I haven't. Have you thought more about what you intend to do?"

"Oh, yes," Daria said as they began walking. "Indeed, I have thought of nothing else."

"And your mind is . . . unchanged?"

"Unalterably. I have waited for this far too long to consider any other course."

She was smiling again or perhaps still. Her expression seemed fixed.

"Where would you like to begin?" Krysta asked, hoping this would not take too long. Even knowing that Daria would be leaving Hawkforte did not make her company easy to bear. Still, Krysta was resolved to keep such sentiment to herself.

"First I must find Father Elbert and tell him I will be with you."

Krysta wondered if Daria always felt it necessary to tell her priest of her whereabouts but said nothing. Perhaps they merely had plans. Father Elbert was found coming up the road from the town. He appeared deep in thought and started when he saw them.

"Father," Daria said very clearly, "I shall be showing Lady Krysta around the manor. I do hope that it will not inconvenience you?"

The priest's gaze darted to Krysta and just as quickly darted away. He frowned. "No . . . I suppose not." He met Daria's eyes, swallowed, and went on more firmly. "Of course not, my lady, no inconvenience at all."

"Good." Daria looked at him for a moment, resumed her fixed smile, and turned to Krysta. "I suggest we start with the storerooms."

Already well acquainted with them and not eager to spend the last few hours of daylight roaming the dark chambers below ground, Krysta nonetheless agreed. She followed Daria around to a back entrance behind the great hall and from there down a flight of stairs. The foundations of Hawkforte's stronghold were sunk deep into the ground and walled in stone. At the bottom of the steps, Daria took tinder and flint from the small alcove where they were kept, and lit a torch kept in an iron bracket. Its light was welcome but could not dispel the chill air, so very different from the pleasant warmth above.

"I do have a fairly good idea of what is down here," Krysta said, hoping to avoid an extended stay.

Daria smiled. In the long shadows cast by the torch, her face looked as though it were cracking. "I'm sure you do, but there are one or two things I doubt you've found yet."

She led the way briskly down a passage. Krysta had no choice but to follow.

TWENTY-ONE

T HE STONE FLOOR SLOPED DOWN STEEPLY.
The air grew ever more chill and dank. Something skittered away around a corner. Krysta
shivered and wished she had thought to bring
a cloak. She had been down here only once before, with
Edvard, and they had not lingered. She and Daria were already beyond the area where barrels of mead and ale were
stored, yet Daria did not slow her pace. Krysta was bewildered, wondering what could possibly be kept so far
removed from everything else and in such damp surroundings. Most anything would rot, and that which
would not would still be very inconvenient to reach.

"Are we going much farther?" she asked as Daria
showed no sign of stopping.

The older woman glanced back over her shoulder but
her face was obscured by the shadows. "Not too much
now. I think you'll find this very interesting."

Krysta heard the lapping of water up ahead and
frowned. She tried to determine their direction but the
passage had twisted and turned so many times that she
was disoriented. "Are we near the sea?"

Daria held up the torch. Water glinted just ahead. "Not the sea, an underground river that runs to it. This is the way out of Hawkforte should it ever come under siege. I'm surprised Hawk hasn't shown it to you yet." She came closer so that the light of the torch shone directly on Krysta. "He hasn't, has he?"

"No, but he did say something about showing me an escape route. We just haven't had a chance yet."

"Well, good, I've saved him the trouble. But this is only the beginning. There is much more of interest right near here." They moved off along the course of the river where the ground climbed slightly. "Did you know that there was a stronghold on this site long before Hawkforte was built?"

"No, I didn't." Krysta was genuinely pleased to be learning so much. She was about to say so when Daria went on.

"Likely it belonged to the Romans. They were idolaters, you know, before they converted to the true way. Signs of their pagan worship are still to be seen down here." She pointed to an elaborately carved stone well sunk into the ground. The stone face of a horned man seemed to gaze back at them. "A place where such worship takes place remains doomed forever."

"It must have been a very long time ago," Krysta said gently. She did not wish to contradict Daria, and she did admit that the dark underground passages had an eerie feel to them, but she doubted they were cursed in any way.

"I tried to tell Hawk that," Daria went on as though she had not heard. "I said this was not a place to be held by decent men but he refused to hear me."

"He may have thought it most important to hold this land against the Danes no matter what happened here in the past."

"Perhaps," Daria said, then fell silent as they came to

a place where the passage turned off to the left. She stepped back against the wall. "Go ahead, I will hold the light for you."

Krysta looked at her quizzically. "What is there to see?"

"I wouldn't want to spoil the surprise." Daria gestured with the torch.

Krysta turned the corner. At first, she saw nothing. Daria was no longer close behind her, and the dimmer light of the torch did little to illuminate the chamber ahead. Only when her eyes had adjusted to the darkness could Krysta make out the contours of a room hewn out of rock. It was small and dank, chill with a wind off the sea creeping around the rocks.

"What is this for?" she asked, turning, and was surprised to see that Daria had stepped even farther back. The walls of the chamber narrowed near where she was standing, almost as though fitted for a—

Clank.

The light vanished, save for a tiny sliver left just barely visible. Krysta rushed forward, slamming up against a heavy wooden door. At the level of her eyes, an opening had been cut but it was so small she could see very little.

Yet she could make out Daria's twisted face, contorted with glee.

"Fool! Stupid, ridiculous fool! How I prayed this would work and my prayers have been answered! Truly, the Lord smiles upon those who serve Him."

Shock roared through Krysta, disbelief warring with the sickening realization of her peril. Even as her mind screamed, she spoke with forced calm. "My lady, what a good joke this is. Truly I have been played the fool. But now, I pray you, let me out and we will share this amusement with others."

"Silence!" Daria shrieked. "You think to make me the

fool, so sweet and placating you try to be! It will not work. All the weeks of scheming, thinking how it was to be done, playing the simpering dolt and then waiting—waiting and waiting!—for you finally to remember you had promised to go with me. I bided my time, hard though it was, and I have been vindicated. Here you will remain, Norse whore! Here you will rot!"

Terror clawed within Krysta, a cold and clammy horror that almost doubled her over. She fought it with every ounce of her strength. She had made a terrible mistake but this was no time to think of that. Now she must use all the guile she possessed to escape the clutches of the madwoman.

"Daria, please, I am quite frightened enough. Your point is well and thoroughly made. I do not know Hawkforte anywhere near as well as I should. Truly, you must stay on here as long as you possibly can bear so that I may be properly instructed."

"Stay on? Twice times fool! I despise this place! I hate it with every fiber of my being. I, who should have had a great manor of my own, was cast instead upon the pity of my loathed half-brother and forced to play his servant. But no more! I will have my due at last. I will—"

She broke off suddenly, as though aware she said too much. A sneer twisted her mouth. "Don't worry, fool, it will not take you so very long to die. Much as I would like to think of you suffering here, dying slowly of thirst and hunger, I cannot take the risk of that. Only a few hours and then the flames of eternal damnation will consume you."

She lingered a moment longer, staring at Krysta where she stood frozen in the small opening of the door. With a wild laugh, Daria departed. The light faded with her and Krysta was left alone in the utter dark.

Her heart was pounding. She heard it with startling clarity just as she smelled the damp rot of the cell and felt the chill air sink through her gown to bore deep within her body. Perhaps her mind, denied the stimulation of vision, was exaggerating all else. That was a rational thought and she held on to it with all her power, for beyond it, like a beast lying in wait for her, was madness.

She shut her eyes and saw fragments of dancing light behind her lids. When she opened them again, the darkness outside was deeper than that which dwelled within her. Shaking, she reached out a hand and touched the closed door. Contact with the solid wood seemed to anchor her in some small way.

Her rapid breathing and the drumbeat of her heart shattered the silence of centuries. Desperately, she tried not to think of how very far she was from light and hope, weighed down by unknowable tons of rock and dirt, as though buried alive. And so alone . . . so horribly, terrifyingly alone.

Yet not alone. The thought, little more than faint possibility, that had begun in her days before solidified suddenly into certainty. She was with child. Another being shared this cell with her and would share her fate, her tiny and yet so dearly loved child.

Fierce protectiveness such as she had never known surged within her so powerfully as to push aside terror. Krysta took a deep, steadying breath. *Only a few hours.*

Hours in darkness and despair could render her too benumbed to resist. That must not happen. She needed to find something, anything, with which to defend herself . . . and her child.

Slowly, methodically, Krysta began to search the chamber with her hands, going inch by inch from floor to ceiling.

H AWK RETURNED FROM HUNTING IN EARLY EVEning. He and Dragon shared a sauna before parting in front of the great hall. While there yet was light,

Dragon intended to inspect his ship and make sure all was in readiness for his departure the next day. Hawk had it in his mind to find Krysta and pleasantly while away the hour or so before supper.

He didn't get very far in that direction before he was intercepted by Edvard with Aelfgyth close on his heels. "Your pardon, lord," the steward said, "but if I might speak with you?"

Coming up close behind her betrothed, Aelfgyth dug her elbow into his side as though to remind him he was not alone in seeking the Hawk's notice. "If *we* might speak with you," Edvard corrected himself.

Hawk was inclined to look on the young couple with favor. He nodded and prepared to listen with patience, although he ached to find his bride.

"I have told Aelfgyth there is no reason for alarm," Edvard said with a quick glance at the woman who stood at his side. "But she is concerned nonetheless and I thought you might reassure her—"

"I last saw the Lady Krysta full three hours ago," Aelfgyth said. "An hour since I went looking for her. The gown she has so generously given is finished and I wanted her to see it. But I cannot find her. I have searched the kitchens, her own quarters, the weaving shed, the stables, and everywhere else I could think of and still there is no sign of her."

Hawk did think this surprising but in no way saw it as cause for alarm. Hawkforte was a goodly sized manor and Krysta was becoming acquainted with all of it. She could be anywhere.

"She may have gone down to the town," he suggested, "or she could be any number of other places. It is scarcely an hour to supper. She will appear."

"Thank you, my lord," Edvard said hastily. He took Aelfgyth's elbow and turned to go, but she was having none of it.

"But that is just it, my lord," Aelfgyth insisted. "The Lady Krysta would never go off somewhere when supper is being prepared, and this the last evening before Lord Dragon leaves. She would be in the kitchens or dressing. Certainly she would not be far from either place, yet I cannot find her."

She looked from one man to the other, the fast-rising steward she was soon to marry and the powerful lord in whose service they both were pledged. Her own audacity amazed her yet she remembered the many kindnesses of the Lady Krysta and resolved to stand her ground.

"I am telling you," Aelfgyth said on a note of desperation, "something is wrong."

Edvard hesitated, and Hawk looked closely at the young woman. He had never paid her much mind but he knew she had a gentle nature and now he saw that she was also intelligent.

The girl had merit, and therefore, just possibly, so did what she said.

"All right," he said slowly. "Where exactly have you searched?"

Again, Aelfgyth rattled off the list of everywhere she had been in the past hour. When she was done, Hawk nodded. "You realize you may have simply been missing her if she moved from place to place?"

"That is possible," Aelfgyth conceded, "yet I told them in the kitchens to send word to me if she appeared and none has come. It makes no sense that she would not go there."

Hawk had to concede this. He was beginning seriously to wonder where Krysta had gotten off to but he was still far from alarmed. Hawkforte was extremely well protected. The Danes might be able to infiltrate spies from time to time but they could do nothing more than look.

Still, accidents could happen. At the thought that one might have happened to Krysta, his easy mood vanished.

His wife could not be found. The reason was most likely benign and she would emerge safe and sound, surprised to have been the object of concern. Three hours, Aelfgyth had said, and an hour of that spent searching for her. It was enough.

"Summon the servants," he said. "Question anyone who talked with her today. Find out if she said anything about going anywhere."

"As you wish, lord," the steward said. He too looked concerned now. "Where may I report to you?"

"I'll be on the walls talking with the watch. I want to know where she went and who she was with."

As Edvard and Aelfgyth hurried to obey, Hawk strode across the yard and took the nearest steps two at a time to the top of the walls. He found the lieutenant in charge of the watch and questioned him closely. Almost immediately, several other men were summoned and among them they tried to recall if they had seen the Lady Krysta during the day. The problem was that they were charged, sensibly enough, with keeping watch on whoever might be approaching Hawkforte, not on those already within it. Looking outward rather than inward, they saw relatively little of what went on inside the stronghold. Yet there were inevitably times when their attention shifted.

"I was just coming on duty, lord," said a young man-at-arms. He was a bit nervous, called as he was to report directly to the Hawk, but he knew of what he spoke. "As I crossed the yard, I noticed the Lady Krysta take leave of her maid, who went on down to the town in the direction of her mother's house. Lady Krysta herself went toward the chapel."

"Did you see her go in there?" Hawk asked.

The young man shook his head. "No, lord, I reported for duty then."

Hawk nodded, satisfied that he had the best information he was going to get. "Send several men out to see if they can locate that fellow Thorgold, and also, if possible, the woman called Raven."

As the lieutenant barked orders, Hawk left the walls and walked quickly to the chapel. He found it empty save for Father Elbert. The priest looked startled to see him but recovered quickly and adopted his usual expression of vague disapproval.

"You wished something, lord?"

Reminded of how much he disliked the man, and how of late he had thought frequently of replacing him, Hawk spoke sharply. "Have you seen the Lady Krysta?"

The priest raised an eyebrow. "Here, lord? No, I have not. I see her very rarely."

"She came this way in late afternoon."

"I was not here then."

"Who was?"

Father Elbert shrugged, "I have no idea." He looked directly at Hawk as he spoke, the picture of candor. Yet he was unusually pale.

"Where is the Lady Daria?"

Was it a trick of the light or did the priest flinch?

"Again, lord, I have no idea. She is in chapel more than usual of late but not just now. May I suggest you seek her in her quarters?"

Several moments longer Hawk surveyed the priest before he decided there was nothing more to be gotten. Abruptly, he walked out of the chapel.

Daria was in her quarters. She was seated beside a window with a piece of embroidery in her lap. Why was it she always looked posed? Hawk pushed the thought aside and spoke directly.

"I am seeking my wife. Have you seen her?"

"The Lady Krysta?" Daria pondered for a moment, then shook her head. "No, I have not, but surely she will be in the hall soon. It is almost time for supper."

Well aware of that, Hawk took his leave as quickly as he had come. In the hall, he found Edvard questioning the servants. No one had seen Krysta since late afternoon. Hearing this, Hawk's mind was made up.

"I want her found. Separate the servants into groups and start them searching." As Edvard hastened to do as he was bade, Hawk summoned his lieutenants and gave the same orders for the garrison. With darkness rapidly approaching, dozens of torches were lit and handed out to the search teams.

In the midst of all this Dragon returned, and hearing of what was happening, he immediately joined the search. At the hour when Hawkforte should have rung with laughter and song, there were only the quick tread of feet and low-voiced murmurs of concern that slowly darkened to something worse.

HER HANDS WERE BRUISED. SHE FELT THEM THROB-bing in the darkness. Her fingers were scraped and bleeding. Her legs ached and her heart beat painfully. Beyond exhaustion, Krysta sagged against the wall. For more hours than she knew, she had searched the chamber, feeling over every inch of stone trying to find something she could use as a weapon. All she had encountered was slick, damp rock and hopelessness.

Chilled to the bone, she was shivering helplessly, and the strength of her mind that had carried her so far was beginning to crack. The darkness pressed in on all sides, unrelieved, unrelenting. Daria truly had buried her alive and soon she would return to finish the job. Without a weapon, Krysta would have little chance against her.

Her face stung and with a start she realized that it was because of the hot tears trickling down her cold cheeks. So weary was she that she did not sob or in any way cry out, she simply wept silently and helplessly. Leaning against the wall, hugging herself, she thought again of the child asleep within her.

"I'm so sorry," she said brokenly. "I know I have to save us and I've tried so hard."

Her voice sounded very odd in the darkness, as though it came from some source other than herself. Yet she felt less alone for having spoken.

"Daria will come back. She is mad and she means to kill us. I will fight her, even without a weapon, but we have little chance."

She pressed her hands to her flat belly and imagined she was touching her child, a small, smiling baby with hair the tawny shade of Hawk's and eyes as green as her own. A baby who would grow to be a sturdy toddler, racing about Hawkforte, learning at his father's side until one day he, too, would be a strong man and noble leader. There in the darkness, sorrow a bottomless hole within her, she imagined she could almost see him, not Hawk yet very like him, so young and yet confident, reaching out a strong arm even as he smiled at her with gentle reassurance.

This baby who had little chance of coming into the light of the world, yet he seemed a man grown and so very real. As though she had called him into being.

Dazed, she stared into the darkness. Her eyes were open, tears still flowing from them, yet there he stood like a bright, shimmering vapor in the unmistakable shape of the man she knew to be her son.

"Falcon," she murmured, and his smile deepened.

A sob broke from her. She stretched out her arms, frantic to touch him just this once before eternal darkness closed over them both. If only her love was strong enough to withstand death, to give him the chance to live as he was surely meant to. If only . . .

Yearning for her son, Krysta reached too far and

stumbled. She went down hard on her knees, gasping in pain. When she looked up again, the vision was gone.

"*Nooo!*"

The cry was ripped from her heart. What torment was this to show her a glimpse of a future never to be? Why this added torture when there was already so much to bear? Was God truly so cruel?

Sobbing, she struggled to rise from the floor but weakness overcame her. Why bother to stand, why keep fighting, why not just give up now? Surely death would close around her as easily as the darkness did.

Or perhaps not . . . for what was this just within the touch of her fingers, this solid something she had fallen beside? Slowly, Krysta lifted her head. She still could see nothing but by carefully feeling what she had just found, her despair gave way to hope. Hard within her grasp, firm and real, was what gave every evidence of being a solid iron bar of a kind that might be used on the windows of a cell. This one had no windows but there was that small opening in the door. Had it once been closed over by the very bar she now clutched?

Carefully, Krysta got to her feet. She fumbled into the darkness, finding her way back to the wall. Without it, she would have been lost entirely. Moving slowly along it, she positioned herself to the side of the door where she would be best concealed when it opened.

Holding the bar in one hand, she touched the other to her sleeping child. Her tears were gone. In their place was a smile identical to her son's.

"Thank you," she murmured and felt her fear flow away. In its place was hard, clear resolve.

HAWK HAD BEEN AFRAID BEFORE. ANY MAN WHO didn't know fear in battle was an idiot and probably a dead one at that. Fear could be good. It could stop you from doing insanely stupid things and even sometimes keep you alive for another moment, another breath, another hour, another day, another battle.

This was different. Terror ate at him, making his soul burn. He wasn't sure which was worse, the sickening anguish he felt or the rage that accompanied it.

She was gone. After hours of searching, he was convinced that Krysta was truly gone. But how and why remained unknown to him. He had questioned every guard, seeking any hint that someone might have done at Hawkforte what Udell had managed at Winchester. But that had happened at night, and Krysta had vanished while yet it was day. The guard had been vigilant as always and no one had seen anything. Not a person out of place, not a single suspicious action, not a hint that his life was about to come crashing down around him.

This was worse than Udell. Then, he had known who had taken her, the danger she faced, and what he must do. Now he knew nothing except that the pain he felt was not to be borne.

Was it possible she had gone of her own free will?

The question had first come to him hours before when he learned that Thorgold and Raven were also not to be found. He had dismissed it at once, stunned even to have thought it. But over and over again as the night wore on, the same doubt flared. Could she have lain in his arms, shared the heights of loving passion, laughed and teased, tantalized his mind as well as his body, and it all meant nothing? Had she clung to her determination that they should not be man and wife?

He shook his head, struggling to clear it. The very notion was absurd, a sick figment of his tormented imagination. Krysta loved him as he loved her. She had put aside all her doubts and fears when they wed. Besides, were that not so he would know it, for she had no subterfuge in her. She was as guileless as clear, sparkling water.

And she was gone.

Not of her own free will, of that he was certain. Someone had taken her, somehow, somewhere. Taken her and, he recalled as a fresh bolt of agony ripped through him, their child.

He would take Hawkforte apart stone by stone if need be. He would scour the surrounding land, put aside his love for it and strip it bare if he must, but he would, by God and all the saints, find her.

"Brother . . ."

He turned, seeing Daria yet not truly seeing her until he forced himself back from the dire vision of destruction he had conjured and stared into the grave face of his half-sister.

"Brother," she said again, "it is very late. Surely everyone is exhausted, yourself included. Would it not be better to resume in the morning when there is light to see by?"

Light? There was no light and would never be again without Krysta. He was not tired, such consideration did not exist. If it did for others, so be it. It made no difference to him.

"Go to your bed."

She stared at him and he noticed yet again the flatness of her eyes. "I only meant . . ."

"I know what you meant." He did not want to be unkind. There was too much pain already to add to it. "Those who wish to do so will continue to search."

She frowned. He wondered if it could really be out of concern for him and felt the thought slip away. Nothing in his experience with her said it could be so. Nothing.

Her husband had rebelled against Alfred and died for it. Daria had been thrown from the heights of anticipated power to sufferance in her half-brother's household. She had no reason to want Krysta found.

Did she have reason for even more?

He stared at her, trying to think, but his mind moved sluggishly before the onslaught of raw emotion. His marriage to Krysta had stripped her of what power she had enjoyed at Hawkforte. What was left for her, then?

His marriage . . . But there had been another marriage before his, that of his sister Cymbra and the Norse Wolf. A marriage begun in violence and intended revenge that, grace of God, turned swiftly to true love.

Wolf had proposed the alliance of Norse and Saxon against Dane. Wolf had suggested his own marriage to Cymbra to solidify that alliance.

An answer had come back to Wolf, insulting him deeply, rejecting both marriage and alliance. An answer sealed with the Hawk's own sign yet never written or known by him.

The mystery of who had sent the message that could so easily have provoked war remained unsolved.

He shrugged impatiently. Why think of such things now when Krysta's fate hung in the balance?

"Go to your bed," he said again and turned away.

H OW COULD THIS BE? IT WAS WELL AFTER MIDNIGHT *yet Hawkforte blazed with light. Not a man, woman, or child had sought rest. In every nook and cranny, every outbuilding and dependency, every passage and every chamber, people were searching. The night air resounded with the constant calls: "Lady Krystaaaaa . . . Lady Krystaaaaaaa . . ." On and on, enough to drive her mad.*

Why did they care? What did it matter to them whether the Norse whore was found? Why was Hawk not raging with anger for all the trouble she was causing and had caused

*from the very beginning? Why was he not glad to be rid
of her?*

*Not that it mattered. She had waited far too long to
consider any change in her plans. She would just have to be
more careful but she was clever enough to manage that. Far,
far more clever than any of them.*

*Best not to wait any longer though, have it done and en-
joy the anticipation of the discovery, the fury that would
erupt. Oh, yes, that would be very good indeed.*

KRYSTA BLINKED ONCE, THEN AGAIN BEFORE SHE WAS
certain of what she saw. Still very dim but growing
stronger, a light was approaching. Her stomach clenched
and she took tighter hold of the iron bar. The impulse to
cry out on the chance that the light belonged to rescuers
was very strong but she forced herself to remain quiet.
Rescuers would likely be calling out to her. In the utter silence of the cell and the passage beyond, she heard
nothing.

Nothing save for her own prayers offered up for the
safety of her child in the moments before the light grew
brighter.

Daria's face loomed at the tiny opening in the door.
Her mouth twisted and her voice was very high.

"There now, you've waited long enough. Did you
fear I would not return? But I have and look what I've
brought you."

She held an object up to the opening. It glinted with
the sharp sheen of metal.

"Do you recognize it? You should. It is Hawk's own
knife. You will die by it and he will be blamed."

Despite herself, Krysta could not prevent the sharp
inhalation of her breath. Daria heard it and laughed. "So
surprised? But how else would I do this? It's perfect,

really. Hawk never wanted peace with the Norse, not really. He rejected Wolf Hakonson's offer of alliance, he sent the message saying he would never allow his sister to be wed to a filthy Viking, then he raged when the Wolf took her anyway and made her his wife. Did Hawk not go to Sciringesheal himself and steal her from there, only to finally have to return her to the Wolf when he came upon Hawkforte with a mighty army? The peace they pledged then was false in the Hawk's heart, he wanted only revenge. As for marrying you, he loathed the idea but was forced into it by Alfred. Now our *great* king will have every reason to be enraged at Hawk, as will the Norse themselves. He will be disgraced, cast down, just as he deserves to be. Alfred will kill him even as he killed my own foolish husband."

"No!" Krysta exclaimed. "All this is lies! Hawk never rejected the alliance and he would never betray it. He did not send that message to Wolf and no one would believe him capable of killing me!"

"Why? Because he has pretended affection for you? That's all it is, you stupid girl! When you are found with his knife in you, and people remember what went before, he will be blamed."

Dread filled Krysta. Beyond question, Daria was mad. Her mind was so twisted that she truly believed what she said. And that meant she would have no hesitation to act upon it.

"Step back!" Daria ordered shrilly. "If you give me no trouble, I will make it quick. Otherwise, I promise you will linger."

Krysta said nothing, only looked inward and summoned all her courage. She gripped the iron bar in both hands.

The door opened. Daria thrust the torch into the darkness, trying to locate Krysta. Huddled in the shadows off to the side, she managed to remain out of sight.

"Come forward and show yourself! By God, if you do not, you will beg for death!"

Only a little more, just let her take a few more steps into the chamber . . .

Light inched across the dirt floor. Krysta drew a breath, held it . . .

"Where are you! You cannot hide!"

The knife was raised, cold steel shining.

Gripping iron, Krysta sent up a quick prayer and lifted both hands over her head. She took a quick step forward, into the light, and swung her arms down hard.

"Aaaaaggghhh!"

Daria's legs gave way. She went down hard but the blow had only struck the side of her head. She was still conscious, screaming, and struggling to her feet.

"Kill you! I'll kill you! How dare you—!"

Cold steel shining. The knife had been flung loose from Daria's hand and fallen across the far end of the chamber. Without hesitation, Krysta dropped the iron bar and lunged for the knife. She had to get it before Daria did . . . had to—

Her fingers were closing on the hilt when mad laughter filled the chamber. She looked over her shoulder and was struck numb by terror. Daria loomed above her, clutching the iron bar.

"Think to thwart me, do you? I will kill you any way I must and still Hawk will take the blame. You stupid, stupid f—"

Her eyes were bulging. She dropped bar and torch together, both hands clawing at the steely arm that had come suddenly around her neck and was choking the life from her.

Hawk. Yet a Hawk such as Krysta had never seen, his features tight with rage, his gaze empty of mercy, the warrior who haunted the nightmares of the Danes.

Krysta dropped the knife and flung herself at him,

pulling desperately at his unyielding arm. "She is your half-sister, you share the same father! Do not kill her!"

He looked at her in disbelief. "She sought to kill you and our child yet you ask me to spare her?"

"To spare yourself! Do not stain your hands with her blood! Do this and it will follow you all your days. Think, Hawk! It is peace you want, not more death!"

Daria's feet were kicking futilely in the air. Her eyes rolled back in her head. She was moments from eternal judgment. Slowly, his gaze never leaving Krysta, Hawk eased his strangling hold.

"I think I have always known there was something wrong with her."

He spoke so sorrowfully that Krysta's eyes stung with tears. She reached up and touched his face. On the ground the torch still burned, throwing writhing shadows across the chamber.

"She suggested we call off the search until morning," Hawk said. "I fell to thinking about how much she stood to lose with you here yet how cheerful she had seemed about it. She was never a cheerful woman, not for any reason. It did not stand to reason she would be now." He sighed deeply. "Praise God I followed her."

Krysta nodded. Reaction was setting in and she could do little more. All her strength was needed to stumble after Hawk down the long passage and back up into the manor, where they were instantly seen and surrounded by frantic searchers.

Chapter

TWENTY-TWO

A LIGHT WAS SHINING IN HER EYES. KRYSTA turned her head, trying to escape the brightness, only to find she could not. The fog of sleep had lifted and in its place came awareness that something was out of place.

She sat up slowly and took a long look around. She was in her chamber, the one she shared with Hawk, lying alone in the vast bed. Her body felt unusually heavy as though she had slept a long time without moving.

A long time, indeed, for she remembered it had been after midnight when Hawk carried her up the stairs, and now the room was filled with angled sunlight streaming through the windows. Off to the west, she could just make out the riotous colors of sunset. She had slept almost a full day. She was throwing back the covers to rise from the bed when memory flooded back.

Daria . . . the cell . . . the terrible hours of darkness . . . the beautiful vision of her son . . . and then the final struggle with the madwoman whose life she had found herself driven to save.

"Oh, my," she murmured, for there seemed nothing else to say. She was hurrying to dress, anxious to learn what had happened while she slept, when Raven appeared.

"Thank heavens!" Krysta exclaimed. "I've been wondering where you were and Thorgold as well. Daria didn't try to harm you too, did she?"

Raven gave herself a good shake and glared at the mention of the madwoman. "And how could you think she did not when neither of us was there to see to your safety? That horrible priest, Father Elbert, lured us into the woods and trapped us within a circle of iron. Villainous foe! Try though we did, we could not free ourselves."

"Does Hawk know about him? I should have told him last night but I was so tired. Father Elbert knew I was with Daria but he said nothing, did he?"

"Nary a word, and yes, indeed, your lord knows all. That fine fellow, Lord Dragon, found and freed us, bless his soul, and let no one be surprised when special favors come his way. He told the Hawk what happened but Dreadful Daria was already proclaiming for all the world to hear that it was Father Elbert who had led her down treason's path. She claims he is working for the Danes, pledged to destroy the alliance in return for wealth and honors from them."

Krysta went very still. She looked at Raven closely. "Do you think that is true?"

The older woman shrugged. "The priest claims not. He said it was all her idea right back to the beginning. According to him, she stole Hawk's seal and forged the letter rejecting the Lord Wolf's offer of marriage to the Lady Cymbra. Thus she set all in motion, so says Father Elbert. But she disputes him, claiming he was the one behind it all even unto the plan to kill you, and she but a pawn duped into believing, she obeyed the will of God."

"So they denounce each other and there is no way to know who is telling the truth."

"Thus it seems," Raven agreed. "Not that it matters. They are both sent away, Father Elbert back to his monastery to be judged by the good priests there and Lady Daria to close confinement in a convent."

Krysta's shoulders sagged with relief. Glad though she was to be free of them, she was gladder still that Hawk had not soiled his hands with blood. There had already been so much of that in his life. Now was the time for him to enjoy the fruits of peace.

Beginning with the greatest fruit of all, their son . . .

She sought to kill you and our child . . .

The words rang clear in Krysta's mind. Last night she had been too exhausted and terrified to heed them but now they returned with stark clarity. He knew. Somehow, Hawk knew she was with child and he had said nothing to her. That devil!

"I must dress," Krysta said firmly, "and find my dear husband. There are one or ten things I need to say to him."

Raven chuckled but a moment later she was gone, just before Aelfgyth bustled into the room.

"I knew it!" the maid exclaimed. "I go off for just a few minutes and you're out of bed, trying to do everything by yourself." Without giving Krysta a chance to reply, she hurried over, took the gown from her hands, and dropped it over her head. "You've been through a terrible time," Aelfgyth informed her. "I can't even bear to imagine what it was like but I'm dead sure that it was hideous." She turned Krysta around briskly and began doing up her laces. "You can't expect to go through something like that without it taking a great toll on you, which is why"—she urged her bemused mistress toward a stool, sat her down, and went to work on her hair—"why you cannot expect to be doing for yourself like this. If the Lord Hawk found out you were up and about, trying to manage on your own, I know what he'd say. That dear man has already been through so much, you don't want to worry him any further, do you?"

"Well, no, of course not but—"

"My mother always says butts are for the rear ends of pigs. Which hair ribbons would you like? The rose and mauve would look lovely with this gown, don't you think?"

Krysta nodded, for there seemed nothing else she could do, so intent was Aelfgyth on seeing to her.

"There," Aelfgyth said when she was satisfied with the results. "You look beautiful. Would you like me to bring you something to eat?"

Krysta shook her head. "Thank you, but no. Where is Lord Hawk?"

"Downstairs. I'll just tell him you're awake. He'll be so relieved that you're feeling better. He was right here most of the night, wouldn't leave your side. He did fall asleep for a few hours, holding your hand, but he was awake before dawn. There's so much to see to, of course, but even so he should have some rest—"

Aelfgyth broke off as Krysta headed toward the door. If anyone was going to tell Hawk anything, it was she. When she thought that he hadn't said a word to her, probably going all the way back to Winchester when he'd had that decidedly strange look on his face just because she was nauseated. Even when they made love, he had never mentioned it, only touched her with such gentle passion. . . .

A blush overtook her. She was not so annoyed with him after all. She could think of nothing save how much she loved him and how truly blessed they were to be together.

Speeding down the steps, Krysta wondered if she would tell Hawk of the strange vision that had come to her in the cell. Had she not tried to reach out to the young man she believed to be her son, she would never have stumbled over the iron bar and could not have delayed Daria's attack long enough for Hawk to arrive.

She paused just before entering the hall and touched a hand gently to her belly. As yet there was no sign of the life that dwelled there, yet she already knew her child well. "Let your wings grow strong, little Falcon," she murmured, and felt the pearl of her happiness glow brightly.

When she stepped into the hall, her eyes found Hawk at once. He was seated at the high table, deep in conversation with Dragon and Thorgold. All three saw her and broke off their talk. Hawk stood and went to her. He was frowning.

"Should you be out of bed? Are you rested enough? Aelfgyth was supposed to come and get me. You have suffered a terrible ordeal and—"

"Enough," Krysta murmured. She raised herself on tiptoe and touched her lips lightly to his. Against them, she said, "I am the most fortunate of women. Whatever ill I have experienced is naught compared to the joy you give me."

He sighed deeply into her mouth and clasped her to him. Around them, the men and women of Hawkforte assembling for their evening meal grinned and nudged one another. The kiss deepened, all else forgotten, as the two fated lovers put aside the tumultuous past and looked to their blissful future.

Only when the laughter and encouragement of the crowd finally reached him did Hawk recall himself. He smiled broadly. Looking over Krysta's head back toward the high table, he said something drowned out by the din of the cheering crowd. It took a moment for Dragon to realize what it was, and when he did, a shiver ran down the back of that stalwart warrior. For the Lord of Hawkforte, his beloved lady nestled in his arms, had spoken the words most guaranteed to strike dread into the foot-loose, fancy-free heart of the Dragon.

"You're next."

Turn the page for a
sneak preview of

TO ME

available November 2001
wherever Bantam Books
are sold

DAMN, DAMN, AND DAMN AGAIN! THE cursed habit had followed her all her life since tenderest childhood. How she loathed being different, how she despised always *knowing*. Lie to her and she would be happy, trick her into believing what was not and she would be delighted, prevaricate, falsify, fib, and palter, nothing would thrill her more. To be in blissful ignorance, never to know or at least not to know beyond the ordinary ken whether someone spoke the truth or lied, that was her great dream as much as freedom itself, for it was a kind of freedom all its own. Let her be done with truth!

He was a man, nothing more. A stranger and a threat. She was glad to be done with him.

Lies.

Her mouth set thinly, she came away from the moss-draped rock and launched herself back upon the course of least resistance through the wood. She would reach Hawkforte before dark. She would wrangle her way upon a merchant ship bound for Normandy. She would find

Thurlow there and together they would make a new life far from the loathsome threat that hung over her were she foolish enough to remain in England.

And that, for anyone who cared, was *truth*.

There was silence in her mind and in the wood, as though nature itself stilled before her blind determination. She drank it in, nodded once and hurried on. It did not occur to her to glance back or even train her hearing in that direction. Not that it mattered. Had she done so, she would have perceived nothing. The Dragon moved over the land like smoke, fathomless and irresistible.

He caught up with the lad scarcely an hour after the first sign of movement. It would have been quicker but he'd hung back awhile, making sure he hadn't been spotted and waiting for the right moment to take him by surprise. He intended to make this quick and get it done with before the boy could hurt himself struggling. After that there would be time for the customary courtesies.

And so it would have been but for one of those vagaries of nature that can never be anticipated. A family of grouse was at home in the underbrush. Dragon's sudden passing roused the parents to protective fury. The male flew from the nest batting his wings and squawking furiously. The female arched her neck, stretched out her wings protectively, and hurled her own dire threats.

The clamor was answered by a slew of other birds who lifted into the air, cackling, cawing, hooting, shrieking and scolding until the hitherto tranquil wood fairly rang with their outrage. The noise penetrated even the fog of Rycca's fatigue and made her look round in surprise.

Surprise that turned swiftly to shock.

The handsomest man she had ever seen.

A shiver of disbelief rippled through Rycca. She did not linger to contemplate the stranger's sudden reappearance or her own absurd thoughts. Instead, she turned and ran with all the desperate speed her weary body could muster.

Dragon followed swiftly. He saw no reason to let the boy exhaust himself any further. Best he face what he rightly had coming and be done with it. Then they would settle the matter of why he was alone and where he was heading. Dragon would see him safely there whether his destination be Hawkforte or not, and whether the lad wanted the company or not. Not mere protectiveness alone dictated that he do so. There was also the matter of curiosity. He sensed a story behind the lad's solitary journey, and if there was one thing Dragon loved, it was a good story. Indeed, people claimed he had a collection of them to rival that of any skald or bard. There were even some who said Dragon should have been one of that happy fraternity, traveling from manor to manor proclaiming the great tales of the age. Fate had called him to a different life, that of warrior and leader. So be it. He still enjoyed those evenings spent round the fire when the ale flowed freely and he held an audience spellbound in the magic of his words.

The lad truly was desperate, Dragon realized suddenly, for he was moving far more quickly than he should have been after the miles he had already covered. With a shake of his head, Dragon closed the distance between them. The boy had strength and stamina, there was no doubt of that, but Dragon was a man full grown, trained to hardship and war, at the peak of his powers. His legs were steel, rippling with muscle, devouring ground. He ran without effort, moving easily over every obstacle, remorseless and inescapable.

The boy seemed to realize that suddenly as he darted a glance over his shoulder. Dragon was so near that he could see the shock in eyes so wide and thick-fringed they must surely provoke teasing. A sudden, dark thought flashed through his mind. Perhaps the boy had a particular reason for taking such desperate measures to escape. A memory rose sharply despite its being long years old. Little more than a child, torn from his home by the ravages of war, Dragon had set sail upon the world's seas in the company of his older brother. In the hold of a ship, at night, a man . . . Even now, Dragon grimaced in disgust. He had fought and fiercely so, but alone he would not have escaped. It was Wolf, already big for his age and with the skill that would make him one of the most renowned warriors of their day, who had saved him. Striking with savage intent, he gutted the attacker, leaving him to writhe in his death throes as he hugged Dragon fiercely and swore they would survive against all enemies and all dangers.

So they had done, rising to vast wealth and power, but not climbing quite so far that Dragon had forgotten how it felt to be young, helpless, and very afraid.

Mildly chagrined by his own kinder self, he nonetheless called out to the boy, "There's no need for this. I'm not going to hurt you. Just stop and we'll talk."

The look this earned suggested Dragon must have suffered a recent head injury in addition to that done to his nether parts. With a last backward glance, the boy redoubled his efforts to get away.

Dragon sighed. He took half a dozen more strides and flowed smoothly into the air, bringing his quarry down in a single motion. Even then, he rolled as they hit the ground, taking the impact himself and sparing the boy all but a simple jarring. He might have done better to knock the wind out of him for the brat struggled furiously, kicking out in every direction and doing his damnedest to get his teeth into any portion of Dragon that presented itself.

"Oh, no, you don't!" Dragon exclaimed. "I've had enough from you." He bounded to his feet, hauling the boy up with him, and gave him a good shake. "Calm down! All I want to do is talk."

That accomplished precisely nothing. Flush-faced, wide-eyed, the lad continued to struggle with all his might. Prudently, Dragon held him off at arm's length and even so kept a careful watch on his flailing limbs as they slowly but inexorably wound down. He waited until the miscreant had scarcely enough strength left to twitch before he tried again.

Pleasantly, he asked, "Are you ready to talk now?"

The boy was panting so hard he probably wasn't capable of speech but he did manage a glare of pure venom.

"No? I can wait." He continued to hold the boy a few inches above the ground, dangling at the end of a very long, very strong arm. At the same time, he repeated quietly, "I am not going to hurt you."

When the boy looked at him in utter disbelief, Dragon added, "Oh, I considered it rightly enough. You deserve a thrashing for what you did. But I'm willing to allow that you may have thought you were acting in self-defense, even as I myself was when I seized you. Any man has a right to protect himself." Deliberately, he awarded the stripling a title he would not merit for many years yet. On closer appraisal, the lad might be even younger than Dragon had thought. Cheeks that had been red with exertion were paling rapidly, revealing damask smooth skin without the slightest trace of even an infant beard. The boy's features were delicately drawn, a straight and slender nose sitting above a full mouth and gently rounded chin. But it was those eyes, those huge, slightly uptilted eyes the precise shade of clover honey that sent a prickle of apprehension down Dragon's back. A sudden, hideous suspicion stirred in him.

Without warning, his free hand darted out and snatched the cap that swaddled the imp's head.

"*Noooo!*" Slender fingers flew to stop him, too late. Masses of silken hair glinting with the sheen of copper tumbled free. Dragon stared in disbelief. A girl. He had been brought to his knees by *a girl*. The realization stunned him if only because in all his experience with women—his very long, very considerable experience—nothing remotely similar had ever happened. In all modesty, no female had ever looked upon him with other than warm encouragement and affection. That may have been because of his appearance although he'd never thought anything of how he looked one way or another. And perhaps his wealth and position had impressed some. But he suspected it had much more to do with the simple fact that he adored women. Utterly, completely, unreservedly *adored* them. Women were the greatest of the gods' considerable accomplishments, the best gift, the most marvelous delight that could be bestowed upon the earth and upon man, including his own lucky self. Women were soft and strong, they smelled good and had beguiling smiles, they gave life and made it count for something. In bed, out of bed, he delighted in them. Old, young, in between, he found their presence a constant source of comfort and enjoyment. That one of these marvelous creatures might actually seek to do him harm left him stunned.

Not that he could blame her. She must have been absolutely terrified and while he was thinking about it, what in hell's name was she doing traveling alone? No wonder she was gotten up as a boy, but that was scant protection. If he'd had more than a few seconds to look at her earlier he would have realized at once what he had finally discovered. *A girl.*

"It's all right, sweetling," Dragon said gently. He set her down with the utmost care, watchful lest in her exhausted state she topple over. "There's nothing for you to be afraid of. No one's going to hurt you. I'll see you safely to wherever you're going and—"

She turned and, fleet as a young doe, ran. He stared after her in amazement. Where had she possibly found the strength to try to escape yet again? It was truly amazing and just one more testament to the extraordinary mystery of women. Not that he could let her go, of course. She might get lost, or have trouble finding food, or be cold once night came, or run into some man with altogether the wrong sort of attitude toward women. Dragon couldn't allow any of that to happen. Nor could he allow her to harm herself by dashing through the woods probably paying no attention at all to her surroundings.

Frowning with concern, he hurried after her.

Rycca's breath came in labored gasps. Her legs were lead, the effort of running agony. Only the desperate courage deep within her kept her from slumping to the ground in defeat. Of all the cruel tricks for fate to play upon her. She had escaped the brutality of her family and their nightmare plans for her future only to find herself in the hands of the most terrifyingly powerful warrior she had ever seen in her life.

And the handsomest man.

If she had possessed even a whisper of breath to spare, she would have laughed in sheer disbelief at herself. Even now, fleeing for her life, she could harbor such a thought. She must be possessed of some inner demon.

Only truth.

Truth be damned! And with it all the rest that life had inflicted upon her. She would not fall to the warrior or to her own weakness. She would run until her heart burst if she had to but she would never, *ever* give up. Surrender was for the craven and meek. She was neither. Heedless of the tears of exhaustion and fear that streamed down her cheeks, Rycca ran on. She did not see the ground change around her, did not notice the trees thinning away, paid no heed to the sea shining below the cliff that suddenly loomed before her. Nor did she hear Dragon's frantic shout. Drained of strength, bereft of hope, driven only by despair, she tumbled straight over the cliff face. A strangled scream broke from her. Grasping at bushes, she tried to halt her headlong plunge. The effort failed and with a last sob of terror she glimpsed the white-foamed breakers rushing up toward her.

Dragon saw the girl disappear over the cliff and

fought the wave of sickness that clawed at him. He could scarcely believe what his stubborn pursuit had wrought but there was no denying the brutal result. The girl was gone, might even at that moment be dead or dying, and it was his fault. With a horrified groan, he flung himself down the cliff side, scarcely controlling his fall as he slipped and slid until leaping the last dozen feet to the beach.

The sight that greeted him made bile rise in his throat. She lay crumbled at the edge of the water against the boulder that had finally stopped her. Tendrils of copper hair drifted on the incoming tide. Another few minutes, and the water would be deep enough to drown her. As it was, her slender form was unmoving. A thin trickle of blood oozed from a wound on her forehead, flowing away into the sea.

Scarcely breathing, Dragon lifted the girl and carried her a safe distance up the sand. He laid her down carefully, then hesitated, momentarily uncertain of what to do. The man who had seen more injuries on the battlefield than he could count, and who had prevented his own death a year before by swiftly dealing with a wound that would have killed him, found himself at an utter loss. She looked so fragile lying there, all the strength and courage suddenly gone from her. Swallowing thickly, he opened the small pack hanging from his belt, drawing from it the supplies that good sense and his sister-in-law, herself a renowned healer, assured he always carry with him. The soft, clean cloth he pressed against the wound on the girl's forehead slowed the bleeding. He left the makeshift bandage in place and quickly checked her limbs, relieved to find none of them broken. In the process, he could not help but discover that the loose boy's clothing concealed a body of strong, flowing curves. Firmly putting that discovery from his mind as best he could, he carefully slid his hands beneath the tunic and, ignoring the odd trembling that inexplicably struck him, confirmed that her ribs were also intact.

With a deep breath, the first in several moments, he drew back and regarded her cautiously. Her only injury seemed to be the blow to her head. She might recover from that completely . . . or she might never wake and simply slip away into eternal sleep. He had seen both happen with men similarly struck down. Only time would tell.

Fortunately for Dragon's peace of mind, before he could do much more than begin to consider how he might get her to a place of greater comfort and safety, the girl moaned softly. Thinking perhaps he had imagined the sound, indeed had merely willed it into being, he leaned closer and closer still until the soft exhalation of her breath brushed his bearded cheek. His gaze focused on her intently, he watched as her eyes slowly fluttered open.

H ER HEAD HURT. RYCCA WINCED BUT HER INSTINCT was to move, to get up, to get away even if she couldn't quite remember what she was fleeing from. She tried to rise only to be pressed gently back onto the sand.

"Easy, sweetling. You had a bad fall. There are no bones broken but you need to take it slowly."

The voice was a deep rumble, soothing, seductive and . . . all too familiar. *Him.* He had done this to her, chased her down, driven her right off the edge of the cliff. He'd damn near killed her and now he thought her help-less, prey no doubt to whatever it was he had in mind.

He had a nasty surprise awaiting him.

But not, unfortunately, until her head stopped spin-ning. With a frustrated moan, Rycca subsided. Dragon took the sound to mean she was suffering and bent over her in concern.

"Does something hurt besides your head? I checked and you seem to be all right but I could be wrong."

He had checked. What did that mean? She stared directly into his eyes, which looked like ancient gold suddenly revealed to sunlight. Worse, his voice rippled through her, setting off odd little shivers at the same time as it made her feel strangely content.

His hand touched her brow very lightly. She scarcely noticed, so absorbed was she in his look of tender concern. Not that she was fooled by that for a moment. She knew warriors, had lived among them all her life. They were rough, crude men who took what they wanted with no thought but the satisfaction of their own urges. To have fallen from the heady heights of freedom into the very hands of such a man was worse even than falling from the cliff. That, at least, she had survived.

Long experience had taught her the terrible folly of ever showing fear or doubt. Accordingly, she met the warrior's gaze squarely, ignored the strange fluttering of her heart, and snarled, "Get away from me."

Dragon sighed. He didn't blame her in the least for being angry with him; she had every right to feel that way. What he regretted was his inability to do as she wanted. "I'm sorry," he said sincerely, "but I cannot. You've been hurt and you need help."

Truth.

No, it couldn't be. Men didn't apologize, at least not to women. Nor did they extend themselves to help someone unless they expected something in return. The candor and compassion she felt in him had to be false. And that prompted a sudden thought: The tumble down the cliff might have done something to her strange, unwanted gift. Perhaps she no longer had any greater ability to tell truth from lie than did any other person. For that, she would fall down a dozen cliffs.

Yet was there still the tantalizing possibility that the warrior meant exactly what he had said. She eyed him cautiously. "I need no help. Let me up and I will be on my way."

Patiently, he shook his head. "It is not safe for a woman to be traveling on her own."

"I was perfectly safe until you crossed my path."

"Well may you see it that way, but if I hadn't come along, someone else would have and you could be in great difficulty right now."

If she hadn't known it would hurt, she might have laughed. As it was, she had to content herself with a grimace. "Oh, you mean I could have been chased over a cliff?"

The warrior reddened, not with anger, which she would have understood in response to her derision, but with what looked very much like regret.

"I thought you were a boy in need of better manners. Had I realized you were a girl . . ." He paused and shrugged. "I would still have come after you because you really should not be without escort. But I would have tried to take you by surprise so you would not run off and get hurt."

Truth.

"Yes, well, that's fine, but there is no need for you to be concerned. I am meeting my . . . my brother just a short distance from here."

Strictly speaking, Normandy was a far journey. But there were much greater distances to go, all the way to fabled Byzantium or even to the lands farther to the east and south. If that weren't enough, there were tales of a land to the west where mountains ran with molten fury and vast vents of steam rose from the sundered earth. Some of those who claimed to have seen such a place told stranger stories yet of a land yet farther to the west, endowed with rugged coastlines and endless forests. Besides all that, Normandy might as well be the neighboring village. So she wasn't really lying . . . not entirely.

"Fine," the warrior said. "I will take you to him."